Prais‹

EX
AN ~~AX~~ TO GRIND IN DEADWOOD

"Ann Charles has done it again. *An Ex to Grind in Deadwood* is a madcap adventure full of real estate, romance, and laugh-out-loud moments, with just enough suspense and ghostly gruesomeness to keep you on the edge of your seat. You'll love it!"
~Jenna Bennett, USA Today Bestselling Author

"A wickedly funny paranormal mystery romance with clever surprises at every twist and turn. Get ready for another hilarious and spooky read from Ann Charles."
~Chanticleer Book Reviews

"When Violet Parker stumbles, you just know it's going to be over another dead body. *An Ex to Grind in Deadwood* makes your hair stand on end one moment and tickles your funny bone the next. Ann Charles gives us another sexy, funny mystery you won't want to put down!"
~Jacquie Rogers, Award-winning Author, Hearts of Owyhee Series

"Smart, funny, and feisty. The Deadwood Mystery series just keeps getting better and better."
~Wendy Delaney, Award-winning Author, Working Stiffs Mystery Series

"*An Ex to Grind in Deadwood* will make you laugh out loud and shiver with fear. Full of gutsy characters, creepy ghosts, and a dash of gore, this next segment of the Deadwood Mystery series comes with a jaw-dropping ending that will render you speechless."
~Sue Stone-Douglas, Native of Lead, SD

For more on Ann and her books, check out her website, as well as the reader reviews for her books on Amazon, Barnes & Noble, and Goodreads

Dear Reader,

Of all of the crazy things I could've decided to try while writing this fifth Deadwood book, I opted for moving. On top of that stressful life event, my husband and I decided to double up on this dose of insanity and buy a house 1500 miles away in Arizona.

In spite of all the highs and lows of dragging our two kids and ornery cat across the West, I finished the book. I wrote through weeks of painting the old house, weeding our many gardens, shopping for a new house both in person and online, jumping through the financial hoops of buying, and pulling my hair out as we lined up the closing of our old house only five days before the closing of our new house several states away.

Two days before we hit the road for Arizona, I wrote, "The End ... for now," finishing the first draft. When I finally got a chance to go through the whole book in one read through, I was amazed that not only was it legible, but it even made sense.

Today, after more editing and polishing, I'm happy to share with you the next chapter in Violet's crazy life.

On a side note, I'm a huge fan of James Garner, as some of you may have figured out via my stories (where do you think Mac Garner from my Jackrabbit Series got his last name?). I had no idea this year would be James' last. I'm sad to say good-bye to such a charming, charismatic screen legend. I'm so glad we have many movies and television shows to keep him alive in our hearts and memories.

Now, as old man Harvey says, "Pull your hat over yer ears and hold on for dear life," because you're in for another wild ride in Deadwood with Violet and her friends ... and her enemies.

Ann Charles

www.anncharles.com

EX
AN ^A̶x̶ TO GRIND
IN DEADWOOD

ANN CHARLES

ILLUSTRATED BY C.S. KUNKLE

Cover Art by C.S. Kunkle (www.charlesskunkle.com)
Cover Design by Sharon Benton (www.q42designs.com)
Editing by the "Grammar Chick" (www.grammarchick.com)
Formatting by Biddles ebooks (www.biddlesebooks.com)

E-book ISBN-13: 978-1-940364-12-4
Print ISBN-13: 978-1-940364-13-1

Dedication

To my husband.

You still laugh at my silly wisecracks and screwball antics.

Te amo.

Also by Ann Charles:

Deadwood Mystery Series
Nearly Departed in Deadwood (Book 1)
Optical Delusions in Deadwood (Book 2)
Dead Case in Deadwood (Book 3)
Better Off Dead in Deadwood (Book 4)

Short Stories from the Deadwood Mystery Series
Deadwood Shorts: Seeing Trouble
Deadwood Shorts: Boot Points

Jackrabbit Junction Mystery Series
Dance of the Winnebagos (Book 1)
Jackrabbit Junction Jitters (Book 2)
The Great Jackalope Stampede (Book 3)

Goldwash Mystery Series (a future series)
The Old Man's Back in Town (Short Story)

Coming Next from Ann Charles:

Look What the Wind Blew In
A Dig Site Mystery
(A novel starring Quint Parker, the brother of Violet Parker from
the Deadwood Mystery Series)

The Rowdy Coyote Rumble
Jackrabbit Junction Mystery Series (Book 4)

Title TBA
Deadwood Mystery Series (Book 6)

Acknowledgments

By this point in the series, you know that I can wax on and on in thank-you verbiage. This time, I'm going to try to keep this short and sweet.

Thank you to my wonderful critique partners, first-draft and second-draft readers, editor, and beta readers. You all have helped make this book a romping fun ride for other readers.

I also want to thank the following marvelous people who helped make this book come together:

My husband, kids, and mouthy cat who fill my life with laughter and joy.

Mimi "The Grammar Chick" (my editor), and Marguerite Phipps (assistant editor), who both make me look so smart.

My brother, Charles (C.S.) Kunkle (cover artist and illustrator) for his ability to draw what I write on the page, and his wife, Stephanie, for helping pick what to illustrate.

Sharon Benton (cover graphic artist) for being so easy going.

My publicists and promoters—my mom and brother (Margo Taylor and Dave Taylor), my aunt (Judy Routt), and my sister (Laura Rensberger).

Wendy Gildersleeve for taking such good care of me and helping me reach for the stars.

Diane Garland for her amazingly detailed spreadsheets and timelines, and for her quick answers every time I bugged her.

Jacquie Rogers, Wendy Delaney, Amber Scott, Gerri Russell, and Joleen James for being awesome author buddies.

Bill and Dixie Evans, Sara Ruth Kane Nikont, and Jerry Bryant for sharing tidbits of Black Hills history with me.

My ex-coworkers, my family, and my Facebook and Twitter friends. I can't thank you all enough for being there day after day.

My brother, Clint Taylor, for telling all of his coworkers about my books. I can't believe you still like me after all of these years, Clint. Ha ha!

EX
AN ^A̶x̶ TO GRIND
IN DEADWOOD

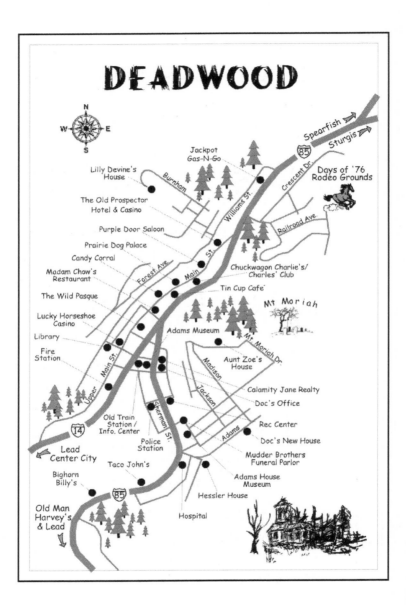

DEADWOOD

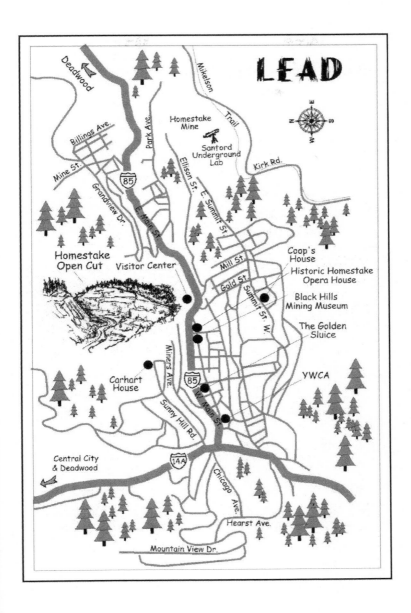

Cast

Violet Lynn Parker (1,2,3,4,5)—Main heroine of the series, Doc's girlfriend, Aunt Zoe's niece

Willis "Old Man" Harvey (1,2,3,4,5)—Violet's sidekick and so-called body guard

Dane R. "Doc" Nyce (1,2,3,4,5)—Main hero of the series, Violet's boyfriend

Detective "Coop" Cooper (1,2,3,4,5)—Deadwood and Lead's only detective

Zoe Parker (1,2,3,4,5)—Violet's aunt and mentor in life; Violet lives in Aunt Zoe's house

Layne Parker (1,2,3,4,5)—Violet's nine-year-old son

Adelynn Parker (1,2,3,4,5)—Violet's nine-old daughter

Natalie Beals (1,2,3,4,5)—Violet's best friend since childhood

Jerry Russo (4,5)—Violet's boss, owner of Calamity Jane Realty

Mona Hollister (1,2,3,4,5)—Violet's co-worker and mentor in realty

Ray Underhill (1,2,3,4,5)—Violet's co-worker and nemesis at work

Benjamin Underhill (1,2,3,4,5)—Violet's co-worker and previous secret admirer

Cornelius Curion (3,4,5)—Violet's client; self-acclaimed ghost-whisperer

Jeff Wymonds (1,2,3,4,5)—Violet's client; father of Adelynn's best friend

Beatrice Geary (1,2,3,4,5)—Violet and Aunt Zoe's neighbor across the street

Reid Martin (2,3,4,5)—Captain of the Fire Department, Aunt Zoe's ex-lover

Tiffany Sugarbell (1,2,3,4,5)—Violet's rival Realtor; Doc's ex-girlfriend

Susan Parker (1,2,3,4,5)—Violet's evil sister; aka "the Bitch from Hell"

Quint Parker (1,2,3,4,5)—Violet's supportive brother; Layne's hero; giver of her famous purple boots

Freesia Tender (5)—Owner of the Galena House

Stone Hawke (5)—Cooper's ex-partner; detective called in to help solve cases

Dickie Dowdin (5)—Host of TV series called "Paranormal Realty"

Honey (5)—Dickie's assistant

Rex Conner (3,4,5)—The biological father of Violet's children

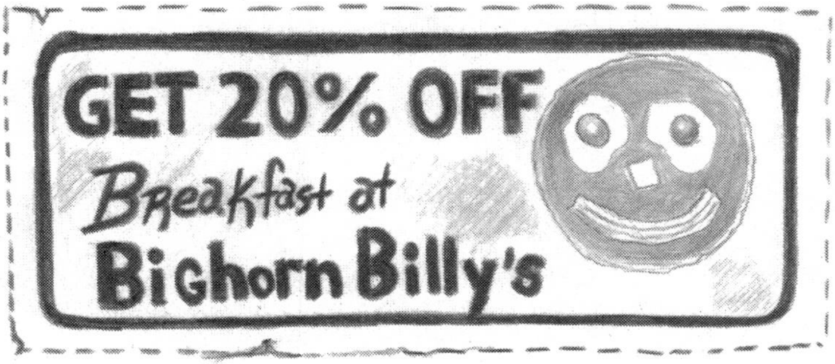
GET 20% OFF
Breakfast at
Bighorn Billy's

Chapter One

Just when I thought my career couldn't sink any deeper, some asshole flushed it down the toilet.

"Jerry had another one of his genius marketing ideas," I said into my cell phone. "He's decided he's going to make me a freaking reality TV star." I rattled off a drumroll of curses to my best friend on the other end of the call, in case she couldn't hear how pissed I was about this latest swirling mess.

A pair of skateboard-toting teenagers dragging their pant hems across the parking lot of Bighorn Billy's Diner gave me a pair of thumbs up on my medley of swear words. I waved back. I appreciated the positive reinforcement after spending the last hour choking down a burger with a side of my boss's newest promotion plan.

"No freaking way," Natalie replied without the emphasis such a disaster required.

I'd already used the word *freaking*. Was she paying attention? It didn't sound like it. Damn it, she needed to get her butt home from Arizona so that we could slam tequila shots over my current problem until we came up with a solution ... or passed out trying.

A cool fall breeze blew through the parking lot, fresh with the scent of pine trees. The Black Hills oozed pine perfume since they were covered from head to toe in the evergreens. The wind stole my warmth—but not my fire.

I pulled my thick sweater tighter around me, the faux-fur trim tickling my chin. "Nat, did you hear what I said? This is bad, like getting caught picking my nose on national TV bad."

Okay, so maybe it was only a regional television program, but it could muddle up my world like a paint can shaker at the hardware store. I kicked the tire of the Picklemobile, the old green dilapidated pickup that I was borrowing to get me from here to there until I could afford a new set of wheels.

"Jerry is determined to turn my career into a circus side show," I continued, "complete with clown hair and makeup. Next he'll have me swallowing swords. I'll be damned if ..."

"Wait, wait!" Natalie said, her voice louder, her attention finally mine. "You need to back the truck up and tell me how all this started."

Tell her how it started? Had her brain turned into a tumbleweed and rolled away into the desert? "My old boss was murdered, remember? Then her giant ex-husband rode in on Paul Bunyan's ox, took over Calamity Jane Realty, and turned me into a billboard bimbo."

I'd almost driven off Interstate 90 when I saw the billboard yesterday on my way down to Rapid City. There I stood, larger than life in that god-awful pink silk suit Jerry had bought me for the photo shoot. My blonde hair spiraled every which way and my lips glistened with a red coat so glossy it looked like I'd just finished sucking the blood from my last victim. As if that weren't enough to make me want to flee the state, the caption underneath my image made me scream loud enough to rattle the Picklemobile's windshield:

Looking for love in all the wrong houses?
Call Violet at Calamity Jane Realty. She'll show you a magical
place you'll love coming home to every night.

"I know all of that, Violet," Natalie said, adopting the calming voice she'd used while talking me through delivering my twins into the world almost a decade ago. "I left the state, not the universe."

"After seeing that billboard, I'd like to leave the universe."

"The billboard isn't that bad. You look good with crazy curls."

"Liar. I look like a vampire poodle that just peed on an

electric fence." I'd sent a picture of the billboard to her phone last night. She'd called back laughing so hard she could barely speak.

Natalie chuckled. "Anyway, what I meant was did Jerry explain why he thinks this will help your career and how soon they will begin filming?"

I pinched the bridge of my nose, trying to breathe through my anger before my skin turned green and I went on a rampage. "I don't know."

"You don't know the *why* or the *how* part?"

"Either. Both."

"Did he tell you about his idea over the phone?"

"No. He was sitting across the lunch table." All three of my coworkers had been there, too. Judging from their reactions, which ranged from a growl of disapproval to a gasp of surprise, none of us had expected this to be the reason Jerry had insisted on a work lunch meeting today.

"Were you daydreaming about Doc again at the time?" Natalie asked.

"Doc was the furthest thing from my mind," I fibbed.

Yes, my boyfriend had been on my mind throughout the meal, especially after last night, but not at the moment Jerry had dropped the bomb about the TV show. I wasn't going to admit that to Natalie, though. She said she was over the betrayal of my sleeping with Doc, but I wasn't entirely convinced by her "we're good" claim.

"Then how come you weren't paying better attention?"

"Old man Harvey sent me a text." I didn't elaborate that it was actually a picture of a dead cow. At least the bigger chunks appeared to be bovine—hooves, head, and sections of hide.

After my eyes had registered what I was seeing, it had taken me a few gulps of water to keep my burger and salad contained in my stomach. During the internal struggle not to vomit, I'd missed everything Jerry had been telling us.

"Harvey has a cell phone now?" Natalie asked. "That's gonna make him more dangerous to the local female population."

"Doc got it for him a few days ago."

"Why?"

"Because Harvey insisted he needed it to protect me better when Doc wasn't around."

"Jeez, Harvey's really taking this self-appointed bodyguard duty seriously."

"Yeah, well, after that creepy shit at the Opera House." And the even weirder stuff going on out at Harvey's ranch. "I don't mind the company and you're like five states away. When are you coming home?"

"I told you last night that I leave in a week. Do you still have Harvey's booby trap set up outside the back door?"

"No, Aunt Zoe made him take it down. She didn't like having a stack of old truck batteries wired to her porch light." A Deadwood police car slowed on the road in front of the diner. I ducked out of view behind the Picklemobile. "I can't see this ending well."

"You mean old man Harvey and his phone or Jerry and his big idea?"

"Both. If I didn't have two kids to support, I'd ..." My phone beeped in my ear. "Hold on, Nat. I have another call."

I looked at the screen. An unknown number with the local area code appeared. My finger hesitated over the IGNORE option. What if it was an emergency about one of my kids?

I accepted the call. "Hello?"

"Violet Parker?" a woman whispered with a hitch in her breath.

I plugged my other ear to block out the sound of passing traffic. "Yes?"

"I need to talk to you." There was an accent there, but I couldn't quite place it.

I pressed the phone harder against my ear. "Is this about a house to buy or sell?"

"It's about what you are."

What I was? I doubted she was referring to my status as a single parent with an ever-shrinking savings account. Maybe she'd heard about my ghost-loving reputation ... or seen my billboard. "Have we met?"

"*Nein, Scharfrichter.*" The engine growl from a passing diesel pickup made the caller's words sound garbled.

"Nine what?" I asked.

"I must see you immediately. Come to the Galena House on Williams Street, apartment four. Knock seven times."

Right now? "I'm kind of busy at the moment."

I wasn't finished venting to Natalie. Not to mention that I'd planned to head up the road to the grocery store after hanging up to grab a gallon of milk for the kids and a tub of peanut butter fudge ice cream for me. It was going to take more than a spoonful or three tonight to lull me into subordination so that I didn't start my day tomorrow with a hard kick to Jerry's shins.

"You will come now," the woman said, louder, no longer whispering. "I will be dead soon."

I blinked. "You what?"

"Do not delay!"

Sheesh! "Who is this?"

"I will be waiting." She hung up, leaving me standing there coated with a layer of goosebumps.

I frowned down at my phone and then realized Natalie was still holding on the other line. "Nat? You still there?"

"Yeah."

"That was really bizarre."

"What? Did Harvey find another decapitated body?"

"No." Well, yes, sort of, only the reverse being that there was a head but not much else, and the victim was a cow. But I didn't want to think about that after that unnerving phone call. "It was some woman. She insisted on seeing me immediately."

"Who?"

"She didn't say. She told me to meet her at the Galena House on Williams Street."

"The old boarding house? You know that's haunted, right?"

"Whatever." I was tired of hearing how everything in this town was haunted.

"Maybe it was a ghost calling you." She hummed the *Twilight Zone* theme in my ear.

I shivered, peering around the parking lot, feeling like I was lined up in someone's crosshairs all of a sudden. "That would be just my luck."

"Are you gonna go over there?" she asked.

"Yeah, I guess. She sounded desperate." Or insane.

"Maybe you should call your bodyguard and have him go with you."

"I think I can handle visiting a boarding house in broad daylight."

"Fine, but you better call me tonight and tell me what she wanted."

"Deal. Say 'Hi' to your cousins for me."

"Will do. Be careful, loony-toon. You have a way of stumbling into the kind of trouble that ends with you standing waist deep in guns and bullets."

Actually, firearms weren't even cutting it these days.

The Picklemobile smelled like cinnamon and old grease. The former thanks to an air freshener I had hanging from the rearview mirror, the latter because it was an ancient truck that belonged to old man Harvey. It grumbled and hiccupped to a start, belching black smoke as it got humming, reminding me of its owner.

I thought more on Natalie's warning as I twisted and turned my way into Deadwood and decided to give my bodyguard a call after all. I pulled into the lot across from the hospital and let the Picklemobile idle while the phone rang.

"Where you been, girl?" Harvey answered. "I've been sendin' you twits for the last hour."

"Twits?"

"Yeah. You know, those lil' notes on your phone."

"Those are called *texts*, Harvey."

"You sure about that? I think 'twits' sounds 'bout right."

I was not going to talk technology with one of Deadwood's pioneers. "I was at lunch with my boss."

"Where are ya now?"

"Heading to the Galena House on Williams Street."

"That there's a bad idea if I ever heard one."

"If you're going to tell me it's haunted, I already know about that."

"It's *extra* haunted and more."

Being that I was a big fat dud when it came to seeing, hearing, smelling, or feeling ghosts, the degree of haunting made little difference to me. "Good for it."

"Pooh-pooh all you want," he said, "but the last time you visited a ghostie, she turned a live woman into a ventriloquist doll."

I shuddered. My queasiness around those talking dummies had been amplified lately, thanks to the particular ghost up in Lead he was referring to who had insisted upon reaching out to me when I'd least expected it.

Pushing my neurosis aside, I focused on the haunted house I was about to visit. "What do you know about the Galena House besides it being haunted?"

"I know that you shouldn't dilly dally there without your bodyguard."

"Dead people can't hurt me, Harvey." At least none had yet; only live ones had left bruises and scars.

"It's not the ghosts I'm thinkin' about. It's the shrunken heads."

I pulled my phone back and frowned down at the screen. Was he for real? I put it back up to my ear. "Shrunken *what*?"

"You heard me—heads."

"Are you going to leave me hanging here or explain that?"

"Years back that place had a run of residents turn up dead, their heads all shrunken up weird like. The cops never could figure out who was behind it and how they'd gone about shrinkin' the skulls."

"You mean shrunken like what one of those tribes does down in the Amazon?"

"Sorta. From what I was told, they didn't look the same as those, though."

"Shrunken heads?" I repeated, feeling dazed.

"Did you stop off at The Golden Sluice after lunch to bend an elbow, girl?"

"I wish I was drunk." This day was turning into a long

unbroken string of bad moments. "What did they do about the dead residents?"

"The paper said their deaths were ruled as heart failure, callin' them 'natural.' Now I don't know about you, but I sure don't figure someone's head shrinkin' up into a dried skull raisin is anything close to natural."

His words painted a picture I didn't want to think about so soon after a lunch of choked down rage followed by gut burning indigestion—and nausea thanks to a picture of cow pieces. Speaking of …

"What's the deal with that dead cow picture?"

"I found that carcass out at the back edge of my pasture."

"What did that? A mountain lion?"

"I don't reckon, the bite marks are too big. Coop wanted me to take some photographs of it because he was tied up in meetings and couldn't come out to see it until later."

"Your nephew is keeping busy these days." Detective "Coop" Cooper had his hands full with a slew of murders and unanswered questions. I was happy that he hadn't been knocking on my door lately looking for more answers, since the ones I gave him usually made him grind his molars and glare holes through the back of my eyeballs.

"That's your fault," Harvey said.

A group of four Harley Davidson motorcycles rumbled past on the main road.

"You must be close," he said. "I could hear those motorcycles in both ears."

"I'm parked across from the hospital."

"What are you doin' there? Come get me at your aunt's place. If you're going to the Galena House, I'm comin' along."

Rather than argue, I did as told. Those shrunken skulls had me feeling edgy about walking into the haunted boarding house on my own. Three minutes later, he climbed into the Picklemobile.

"Head 'em out, Rawhide," he said, flashing me his two gold teeth. He smelled like soap but looked scragglier around the edges than usual.

"Your beard could use a trim."

"I ain't got no woman to impress right now, so I'm giving my trimmer a vacation."

"I'm a woman."

"Nah, you're still a filly to me. Besides, you got your own stallion to nag. How's sex treating you these days? You sure seem to be riding a lot looser in the saddle. I take it Doc is gettin' the job done."

That was a subject we were not going to touch. Ever. I answered with a squint and changed the subject. "How many residents had their heads shrunk?"

"I can't remember. Two, maybe three."

Turning onto the main drag, I headed for Williams Street. "How long ago?"

"I must have been knee high to a buffalo when the story came out. I remember my folks jabberin' about it during a meal or two."

They talked about shrunken skulls during dinner? That explained why no subject seemed off limits with Harvey while eating, including castration techniques and the ins and outs of two-dollar whores.

Williams Street ran the length of Deadwood up above Main, behind a row of southeast facing brown and burnt red brick buildings. I drove up the hill past the historic Franklin Hotel and made a right.

"Did they ever figure out why?" I asked.

"Nope. Like I said, they ended up calling it 'natural' and went on to the next crime."

A Victorian boarding house loomed in front of us, reminding me of an unkempt gentleman down on his luck. Weeds stuck out of the wrought-iron fence like loose threads. White paint flaked onto the brown grass around its foundation joined by torn asphalt shingles from the roof. A faded rectangular sign confirmed I was at the Galena House.

I parked, squeezing as tightly as possible against the concrete wall in front of the house to leave room for passing cars. Streets on this side of Deadwood were made for horse carriages, not old pickups with side mirrors.

"Well, the woman who called and asked me to meet her here didn't sound like she had a shrunken head," I told him, "so we might as well see what's going on."

"A woman called you? What'd she say?"

"Something about nine sharks and that she needed to see me now because she'd be dead soon."

He grunted. "No shit."

We sat there staring up at the boarding house in silence. It was an old style Italianate. Some of the fine cornices had crumbled, but the two columns bracketing the porch stood tall and bright like they'd been recently painted. A shadow moved across the upstairs window. Was that the woman? As I watched, the shadow returned, obscured behind a white gauzy curtain.

Someone was waiting for me.

I pushed open my door as far as the wall would allow, still wondering how heads could be shrunken and then written off as something natural. Harvey joined me on the sidewalk leading up to the house.

"Let's go see what this mystery woman wants," he said.

The gate opened without a sound, giving me pause. I'd expected a squeak of resistance. The porch creaked something awful as we crossed to the front door.

I held up my knuckles to knock and Harvey bumped me aside, turning the knob and pushing it open.

"Harvey!"

"What? They're apartments. Nobody knocks on the outside door. You have to go inside."

Surprisingly, apartment number four wasn't up the wide, oak staircase that looked to have been refurbished, the varnish still glossy. It was at the end of a long white hall that smelled like fresh paint. I could see drips of white here and there on the edge of the dark blue carpet.

An old-fashioned brass knocker in the shape of a grandfather clock made a solid thwack on the wooden door thanks to Harvey.

"I'm supposed to knock seven times." I added six more

thwacks.

His bushy eyebrows rose. "Any other instructions I should know before we step inside?"

"Yeah, stay out of trouble. I don't need Detective Cooper harping on me about dragging his uncle into any more of my schemes."

I looked back down the hall. The light coming in through the front door windows seemed to lessen. Rain must be moving in, the gray clouds thickening even more. That or it was an omen. I chewed on my lower lip. I preferred the rain prediction, even if it would give me a helmet head of frizzy curls.

Harvey knocked again with the brass clock, seven more times. We waited, passing shoulder shrugs and frowns back and forth.

I put my ear to the door.

"What do ya hear?"

"Ticking," I said.

"Like a bomb?"

"No. Like a clock ticking." But there were no footfalls. No floorboards creaking either. Nothing but tick-tock, tick-tock.

"Are you sure she said apartment four?"

"Positive."

"Is her number still on your phone?" When I nodded, he pointed at my purse. "Give 'er a call back."

"Good thinking."

"That's why you need me along. I'm the brains of this operation. You need to focus your purty head on smilin' for more billboards."

I wrinkled my nose at him. Pulling up her number, I hit the call button and listened. My phone rang in my ear. On the other side of the door, a phone trilled in response. After the tenth ring, I hung up.

"Maybe she had to run out," I said. "We can come back some other time."

Harvey reached out and turned the knob. The door creaked open. "Or we could let ourselves in and wait for her to come home."

I stepped back, my heart picking up speed. "Harvey! We can't go in there. I'll end up in jail again if Cooper finds out."

"She called you. We're just bein' friendly and lettin' ourselves in to save her the trouble."

He walked inside the shadow-filled entryway and then stopped short. "Well, I'll be a frozen cow pie."

I inched up behind him. The ticking sound was much louder on this side of the door. "Wow."

Covering every square inch of the walls in the foyer and living room beyond were clocks. Ticking, ticking, ticking.

"I've heard the sayin' timeliness is next to godliness," he said, "but this is taking things a little too far."

"That's not how the saying goes."

"It was in my grannie's house. She threw pots and pans at us when we were late for dinner." Harvey moved further into the apartment. "Hello? Anybody home?"

I followed, still gaping at all of the clocks. The constant noise in the room would drive me to drink. "It's no wonder she sounded cuckoo on the phone."

Harvey snorted. "You need to work on your stand-up comedy routine."

Something smelled funny in the place. "You smell that, Harvey?"

"Hard to miss." He hit the light switch on the wall. A clearer view of the clocks didn't make me feel less like running back out the door.

The longer I stood there, the more the smell made me want to gag. "We need to get out of here."

He glanced my way. "You feelin' itchy?"

Clear to my toes. "Uh-huh."

"Me, too."

"I think it's all of these damned clocks." And that odor.

"Nah, that's not what's got my boots itchin' to skiddaddle." His voice sounded wheezier than usual, hesitant. "I'm more worried about that thing over in the corner."

"What thing?" I followed his gaze, frowning at a wrinkled pile of clothes in the corner near a rocking chair. A pointy-toed shoe stuck partway out from under the fabric on one side, an L-shaped gnarled stick jutted out on the other.

"What is that?" Grabbing onto one of Harvey's suspenders, I led us closer.

Harvey reared back when we drew near. "Yep, that's what I thought," he said.

My breath caught as my eyes registered what was mixed in with the pile of clothes. That wasn't a stick; it was an arm. A bony, gnarled arm.

And there was a leg sticking out from under the end table.

Harvey kicked the shoe aside.

There was the other leg.

I couldn't look away from the gnarled flesh and bones. It was so macabre that it seemed unreal. Except for that smell. I retched and covered my nose and mouth with my arm.

"Didn't she say something about being dead soon?" Harvey asked me.

I let out a squeak, which was all my vocal chords would allow in their frozen state.

"She wasn't lyin' then, was she?"

Harvey bent down and pointed at something small and round that rested against one of the rocker bases of the chair. "You see that?"

"Oh, my God!" I clutched his arm. "Is that …"

"Looks like we got us another skull raisin." He stepped back, dragging me out the door into the main hall.

I fumbled with my phone, my hands trembling, and held it out to him. "You need to call Cooper, Harvey."

"Me?" He pushed my hand away. "I ain't callin'. That boy's gonna be all horns and buck snorts when he hears you found another dead body. This is your show, girl. I just came for the dance."

"Fine, you big chicken." I called Cooper.

"What do you want, Parker." He sounded bristly, as usual.

"I need you at the Galena House on Williams Street."

"I'm busy here. Someone has to solve these damned murders you keep stumbling into. Why do I need to come there?"

I cringed, anticipating the explosion that was sure to follow what I was about to say.

Harvey nudged me. "Just tell him, girl."

"Parker," Cooper's voice grew growlier. "Is my uncle with you?"

"Yeah, and … uh … he wants me to tell you that he found a dead body." I hung up as the shit hit the fan.

Chapter Two

The sky had fallen.

Outside, the rain dumped in buckets. Mixed with pellets of hail, it pinged on the Galena House porch roof and plunked off the hood of the Picklemobile.

Inside, Detective Cooper thundered. I could hear him barking orders to his buddies in blue, his rumbles resounding down the long hallway and pouring out the front door.

"I can't believe you pinned this tail on my ass," Harvey said from where he leaned against one of the white pillars, his arms crossed over his chest.

"What?" I pulled my cell phone from my sweater pocket. "You found her first."

"I was here helping *you.*"

"If you're gonna be my bodyguard, you're going to have to get used to getting your hands dirty."

He stuck out his chin. "I'll play in the mud any day, especially if bikinis are involved, but I don't like blood on my hands."

"I didn't see any blood." How could there be no blood?

"You know what I mean, girl."

I joined him at the column, frown and all. "Seriously, did you notice any blood?"

"Nope. But that corner had a lot of shadows."

"I didn't smell blood either."

Harvey nodded. "That other stink hid everything else."

"It's like all of the juice was sucked right out of her." I cringed, thinking about how her arms and legs had looked like gnarled twigs covered in flesh. "How can that be? She was just talking to me."

"Are you sure she and your caller are one and the same?"

Now that he mentioned it, no. "You think someone else might have called me from her phone?"

"It's a possibility."

"Why? To lure me here?"

He stroked his beard, taming some of the stragglers. "That's another possibility."

I rubbed the back of my neck, pondering Harvey's question some more. "What? A setup then?"

"Could be. Or a warnin'."

A warning? I shivered, tightening my sweater belt.

"You have been meddlin' in some kooky shit lately, what with those white-haired weirdos."

"Those white-haired weirdos have been meddling with me not the other way around." Ever since I had run into two of them at Mudder Brothers Funeral Parlor, I'd turned into a magnet for the super pale population in the hills.

My phone vibrated in my pocket. I pulled it out. "It's Doc."

"Coop said no phone calls." Harvey checked over his shoulder. "He'll bust your balls if he catches you gettin' all leaky-mouthed on the phone."

Yeah, but it was Doc. For him I'd take my chances with the detective's temper. "Run interference for me."

"Fine, but you better be quick as a hiccup." He left the column and slipped between the yellow strips of police tape crisscrossing the doorway.

I held the phone to my ear. "Hi, Doc."

"What do you mean you found another body?" The sound of his baritone voice warmed my chills even if it was tight with tension.

"You got my text." It wasn't a question. I'd sent him a message as soon as I'd hung up on Cooper's curses.

Doc didn't bother with an answer. "Where are you?"

"The Galena House."

"That's up behind the old Fairmont Hotel, right?"

I leaned my shoulder against the column, looking out over the backsides of the buildings bellied up to Deadwood's Main Street. They didn't look so fancy from behind, more cluttered and disheveled, like the back of a film studio where real life took place. "Yeah, on Williams Street."

"I'm on my way."

"You can't come right now." As much as I would have liked his company at the moment, he needed to stay away.

"Why not?"

"Detective Cooper and his pals are here asking questions and taking pictures. I'm not even supposed to be talking on the phone. If Cooper finds out—"

Someone plucked my phone from my grip.

I whirled around. There stood Cooper. He'd confiscated my phone. His steely eyes had a frosty sheen, reminding me of the little balls of hail bouncing on the lawn.

"I said no calls." He held the phone up to his ear. "What did she tell you, Nyce?"

I jammed my hands on my hips, hitting him with a glare of my own. Why did he assume I was on the phone with Doc? It could have been a client or my boss. And what happened to my bodyguard running interference for me?

The detective's gaze narrowed as Doc told him something that I hoped wasn't the truth. "I'm sure I don't need to tell you to keep this information to yourself for the time being."

"Doc isn't going to say a word," I said under my breath. Nobody kept secrets like Doc. He hid a doozy of his own that would ruin his livelihood as a financial planner if it were leaked.

Cooper's head cocked to the side as he listened some more, then he snorted. "As a matter of fact, she did."

I did what? What had Doc told the detective about me? I held out my hand for my phone.

Cooper smirked at my hand, my phone still pressed against his ear. "Sounds good. I'll see you Wednesday night. It's your turn to bring the beer." He handed the phone back to me. "Say goodbye, Parker."

I took my phone. "What did you tell him, Doc?"

"Nothing he doesn't already know."

"Parker!" Detective Cooper wasn't playing nice today.

"You're being extra pissy this afternoon, Detective," I poked him in the shoulder. "And here I was kind enough to bring you more work to help you feel useful."

That went over like a six-hundred-pound pole vaulter.

Cooper's eyes narrowed into two coin slots. "I'm going to count to five, Parker. One."

Doc chuckled in my ear. "Call me when Cooper's done chewing on you."

"Two."

I squinted back at the detective. "Will you look up the definition of *excessive force*, Doc? I think we're crossing over the 'reasonably necessary' line here."

"Three."

"I'll bring you some bandages tonight and stitch your wounds," Doc said.

"Four."

Anything involving his hands touching my skin sounded like a brilliant plan, especially after the day I'd had. "I … "

"Five." Cooper reached for the phone.

I ducked his grasp. "I gotta go, Doc."

"Be careful, Trouble." Doc hung up.

I lowered the phone. "Happy now?"

Cooper snatched my phone from me and shoved it in his front pocket. "*Now* I am." He pointed at the floorboards. "Stand here and talk to nobody, understand?"

"I have a right to free speech."

"Consider it temporarily revoked." He stalked back inside, tearing a piece of police tape loose on the way.

Harvey joined me back on the porch a few huff-filled moments later.

"What happened to you?" I attacked. "You were supposed to be running interference for me."

"Whoa, tiger. Retract those saber teeth." He held up both hands in defense. "I had to drain the sleepy weasel."

I groaned. "Why does that not surprise me?"

"My ornery old prostate got stubborn and dammed up the flow." He checked his zipper.

"I don't like your ornery prostate." The last time it got

uppity, I had landed in jail.

"That makes two of us." He pulled on his suspenders, grinning. "What'd I miss?"

"I got busted by Cooper for talking to Doc."

"I told you so."

I wrinkled my lip at him. "Whose bathroom did you use?" I lowered my voice. "The dead woman's?"

"No. There's some young whippersnapper standing guard at the door. A new kid."

I raised both eyebrows. "You don't know his name?" Harvey knew everyone in town, and their parents, aunts, uncles, and cousins—especially the kissing ones.

"Well, he and I haven't shared water at the same trough yet, but give me a week or two."

"So he wouldn't let you in?" It would be out of character for Harvey not to try to sneak a peek at what Detective Cooper was up to behind closed doors.

"Not even for two free tickets to the next mud wrestling night over at the Prairie Dog Palace." Harvey shook his head. "Coop probably threatened to remove one of the kid's testicles if he let either of us come near that apartment."

I should've taken some pictures before Detective Cooper raced in and barricaded it. However, between the way the body had looked all wadded up in the corner, the ticking clocks, and that peculiar stink, I'd wanted nothing more than to get the hell out of there.

Why so many dang clocks? "Those wooden clocks reminded me of something I'd find in one of those Bavarian tourist towns." I paced the length of the porch, wishing I were back in the parking lot of Bighorn Billy's with my only problem being a maddening boss.

"They're called Black Forest clocks," Harvey said. "They had a run on them on the QVC channel last Christmas. Real Black Forest timber and authentic German craftsmanship. I would've bought one if they'd thrown in a case of Fürstenburg beer."

"She must have been watching QVC, too."

"Too bad she didn't know how to keep time."

"What do you mean?" I paused in front of him.

"Didn't you notice that none of them had the same time?"

"No. I was a little overwhelmed by how many there were and all of that ticking, not to mention the dead body."

"I only saw one that was even close to the actual time."

"Maybe they're broken." I went back to pacing. "What are the chances of Cooper letting us go back in there later to take another look?"

"You'd have better luck saddlin' a snortin' stallion."

"Stupid question, huh?"

"There's nothing wrong with wishful thinkin'."

I rubbed my hands together, trying to warm them. "Why did she call me?"

"That's a question I'm purty sure Coop will be askin' you a few more times before the day is done."

"I should've had the sense to ask her a few things before agreeing to come here."

"Keep in mind we're not even sure it was her who called."

"Well, if it was her, I should have been more thorough." Unfortunately, I'd been too busy whining on the phone to Natalie about a television crew following me around to think about playing Twenty Questions.

"What would you have asked?"

I replayed our short conversation in my head. "Her name for one." And if her need to talk to me had something to do with all of the trouble I'd stumbled into lately.

"Don't beat yourself up too much. Coop will do plenty of that later." Harvey jangled change in his pocket as I walked back and forth in front of him. "You're not thinkin' about doin' something harebrained, are you?" Harvey asked.

"That depends on what you mean by harebrained."

"Gettin' yourself all tied up in a knot over something you should let Coop unravel."

"I'd prefer to let Detective Cooper and the Deadwood Police Department handle this one without me being mixed up in it any more than I already am." That was the truth.

Harvey's forehead scrunched up. "That's not exactly a 'no'

comin' from your lips."

I truly wanted to leave it to Cooper to figure out this whole mess, and I was sure Doc would be reinforcing that very idea, but what if the dead woman had left me some clue as to why she'd insisted on seeing me immediately? Something in that apartment that I was meant to see. Something that Cooper skimmed over in his search for evidence.

As much as it pained me to admit it, Cooper was a good detective. But even Jim Rockford wasn't infallible, although James Garner sure made him look damned good on the small screen. Cooper was human ... at least his nose broke like he was. I'd witnessed him overlooking evidence first hand. What if he passed over the key that unlocked the answers to why I had been called into this mess?

"Whose bathroom did you use?" I changed the subject.

"He used mine," a soft voice said from behind us.

Harvey and I both turned.

A young woman stood in the doorway behind the crime scene tape. Her smile seemed hesitant, like she wasn't sure if she'd get busted by Detective Cooper for letting her teeth be seen. Her eyes and hair were dark brown, her skin a smooth mocha blend. She reminded me of Halle Berry, only her face was more heart-shaped, her cheekbones not so defined, and her curves a tad more shapely.

"That's Freesia," Harvey told me, pointing his thumb in the woman's direction. "She owns this place."

Owned it? She looked to be in her late twenties. That seemed pretty young to own a big white elephant like the Galena House. I smiled back as if we weren't all standing on the porch while policemen milled about down the hall.

"Hello, Freesia, I'm Violet. We have flower names in common." I'd gotten mine from my hippy mother, who used me as a placeholder for her flower child memories.

"You're Violet Parker, aren't you?" Freesia ducked through the remaining strip of yellow tape and joined us on the porch. Her shoulder length waves of thick hair trembled in the cool breeze. She buttoned her jean jacket. "You're that Realtor who sells haunted houses."

I resisted the urge to roll my eyes. Jerry was going to have a hell of a time changing my marketing brand from "spooky" to "sexy," no matter how much makeup and hairspray he doused me in.

"That's Violet all right," Harvey answered for me.

I shot him a quick scowl for his help.

"I've heard about you," Freesia said.

"None of it's true." I tried to laugh, but it came out as more of an awkward titter.

What had she heard? That I had tea with the dead? I talked to ghosts? I had sex with my clients? All of which were true, except for that last one. I'd had sex with only one client, and I was still not done between the sheets with him.

In fact, my relationship with Doc seemed to have graduated to the next level—sex *and* food, shared on a semi-regular basis. If only my kids would stop trying to muck up the good thing I had going with him, all would be sunshine and fields of dandelions for us. Well, almost. But my relationship pitfalls were subjects for another time with an audience who had more in common with me than the acquaintance of a shriveled up dead woman.

Freesia's eyes crinkled in the corners when she smiled. "I heard that you are good at what you do."

What did she mean? I was good at selling real estate or conjuring wispy folks? If she'd been trading stories with my ghost-whispering client, Cornelius Curion, and our fellow séance buddies, I needed to clarify a thing or two.

I searched her face, looking for signs of a half-hidden sneer or veiled mockery but saw none. Still, I played along with caution. "What do I do?"

Her brown eyes searched back. "Sell houses?" she said, ending with a questioning note.

Okay, now I knew whoever had been talking to her was full of crap. I sucked at selling houses. I had yet to sell a single one of my listings. The house Doc had bought through me didn't count because Mona, my mentor, had pretty much held my hand through it all while acting as the selling agent.

"Why are you making that face?" Freesia took a step back as if I might morph into a turtle and snap.

I had a reputation for scary smiles that sent children shrieking away. Evil clowns had nothing on me. I shook off my expression and painted on what I hoped was a pleasant smile. My eyes felt like they were bulging, though. "Sorry, my mind was elsewhere."

"What did you think I meant?" Freesia asked, her expression still guarded. "Do you do something besides sell houses?"

Boy was that a loaded question.

Harvey laughed outright, his gold teeth shining through his grizzle.

"Shhhh," I poked the old coot in the ribs. "You're going to get Cooper to come out here and snarl at the end of his chain again."

He waved me off. "He's all bark."

"Oh, yeah? Then why do I keep ending up with teeth marks?" I turned back to Freesia, whose gaze bounced between my bodyguard and me. "I don't do anything besides sell houses. Harvey was just being a wiseacre."

"I get the feeling he does that often."

"Violet has a way of making me grin like a mule eatin' thistles, especially with all her wild hairs."

"Wild hairs, huh?" Freesia's gaze traveled up to the curly mess that was trying to escape from my combs and bobby pins thanks to the damp air. "Every woman should have at least a few. Where's the fun in life without them?"

I had a feeling that Freesia and I were going to be pals.

"Were you born with all those curls?" she asked me.

"Yep, but the color needs a touch up every six to eight weeks thanks to life with my two nine-year-olds."

"How can you have kids that old? I'd have guessed you're in your mid-twenties."

Harvey's guffaw turned into an "oomph" when I elbowed him in the breadbasket.

"Thanks." *I think I love you.* Move over, Natalie, I found a new best friend forever. "How long have you owned this place?"

"I took it over about three years ago when my parents decided they wanted to enjoy the sun in Nevada year around."

"Did you grow up here?"

"No. I'm from Ohio, near the Kentucky state line. This place belonged to my great great-uncle." She squinted and held up her fingers, counting under her breath. "There may be another 'great' in there yet."

"Did he come out for the gold rush?"

"No, he came in the late 1890s looking for work on a ranch. From what I've been told, his parents were freed slaves. As soon as he was old enough, they insisted he head out West where there was more opportunity and money for a man like him. My pop could fill your head with tales about him and how good he was on a horse."

Harvey leaned back on his heels. "From the stories I remember, your great-uncle wasn't just good on a horse, he could do the job of three cowpokes and cook a mean chuckwagon stew to boot."

"You've heard of him?" Freesia asked, clutching her jacket collar tighter as the hail came down harder.

"Of course. Big Jake Tender was a legend around these parts, tall as a mountain and strong as two oxen. I remember a story from back when I was still a seedling 'bout how Big Jake took on a bull that had wandered into town and was causin' a ruckus, chasin' folks down the street, crashin' in windows. Folks said he grabbed that mean old bull by the horns, did some fancy footwork, and dropped it to the ground so fast the beast had the wind knocked clear out of it. It took six men to load it up and haul it out of town."

"I remember hearing that one." Freesia's grin was proud.

"Big Jake was also pretty popular with the ladies down in the Badlands," Harvey winked at her. "But then he went and fell in love and broke their hearts."

Freesia's laughter almost made me forget why I was standing on the porch of the Galena House. "My pop saved those tales until I hit my teens."

Harvey shook his head. "Too bad she never loved him back

enough to wear his ring."

Big Jake's great great-niece patted one of the columns; her smile grew wistful. "He built this place for her. Poured his heart and soul into it."

"It's a beautiful house," I said, feeling sad for Big Jake Tender and his unrequited love. All the Galena House needed was some TLC from a deep checkbook and it would be quite a knockout. "From the looks of the craftsmanship, Big Jake must have been quite a carpenter, too."

"Pop always called him a 'Jake of all trades' and aspired to be just like him … well, except for all of those painted ladies. My mom would've had his hide if he even thought about sowing a single wild oat." She trailed her fingers down the column, a lover's touch. "They fell head over heels for each other right out of college, and as soon as my brother and I were out of the house, they moved out here to take over the family legacy. This place was in really bad shape when they got here. Pop poured years and lots of money getting it this far, but then they spent a January down in Nevada and fell in love with the desert. That's where I come into the story."

"So, you've been living here on your own?"

"Mostly. My name is on the deed, but my parents come up in the summer. They help me with odds and ends, like fixing the roof, replacing the lead plumbing with copper, painting and staining, and whatever else they're up to tackling."

I glanced back at the doorway, making sure Detective Cooper wasn't loitering within hearing distance. "How long had the woman in apartment four lived here?"

"Ms. Wolff?" Freesia lowered her gaze. She kicked at a raised nail head in the porch floor boards. "She moved in about a year after my parents took over the place. They'd changed it from a boarding house into an apartment building, and she was the first to rent a unit. She told my pop that she'd lived here years ago, too, back before it fell into disrepair."

I wondered if Ms. Wolff had been around during the last round of murders and shrunken skulls. Now didn't seem like a good time to ask that question aloud. Freesia probably wouldn't know the answer anyway.

"What was Ms. Wolff like?" I pressed, trying to see if she had a history of crazy or if her phone call to me had been a one-off?

"Violet," Harvey warned, nudging his head toward the front door. "Coop's wrapping up."

I needed to hurry it up if I was going to pick Freesia's brain before Cooper bullied her into keeping her lips sealed around anyone without a badge. "Ms. Wolff called me today," I said quietly to Freesia. "She insisted I come and see her immediately."

"I know." Her volume matched mine. "Willis told me."

Her use of Harvey's first name inspired a raised brow for the old man. "What else did you tell her?"

He shrugged. "She had a right to know since she owns the place."

"Anyway ..." I turned back to Freesia, catching sight of Cooper in my peripheral. He was talking to the cop guarding the door to Ms. Wolff's apartment. "What I'm wondering is if Ms. Wolff was in her right mind when she called me or if she was prone to eccentricity."

Like calling a Realtor out of the blue and scaring her with talk about the Grim Reaper.

Freesia pulled her jacket tighter around her and buried her hands in her pockets. "Ms. Wolff had a mind like a steel trap. She knew the history of the Black Hills inside and out and could tell you the names of people who had come and gone since back before Big Jake came to town. Her bedroom has a long shelf filled with one history book after another, as well as some personal journals she'd acquired over the years. I asked her once if she was a retired teacher, but she shook her head and changed the subject."

Harvey shouldered me over a step. "What's with all of those cuckoo clocks?"

"She liked to collect them."

"How come none of them have the right time?" Harvey prodded some more.

"I asked her about that when I first took over. She said that if they all were to go off at the same time, the commotion would keep her up day and night."

The ticking alone would make me climb the walls. "It would be pretty loud. There have to be over fifty clocks in there."

"One hundred and thirteen last time I counted," Freesia corrected me.

"Did she have any friends who'd visit her?" I asked. "An ex-husband? Or a boyfriend even?"

"Or a girlfriend?" Harvey asked. When I frowned at him, he shrugged. "What? Maybe she didn't like boys."

Freesia's forehead furrowed as she looked toward Main Street. "Every now and then she'd talk about a man she used to go on picnics with years ago and this forlorn smile would creep onto her lips; otherwise, she was a textbook version of a loner. Most days, she went out only if she needed groceries. My parents would take her to the store in the winter. After they moved away, I drove her around when she needed a ride. When I was busy, she'd ask the other residents."

"Did they get along with her?"

"Sure. She was very kind. She baked for us as a 'thanks' for helping her. Her rum cake was to die for, and her homemade peppernut cookies would make this place smell great for days."

"What was her first name?" I asked.

"None of your business, Parker," Cooper answered, his voice hard and tight. He grabbed my elbow, a gesture that appeared polite, but his grip was all dominance and irritation. He pulled me several steps away from Freesia. "I thought I told you to stand here and not talk to anyone."

"I thought you specified no phone calls."

"I said talk to nobody."

"Freesia's not a nobody. She's the house's owner." I tugged my arm free. I was allergic to dominant males. They made me break out in fights. "Besides, it would've been rude for Harvey and me to ignore her, right, Harvey?"

The old buzzard held up his hands. "Don't make me the monkey in the middle on this one."

Cooper looked at Freesia, his scowl dissipating. "How are you doing, Ms. Tender?"

The sound of Big Jake's last name reminded me of what I'd learned about the Galena House. Suddenly the old place seemed more forlorn than unkempt.

"I'm okay, just sad. Ms. Wolff was a sweetheart. Were you able to determine how she was killed?"

Harvey and I exchanged a wide eyed glance. The detective must not have filled her in on the condition of the body. I turned back and caught a steely look from Cooper, warning me to keep it that way.

The detective's focus returned to Freesia, his rigid features softening. "If you're up to a visit to the station, I'd like to have you come with me to answer a few more questions."

A few? No fair. He was going to take it easy on her. I usually got the full shakedown followed by a rubber glove inspection.

A few weeks back, Harvey had mentioned that Cooper had the hots for someone. Maybe Freesia was that someone. She was young for the detective by about fifteen years or so I guessed, but age might not matter to either of them. I hoped she used protection when getting naked with him. Chainmail underneath a hazmat suit should be enough.

Harvey joined me off to the side while Cooper treated Freesia with kid gloves. I watched with a pout, waiting for him to offer her milk and cookies. I leaned over and whispered, "How come he's so nice to her?"

"Probably because she didn't drop another murder in his lap that could cost him his job if he can't solve it."

"It wasn't my fault. Ms. Wolff called me."

"Maybe so, but why?"

Cooper shouted for one of his men, who shielded Freesia under an umbrella and led her to a police car. The hail had stopped, replaced by a steady drizzle. Freesia waved goodbye to us before sliding into the passenger seat.

After speaking in grunts and growls on his cell phone, Cooper hung up and stalked back to where his uncle and I waited for our flogging. "You can leave for now, Parker. I'd advise you to stay in town for a few days."

What? "You're not hauling me to the station, too?"

"Not now but don't get too comfortable."

I couldn't remember the last time I'd felt anything even remotely close to comfortable since making the detective's acquaintance back in July.

"What about me?" Harvey asked.

"Keep your phone handy."

"Did you see the twits I sent you earlier?"

Cooper did a doubletake. "You sent me what?"

"He calls texts 'twits,'" I explained.

"The pictures of the cow," Harvey added.

The canyons in Cooper's forehead deepened. "I'll call you later about those."

I palmed the keys to the Picklemobile and pulled the neck of my sweater up over my head to shield my hair. Rain tended to morph my curls into a clown wig. "Let's go, Harvey."

"Parker!" Cooper stopped me halfway down the sidewalk.

My shoulders tightened. I turned. "What?"

He joined us in the rain, his dark blond hair, crooked nose, and windbreaker dotted with water drops. "I cannot emphasize how important it is that you keep your big mouth shut about this damned mess until I get to the bottom of it."

Now that I thought about it, chainmail wasn't enough. "What do you think, Cooper? I'm going to place an ad on the front page of the *Black Hills Trailblazer*?" I took a step toward him, thinking it might be nice to add another crook to his nose with my fist. "Having another murder on my résumé is not exactly going to help my reputation, you know."

He held his index finger to his lips. "Not a word to anyone other than Nyce. Not even to your boss."

Harvey tugged on my sweater. "Unless you two wanna slice thumbs and share blood over it, I suggest we get goin'."

"I don't want to hear about either of you sneaking around this place later," Cooper hollered at our backs. "Leave this one to the police, Parker."

"I'd be happy to," I yelled over my shoulder while Harvey dragged me along. "It'd be wonderful if you could actually solve it before I'm forced to!"

Chapter Three

"Where can I drop you?" I asked Harvey as we headed back across Main Street.

"There's only one place I can think to go right now."

"Where's that?" I knew where I wanted to go to unload the weight of Ms. Wolff's death.

"Doc's office, our pow-wow headquarters."

He must have been reading my mind.

I parked the Picklemobile behind Calamity Jane Realty. The exhaust pipe announced our arrival with a loud bang; the backfire was its version of a car alarm's *beep-beep*. Jerry's Hummer wasn't in sight, nor Ben's Subaru; only Mona's and Ray's SUVs were parked in their usual spots.

"I need to go into the office and touch base." I hoped Mona wouldn't ask too many questions about my whereabouts for the last two hours. I hated to lie to her, but Cooper had insisted, so this one was on his conscience, not mine. "I'll be over there in a few."

"I'll fill Doc in on the mess we waded into back at the Galena House while we wait."

"Don't let Detective Cooper find out you were talking about Ms. Wolff."

Harvey reached for the door handle. "Coop told you to keep your big mouth shut. He didn't say a peep about stopping my chin from waggin'."

We crawled out of the pickup and dodged raindrops all the way across the lot. Harvey veered next door to Doc's as we neared.

I stepped inside Calamity Jane's and shook out my sweater, hanging it on one of the pegs lining the back wall. I could smell remnants of my boss's cologne as I passed his office, but as I'd figured when I hadn't seen his Hummer, there was no sign of him. The overhead lights were on, but nobody was home. After his latest absurd marketing idea, I was beginning to think that was true inside of his head, too.

Mona looked up from her laptop as I stepped into the front room where four desks formed an open circle, like Conestoga wagons ready for an ambush. Our desks used to be lined up like school children, but Jerry didn't think that inspired a team atmosphere. Now we were huddled together so that we could gaze into each other's eyes in between clients coming and going. Lucky me, I got to face off with the scowl of my favorite coworker, Ray the Horse's Ass, hour after hour. I could only imagine what fun form of torture Jerry would come up with next for us. Thumbscrews? Matching iron maidens? A company retreat?

I looked over at Ray's desk, noting his cell phone and keys weren't in their usual corner. The bathroom door stood open, the room dark. He must have taken off with Ben, his nephew, the newest member of our "five-man team."

"Where'd you disappear to after lunch?" Mona asked, her red fingernails clacking on her keyboard. As much typing as Mona did every day, I had a suspicion she was either writing a book or having a torrid email affair with some lovesick prison inmate … or maybe a cell block full of them.

I tucked my purse into my desk drawer, glancing at the clock. Only two hours had passed since I'd left Bighorn Billy's. The fire in my gut over Jerry's reality TV idea had been stomped on and doused by a dead woman.

"I had a few errands to run." Guilt warmed my cheeks at my lie. "Where's everyone?"

"Jerry had to meet with Jane's lawyer about some title paperwork. Apparently her being murdered gums up the transfer of ownership."

Melancholy plopped down on my chest. There wasn't a day that went by that I didn't miss Jane with her level-headed career plans and her ability to converse without a single sports-based metaphor. I crossed my fingers that this paperwork problem acted as tar under Jerry's marketing machine.

"Ray and Ben headed out after lunch to meet a client who is interested in purchasing the High Stakes Casino."

My desk phone was blinking. Because it was Sunday, I suspected my son had called to ask me to pick up some household chemical, superglue, or pizza before coming home. I sat down and scanned through a few new listings posted to the MLS database. My eyes glazed over, my brain still back in apartment four with all of those clocks. Why had there been no blood? "That casino closed down last winter, right?"

"Yes," she paused to shuffle some papers around and then returned to her keyboard. "One of the pipes burst during that below zero spell we had and flooded the second floor, ruining a good portion of the first floor's ceiling. Not to mention the wreck it made of the carpet and underlying floor boards on both levels."

What had Ms. Wolff said, or whoever it was that had called me to come over? Something about "nine shark trickster"? Or was it "nine shaft rigger"? No, there was a "kst" sound in there, I was pretty sure. If only a damned pickup hadn't driven by at that very moment.

"Some of the original molding was warped," Mona continued, "which is too bad because it was really ornate."

What were we talking about? Oh, yeah, the High Stakes Casino. "This client of theirs must have an impressive bank account."

"Or a group of investors in his back pocket. Ray said the guy wants to turn it into a high-end gentlemen's club reminiscent of the old days, including a cigar smoking lounge, pool hall, dance stage for vaudeville type performances, and a high roller gamblers' den."

"In Deadwood? He has us confused with Vegas."

"According to Ben, the buyer believes the future of the gambling industry is in returning to successful methods used in the past. He wants to have the place reminiscent of old style Vegas, with Dean Martin, Frank Sinatra, and Bugsy Siegel."

"I'm sure Detective Cooper will love taking on the mob." Maybe he'd quit harping on me so much if tommy guns and pinstripe suits filled the streets of Deadwood.

I locked my computer and pushed back from my desk, wondering if Harvey had finished filling Doc in on our discovery in apartment four.

Mona lifted her rhinestone reading glasses, resting them on top of her auburn tresses. "Hold on a minute while I picture Cooper with sweat trickling down his sideburns, guns a'blazin." She purred in her throat. "It's too bad he's a little young for me. What about you?"

"What about me?" I pulled out a compact mirror and tube of lip gloss from my desk drawer, tucking my hair back, freshening up for Doc. Even if he had seen me first thing in the morning a few times now, he hadn't seen me in all of my frizzy glory.

"I know Detective Cooper is not your favorite person, but you can't tell me you've never thought about hitting that?"

Hitting that? I paused mid-gloss and shot her an open-mouthed look over the mirror. "You've been hanging around Ray too much. His vernacular is rubbing off on you."

She leaned back, crossing her arms over her chest. "Answer the question, Vi."

I finished touching up my lips. "Sure, I've thought about 'hitting that' many times."

"Ha!" Mona grinned wide. "I knew it."

I tucked the mirror and gloss back into my desk. "In most of my fantasies, I use my shoe. Sometimes it's with a wooden spatula or a serving tray. Once I even daydreamed about using a rubber chicken on him until he cried like a baby." I sighed like a lovesick groupie. "That one really got me all jazzed up."

She chuckled, lowering her glasses back onto her nose. "You can joke all you want, but he's one hot cop."

"That's true. I've seen him spit fire with my very own eyes, and then had to be treated for the burns."

"You really don't like him, do you?"

What I felt for Detective Cooper was much more complicated than circling YES or NO on a do-you-like-me note.

There were levels of frustration and anger sandwiched with humiliation and fury, yet slices of respect and trust were melded in between it all. However, it would take way more time than I had at the moment to explain it all, so I kept it simple. "Mona, I can't emphasize enough how much Cooper does not ring my bell." Except for the one signaling the end of yet another round of fighting between us.

"He's such an alpha male, all dominant and chest pounding." She leaned her chin on her palm. "And so big."

Big? Cooper was long-legged, rip-corded, and lean, built like an old West gunfighter, but not really "big." I was beginning to wonder if we were still talking about the detective or if Mona had moved on to another alpha male who was messing up my world with his marketing schemes.

"I bet he's an animal in the sack," she said.

I stared at Mona, taken aback at our topic of conversation this afternoon. This was the first time she and I had delved into the subject of sex. Until now our friendship had been centered on work and my kids with her sharing only brief snippets of her family and past. What had changed? Jane dying? A camaraderie because we were now outnumbered by men in the office? Maybe she had something she needed to share about a certain man and I was replacing Jane as Mona's new confidante.

"An animal, huh?" I shrugged, playing along. "He definitely has sharp, pokey parts. Personally, I prefer to be bitten, not clawed."

"Doc's a biter, huh?"

I'd filled her in last week on the situation between Doc and me while sipping on lattes at the Tin Cup Café. I'd been afraid she'd shake her head about me getting involved with a previous client, so her smile had been a relief.

"He bites some," I grinned, "but he licks a lot more." Enough about Doc. "What about Jerry?"

"Jerry?" She jerked upright, her eyes glancing toward his office. "What do you mean? We're talking about Cooper."

"Come on, Mona. I'm not blind. There's something going on between Jerry and you." Something that had her wanting to exchange locker room talk about sex and boys with me.

"You're reading things wrong. He's my boss and that's it." She returned to her keyboard, clacking away, but her cheeks were full of roses.

"Sure, Jerry is your boss right now. What about before?"

"Before, he was Jane's ex-husband."

"And?"

"And nothing. That's all there ever was and all there ever will be."

She wasn't going to budge today. Fine. I wasn't going anywhere and neither was she or Jerry. I'd try again later. "If you say so." I headed toward the front door. "Speaking of Doc, I need to run over to his office for a few minutes."

Her eyes remained glued to her screen. "Got it."

I jangled my keys. "If you need to leave, lock up."

"Will do. Say 'hello' to your biter for me."

Chuckling, I pushed outside. The cold, damp air chilled my skin, making me wish I'd grabbed my sweater even if it was still soggy. The change in seasons had cooled things down quickly up in the hills, where Old Man Winter always nipped at autumn's heels right out of the gate. Most years, snowflakes started falling in October and kept flurrying off and on all of the way into May. That reminded me that I needed to dig the kids' winter coats out of the boxes I had stacked down in Aunt Zoe's basement and see if they still fit.

I didn't waste time watching my breath turn to steam and dashed into Doc's warm office closing the door behind me, shivering in my damp silk blouse.

"It's 'bout damned time, girl," Harvey twisted in his chair opposite Doc's desk. "We gotta hit the road soon. Coop and I need to figure out what to do with that cow mess."

Doc rose from his desk chair and shrugged off his tan corduroy jacket. "Here," he said, coming around and draping it over my shoulders. His dark brown gaze lingered below my chin until I pulled the jacket closed over my chest.

Warmth cocooned me; the scent of his skin and woodsy cologne were exactly what I needed to soothe some of the scrapes left after my brush with Cooper's scratchy personality.

"Thanks," I looked up at him, hungry for more of his body heat. His black hair looked finger plowed, his chin and jaw shadowed with stubble.

"You're welcome, Boots." Doc's focus stayed locked on my lips for a heartbeat or five, making me glad I'd taken the time to gloss them up for him. "Is that the cherry flavored stuff or strawberry?"

"Ah, shitfire." Harvey pushed out of his chair. "Come on you two horny toads, don't make me get a hose." He caught my arm and led me to his seat, shoving me down into it.

It wasn't my fault. Doc did things to me, all kinds of things, sometimes with his fingers, often with his tongue, especially when we were alone. If Harvey looked up the words *hopeless*, *pathetic*, and *lovesick* in the dictionary, my picture would be smack dab in the center, my grin goofy and sappy as hell.

I did my best to keep my heart from popping up into my eyeballs when I stared at Doc. Knowing that he'd dumped his last girlfriend at the mention of marriage, I had to play it iceberg cool. If he knew I'd gone and fallen head-over-boots for him in three short months, he might kick me to the gutter, too. Aunt Zoe kept telling me that Doc wouldn't do that, claiming I was "special," which I interpreted as *mental but harmless and means well*. Clearly she was biased due to our shared DNA. When it got down to bedrock, I didn't want to take any chances with the M-word. I had two kids to take care of, so drowning my broken heart in tequila was not an option.

"I already spread my manure, fillin' Doc's ears with what I know and saw." Harvey lowered into Doc's desk chair. "It's your turn now."

Doc waited for me, one of his dark eyebrows lifted higher than the other. "You doing okay?"

"All things considered," *reality TV show, dead woman, asshole coworker, lonely nights*, "I'm good." I cinched his jacket tighter since Harvey wouldn't let me wrap up in Doc's arms.

"What'd the lady on the phone say to you?" he pressed.

I repeated what I remembered, mangling her "nine"

comment even more. Clouds passed over Doc's face as he listened to my account, settling on his creased brow. When I finished, he scrubbed his hand down his face, scratching over his five o'clock shadow.

"Christ," he muttered and walked over to the front window, his back to Harvey and me.

"What do you make of it?" Harvey asked.

"Something that is going to keep me awake all night."

I picked at lint on my black pants, wishing we were sitting around planning a picnic instead of discussing a dead woman.

Doc's cell phone rang. He pulled it out of his pocket, looked down at it, and then turned to me. "It says you're calling me."

"I am?" Had I butt dialed him when I'd sat down? I felt for my phone and came up empty.

"Hello?" he answered, his eyes locked onto me. "Yeah, she's here." Another pause. "Sure." He walked over, his phone held out for me to take, and mouthed the name *Cooper*.

Crap, right. In my haste to escape without having to take a trip to the police station, I'd forgotten he'd pocketed my cell. "You stole my phone, Detective."

"I confiscated it. There's a big difference."

"I call bullshit."

"What a coincidence, because I called you, and time and again you're full of it."

He was turning into a real comedian. "I want my phone back, Cooper."

"I figured you might. By the way, Natalie called and left a message for you."

I pinched the bridge of my nose, wishing I could pinch him instead. "Don't you need a warrant to go through my phone records?"

Harvey snickered, which earned him a glare from me.

"All I did was answer a ringing phone."

I growled at him. Doc placed his hand on my shoulder, squeezing slightly.

"Are you up on your rabies shots, Parker?"

"What did Nat want?" I cringed in anticipation, wondering if

Natalie had had the sense not to let on to Cooper that I'd told her about Ms. Wolff's creepy call this morning. I imagined having Cooper answer my phone had knocked her back a step.

"She wanted to check in and see if you had called on her mother like you two had discussed earlier."

Whew! She'd gone into code mode. Quick thinking on her part. "When can I get my phone back?"

"Did you?" Cooper asked.

"Did I what?"

"Check in on Natalie's mother?"

I hesitated, trying to figure out if he were seriously concerned or being a nosy detective. "Why do you care? Are you working part-time for a nurse hotline now?"

"Answer the question, Parker."

"I don't know that it's any of your concern."

"It's a simple question."

"Not when it's coming from you, Detective."

"Jesus, Violet." His voice sounded tired this time, not so barky. "Why do you have to make every conversation we have a battle?"

I hated it when he let his human side show through. It was hard to be snappy with him when I knew he'd been working day and night on these unsolved cases and probably needed his binky and a nap. "Maybe if you'd use the words 'pretty please' every now and then, I wouldn't feel the need to come out swinging."

"You push your luck with me and then bitch when you end up in my jail. You're so damned hard-headed. How does Nyce put up with your mouth?"

"Doc's quite fond of my mouth." That earned me a wink from the man in question. "Funny, Cooper, I didn't hear a 'please' at all in there."

He sighed through the line, sounding more pained than frustrated. "Would you *please* tell me how many people besides Nyce and your buddy, Natalie, know about this morning's phone call from Ms. Wolff?"

"To be fair, when I told Nat I didn't know anyone was dead."

"I need names, Parker. Not excuses."

"Natalie, Doc, and Harvey. That's it."

"You're sure this time?"

It was my turn to sigh. "Yes, Detective. I'm positive."

"Good. Let's keep it that way then."

"You actually think you can keep the town of Deadwood from finding out Ms. Wolff was murdered?"

"No, but if I can keep you from being connected to her in the public eye, both of our careers may still have a future."

Good point. "I'll be by to get my phone in a few minutes."

"Don't bother. I'll send it by this evening. Your aunt's place or Nyce's?"

"Aunt Zoe's."

"Before you hang up, I have a couple more questions."

Harvey waved at me to hurry up. I pointed at the phone and shook my fist. "I'm waiting with bated breath, Detective."

"Is there anything else I need to know about today's events? Anything you've withheld ... by accident, of course?"

I thought about the phone call, the apartment, my conversation with Freesia, all of those clocks.

"Parker?" his voice had the hint of a snarl to it again.

"I'm thinking." I had recounted everything to him, I was sure. I didn't want to get pulled into this mess, especially not with shrunken heads involved. "No."

"You're absolutely positive."

"Cooper!"

"Okay, okay. It's just you don't have the best record for total honesty in the past."

That was his fault for being such a frustrating prick. "Will there be anything else, Detective?" Or was he done with his rubber glove?

"Yes. Why is there a picture of a horse's skull in your phone?"

"You looked at my pictures?!!" My cheeks burned as I remembered a picture I'd taken last week of a weird mole on my back where my bra strap rubs and sent it to Natalie to check out. Thankfully Doc and I kept our phone sex to verbal stimulation, not photos of me in compromising positions.

He chuckled. "Goodnight, Parker." He hung up on me.

"I'm going to shoot him in the foot with his own gun, I swear." I handed Doc his cell phone.

"That's been done before," Harvey said. "If you want to be original, you'll need to aim for his knee."

Doc pocketed his phone. "Violet, tell me again what the lady said to you during the phone call."

I repeated what I could recall, including the various "nine" lines, which had now morphed into three garbled possibilities.

"Does she have one 'F' or two in her last name?"

Harvey and I shrugged as one. "I didn't ask," I told Doc.

"The clocks in her house were Black Forest designs?"

"Yep," Harvey said. "Over one hundred of them."

"And this Freesia woman who owns the Galena House said the victim made peppernut cookies?"

I nodded, still worrying about what other pictures I had stored on my phone. I vaguely remembered taking a picture of Cooper's case board of Jane's murder in his basement last month. That would surely have made his blood boil if he'd found that one. Had I taken a picture of the crate full of bottles of mead that was stashed at Mudder Brothers?

Doc leaned his hip against the desk, rubbing his jaw. "She wasn't saying 'nine' like the number, Violet."

Wait! Those were all on my *old* phone, the one I'd dropped in the toilet at the Opera House. I sat back, relieved. Putting aside all worries about what Cooper might have seen on my phone, I absorbed Doc's words. "She wasn't?"

"No. She was speaking German. 'Nein' means 'no.'"

"Of course!" Once he said it, everything clicked. "I'm an idiot."

"You were distracted by everything going on today," Doc said. "You would've figured it out once the dust settled."

"So what does 'shark trickster' mean in German?"

"It means you don't hear for shit." Harvey grunted to his feet. "And knowin' your luck, whatever she said is not gonna help you get some much needed beauty rest anytime soon."

I stuck my tongue out at the old bugger.

"I have just the sleep aid for you, Boots." Doc said, locking the front door and turning the sign to Closed.

He sure did. Too bad his bedroom wasn't just down the hall from mine. "If only Ms. Wolff had been calling about a house. Now there's a whole new mystery to figure out."

"For Cooper or you?" Doc asked.

"This one is all Cooper's. I'll even wrap it up and put a bow on top."

"Well, hunky dory, it's agreed then." Harvey knocked twice on Doc's desk. "We're leavin' this one to Coop. You ready to go, girl? I have a cow mystery to piece together."

I stood, pulling out my keys. "I'm worried about you staying out there alone."

"Don't be. I'm not stayin', just headin' out to take care of chores and wait for Coop's instructions. I'll be back in a bullwhip snap."

"Should I make up the couch?"

"I'd appreciate it. I'll twit ya later, Doc."

Doc followed Harvey toward the back hallway. "Twit?"

"Don't ask," I said.

Doc caught my arm. "Hold on, Violet." He looked at Harvey. "You have your spare set of keys to the Picklemobile on you?"

Harvey nodded.

"Why don't you head out. I'll take Violet home."

"Works for me." Harvey opened the back door. "Stay out of trouble, girl," he called.

"Be careful at your ranch, old man."

Doc locked the door behind him. Then he leaned against it and crossed his arms over his chest. "This isn't good, Violet."

I held up the wall at the other end of the hallway. "I know. You're standing way too far away from me. Come closer." I tried to make light of a dark subject.

"You make it hard for me to stay focused when you wear soft shirts that I like to touch."

"My bra is even softer."

"So is your skin, especially under your bra."

"I've been told the back of my knees are pretty smooth, too. And my inner thighs."

"Stop distracting me, vixen. Have you thought any more about what we talked about last night?"

Yes, I had, plenty, mostly during the early morning hours when I was supposed to be getting that beauty sleep. "You really think it's a good idea after last time?"

"We need to figure out your role in all of this."

"I'm fine with being blissfully ignorant."

"If that were true, Cooper wouldn't be pissed off at you."

"Cooper needs to get laid, take a vacation, and relax."

"Funny, I was thinking about you naked this morning, writing myself a prescription for that very trifecta."

"Oh, yeah? Where would we go?"

"I don't know. I got fixated on that first part." He shoved his hands in his pockets. "Ms. Wolff didn't call you on a whim. You must realize that she sought you out for a reason."

"Yeah." I pulled his jacket tighter around me. As much as I wished it wasn't so, I'd have to be naïve to think otherwise. I leaned my head against the wall. The energy drain of today's emotional highs was taking its toll on me, making my head ache. "I don't know what to do, Doc. I feel like I'm tiptoeing through a haunted house while blindfolded. I have to keep feeling my way along, waiting for the next monster to slime my hand."

"I do. Call Cornelius."

"But what if ..." I hesitated.

There were too many what-ifs for my comfort, the most worrisome being that Cornelius would figure out Doc was the medium, not me. Then word would get out, tarnishing Doc's reputation and potentially ruining his business.

"We can what-if this all day long, Violet. We need to know if you are the key, and the only way to do that is experiment."

"We're playing Dr. Frankenstein here. Next thing I know, you'll be sending me to the graveyard to pick up a fresh brain. Grave robbing will really dress up my rap sheet."

"Nah. Your big brain will do fine." He closed the distance

between us in a few strides, grasping the lapels of his jacket. "Violet, please call Cornelius and set up another séance for just the three of us."

"What if he finds out your secret?"

"Trust me, it's worth the risk." He ran his finger down my cheek, his gaze serious. "I've been dealing with paranormal activity all my life. This is the first I've ever come across so much disturbance in one place. There's something going on here, something much bigger than random hauntings. We can't let fear stop us from figuring out how you fit into it all."

"I don't think I want to know."

"I used to feel that way, too. But if you really do possess some sixth sense ability, the best course is figuring out what it is and accepting it."

I rested my forehead on his chest and wrapped my arms around his waist, leaning on him. "Doc," I breathed his name, his scent calming. "Why did she call me?"

He massaged my shoulders, his hands melting away the day's tension. "Maybe Cooper will figure it out."

"You really believe that?"

"Not at all."

I pulled back and frowned up at him. "You could have at least hesitated."

"We agreed to be honest with each other about everything, remember?"

"Why don't you believe in Cooper?"

"I think this is outside of his realm, but it doesn't hurt to have him and his guns on our side."

"Doesn't hurt you maybe, since you two are poker buddies now, but he chafes my hide."

"Really?" Doc's eyelids lowered, his smile flirting with me. "Where are you chafed, Boots?"

"In a few spots."

"I should probably have a look at them. Kiss them better."

"I thought you said you weren't a doctor."

"I'm not." His hands slid under my shirt, his palms warm on my skin. "But I'm good at playing one. If only you were wearing one of those gowns that opens in back."

I eased my hands around his neck. "Here you are thinking about getting me mostly naked and you haven't kissed me 'hello' yet."

"My fantasies vary in the amount of clothing you have on." His fingers climbed my rib cage. "Take this shirt."

"What about it?"

"No, I meant take it off."

"And then what?"

"We'll discuss the situation with your bra." He tipped my head back and kissed me, slow, teasing, tantalizing. "Hello, Boots," he whispered when he finished.

"I missed you today," I said.

"Good." His thumbs brushed over me, zinging me clear to my toes. "How about you take me to a magical place that I'll love coming home to every night?"

"That stupid billboard!" I huffed at his quiet laughter. "I'm going to hurt you for that one."

He backed me into the wall, his hips pressing into mine. "Did you bring your spurs?"

His cell phone rang, vibrating against my thigh. "You want to get that?"

"Not really," he said, but pulled his phone out anyway. "It's Cooper again."

"Damn that man."

Doc pulled away from me. "Hello, Cooper." As he listened, his dark eyes moved from my eyes to my lips and back again. "Okay, I'll let her know." He listened for another few seconds and then hung up.

"What now?"

"Your Aunt Zoe called. She wants to know when you'll be home for supper and why Cooper is answering your phone."

I'd have to figure out a good way of avoiding the truth about Ms. Wolff and that whole mess while trying to explain why Deadwood's detective had my phone. But more importantly, "Are you joining us tonight?"

"What are you having?"

"I saw some pork thawing in the sink this morning. I think Aunt Zoe was going to turn it into pulled pork."

"What can I bring?"

"Yourself."

"Plus wine and bread?"

"I've never turned down either."

He grabbed my hand and laced his fingers through mine. "I forgot to mention one other thing Cooper said."

"What's that?"

"Your Aunt Zoe invited him to dinner."

"No!"

Chapter Four

Tuesday, October 2nd

Four score and seven years later, Abraham Lincoln called me bright and ugly in the morning. Actually, only two days had passed, and the caller who had the gall to wake me at dawn's early light was Cornelius Curion, the Abe look-alike who claimed to be a ghost whisperer and also happened to be my single buying client at the moment. The latter fact kept me from wishing ten thousand locusts would swarm his head.

"Good morning, Cornelius," I mumbled, my tongue still asleep.

"I NEED TO TALK TO VIOLET PARKER!" he yelled through my phone, making my ear ring and my eyeballs almost pop out of my skull. Apparently, today he was saving his whispering for ghosts only.

In addition to the odd belief Cornelius had that he could share sweet nothings with the ectoplasmic crowd, he was also under the misconception that I had a personal secretary—such as Jiminy Cricket in my freaking pocket. No matter how many times we played this game on the phone, the damned man couldn't get it through his stove-pipe hat that if he called me on my cell phone, I was the one answering the call.

Well, at least when Cooper didn't have my phone.

I'd received my phone back Sunday evening as promised. Fortunately, Cooper had been too busy trying to solve Ms. Wolff's murder to join us for what I'm sure would have been a fun-filled family dinner.

"This. Is. Violet." I growled at the end for emphasis.

A loud clanging rang in the background from his end of the line, sounding like twenty pans had all fallen to the floor at once.

"GOOD!" he yelled. "IT'S YOU THEN!"

"And it's me now, too." A sharp *thwack, thwack, thwack* came through the phone. I sat up, shoving my hair out of my face. The smell of pancakes and coffee filtered through my bedroom doorway, making my stomach growl along with my brain.

"Where are you, Cornelius?" My volume increased to match his with all of the commotion in the background. Lurching out of bed, I shut my bedroom door. The kids didn't need to wake up for another fifteen minutes.

His reply was drowned out by what sounded like a saw cutting through wood.

"I can't hear you, Cornelius."

"HOLD ON!" he yelled.

I dropped onto the bed and stared at the ceiling, trying to figure out how I would broach the subject of the séance to Cornelius.

The racket coming through the line began to fade. I heard a door shut and then there was silence.

"There," he said at a normal level. "Now you can quit shouting at me. Would you look at that! There are two ravens sitting on the fence by my car. I can never remember if seeing two ravens is a bad omen or good. My grandmother had a poem she'd recite to help me remember, how did it go ...? I can't remember."

I covered my eyes. "Cornelius, where are you?"

"Goldwash."

Was that one of the casinos on Main Street? Or was that the Golden Spur? I needed coffee to clear the spider webs leftover from my nightmare about shrunken heads. "Where?"

"Goldwash." I heard a bird screech from his end. "It's an old mining town in Nevada. Surely you've heard of the famous haunted hotel here in town."

"Can't say that I have." My eyelids snapped open. "You're not trying to buy that hotel, too, are you?" His lack of funding had held up the sale I was working on for him for The Old Prospector Hotel, Deadwood's own haunted playground. If he was trying to get money for another hotel and was screwing up my sale because of it, I was going to go down there to this Goldwash town and sic the ravens on his bony ass.

"I wish!" he said. "But this place isn't for sale. A friend of mine bought it years back. He's fixing it up, hoping to make it a mecca for paranormal lovers. Buffalo was my inspiration for buying the hotel in Deadwood."

"Buffalo?" I scratched my temple. "You mean the buffalo

down in Custer State Park inspired you to want to have a place here in the Black Hills?" I thought it was The Old Prospector Hotel's ghost stories that had inspired him to come north.

"No, *Buffalo* is the name of my friend down here, but did you know that the white buffalo is a sign of good luck? So is a desert tortoise. I think two ravens may be, too. Isn't one raven considered a sign of impending death? Like a flying grim reaper?"

"You know what? Just stop. Please. It's too early for this."

"You sound tense, Violet. Have you been reaching your hand into dark places again? You really shouldn't tour the shadowed recesses of your mind without me there to guide you."

Right now I was thinking about reaching my hand through the phone and beating him with his own hat.

"When are you coming back to Deadwood?" I asked, cutting through the fog of befuddlement that rolled in whenever Cornelius came within my hearing range.

"Is there a problem with the sale?"

"No." There was a problem with dead people, but if I came right out in the open about wanting to set up a séance with Doc, that could start a chain of events that might end up in some sort of negative social explosion for Doc. I waded in on my tiptoes. "The sale is going through without a hitch at this point, but I need to see you."

"Ohhhh. You've fallen in love with me, haven't you?"

His question stunned me into a total silence rivaling that of deep space.

"I should've seen this coming. It happens all of the time."

Was he serious? "All of the time?"

"Yes. Women get attached to me very quickly. My hypothesis is that it's due to my ability to communicate with ghosts."

"So you think that makes you a rock star in their eyes?"

"No, of course not," he said, as if I were the silly one this morning. "I believe that they see how good I am at communicating with ghosts and it appeals to their need to find a man whose communication skills are on an equal playing field with them. Time and again, women complain about how their husband or boyfriend won't talk to them. I'm the answer to their prayers—the answer to *your* prayers."

Actually, he'd been more the cause of my nightmares.

"Cornelius, I have not fallen in love with you, so it's your lucky day."

"That would explain the two ravens."

At this point, I figured the best course was to continue with my initial reason for calling him last night and leaving a voicemail to get back with me ASAP. "I need to see you about a ghost."

"You have been reaching out, Violet. I knew it. I could feel the ripples in the other realm. Bad girl!"

I hit my phone on the bed a few times. Doc owed me big time for this. "No, Cornelius, those ripples weren't caused by me. But when you return, I'd like to discuss another meeting with you like we had up at Mount Moriah." Just thinking about how I'd reached into the darkness and torn out that thing's tongue still made me tuck in my knees and tremble.

"You mean a séance, Violet?" I could hear the excitement in his voice. He was probably hopping around down there in Goldwash like a grasshopper in tall weeds.

I cringed. "I'd prefer we call it a reaching out session."

"It's more like a type of reaching inward therapy. Should we reserve the jail cell at the police station?"

"No, we definitely should not." Cornelius had been leaning on me to have a séance in one of the jail cells in Detective Cooper's lair since he'd found out a prisoner had hanged himself there and was said to still haunt the place. I could only imagine the slew of nicknames I'd incur if I toted candles and an EVP monitor into the station and started talking to the walls.

"I'd prefer to be in the privacy of your hotel suite again," I told him. The last two séances—the only two I'd ever taken part in—had been in his hotel room. Mt. Moriah wasn't really a séance, more of freaky-ass accident. "Only this time, Safari Skipper and her biker boyfriend can't join us."

"Who will run my equipment?"

"You said that it could practically run itself."

"That's true, but there's safety in numbers when it comes to the paranormal world."

Not in my experience. One seemed to be the magic number, unfortunately, but there were no witnesses to back up my story and keep me from appearing temporarily insane.

"We'll take our chances." I'd surprise him with Doc's presence. Since Cornelius was of the mindset the-more-the-merrier, he wouldn't mind a third party attendee.

"I'll be back up there this weekend."

Good, that gave me time to prepare for this mentally so the anxiety wouldn't strangle my heart in the meantime. "Call me when you're settled in."

"I'm going to go catch one of those ravens and pluck a few of its feathers to bring with me for the séance."

"Excellent. I'll pick up some eye of newt the next time I'm at Piggly Wiggly." I wondered if he could hear how deep the sarcasm was flowing on my end.

"Don't waste your time, Violet. They don't sell eye of newt there," he said and hung up on me.

I threw my phone down on the bed and flopped back on my pillows. Conversations with Cornelius had a way of leaving me feeling like I was dangling upside-down from a tree limb.

A door slammed out in the hall. Seconds later, the yelling began.

"Dang kids!" I hopped out of bed, stomping out into the hallway to blow my whistle and play referee.

Twenty minutes and two timeouts later, Addy and Layne marched down the stairs in front of me, heads lowered in pouts.

"The kitchen. Now!" I said when we reached the bottom step, in case one of them thought they could make a break for it.

Happiness awaited me in Aunt Zoe's lemon colored kitchen in the form of caffeine and carbohydrates. Old man Harvey stood at the griddle watching pancakes bubble while Aunt Zoe poured two cups of coffee.

"Good morning," she said, setting one of the cups down in front of me. She pulled a plateful of pancakes out of the oven and placed it in the middle of the table. "Has the storm passed?"

"What storm?" Addy asked, sliding two pancakes onto her plate.

"The one causing all of the thunder upstairs."

"Duh, Addy," Layne said, his mouth full.

Harvey flicked Layne's ear. "Didn't you learn anything this mornin', boy? Don't mess with girls before they've had their feed. The only thing ornerier than a sore-toothed grizzly bear is a hungry woman."

"Bite your tongue, old man." I hit the buzzard with a mock glare since I didn't have a wooden spoon handy. "You're outnumbered by hungry women this morning."

He grabbed two pancakes and dropped them on the plate in front of me, tossing three pieces of bacon on top. "Eat."

"I can't put all of this away."

"Cut the crap, girl. Doc isn't here, so you can fill your gullet. Besides, you're gonna need a full stomach to face off with my nephew this mornin'."

Detective Cooper had called last night while I was washing dinner dishes and ordered me to be in his office first thing this morning. As he'd warned back at the Galena House, he had more questions for me. My flat out *NO!* was met with a slew of cursing. After we'd traded a few terse insults, I'd proposed his interrogation take place at an offsite location, aka his house. I'd also insisted on Harvey coming with me since he'd been standing right there next to me in that apartment when we'd found Ms. Wolff. Cooper agreed, saying he could kill two birds with one stone that way. As high strung as he was these days, I hoped he was using a turn of phrase and didn't plan on aiming his loaded, authentic Colt .45 bedside lamp in my direction.

"Why are you going to see Detective Cooper?" Layne asked in between slurps of orange juice. "Is this about that foot I found in the tree last summer?"

"No." I wasn't sure I ever wanted to find out why there'd been a bare foot with mistletoe stapled to it hanging from a tree on the hill behind Aunt Zoe's house. Nor did I want to think about it while eating bacon. "It's about something else."

Layne was an ace gumshoe who couldn't be distracted with a handful of candy like his sister. A few weeks ago, he'd brought home a library book on the art of spotting clues that a person was lying. Ever since, I'd had to be on my game when he drilled me with questions ranging from if I'd hidden the superglue from him again to how long I planned to keep dating Doc. He hadn't been happy with either answer, even though I'd told the truth.

"Kelly's dad wants us to come over for pizza tomorrow night," Addy said.

"You and Layne can go if you promise to listen to whatever Jeff tells you to do."

"He wants you to come, too, Mother dear."

"I don't want to go," Layne said. "He just wants to make Mom his girlfriend."

"That's a good thing," Addy said.

"I already have a boyfriend, Adelynn. How many times do we need to go over this?"

"Why can't you have two boyfriends?"

Harvey snickered. "Because boys don't like to share."

Speaking of sharing, I frowned over at him. "Did I see that black Jaguar leaving Miss Geary's drive again this morning?" The rumble of the engine had drawn me to my bedroom window, wondering if Doc had pulled up. I'd gotten there too late to see the driver through the shaded windows, only his taillights.

Harvey flipped a pancake and smacked it. "Yep, you did. Looks like that poacher is back settin' his traps."

That was too bad. I was hoping Miss Geary had had a change of heart and kicked her new man to the curb. Ever since she'd sent Harvey and his suspenders packing, he'd been sleeping over at Aunt Zoe's. When he wasn't mooning over Miss Geary through the window, or cursing at her new stallion, he was nosing in on my after-bedtime moments with Doc.

There was nothing like a busybody old man sitting on the end of the sofa to dampen the mood. It was too bad they'd shut down the brothels in Deadwood. I'd pay for company for him at this point to score some alone time with Doc.

"You didn't answer me, Mom," Layne said. "Why do the cops want to talk to you?" He lowered his fork and eyed me closely, his lie detector vision activated. Maybe I should have bargained to take him with me to Cooper's instead of Harvey.

He'd really give the detective a run for his money.

I shrugged. "He wants to ask me some questions."

"About what?"

"Probably his house," I lied, holding steady eye contact. "You know I'm selling Detective Cooper's place for him."

"Why is Harvey going with you then?"

I shrugged, lifting my coffee cup too quickly and banging the rim into my front tooth. "He wants to visit with his nephew," I said, rubbing my tooth with my finger.

"That sounds fishy." His eyes narrowed. "Last night, you yelled you wouldn't go unless he let Harvey go, too."

"I didn't yell."

"Yeah, you kinda did, Mom," Addy said.

"What have I told you kids about eavesdropping on my phone calls?" I said more defensively than I meant to.

My total lack of privacy these days thanks to two children who were unhappy with my having any kind of love life, an over-protective bodyguard sleeping on the couch each night, and a damned chicken who found my bed "just right" had me snapping my teeth at flies.

"Hmmm, that seemed extra defensive."

I nodded at Layne's plate. "Eat your breakfast, son."

He took a bite, his eyes still on mine. "I wasn't eavesdropping on purpose. You were yelling so loud I couldn't hear the TV."

I stabbed three pieces of pancake onto my fork. "Golly gee, I'm so sorry to have interrupted your regular programming."

"Sarcasm, too." He set his glass down and pointed his fork at me. "Guilty! In the last few minutes, you've shown five of the top seven signs of lying."

I swallowed the wad of pancake and syrup. "What sign is this, Snoopy Snooperson? You're grounded!" My voice sounded strangled thanks to the frustration knotting my throat. I didn't need this shit from Cooper, let alone my son.

Addy laughed, which earned her a punch in the arm from her brother.

"For what?" Layne asked me, his voice whiney.

Now who was being defensive? "For grilling your mother at breakfast."

Addy stuck her tongue out at her brother.

"Knock it off Adelynn Renee or you'll be grounded, too."

"What! What did I do? He's the one who punched me."

"She started it when she—"

Aunt Zoe let out a shrill whistle, silencing both kids. I needed to practice my whistling.

"Layne, don't you have library books to turn in today?" When he nodded, she pointed at his plate. "Take that to the sink and go get them."

Layne shoved the last bite in his mouth, racing out of the room after shooting his sister a wrinkled upper lip.

"Addy," Aunt Zoe zeroed in on my daughter. "You promised you'd clean up the chicken's cage this morning and fill her feed bowl. You know what happens if you don't follow through on your word, right?"

Addy gulped the last of her juice, scooped up her plate, and deposited it in the sink on her way over to the basement door. "Don't leave without me, Harvey."

"You better get those tail feathers moving, kid," he said, pretending to chase after her with the spatula.

With my children gone, peace and quiet returned to my world. I covered my face. "I'm a shitty mother."

"What are you jawin' about?" I heard the chair Addy had left scrape back and then creak. I peeked out as Harvey began scooping forkfuls of pancake into his mouth.

"You are not a shitty mother," Aunt Zoe said, reaching over and tugging my hands away from my face.

"Baloney! In seconds, you were able to redirect their aggression and get them busy doing tasks that I have to tell them to do five times before they even acknowledge I'm speaking."

"It's only because I'm not you. Kids are wired not to hear what their parents are saying half of the time."

"Make that ninety-nine percent of the time," I corrected.

"Those two kids are lucky to have you," Harvey said.

I raised my eyebrows. "Was that an actual compliment?"

"Yemph," he spoke through pancake then washed it down with a gulp of coffee. "But don't get used to it. Your noggin' is big enough with all of that hair."

"Leave my hair out of it." I pinched his arm. "You sure you have time to take the kids to school today?"

"You mean in between shoving food in my mouth here and listening to the birds?"

"Don't you need to go out to your ranch, take care of your herd or something like that?"

"I already did that. Some of us don't wait for the sun to rise to get our lazy asses out of bed."

"Violet," Aunt Zoe traced the rim of her coffee cup with her finger. "I was looking through my old German dictionary last night."

"Why do you have a German dictionary?" Had she taken German in school? Her grandmother had taught her Latin, but this was the first I'd heard anything about German. Then again, Aunt Zoe had been dropping bombs about her past lately, surprising me with truths and events that I hadn't a clue existed … until now.

"That's not important." She deadpanned me, making me feel like I'd sworn to tell the truth and nothing but the truth. "What did you say Ms. Wolff said on the phone?"

"Which part?"

"After the word *nein*."

I shrugged. "It sounded something like *shark trickster*."

"Or did it sound like *Scharfrichter*?"

I repeated what she said slowly, trying to replay Ms. Wolff's voice at the same time in my head. "Shahf-riks-ter. Shark trickster." I frowned up at her. "That could have been it. What does it mean?"

"Executioner."

"What? That makes no sense." I crossed my arms over my chest, thinking back to more of the conversation. "That would mean that when she said she wanted to talk to me about what I am, and I asked if we'd met before, she'd replied with, 'No, Executioner.'"

Aunt Zoe nodded. Harvey's brows merged into one long bushy caterpillar.

"Are you sure that's not the German word for Realtor?" I asked.

"Yes."

"Could it be some kind of urban slang word for a prostitute?"

Harvey smirked. "Now why would she be callin' you a prostitute, girl? You think she spends her nights sittin' next to Jeff Wymonds?"

I wrinkled my nose at Harvey. "I wish you'd never heard him proposition me that day."

He grinned. "I wouldn't have missed that for a free beer and a poke."

Aunt Zoe frowned at me. "This worries me, Violet."

"That an old confused woman called me an executioner?"

"Oh, I don't think she was confused at all."

"What do you think? This is my new reputation? First there was Spooky Parker, then Four-Alarm Parker, and now Sharf trickster Parker?"

"*Scharfrichter*," Aunt Zoe corrected my lousy attempt at German.

"It almost rolls off the tongue," Harvey said.

"What aren't you telling me about this woman, Violet?" Aunt Zoe asked.

"I don't know what I'm not telling you." That was the truth. Between Layne and Aunt Zoe this morning, they had me questioning my own name. "Why? What do you think I'm not telling you?"

"That you saw something in your dreams. Something very bad." She leaned forward, her eyes piercing holes into mine. "And you killed it."

Chapter Five

Cooper's department-issued sedan was sitting in his drive when I parked the Picklemobile curbside in front of the detective's place. A square, one-story 1940s era bungalow painted pale blue, the house reminded me of its current owner—made up of all fixed right angles, looking impenetrable. All it needed was a flagpole running up through the center of it and we could have named it Fort Cooper. The last time I was in his basement storage room, I should have looked for a cannon or two.

The big doors on the detached garage were closed and locked tight, Coop's chromed-out Harley Davidson probably penned in for the day thanks to dark western clouds threatening to lighten their load. My Calamity Jane Realty sign waved in the stiff mid-morning breeze, creaking this way and that like a loose shutter. I double-checked the front porch, half expecting to find the clench-jawed detective standing there with rifle in hand, holding down the fort. But there was no sign of life ... nor Cooper.

I chuckled at my own joke.

"What's so funny?" Harvey asked, pushing open the passenger side door.

I thought about the reason why we were parked in front of Cooper's house and felt my grin melt. "Nothing."

"You ready for this?"

I shoved open the truck door. "Sure, what's the worst that can happen? I'm innocent on this one."

"Not really," Harvey said. "We did sorta push our way into that apartment without an invitation."

Shutting the door, I skirted the front of the truck, buttoning my blazer. The Picklemobile's engine ticked. "No, *you* opened the door and walked in, I just followed."

"You stickin' with that story today?"

I met him on the sidewalk leading up to Cooper's front door. "Yep. Unless I need to come up with a better one to stay out of jail." I shot him a wink. "Cooper won't arrest his own uncle, but I bet he'd love any reason to throw me back in that piss pot of a cell."

"Don't be so sure 'bout that. I've seen him drag his own grammy to the hoosegow."

I led the way up the porch steps, my brown boots keeping my calves warm while cool air froze my knees under my dress. "Yeah, but only after she shot him."

During one of the last few times I'd visited Cooper at home, he'd been wearing a hole-filled T-shirt that he'd acquired after standing at the wrong end of a shotgun barrel. I paused on the top step, frowning down at Harvey. "You didn't bring Bessie along, did you?"

"Sure did. I never leave home without her these days. Too much wacky shit is goin' on in the hills lately. You never know when a shotgun is gonna come in handy."

"You're going to get *us* shot one of these days."

"Said the girl who keeps stirrin' up trouble and insists on draggin' her bodyguard with her all over God's green earth this week."

"Stop the bullshit train right there, old man. First of all, trouble keeps finding me. Second, you're the one who wanted to go with me to the Galena House, not the other way around."

"Aren't you glad you had me along, though?"

"The jury is still out on that."

Cooper's front door swung open at the same time I raised my fist to knock.

"You're late, Parker." Detective Cooper filled the doorway, dressed in a creased shirt, blue tie, and dress pants. Not a single shotgun hole to be seen. He actually looked almost handsome in a rigid, carved from granite way—except for the fact that his gray eyes were glaring at me like usual, which ground any kind thoughts right out of my head.

"Really, Cooper? Is that your official greeting?" I pushed past him, shouldering him aside, walking through a cloud of his citrusy cologne. "Just once, would it kill you to be civil?"

"I was civil once, and then you broke my nose."

"Oh, right. Hold on." I patted my blazer pockets. "Shucks, I left my teeny tiny violin at home. Guess you'll have to save your crybaby story for another day."

"Now who's not being civil?"

"If you two are gonna circle and snarl at each other for a bit," Harvey said, "I'm goin' in search of somethin' to wet my whistle." He left me alone with Cooper.

"I hope this is worth the hassle of dragging us here," I said to the detective.

"Trust me, Parker, I'd rather keep you and your big nose on the other side of the Continental Divide when it comes to this murder. But since you were the last one Ms. Wolff talked to, I'm stuck dealing with you again."

From the tone in his voice, it appeared my presence rated up there with intestinal tapeworms.

I followed him into his living room. "The feeling is mutual," I grumbled. A glance at the bar that divided the kitchen from the dining room turned into a doubletake. I went over and scooped up several business cards scattered on the counter. "You've had more walk-throughs, I see."

He nodded. "This place needs to sell soon. I'm tired of having to hide my weapons every day when I leave."

"Just take 'em with you like I do," Harvey said, rejoining us with a glass of water. He grabbed a handful of cookies meant for potential buyers from a bowl on the bar. "Or lock 'em in your basement storage room with the rest of your whatnot."

Cooper's gaze narrowed on me. "I tried that once, but someone got curious."

I rolled my eyes. "Are we going to spend all morning rehashing old times, or are you going to ask me some questions? I do have a job to get to, you know." I'd lied to Jerry and told him I was heading to Cooper's to discuss ideas on more ways to market his house since the detective had insisted I keep my lips sealed about Ms. Wolff.

"I'll remind you, Parker, that we could have been right across the street from your place of work, but you had to play hard ball and make us all waste time coming here."

"And I'll remind you, Detective Cooper, of what I said on the phone—there's nothing more to tell. You'd have better luck consulting my Magic 8 ball. Would you like me to run home and grab it for you?"

He pointed at his black leather couch. "Sit. Both of you."

Harvey and I obeyed. I resisted the urge to give the detective a "Woof!" As much as I didn't like Cooper's bossiness, I wanted to get this over with. A pap exam by a group of brand new interns was preferable to Cooper's rubber glove treatment.

The detective dragged one of his dining room chairs across from us, dropped onto it, pulled out a notepad, and started clicking the end of his pen.

"What was the Chief's reaction to this one?" Harvey asked in between his cookie chewing.

"Volcanic."

Harvey had informed me recently that Cooper's inability to solve these bizarre murders that kept happening had his boss snorting fire. The detective might chap my ass, but I didn't want him to lose his job. There was something comforting knowing that Cooper was out there. Sort of like a gun tucked under the mattress for the towns of Deadwood and Lead ... or rather an arsenal of guns, knowing what I did about Cooper's firearms collection.

Harvey chomped on another cookie, getting more crumbs in his beard. "What are you gonna do?"

Cooper clicked the pen a couple more times. "Well, since I can't legally deport Parker to another state, I'm going to have to throw everything I can think of at this one and hope something sticks for once."

I cocked my head to the side. "Now why would you want to deport the one person in town who has managed to solve several of your recent cases?"

Click, click, click. "Not several."

I held up my fingers, counting off. "Hessler, the Carharts, George Mudder ..." I paused, raising my eyebrows. "Should I keep going?"

He adjusted his jaw. "Your method of solving cases causes an even bigger mess with more headaches than if you'd just let me do my goddamned job."

Harvey snickered. "You two should try workin' together instead of wastin' so much time and energy lockin' horns. Although it won't be near as entertainin' for the rest of us."

Work with Cooper? The man spelled *team* with a bunch of capital I's.

Click, click. The detective smiled at us. I could have sworn I heard his cheeks splinter. "I agree, Uncle Willis. Working together is the best strategy on this new case. Why do you think you two are sitting here with me this morning?"

Come on! I snorted. Who did he think he was fooling with this go-team song and dance? Next he'd be doing cartwheels and backflips. "Because last night on the phone you threatened to drag my butt to the station if I refused."

"I didn't threaten. I merely suggested in a strong tone."

"I distinctly remember the word 'jail' coming from your end of the line."

"My intent was conversational only. If you'll recall, I mentioned that we'd recently painted the walls of our jail cells. That was it. I can't help it if you misinterpret my words, Parker, and assume the worst at every turn."

I threw up my hands. "You're impossible." I stole a cookie from Harvey's hand. "Your nephew's impossible, Harvey. There's no working with him. I'd have better luck carving the statue of David from a chunk of marble with a plastic butter knife." I shoved the whole cookie in my mouth at once. The lemony sweetness reminded me of my Aunt Zoe's lemonade and happier days than sitting here under Cooper's glare.

Harvey grinned back at me between the crumbs in his beard. He turned to Cooper, pointing his thumb in my direction. "When she gets feisty like this with her cheeks all hot and bothered, you can really see why Doc keeps chasin' her tail."

Cooper's cool gray gaze scrutinized my face like I was something in a petri dish. He shook his head. "I'm sticking with my theory that Doc is magnetically attracted to chaos in the universe."

Oh, the irony. If they only knew which one of us kept her lips sealed while the other dabbled in all things *ghosts*. Putting together jigsaw puzzles had often been the highlight of my evenings before Doc had shown up on my doorstep.

I made a point of looking at my wrist where no watch existed and then up at the detective. "Let's skip the Tupperware party social hour and move on to the interrogation. Why exactly are we here?"

Click, click. "I want you two to go over everything again." He pointed the pen at me, "Starting with you. Go."

After a snarl and a growl, I went.

Then Harvey went.

Then I went some more, repeating everything I'd already told him.

When we finished, he ordered me to start again. When I grabbed that damned clicking pen from his hand and threw it across the room, he threatened to take me to the station so I could tell my story to his boss. I relented after some face scrunching.

After I finished, he collected his pen from the floor, then pulled several photos out of his shirt pocket and splayed them on the coffee table in front of us.

"Take a look at those and tell me what you see."

I glanced down. "Photos."

"Humor me here, Parker. I'm *allowing* you to look this time. There's no need to go sneaking into my locked basement room to see what's on my case board, most of it is right here."

This sharing was new for Cooper. And disturbing. Was I on one of those hidden camera videos like the old *Candid Camera* show? "Are you ill, Detective?"

"Probably." He tapped his finger on the top photo.

I picked it up, grimacing at the folded mess of skin, legs, and arms.

Ms. Wolff's body reminded me of a deflated blow up doll draped in clothing. Everything was the way my nightmares had been replaying it, except for the part where her body rose up and lurched toward me, one arm outstretched while the other searched for its missing head.

"Where's Ms. Beals?" Cooper asked.

Blinking away the zombie-ish scene, I raised my gaze to him. "You mean Natalie?"

He nodded and clicked twice.

"In Arizona. Why?"

"I'm covering all of my bases, making sure I've interviewed all involved in this case."

"You mean interrogated, not interviewed." The word *interview* implied a formal question and answer session, not being drilled and threatened while tortured with a clicker.

He pointed at the photo in my hand. "Focus."

I handed the one I'd started with to Harvey and picked up the next. It was a picture of the wall with all of the clocks. "What am I focusing on?"

"Anything that strikes you as odd."

A strangled laugh escaped between my lips. "Besides a headless body and a shrunken skull?"

"Exactly." His serious voice calmed the hysteria that had bubbled up inside me while looking at Ms. Wolff's corpse.

I focused, as he ordered. There were more clocks than I remembered, all spaced evenly like they were part of a wallpaper pattern. I wondered if she had written anything on the back of them, like where she had bought them or when. Or if there were a reason for the time each was set to. Had she stuffed any notes inside of the little doors some of them had? Had Cooper's crew checked for any treasures left behind? Any clues?

"When will Ms. Beals be returning?" the detective interrupted my train of clock questions.

Harvey tossed the first picture onto the coffee table, grabbing another cookie while he waited for me to finish looking at the one in my hand.

"Natalie should be home next Monday, I think."

I handed the wall of clocks photo to Harvey and picked up the next. It was a shot of an old fashioned rotary dial phone. It sat on an end table next to the chair that I was pretty sure had Ms. Wolff's crumpled body at its base. Was that the phone she'd used to call me? Or the one someone else had used to call me while Ms. Wolff lay dead below on the floor? Goosebumps formed on my arms.

"Did she drive down to Arizona?" Cooper asked as I handed the phone photo to Harvey.

"Yeah. Her cousin needed her to take along her tools."

"A workin' vacation," Harvey added, eyeing the phone picture. "Her grandpa broke his leg. Natalie had to help finish a building he'd started." He pointed down at the phone. "Your Great-Aunt Juniper used to have a phone like this back when I was a tadpole."

I grabbed the next one from the stack without looking at it, staring at Detective Cooper instead. "I can tell you right now that Natalie is not going to be able to give you any information on this. She only knows what I told her right after the phone call, and I've already told you that part of the story multiple times."

He leaned forward and tapped the picture in my hand. "What do you notice in this one?"

I looked down at a picture of what looked like a closet. Dresses, shirts, and jackets hung with one shoulder sticking out. Shoes were lined up below like foot soldiers. On the two shelves above the clothes hangers, mannequin heads lined the lower and hat boxes filled the upper.

"She must have been quite a fancy dresser. If the hats in those boxes match the brand names on some of the lids," the ones I could read anyway, "those are not cheap hats."

I wondered why the mannequin heads were empty. Maybe she used to keep her hats on the heads but later preferred to store them in the boxes.

"I'd like to take a closer look at her clothes," I told the detective.

"You think there's a clue there?"

"I don't know. Mostly I want to see her taste in clothing, see if she was into brand names. Sometimes clothes can say a lot about a person." Truth be told, I wanted to know what kind of a person Ms. Wolff had been. I felt an affinity with her since I was most likely one of the last people she had talked to.

"Like what?" Harvey asked, taking the picture from me. "Just looks like old lady stuff to me."

I pointed at the detective. "Take Cooper's outfit."

Cooper sat back, straightening his tie. "I'm all ears, Parker."

"Today he's wearing a button up shirt and tie. No holey T-shirts, no torn jeans, no Harley Davidson emblems. He's all business. Don't be fooled, though," I smirked at Harvey. "He didn't dress up for us. We don't rate. He's dressed up for something going down at work. Something that made him actually iron his collar this morning and pick a tie that has no bullets, handcuffs, or anything else fun or threatening. It's just a regular navy blue tie."

Harvey perused Cooper from top to bottom, bending over to tug up the hem of his nephew's pant leg. "Look, his socks even match."

"Well done, Parker. If you ever lose your job at Calamity

Jane's, you should try out as one of those fortune tellers at the circus. With your crazy hair, you'd fit right in."

"Leave my hair out of this."

"What's going on at work, Coop?"

The detective shrugged. "This latest death has drawn some unwanted attention. I have a meeting this afternoon, and I need to dress appropriately for our company."

I wondered whose presence required such a button-up version of Cooper, but I could tell by the rigid expression on the detective's face that he wasn't going to share anything more than he already had.

"Do me, do me," Harvey said, tugging on my arm.

I laughed. "You're easy, Harvey. Today is like every day for you. You dress for comfort, but you always smell good and make sure to brush your hair and finger comb your beard. I'd say that you're out to enjoy life but on the lookout for tail."

"Always on the lookout," he agreed, his gold teeth showing.

"What about you, Parker?" Cooper asked. "What's with the flowery, girly dress under that dark red power jacket?"

"It's a blazer," I clarified, brushing some lint off the lapel. "I chose it because I was cold. As for the dress, I thought some flowers might look nice today, since it was dreary."

"She's lyin'," Harvey said, tugging my blazer aside. "Look how tight her dress is up top. And her hair is down and loose. She only shows off her wares like this when she's on the prowl."

"I'm not on the prowl." Although, it didn't hurt to dress to impress the man who took me to the moon and back when we were alone and sans clothing.

"Who are you having lunch with?" Cooper asked.

"A client." I adjusted my blazer, buttoning a button Harvey's tug had undone.

My lunch with Doc had almost nothing to do with my choice in clothing today. Well, except that I knew he liked boots. Oh, and he might have mentioned last week how sexy it was when I crossed my legs while wearing a dress. And there was a slight possibility my matching underwear and bra were inspired by the hope that Doc would have a chance to see them today—and then remove them. But that was it.

So what if I was a bit pathetic with this need to see Doc's eyes light up when he looked at me. After years of living in a no-man land, was it so wrong for me to like having a gorgeous guy stare at me as if I came equipped with a huge flat screen, a zero turn radius lawnmower, and a decked-out barbecue? Not to mention that it had been over a week since we'd last stolen over to his house and enjoyed some time in his bed … and on his stairs. A girl had needs.

"Tell your so-called client that I need to have a chat with him when he has an hour of free time," Cooper said. "I'll come to his office."

I didn't dignify his assumption with a response.

Instead I picked up the last photo the detective had left on the coffee table. It was a crooked shot of a dresser top with an attached mirror reflecting the flash in the upper corner. I held the picture closer, my nose almost brushing it. "What's this?" I asked pointing at something that looked to be stuck in the mirror's edge.

"Look closer," Cooper said, pulling a magnifying glass out from a drawer in the coffee table.

I took it, did as told, and then gasped, my heart free-falling down a deep, dark hole.

Harvey plucked the photo from my fingers, squinting down at it. "What is it? What do you see? I left my readers at your aunt's house."

"Violet?" Cooper asked, waving his hand in front of my tunneling vision. "Are you okay?"

No. I was far from anything even close to *okay*, but I nodded anyway.

"You should probably continue breathing then."

I inhaled, gulping much needed oxygen down my windpipe. The darkness that had been rising ebbed but still lapped at the edges of my sight.

"What is it?" Harvey asked again. "What's got you skittery all of a sudden, girl?"

I pointed at the square picture tucked into the trim around

the dresser mirror in the photo and handed him the magnifying glass. "Look."

Harvey squinted. "I'm lookin'. Who is that? The shape of his head reminds me of ..." Harvey stopped. His blue eyes locked onto mine, mirroring my fret and worry.

"It's Layne," I whispered.

* * *

"Why would that woman have a picture of your boy?" Harvey asked a half-hour later, his bushy eyebrows scrunched into one long wrinkled caterpillar.

I leaned back into the cushy booth, the whirring of anxiety in my ears blocking out most of the usual lunch time clamor going on around me at Bighorn Billy's Diner. "I'm more concerned right now about how she got it."

I remembered when I'd taken that picture in my aunt's workshop. Aunt Zoe had spent the afternoon with us, teaching the kids how to make blown glass pieces. Both Addy and Layne had made several creations with Aunt Zoe doing the dangerous work, letting the kids choose the material and spin the rods. I'd taken pictures of them and their favorite creations with Aunt Zoe's old film camera, wanting both kids to have the pictures in hand to remind them of that day long after they were grown and gone.

I'd explained this to Detective Cooper and Harvey. Unsurprisingly, Layne had been the main focus of the remainder of our conversation before Cooper nudged us out the door; he needed to get back to work in time to prepare for his meeting with whatever big wigs had inspired him to wear a tie. Most of the theories of how Ms. Wolff had ended up with that photograph had come from Cooper and Harvey; my brain had been too scattered with fear for my kid to think straight.

Before shutting the door in my face, Cooper had asked me to wait on confronting Layne about whether he knew Ms. Wolff until the detective had dug deeper. Then he'd made my eyebrows shoot to the top of my forehead by suggesting he and I take a

tour of Ms. Wolff's apartment together tomorrow. When his
uncle offered to join us, he shook his head without pause, which
made me wonder if Cooper had found some other skeleton in
one of Ms. Wolff's closets that he didn't want his uncle to see.

"Maybe it's a coincidence," Harvey's voice hauled me back to
the present. "Like Coop said."

I stirred sugar into my tea. "You and I both know that's
hogwash."

"What's hogwash?" Doc slid into the booth next to me,
smelling like fresh air and my favorite woodsy cologne. With my
focus mired in worry, I hadn't noticed him come in.

His hair and shoulders were sprinkled with rain, but his hand
was warm when he reached beneath the table and found mine. I
laced my fingers through his, resting our hands on my thigh.
Today I relished the distraction his warm touch brought, wanting
to savor it like hot fudge on vanilla ice cream.

"We just came from Cooper's place," I explained.

"Right, the interrogation you told me about last night on the
phone."

Ranted about until his ear rang was more accurate, but there
was no need to split hairs.

"Coop found somethin' of Violet's in Ms. Wolff's
apartment."

Doc picked up a menu. "Oh, yeah?"

I stirred my tea some more, adding more sugar. "Yeah. Ms.
Wolff had a picture I took of Layne stuck into the trim of her
bedroom dresser mirror."

"What?" Doc lowered the menu. "Layne? Your son?"

"Yep. My son."

Leaning back, Doc pulled my hand into his lap, tugging me
closer. "Did Layne know her?"

"I don't know."

Harvey motioned for the waitress to come over. "Coop's
gonna take Violet on another tour of Ms. Wolff's apartment
tomorrow, have her snoop around with him."

Doc searched my face. "How did you manage to convince
Detective Cooper to agree to that?"

"It was his idea."

His dark gaze narrowed. "Now I'm really worried."

"Why? You think he has ulterior motives?" I always did, but Doc was usually more of a Polly Positive about Cooper than me and my conspiracy theories.

"No, I'm worried because Cooper usually insists you stay as far away as possible. If he's offering to take you on a personal tour of the murder site, something is up."

Yeah, I'd thought that, too. I wasn't naïve enough to think Cooper had plucked daisy petals and had a change of heart about his overall desire to have me booted from the state.

"Maybe his job is hangin' from the noose," Harvey threw out.

"He's the only detective in the northern hills," I said. "The chief wouldn't fire him, would he? You think that's what this important meeting is today?" It would certainly explain him dressing all spiffy and wanting to share notes.

"Could be." Harvey waited while the waitress came and took Doc's drink order. "Or it could be he's finally figurin' out he needs some help to solve these murders. The boy always has been a bit anvil-headed. Takes after his mother that way."

"His mother, huh?" I said, shooting Harvey a crooked grin.

Harvey winked back, then turned to Doc. "Hope you don't mind me joining you two for lunch. Violet wasn't fit to be left alone after seeing that picture of Layne."

"Three's company," Doc said.

I sniffed. "I was fine."

"You were tremblin'."

"From the cold."

"How was I supposed to tell the difference with that blazer coverin' your headlights?"

And yet another reason for me to cover my headlights at every opportunity. "Gee, I don't know, maybe when I said, 'Dang, it's cold in here, why isn't your heater working?' you should have caught on."

"I thought you were makin' small talk about the weather."

"When have I ever made small talk with you?"

"When we first met."

"No, I made small talk with Bessie, your shotgun, until you removed her double barrels from my kisser."

"What'll you have, hun?" the waitress interrupted our tennis match.

When we finished ordering, Doc let go of my hand and lowered his palm onto my thigh. His body heat zapped through my dress like it was made of copper. "Tell me about what happened at Cooper's," he said, squeezing my leg as encouragement.

For the next ten minutes, I took turns with Harvey catching Doc up on our morning fun. We bounced from the speculation about Cooper's meeting this afternoon to what we had seen in each picture and why he had shown them to us. Neither of us believed he happened to have a few photos of the crime scene on him and felt like sharing them over tea and biscuits.

Emptying his drink, Harvey excused himself to go see a man about a mule. Finally I sat alone with Doc.

"Are you okay, Violet?"

"Mostly."

He rubbed my leg reassuringly. "There's probably some easy explanation for Ms. Wolff having Layne's picture."

I puffed my cheeks and blew out a sigh, trying to smile around my anxieties. "I hope you're right."

He removed his hand from my thigh, reaching out to snag one of the longer curls twirling down from my temple. "You wore your hair loose."

"Harvey always tells me that men like women better with their hair down." The same thing had been said by Doc's ex-girlfriend, Tiffany, the Jessica Rabbit look-alike who happened to be the inspiration for my boss's billboard marketing madness. Her sexy ads for a competing real estate company in Spearfish had increased their walk-in traffic by thirty percent according to Jerry's insider information.

"So," Doc wound the curl around his finger, "you're letting Harvey advise you on what to wear now?"

"Only when it comes to dressing to impress."

One of his dark eyebrows inched up. "Were you out to impress Detective Cooper this morning?"

"I have two recurring goals when in Cooper's company—to refrain from poking him in the eye with a sharp stick and to stay out of jail." I shrugged out of my blazer, partly to cool down the furnace growing inside of me thanks to Doc's nearness, partly with the hope of heating Doc up. "I had someone else in mind while showering this morning."

"Oh, yeah?" His gaze lowered, eyes darkening as he openly admired the flower garden stretching across my chest. "Nice dress. Pretty daisies."

"This old thing? I found it in the back of my closet. I'm surprised it still fits after all of these years." The top gaped more than it used to thanks to gravity sucking some of the air out of my balloons, but push-up bras worked miracles these days.

"I wonder what it looks like when you cross your legs in it." His hand returned to my thigh, his fingers pulling up the hem until he found bare skin. "Who was on your mind while you were getting all warm and wet?"

The fire I'd been playing with burned in all sorts of interesting places. "Some guy I know."

"Some guy, huh?" His gaze dipped to my neckline and lower. "You're wearing a red bra."

I pulled open the front and peeked down, as if I hadn't spent too many minutes this morning with him in mind, debating on which bra and underwear to choose. "I guess I am. Are you always so observant?"

Under the table, his hand slid up my thigh. "Matching panties, I'm guessing."

"What panties?" I lied.

I was too chicken to go commando. I even had added a short satin slip. I'd had bad luck with wrap dresses in the past on windy days. The last thing I needed was a wardrobe malfunction in front of Cooper or my boss. Jerry would want to record it and use it for an online marketing ad.

Doc's fingers stilled. "You wouldn't happen to have any free time this afternoon would you?"

"What for?"

"I could use your help."

"With what?"

"Reminding you who you should be thinking about while you're in the shower."

I chuckled. Noticing Harvey weaving his way between the tables, I leaned closer and whispered, "I'd rather go to your place and have a hands-on demonstration with that new soap you bought. What flavor is it?"

Doc sucked a breath in through his teeth. "Peach."

"Where in the hell's our food?" Harvey asked, then looked at me, his eyes drifting down to my neckline. He grinned at Doc. "What do you think about that daisy dress of hers?"

Rubbing the fabric on my sleeve between his finger and thumb, he smiled at me, sort of wicked and sexy at the same time. I should practice that in the mirror to see if it had the same heart-sputtering effect on him.

"It's pretty and soft," Doc said, his fingers drifting down the skin on my arm. "But I'm more partial to violets."

Harvey snickered. "Partial to Violet's what?"

"Order up," I heard come through the window leading to the kitchen. Thank God.

"Here comes our food," I said, changing the subject.

The waitress brought our lunch over, distracting Harvey with a bacon cheeseburger and a wag of her hips.

We spent the next fifteen minutes speculating about Ms. Wolff, Layne, and Cooper. The ten minutes after that were filled with Harvey picking Doc's brain on some investment opportunities. I took that opportunity to zone out and aimlessly chew on cold French fries, battling a handful of 'why me's' when it came to ghosts, albinos, and retired professional basketball players.

As the waitress collected our plates in exchange for the bill, my cell phone rang. It was Mona.

"Hello?" I said into my phone, nodding at the waitress who wanted to take my plate of half-eaten French fry corpses.

"Violet, where are you?" Mona asked.

"Bighorn Billy's eating lunch. Why?"

"There's a gentleman here looking for you. He says he saw your billboard and is interested in talking to you."

"Great." I grimaced, imagining what kind of client that billboard would lure. "Is he legit you think?"

"Ah, sure."

"Is he standing in front of you right now?"

"Yes."

"Is Ray trying to steal him already?"

"Yes."

"That asshole! Stall for me. I'll be there in two shakes."

Doc left money on the table to cover the bill and then some.

"I owe you," I said as he helped me out of the booth and handed me my blazer.

"You can find a creative way to repay me, Boots." His eyes twinkled with a mixture of mirth and lust.

Outside the diner, Doc offered to take Harvey back to Aunt Zoe's where we'd left his pickup this morning. Then he walked me over to the Picklemobile.

"I was serious about coming over this afternoon." His eyes admired me from head to toe, then he buttoned up my blazer. "I would like a chance to unwrap that dress and see for myself what's underneath."

"What's in it for me?" I flirted, looking up at him from under my lashes.

He caught my hands and pulled me closer. "More of this."

He tipped my chin and covered my lips with his, coaxing a moan from me. I pressed into his heat, needing his warmth, his touch, and whatever else he was willing to give to me. When he finished lighting wildfires, he stepped back, his gaze as molten as my insides. "You interested?"

Hell, yes! I licked my lips, trying not to let it be obvious how twisted up and over the moon he had me. "Let me see what this client wants and then I'll be over."

A horn honked.

I stepped back from Doc and glared over at Harvey, who sat waiting in Doc's Camaro. The old codger needed to give us a moment. It's the least he could do after so many nights of sitting at the other end of the couch, keeping me from jumping Doc's bones after the kids went to bed.

Harvey pointed out the driver's side window.

I followed his finger. Standing in front of Bighorn Billy's front doors watching Doc and me with her jaw unhinged, her cheeks bright red, and flames shooting from her eyes, stood Tiffany Sugarbell.

Doc's ex-girlfriend.

My competitor in real estate marketing ads.

The selling agent for the hotel I was helping Cornelius buy.

The woman Doc once told me was obsessed with winning, competitive on every playing field, including the bedroom.

"Oh, shit," I whispered, stepping back into Doc, who wrapped his arm around me.

"What's wrong?"

"We have a problem."

Judging from the snarl now scrunching Tiffany's face into what looked like an ancient Maya mask, she did, too—with me locking lips with her ex-boyfriend.

Chapter Six

There were five different ways that Tiffany Sugarbell could turn my world into a living hell, and probably several more that I hadn't thought of yet.

One, she could try to seduce Doc back between her sheets. The green jealousy monster and I made ugly bedfellows, especially when we spooned.

Two, she could partner with Ray, forming some evil alliance with the aim of ruling over my universe and screwing me out of sales and a job.

Three, she could sleep with Cooper and whisper sweet nothings in his ear all night about how I was guilty of every single thing he had suspected all along. I could see them locking me in jail and then dancing a jig together before Cooper ground the key between his molars and swallowed the metal shards.

Four, she might woo Cornelius ... somehow. If that were even possible. Crazy Caly had managed it without trying, but I strongly suspected she wasn't normal, and that had played a role in his attraction to her. Maybe Tiffany could wrap herself in a boa of raven feathers and convince him to back out of the hotel sale before the paperwork was finalized.

Five, she could blab to everyone in the hills that I wore a pushup bra. *Droopy Boobs Parker* would be my new nickname. Oh, the fun Cooper's crew would have with me every time they dragged me into the station.

During the drive back to Calamity Jane Realty, I tried to come up with a plan on how to handle each possibility. All the while, I kept an eye out for her Jeep in my rearview mirror. I half expected her to chase after me and try to run me off the road for kissing her ex-boyfriend.

Doc might believe I was overreacting about how bad this could turn, but Doc's XY chromosome mix made it hard for him to understand how a pair of X chromosomes plotted and schemed. His reminder back at Bighorn Billy's that Tiffany had moved on and was fully involved with a new man had inspired my scornful laugh in return.

I still vividly remembered the day Tiffany had slapped him across the cheek for walking out on her, leaving her high and dry without an explanation. Only later had I found out it had to do with her mentioning the idea of marriage to him.

Tiffany's rage that day had surfaced with a *ka-boom* at the mere sight of Doc, her usual professional veneer buried under smoking debris. I could have sworn in that heated moment her eyes had flashed fire and her red hair had flamed at the tips. But my memory could be partly skewed due to my envy for her perky breasts and incredible sales numbers.

Either way, one thing was clear today from the pinched expression on Tiffany's face—she didn't like to share with others. Contrary to what Doc might believe about his ex, I had a target on my back now. I sure hoped her aim was as rotten as mine.

I parked the Picklemobile behind Calamity Jane Realty, checking my reflection in the rearview mirror. My lips needed fixing thanks to lunch and Doc; my hair needed corralling so I didn't scare away my potential new client. After powdering my nose back into a matte finish, I was ready to impress.

Whiffs of Mona's jasmine perfume drifted down the office's back hallway. As I passed the bathroom, a heavy dose of green apple air freshener made me grimace—Ray! I was going to superglue his ass to the toilet seat if he didn't stop trying to steal my clients. That would keep him out of the way when new customers came calling.

I pasted on a smile, all set to meet and greet, and stepped out into the front office.

"Too late," Ray called out. His sneer made me want to reach for a sledgehammer.

"Where did he go?" I asked Mona.

"He got tired of waiting for you to finish getting all girly'd up for him," Ray answered.

"I didn't yank your chain," I said without looking at the horse's ass.

Mona smiled at me, warm and reassuring. If Jerry was truly the brilliant marketer he thought he was, he'd figure out how to clone Mona. "He got a phone call and had to leave."

"Dang." I dropped my purse on my desk.

"But he made an appointment to come back tomorrow morning at nine. I wrote it on your desk calendar. You don't have anything going on then, do you?"

Only a walk-through of a dead woman's apartment with Detective Cooper. But meeting my potential client rated higher on my priority list than hanging out with the detective. Coop would have to wait until I was finished playing Realtor. I needed to keep my job as much as he did. "I'll be here by eight-thirty."

"That'll be a first," Ray said.

I didn't bite on his hook. "Where's Ben?" I asked Mona, heading for the coffee pot.

"Jerry took him to meet an old friend he used to play ball with."

Great. Now Ben would have yet another thing in common with our boss besides a set of testicles. I poured a cup of black coffee, debating on sugar or not. Black might be better, adding a sprinkling of hair on my chest so I could compete with Ben on the be-like-Jerry game. Nah. Sugar won.

The rest of the day passed slowly, especially after Doc called and told me he had to run down to Rapid City to help one of his clients and wouldn't be home until tomorrow. I phoned Cooper and left him a message about pushing our meeting back an hour. Then I watched the clock tick one minute at a time, feeling like a mosquito trapped in sap, wanting to go home and hug my son since Cooper wouldn't let me badger the kid with questions. Finally it was time to call it a day.

I spent the evening following Layne around like a puppy. When Aunt Zoe asked me if I were feeling okay, I joked that I was having early separation anxiety.

Doc called my cell phone long after I'd left the kids'

bedroom and crawled under my sheets.

"How are you doing?" he asked, his deep voice velvety. I wanted to wrap myself up in it to fight off the chills and dread that kept breezing through me.

I had a feeling he wasn't making small talk, so I didn't either. "I'm scared about Layne."

"This is some weird coincidence, Violet. He'll be fine. He's a smart kid."

"*And* I'm anxious about Tiffany knowing we're a couple." I winced. Was *couple* too strong a word for his comfort level to describe our relationship at the moment? I felt extra sensitive about his feelings after having Tiffany and his past in my thoughts today. "Well, we're together, I mean. Not necessarily a *couple*, but still boyfriend and girlfriend. Dating exclusively at this moment ... sort of."

I covered my mouth to shut it up.

"Are you done, sweetheart?" he asked.

I took my hand away long enough to answer. "I think so."

"Two things you need to know."

Only two? My hand lowered to my sternum. "What?"

"Don't apply what I said about why I left Tiffany to you."

Which part? As much as I wanted clarification, I kept my lips squeezed tight, afraid I'd sound more stupid and pathetic than I already had. "What's the second thing?" I asked instead.

"You may have been right."

"About what?"

"Tiffany not taking the fact that we're a couple very well."

So we were a couple in his eyes. Whew. *What exactly did being a couple mean to him?* I bitch-smacked my forehead, trying to mute that insecure voice in my skull. "Why do you say that?"

"She called me tonight."

That settled over me like mustard gas. I coughed to clear the constriction in my throat. "What did she say?"

"I didn't answer."

Good! "Why not?"

"I was busy working."

Even better. "Oh."

"And I didn't want to talk to her."

I smiled. "Why not?"

"Violet, don't you get it yet?"

"Get what?"

"The obvious."

"I never assume I understand the obvious." That usually resulted in my cheeks burning and a need to bury my head in the sand.

"That's probably a safe bet."

He was losing me. After the long, brain-bending day I'd had, I needed to keep our conversation at an eighth grade reading level.

"Did she leave a message?" I asked, my throat still burning about Tiffany calling *my* boyfriend.

"Not just one."

I plucked a chicken feather from my comforter and let it drift to the floor. "So she called back?"

"Yes, twenty-three more times."

What! Jeez! Crap! One sighting and she'd gone psycho. "What did she say in her messages?"

"I don't know."

"What do you mean you don't know? Was she speaking in tongues?"

He chuckled. "I deleted them without listening to any."

Really? "Weren't you a little bit curious about what she had to say?"

"Nope."

"Why not?"

"One of the many benefits of no longer being involved with her romantically is that I don't have to listen to anything she says."

"So if I called and left you twenty-three messages you'd listen to every one of them?"

"No."

"Oh."

"I'd play the first one to find out what trouble you'd gotten into again and then come find you."

I leaned back against the pillows, stretching my legs out in front of me, wishing he was sprawled out next to me. "You'd show up as my knight in shining armor?"

"Something like that. Not that you'd let me save you."

"I certainly wouldn't stop you if I was up shit creek."

"Good. I'll make sure to bring paddles next time."

Rubbing my eyes, I sighed. "What are we going to do about your ex?"

"Ignore her. She'll get over this and move on."

I didn't share his optimism. "It's already been three months. It appears she hasn't moved an inch yet. Maybe she's been holding onto the hope that you'd eventually change your mind and take her back."

"No, I think this goes back to her need to compete and be the best at everything."

"Or maybe you're irresistible."

He laughed.

"You are pretty decent in the sack, Doc."

"Pretty decent?"

"I've definitely had worse."

"Name them."

It was my turn to laugh.

"I'm serious, name them so I can hunt them down and warn them to stay away from you."

"You're starting to sound as loony as Tiffany."

"You drive me nuts, Boots."

I grinned. "I think that's the most romantic thing anyone has ever said to me."

"I'm just getting rolling."

I miss you.

I bit my tongue, keeping those three words inside. I was afraid if I said them, then three other words would follow, and Doc would leave me, too. Tiffany and I could become best friends forever and plaster our walls with pictures of Doc we shot through his blinds and curtains.

"Please tell me you're definitely coming back up here tomorrow." I plucked another chicken feather from my comforter. Addy must have let Elvis run loose today after school, dang it.

"I should be hitting the road by noon. Why? You want to finish what you started at lunch today?"

"Maybe."

"There's no 'maybe' about it."

I sat silent for a moment, listening to him breathe, imagining him touching me. "Violet?"

"What?"

"There's something I need to tell you about Tiffany."

My gut lurched. I wasn't sure I could handle this tonight, but before my brain could take a vote on the matter, my lips asked, "What?"

"Are you alone?"

"Yes."

"In your bed?"

"Yes."

"Under the sheets?"

I growled at him. "Damn it, Doc. What haven't you told me about Tiffany?"

"She's not you."

He'd said that before. "What does that even mean?" I already knew she wasn't flabby-bellied with wild hair.

"It means that if Tiffany tries to mess with you about us, remember what I'm telling you right now."

What was he telling me? "That she's not me?"

"Yes."

He was going to need to spell it out for me, because I was tired of the guessing game when it came to us. "Could you be less cryptic, Doc?"

"Not over the phone. Sleep tight, Boots."

He hung up, leaving me wanting so much more.

* * *

Wednesday, October 3rd

I blinked awake. The morning sunlight did not make my

current situation look any better no matter how long I lay there in my bed, wishin' and a hopin'. The smell of bacon lured me out from under my covers eventually.

My morning went the same as every other with periods of yelling and bouts of fighting until Harvey shoved the kids out the front door to take them to school. I spent extra time picking out a power outfit made up of black dress pants and a tiger striped silk blouse. Black leather boots finished off the bottom, a tightly coiled French chignon wrapped up the top. With some eyeliner and a touch of tinted lip gloss, the queen of the jungle was ready to meet her new client.

Parking spots were plentiful when I pulled into the lot, even with Jerry, Ray, and Benjamin's vehicles already there. The "boys" had taken to coming in early to work and hitting the basketball court next door at the Rec Center for some early morning competition to get their testosterone spiking. As for me, I preferred caffeine over sweaty jock straps.

Mona pulled in right behind me.

"Morning, Vi," she said and walked in with me. "How's your aunt doing these days?"

"Okay." We hung up our jackets and went our separate ways to our desks. "Why do you ask?"

Mona opened her laptop. "I saw Reid Martin playing pool last night up at Charles' Club."

"Yeah?" Reid and Aunt Zoe had a history. I didn't know the full details, but it initially involved rejection and hurt feelings, and now included a shotgun aimed at his backside as Aunt Zoe shooed him away. "How's Deadwood's fire captain doing?"

It had been a couple of weeks since I'd run into Reid hustling out Aunt Zoe's screen door while she hunted down her shotgun shells. Since then, I'd heard he was working long hours and drinking during the short ones. Whatever was going on between those two, Reid seemed to be swimming in booze to get through it. I'd been there and done that in the past, so I wasn't one to throw pebbles at anyone's glass house. Hell, much more of this crazy shit going on in my world and I might join him at the bar.

The back door creaked open; male laughter echoed up the

hallway.

"I think Reid's broken," Mona said. "On a positive note, he could write country songs now. If he got himself a three-legged hound dog, he'd be on the road to a Grammy."

Jerry's extra-large shoes thudded into the front room. "Mornin'." His cheeks were flushed, his tie hung loose, and his hair was wet. I caught the glance Mona shot at his backside as he bent over in his khakis and poured himself a cup of coffee. "What's the game plan today, ladies?"

Mona's fingers started their clacking song and dance. "Two showings and a lunch meeting down in Spearfish for me."

"That color looks nice on you, Red," Jerry said, staring at Mona's white cashmere sweater snuggling her chest perfectly. "What about you, Violet?" he asked, his gaze still assessing Mona's front side.

"White always makes me look washed out," I answered, tongue in cheek.

"I think you look nice in white," Ben said, rounding his desk and dropping into his chair. His cheeks were flushed, too, but his tie was straight and tight against his neck. "It turns your hair a pretty golden color, like Kate Hudson's."

"Thanks, Ben. I like that tie."

"What is this?" Ray asked, dropping into his chair and kicking his boots up on his desk. "A hippie love-in?"

Jerry chuckled, dragging his focus away from Mona the siren. "I meant, what's on your plate today, Violet?"

"Your Billboard Bunny caught a mouse," Ray cut me off.

"He's more of a golden-haired lion," Mona said.

"Apparently," I clarified for Jerry, "a customer came in yesterday while I was at lunch and made an appointment to be here at nine." Which was twenty minutes away.

"He mentioned seeing her billboard." Ray crossed his arms over his chest and grinned at me. "That was a brilliant marketing idea you had, Jerry."

Freaking kiss ass. Ray knew my feelings about the billboard ad. He'd overheard me tell Mona the afternoon when I had first seen it that I was going to spray gasoline all over it and burn the sucker down.

"After I finish talking to this new customer, I have an appointment with Detective Cooper."

"Again?" Jerry's blonde eyebrows formed a line on his forehead below his buzz cut.

Ray snickered. "Does it involve handcuffs?"

I ignored him. "Cooper wants me to show him a place in town," I sort of fibbed since he was actually going to show me the place.

"Are you going to show him somewhere that he'll love coming home to every night?" Ray repeated my billboard slogan.

"Ray," Mona warned.

"What? I'm getting our little Violet warmed up for her new customer."

"That's enough, Ray," Jerry said. "Violet, I'll leave you alone to get prepped for your next potential sale then." He raised his coffee cup in salute. "Nice game this morning, boys." He tapped on Mona's desk as he walked past her. "Keep up the good work, Red."

With the coach back in his office, the rest of us did our usual warm up routine. Mona clacked out more of what I suspected was going to be her great American novel, Ray picked up the phone and started schmoozing his clients, and Ben began printing new listing reports for all of the Black Hills and the surrounding area. Meanwhile, I fretted about losing my job, getting thrown in jail, and dirtying my already sullied reputation.

At five minutes until nine, my nerves about meeting a male client who found me thanks to a sleazy billboard were all sparky, my bladder tickling like I might pee my pants. I grabbed my purse and slipped into the bathroom, taking care of business, scrubbing my hands longer than usual, touching up my makeup.

I heard the bell over the front door jingle and then Mona gave her usual "Welcome, would you like a cup of coffee" bit.

Taking a deep breath, I opened the door and stepped out. I took one last moment to smooth my shirt and tuck up some loose curls before heading toward the front office.

With a big smile glued high on my cheeks, I stepped out into the front room. "Hello, I'm ... "

My voice froze and fell over dead.

My smile collapsed onto the floor next to it.

"You're Violet Parker," finished Rex Conner, the low-down, no-good, piece-of-shit father of my children. His smile was working just fine. It creased his brown eyes and showed off his straight white teeth. "I've come to see you about a house."

No. Fucking. Way.

Chapter Seven

Long ago, in a prairie town about forty miles away, a foolish college girl got knocked up by a handsome, smart, charming, slick—*did I mention handsome?*—older college boy. It wasn't a night of drunken debauchery, nor was it her first time. It was a matter of trying a different birth control pill and ending up pregnant. When the foolish girl told the handsome boy about the bun in the oven (not realizing at the time that she should be using the plural version of the word *bun*), his reaction was to sprint in the other direction, running off to pursue his career and never to be seen again … until today.

There was more to this tale, some soap opera drama award-winning shit involving the girl's trampy younger sister and a lot of unscrupulous sex that didn't include the foolish girl. But that was a tale for another time and still necessitated a bottle of tequila to cough it all out.

For now, the moral of the story was that old man Harvey had been right: I should carry a firearm at all times in case my children's sperm donor walked through the door and needed his smug handsome mug blown to smithereens.

"Violet?" Mona rushed toward me. "Are you okay? You look like you've seen a ghost."

More like the devil himself.

"Maybe you should have a seat. Ben get her a glass of water."

Ben sprang to his feet and had a glass ready for me after I fell into my chair.

"If you'll give Violet a minute, Mr. Conner," Mona said to Rex, "she'll be right with you." *Won't you?* Mona mouthed when her back was to Rex.

I nodded slightly. It was about all I could manage at the

moment. My brain seemed to have crashed and needed a few heartbeats to reboot.

"No problem," Rex said, checking his watch. "I don't need to be at work for another hour."

Work? Where in the hell was he working? Here? In Deadwood?

Ray walked over to stand next to Rex, his smirk for me only. "As I said yesterday, Mr. Conner, I can help you. Just let me know what you're in the market for."

Rex patted Ray on the shoulder like they were old chums. Old *chum* was more like it—rotten, stinking, fish head chum. I'd love to take both of them out to sea and dump them overboard for the sharks to eat.

"Thanks," Rex said, "but I'm here for Miss Parker."

Here for what, though? If it had anything to do with the two children I had raised without him, I might end up seeing Detective Cooper today from behind bars.

Schooling my face, I finished the glass of water Ben had brought and took a deep breath. Nobody at Calamity Jane Realty knew that I had a history with Rex and I needed to keep it that way. He'd signed away all rights to his children almost a decade ago, and until I figured out what his angle was for showing up at my job and surprising the life out of me, I needed to play it safe.

"Sorry about that, Mr. Conner," I said, crisp but pleasant. "I've been having some problems with an inner ear issue and it causes vertigo at the most inconvenient times."

One of Rex's dark blonde eyebrows crept up. "That sounds uncomfortable, Miss Parker. I hope you have that looked at by a qualified physician before it becomes more of a problem."

Go fuck a duck, asshole.

My phone started ringing. I hit the forward button, expecting the call to transfer to Mona. Instead I heard the phone ring in Jerry's office. Jerry must have changed the forwarding setup.

Back to the problem at hand—Rex.

Well aware of the audience that sat circled around us listening to every word Rex and I spoke, I indicated the chair opposite my desk. "Why don't you have a seat and we can discuss exactly what you're looking for in detail."

And why you dared to step back into my breathing space.

While he lowered into the chair, I grabbed the small framed picture of Addy and Layne bookending Aunt Zoe and stuffed it into my middle desk drawer. No way in hell did Rex get to even peek at what he'd happily walked away from almost a decade ago.

"Would you like something to drink?" I envisioned dumping a freshly brewed carafe of coffee over the son of a bitch's head.

"No, thank you. I'm fine."

I clasped my hands together in front of me to keep them from throwing something at him of their own free will. My smile felt three sizes too tight, but I forced my cheeks to wear it anyway. I locked gazes with him and held my ground.

What in the hell are you doing in Deadwood? I wanted to scream, but instead asked, "How can I help you?"

Rex's focus drifted down to the neckline of my silk shirt. "I'm interested in seeing what you have available."

Absolutely, positively nothing for him except for my foot, which I'd be happy to plant in his ass on the way out of the door and my life.

"To rent or own?" I asked.

"That depends on how things pan out."

I could show him how they'd "pan out." I just needed a cast iron skillet for demonstration purposes.

Mona's fingernails returned to her keys, her interest in Rex Conner and me apparently over. Good. One down, two to go. I could see Ray over Rex's shoulder, leaning back in his chair, openly watching me. A glance Ben's way caught him staring at Rex, small vertical wrinkles dividing his eyebrows.

"Well, we could start with rentals. If none of them work for you," *you could leave the damned state,* "we can revisit your plans for staying in town."

Rex's smile widened, obviously catching my hint. That was unfortunate; I rather liked the idea of beating it into him. "I'll leave it in your talented hands then."

Talented hands, huh? A memory flashed of the things he used to like me to do with my hands and bile rose in my throat.

"One bedroom or two?"

"Two preferably. I prefer a separate room for my office."

Ben stood and grabbed his keys. "I'll be back in a half hour," he told Ray, who nodded while continuing to watch the Rex and Violet show. Being the rat he was, he must have picked up the scent of Rex's rotten personality and felt like bonding with him.

"I don't like to take my work to bed," Rex added with a wink.

Right. I remembered. He preferred to bed long-legged skanks who were bent on screwing their older sisters' boyfriends to uphold their psychotic vendettas.

I flipped open the available rentals report Ben had printed out yesterday.

Across the room, Ray snickered at me. I aimed a pointed look over Rex's shoulder at the horse's ass, pretty certain Ray's shit eating grin was based on the fact that I'd taken my work to bed—as in Doc.

"Ray," Mona interrupted our showdown before we had a chance to clear leather. "Did you ever send me that information I needed on the Elks' Lodge in Deadwood?"

"It's in my SUV."

"Could you go get it, please." It was more of an order than a question.

Ray shot her a frown. "You need it right now?"

Mona lowered her reading glasses. "I needed it two days ago when I asked you for it," she said as sweet as cherry pie, but her glare was loaded with tartness.

With a grunt, Ray followed in Ben's wake.

Thank you, Mona.

Focusing back on the problem sitting in front of me, I skimmed my finger down the page of rentals available in the area, passing over three that fit his bill. "Hmmm. It appears there aren't any two bedroom rentals available."

"Nothing?" Rex raised one eyebrow. "Really?" His voice was full of disbelief.

Mona's typing slowed, her face turning in my direction. I avoided what I was sure was a questioning look from her. She studied the listings every day and could usually rattle off how many two, three, and four bedroom places were available in a fifty mile radius.

I stared hard at Rex. "Really." *Now leave.*

Mona cleared her throat.

Without looking at her, I held up my index finger in her direction.

Rex rubbed his chin, tipping his head to the side. "That's a bit of a surprise."

"Yes, it is." I leaned back, smiling wide, baring my sharp teeth. "Today seems to be full of them."

"How about houses for sale then?"

"Nothing there either," I said without even a glance at the reports in front of me.

Rex's eyes narrowed. "Deadwood must be a popular place to live."

"We're mired in a seller's market at the moment."

Mona stopped clacking altogether.

"Violet," Jerry called, stepping out of his office and breaking the tension hovering between Rex and me, "I have a mess ..." He looked up from the newspaper he was carrying and noticed I had company. "Oh, I'm sorry to interrupt. Please continue. I'll catch you later."

Unfortunately, instead of returning to his office, Jerry headed for the coffee maker.

"What do you suggest then, Miss Parker?" Rex asked.

Shit! I could sidetrack Mona for now and make up a reason I had blown off Rex later, but with Jerry listening in, I was at a disadvantage.

"Why don't you let me do some more research and give you a call ..." *never ever EVER* "... later."

Jerry strolled towards us, fresh coffee in hand. "Hello," he said to Rex. "I'm Jerry Russo." He held out his hand.

Rex stood and took Jerry up on his handshake. "Rex Conner, nice to meet you."

"I hear you saw Violet's billboard ad."

"I did." Rex's eyes practically sparkled when they settled back on me. "It snagged my attention immediately."

I bet it did. I wonder what other old enemies of mine would be surfacing now that they knew where to find me.

Jerry patted my shoulder. "She's a great Realtor, really knows this area well."

That wasn't quite true. While I'd been coming here in the summer to stay with Aunt Zoe since I was a kid, I'd only lived here full time since March.

"Too bad there isn't much available around here," Rex said. "I was really looking forward to checking out some places and settling in for a while."

"Isn't much available?" Jerry looked down at me, his forehead all crunched. "Didn't Ben print out reports for today?"

I sighed. "He was working on that when he had to step out."

As Jerry strode to the printer, Rex gave me a white-toothed victory grin. Oh, how I wished I carried a battering ram in my purse.

"Here we are," Jerry said, rejoining us, oblivious of the tension crackling out from my head like bolts of electricity.

Ray came stomping down the back hallway. He dropped a folder on Mona's desk. "There you go, Red." He eyed Jerry and then Rex and then me, his suspicion plain as mud on his face.

"Thanks," I said when Jerry handed me today's report on rentals. I glanced down at the paper. "Well, would you look at that. It's your lucky day, Mr. Conner."

"I was thinking just that when I woke up this morning," Rex said, oozing charm again.

I longed to dump him and all of that smarmy charm over Pactola Dam.

"Would you like me to write down the addresses so that you can take a look at the places available?" I offered.

Jerry shot me a quick frown. "Or Violet could show them to you personally."

No, Violet does not want to do that, thank you, Coach Jerry.

"I'd like that," Rex said to Jerry. He turned to me. "Are you available tomorrow afternoon?"

No! Not even for a minute. Nothing available for all eternity either.

"I'm sure she is."

If Jerry didn't stop answering for me, I was going to climb up on my desk and leap onto his back, pummeling him until he whimpered like a spanked puppy.

"Excellent." Rex pulled a set of car keys from his pocket. "Will two o'clock work, Miss Parker?"

I nodded, not trusting my mouth enough to open it in case a ball of fire spewed forth and burned Rex to a crisp right before my boss's eyes.

"It's a date then," Jerry said, clapping his huge hands together.

I jerked at the sound. "An *appointment*," I corrected with a brittle imitation of a smile. "I'll drive," I told Rex. There was no way I was crawling in a vehicle with him unless I had the upper hand.

"Perfect." Rex shook Jerry's hand again, then held his palm out for me to take.

When I hesitated, Jerry nudged me toward Rex. "I'll see you then," I said, letting Rex's hand touch mine.

It was all I could do not to recoil from his firm warm grip. As soon as he left, I was going to race to the bathroom and scald my skin under steaming hot water.

With a nod farewell, Rex strode out the front door.

"Are you feeling okay, Violet?" Jerry asked after the turd had left.

Not even a miniscule bit. "I'm fine." I grabbed my purse from my drawer. "If you'll excuse me, I need to run to the restroom for a moment."

"Sure, yeah." He stepped aside, letting me pass. "Oh, when you're finished, you need to call Detective Cooper."

That stopped me. Cooper must have been the one who was calling when Rex first showed up. I turned back, wondering what Jerry knew about my appointment with Cooper at the Galena House today. "Did he give a reason for the call?"

"Yes. He told me to let you know he'd like to take you for lunch as a thank you for all of the hard work you've been doing to get his house sold."

I glanced beyond Jerry out the front window to make sure there were no pigs flying around outside.

"How kind of him," I said, wondering what in the hell the detective was up to with this ploy.

"You're doing a great job for the team, Violet," Jerry said.

His compliment made me sputter in surprise. Lately, I'd felt like I kept fouling out. "Thanks."

Turning on my boot heel, I escaped to the bathroom. Once there, I stared at the red-cheeked woman in the mirror, surprised to find that my mouth wasn't frothing yet.

Rex Conner.

In the flesh.

Interested in acquiring a house in Deadwood.

I gripped the edge of the sink. How was I going to keep the truth about who he was from my kids? Where was that paper he'd signed that stated he agreed to give up all rights to his children? I knew my father's lawyer had a copy stored away somewhere, but I was sure I'd hidden my copy in one of the boxes stored down in Aunt Zoe's basement. Or had I left it at my parents' place in case Addy or Layne started snooping through my stuff?

Fuck! Shit! Damn!

I scrubbed both of my hands down my face, and then splashed cold water on my hot cheeks.

What was I going to do? I wanted to call Doc and spill my troubles all over him, but I had no idea how the news about Rex looking me up would go over. Not that Doc was the jealous type, but we were still so new in our coupledom that this news might cause problems I didn't realize were even a possibility. We had enough working against us already with all of Doc's freaky ghosts, my pissy kids, and now Tiffany Psycho-bell. Would knowing the father of my children was skulking around me scare Doc off?

God, why did Rex have to show up now? I patted my skin dry and then checked my cell phone. Detective Cooper had left me a message, too. He was quite attentive this morning. Wasn't I the lucky girl?

I pulled up Natalie's number. Her phone rang six times before forwarding to her voicemail. I hung up, wishing she weren't so damned far away. I needed her now more than ever. She was the only one who knew how dangerous Rex being back in town was to my family.

Tossing the paper towel in the trash, I blew out a breath.

Cooper had better be on his best behavior today. Because after facing down Rex this morning, I wanted nothing more than to bite someone's head clean off. The detective's thick skull would do fine.

* * *

Detective Cooper's sedan sat in front of the Galena House when I pulled up. I parked behind it and killed the Picklemobile's engine. The motor did its usual spit and sputter before dying with a loud backfire. *Bang!*

A broad shouldered, black haired man shot out onto the front porch, his handgun pointed at the sky, his gaze darting up and down the street.

What the hell? He had to be one of Cooper's pals.

I climbed out of the Picklemobile and slammed the door behind me.

"Hold it right there, ma'am!" he yelled from the porch, holding his hand out toward me like he was directing traffic. "You might want to stay in your vehicle until I clear the area."

My neck swiveled as I looked around for something or someone suspicious. "Clear it of what?"

Cooper strode out onto the porch. "Would you put that damned thing away? You're going to scare the neighbors." His eyes landed on me, searching my face, narrowing on what they saw there. "Why didn't you answer your phone?" he called down to where I still waited by the Picklemobile, shivering in the cool morning breeze.

"I was busy."

"I called three times."

He had—first my cell phone when Rex was there, then my

office phone which I'd forwarded, and then my cell again about twenty minutes after Rex had left. The last one I'd ignored because I didn't think my blood pressure could stand a conversation with Cooper at the time. Whether or not I had the patience to deal with the detective was still up in the air, but he'd left me little choice this morning by demanding my presence ... or else.

"Three?" I hollered back. "You're beginning to make me feel special, Detective."

"Oh, you're special all right," he said, and then muttered something I didn't catch.

"Can I come up there now?" I asked, planting my hands on my hips. "Or should I wait out here for you to give me a play-by-play of the walk-through?"

Cooper pointed at the porch for an answer. As I started up the walk, he turned back to the guy with the gun. "This is Violet Parker," I heard him say, "the one who received the phone call from Ms. Wolff."

The trigger happy traffic cop stuffed his handgun back in his shoulder holster, saying something I couldn't hear with the truck rumbling past on the street behind me.

"Yes," I heard Cooper reply with an extra dose of terseness, "and I told you not to use my first name. Next time you slip, I'll shoot you in the foot and enjoy a little paid stress leave for my troubles."

Detective Cooper's first name was top secret according to Harvey, akin to the access codes to Area 51.

I climbed the porch steps, my gaze darting between the two men in front of me. Cooper mirrored the gunslingers of the old West—all rigid features and lean length, reminding me of cut and dried rawhide. The other guy looked like he was straight out of an early 1970s police drama with his pork chop sideburns, brown corduroy jacket, and too thick and wavy black hair. James Garner from *The Rockford Files* popped into my brain once again; I couldn't help it, the local station kept showing re-runs after the kids went to bed. However, while Mr. Garner had sex appeal, this new guy just had a square jaw minus the dimple.

Cooper's cohort stuffed his hands in his front pant pockets, tipping back on his loafer heels. He checked out my outfit, spending a few extra beats on my boots and hair.

"Who's your friend?" I stood next to Cooper, wondering if this were his boss.

"Ms. Parker, meet my new partner on this case—Stone Hawke."

Stone Hawke? For real? That sounded like a character from a comic book or one of those gritty movies Quentin Tarantino was famous for making.

I laughed, a sharp barking sound that echoed in the cool morning stillness. I knew it was impolite, but after Rex's surprise visit, I'd sort of lost the reins on my control, and the horses were running away with the carriage while I held on for dear life.

"You find something funny, Ms. Parker?" Cooper asked.

"No," I said, trying to stifle my chuckles with my fist. "There's absolutely nothing at all funny about this morning's events."

Cooper seemed to pick up on the bitterness in my tone. He stared harder at me, his detective x-ray vision contacts sliding into place. "What hap—"

"Ms. Parker," seventies superstar Stone Hawke cut him off, flipping a mini notebook open. "Would you please tell us what happened on Sunday, September 30th around twelve-forty-five p.m.?"

This again? He had to be kidding me. I frowned up at Cooper. "So this guy here isn't your boss?"

Cooper shook his head. "He's just anoth—"

"Ms. Parker," Detective Hawke interrupted Cooper again, gracing me with what I was sure he thought was a warm and fuzzy bear sort of smile. He tugged a pen from an inner pocket in his corduroy jacket and clicked it open, closed, and open again, like he was testing it for quality control purposes.

Each click made my shoulders scrunch a notch tighter. What was it with the Deadwood cops and those damned click pens? Were they issued as interrogation torture devices?

"Would you mind retelling the events of that day," Hawke

continued, seemingly unaware that my eye had twitched at his last click, "including every detail you can think of in that curly blonde head of yours."

"Oh, shit," I heard Cooper say under his breath before he took a step backward.

Click, click, went Detective Hawke's pen.

My eye twitched again.

Then something splintered in my brain.

"No." I spoke in a growl, sounding all demon-possessed like the little girl in the *Exorcist*. At any moment, my head would spin clear around.

Hawke's thick black unibrow scrunched in the middle as the two sides of his forehead collided in a curious display of plate tectonics. "No, you wouldn't mind retelling the events?"

CLICK. CLICK!

I swiped the pen from his thick fingers, dropped it on the floor boards, and stomped on it over and over with my boot heel until it broke into several pieces. Then I scooped up the pieces, grabbed Detective Hawke's wrist, and dropped the remains in his palm.

"No," I said, "I am not going to tell my story one more time." I tucked back some curls that had come loose during my stomp-fest and straightened my coat, taking a moment to calm down, steady my voice. "Detective Cooper has all versions of my story already written down. You can read his notes and catch up."

His jaw unhinged, Hawke turned to Cooper. "Why didn't you inform me that your witness is unstable?"

"She's not usually like this. She's obviously—"

"Pre-menstrual?" Hawke interjected.

Cooper winced and took another step back. Smart cookie.

I stepped really close to Detective Hawke, my fists clenching. I didn't like what I saw, especially all of the hairs in his nose. "Listen you ass-scratching baboon, insult me one more time and it will be your testicles under my boot heel next."

Whirling on Cooper, I snarled. "Are we done standing around out here? Because I have some serious crap to deal with back at work and the sooner we do this, the sooner I can return to what I do best."

"Messing up my cases?" Cooper asked, a grin ghosting his lips.

Actually, it was panicking, but that wasn't very cool sounding and I needed a good exit line. "Selling real estate."

Oh, man, that was so lame.

Cooper's grin fully surfaced. "Is that the best you could come up with?"

I shoved him in the chest as I stalked past him. "I'll come up with something all right. Something you can stuff right up your ying-yang along with that stick."

"*Ying yang?* You're slipping, Parker," he said from behind me, following on my heels.

"Yeah, well I've had a really crappy morning, so cut me some slack."

"What happened? You didn't get another phone call, did you?"

No, this time trouble had walked right through the front door.

Detective Hawke trailed behind us keeping a safe distance. Becoming a eunuch must not have appealed to him.

"No call," I told Cooper. I didn't feel like spilling anything else right now. The burn from seeing Rex again was too raw, still oozing.

"Your family's okay?"

"Uh-huh." I passed the stairwell, heading toward the door crossed off with crime scene tape.

"Doc's fine?"

I hoped so. There was the chance that Tiffany had him tied up and muzzled in her basement by now, though. "Yes."

"Ms. Beals and your aunt are good?"

I stopped in front of the door to Ms. Wolff's apartment, frowning back at Cooper. "What's the deal?"

His eyes widened for a split second. "What do you mean?"

"Are you putting on a show for your new partner or something?"

"A show?"

"Yes. You're pretending to have a human heart and care about my problems all of a sudden." My gaze bounced between the two detectives. "Oh, I get it now. You're playing the 'good cop' role today, aren't you?"

"Violet," Cooper started, crossing his arms over his chest. "I was—"

"If this is the disrespect all of your witnesses show you," Detective Hawke said, all high and mighty toned, "I can see why you're having an issue with solving your cases lately."

"Pipe down, Rockford Files," I snapped. "Cooper's inability to solve murders has nothing to do with me."

"First of all," Cooper grated, "Ms. Parker's disrespect for officers of the law has no correlation with my open cases."

"I do not disrespect all cops," I clarified. "Just you two."

"Second," Cooper nailed me with his steely gray glare, "you have a lot to do with why these damned murders aren't solved yet and you know it."

"Me?" I rolled my eyes. "Oh, jeez. Here we go again with how I keep screwing up your investigations."

"Is she hiding evidence from you?" Detective Hawke asked, his hands back in his front pockets.

Cooper's face pinched. "No, she's not hiding evidence."

Au contraire, but now was not the time to bring up that tidbit about the demon guidebook I hadn't told him about or any of the other stuff.

Detective Hawke's gaze bounced between Cooper and me, his mouth morphing into an ugly sneer. "Are you screwing the witness again, Coop?"

Without warning, I stomped my heel down on Detective Hawke's toe. Hard.

He squealed and did a one-footed jig.

I debated on clapping along.

"Violet," Cooper said, his mouth all wavy lined, hovering between a smile and a frown. "Please try to keep your hands and feet to yourself."

"Fine, but you'd better advise your new partner to filter his comments." I pointed up at Hawke's red face. The fury radiating from his eyes could have heated a small house. "I'm a woman on the edge today, so back off."

His only response was a wrinkle of his upper lip.

Good. At least we both knew where we stood—he didn't like me one iota and I hoped a tornado would blow through and whirl him far, far away. One detective was all Deadwood needed. Two of them would only muck up the murder messes more.

Cooper tore the crime scene tape off the jambs, unlocked the door, and opened it. He held his hand out for me to enter before him. "Shall we begin, Ms. Parker?"

"This is going to be so much fun," I muttered and stepped over Ms. Wolff's threshold.

Chapter Eight

Time had gone on without Ms. Wolff. Her wall of clocks proved it. Each one still ticked away, the hands showing different times as their pendulums swung to and fro.

Ms. Wolff's apartment was shrouded in gloom, which added a cloud of doom to my overall mood as I stood there in the living room remembering how my last visit had gone. I sniffed, glad the odor that had been in here on Sunday was absent. Looking around, it appeared that the body and its smell were the only things that had been removed.

"Holy shit," Detective Hawke said, coming to a stop next to me, his shoulder bumping mine. "This victim had a serious case of OCD."

His comment confirmed my suspicion that this was his first time in Ms. Wolff's apartment of horror. I hoped he'd at least flipped through the pictures before coming along for the tour.

I turned to Cooper, who stood back, giving me breathing space. "What do you want from me?"

He glanced around the room, and then centered his focus on me. "I want you to snoop around, just as you would if you had sneaked in here in your usual style."

The normal, testy Detective Cooper had returned. Good. I preferred fencing with him over holding hands and singing campfire songs. "Where should I start?"

"Here is as good a place as any."

"You sure this is wise, Cooper?" Hawke asked. "She knows not to get her fingerprints on anything, right?"

Hawke must have thought I'd lived under a rock for the last decade. I'd seen enough episodes of forensic crime television shows to know to look and not touch. I shot Cooper a disgusted grimace. "Did you really have to bring Barney along? This would go much smoother without your sidekick."

"The choice was not mine."

What did that mean? I'd have to tell Harvey about Stone Hawke and see what he knew about Cooper's new partner. "So Rock here will be tagging along on all of our future adventures?"

"Lady, the name is Detective Stone Hawke, or just Detective Hawke if that's easier for you to remember. Not Barney, not Rock. And for your information, I happen to outrank your pal, Detective Cooper."

Was I supposed to be impressed? He'd picked the wrong citizen to show off his shiny badge to if so. "You outrank him, all right," I said, strolling over to the clock wall. "You smell like you've been flea dipped in cheap aftershave. If you're looking to entice a member of the female population with that stuff, stick to dabbing it on not splashing around in it like a dog in a mud puddle."

Hawke turned to Cooper. "Do you put up with this kind of mouthy talk from her all of the time?"

"More often than not. But sometimes I arrest her."

That won him one of my middle finger salutes.

"I remember the women in Deadwood being more friendly," Hawke said.

Cooper scoffed. "If you were looking for a farmer's daughter sort of welcome from the local female population, you rode into the wrong town, partner."

"Stone Hawke," I tried that on for size, stepping closer to check out the clocks that were at my eyelevel. "That sure sounds like a made up name for a cop to me, something I'd find in an action-adventure novel. Did your mom like to read, Detective Hawke?"

The detail on each clock was intricate, incredibly so for something carved out of a tree. The wood was polished so much it looked plastic in the low light.

"Leave my mother out of this." Hawke grumbled to himself as he stomped over to the window.

"Cooper." I turned to find his steely gray eyes glaring at

Hawke. It took him a second to return his focus to me. "I'd like a better look at these clocks, but it's too dark in here. Can I open the curtains?" Although, with it raining outside, that probably wouldn't help much.

He seemed to follow my train of thought. "How about a flashlight?" he offered, joining me at the wall.

"That'll do." I held out my hand.

He offered a palm-sized flashlight, handle out. When I reached for it, he pulled it back. "Be careful. If you flick this switch and push that button there, it'll zap you."

"Of course, it will. Even your flashlight is a weapon." I shook my head. "I'm surprised it doesn't shoot bullets, too."

"It never hurts to be prepared." He handed the flashlight over.

"Now you sound like your uncle." I carefully switched it on, making sure I didn't electrocute myself and add another fatality to Cooper's case board.

I shined the light on one of the clocks. From what I could tell, it had wooden hands, dial, and pendulum. I'd bet the cuckoo and all of the decorations on it were made of wood, too, no plastic on this puppy. "What kind of wood do you think this is?"

"Walnut," Cooper said without question.

"How come you're so sure?"

"I'm a detective. They pay me to be sure."

I peered at the next one over. The design was different, this one with leaf carvings—poison ivy from the looks of the three leaf bunches—instead of birds of prey. Again, it was highly polished with wood components. "There's no dust on them."

"Like I said," Hawke came up behind us, making it two too many detectives in one spot, "she had a serious case of OCD. I've seen others with it. They get fixated on something, like washing their hands, and can't leave home because they keep washing and washing. All these damned clocks must have kept the victim busy night and day."

I sidestepped over to one of the clocks that wasn't working, shining the light on it. Carved hunting dogs were affixed to it. But something about them made me uneasy. I looked closer, studying the carved pieces, noticing that they seemed furrier than most hunting dogs, more ferocious, posed in menacing positions with a young girl cowering between them. Then it hit me—they weren't dogs, they were wolves. I shined the light back into the opening in the clock face to see if there were other wolf carvings glued onto the piece that must usually spin, but I couldn't get a clear angle on what was hidden inside the clock. I nudged it with the flashlight, but it was stuck. I looked above the opening and noticed a skull at the apex mixed in with the leaf carvings and almost dropped the clock.

"What are you doing, Parker?" Cooper asked.

I swallowed my unease, getting back on track. "Trying to see something." And trying to figure out why this one had stopped.

"Why are we wasting so much time on these stupid clocks?" Hawke snapped. "We should be going through her dresser, pulling up the carpet in her closet, looking for something worthwhile, not admiring her collection of cuckoo clocks."

I wished good ol' Stone would roll across the room and let some moss gather on him for a bit. Ignoring the new guy, I told Cooper, "I want to take this one off the wall."

"Why?"

"To see if it's battery operated," which I very much doubted. What I really wanted to see was if she'd hidden anything inside the back panel, and having Cooper prove the clock was not battery driven seemed a good way to get him to open the back without showing my hand.

"I'm ninety-nine percent sure this is a mechanical clock that needs to be wound by pulling on the weight chains one at a time." His gaze skated over the whole wall. "I'm betting all of these operate that way. They look like authentic Black Forest cuckoo clocks."

"Humor me this once."

"Just do it, Cooper," Hawke attached himself to my side again, his arm bumping mine. The man seemed to have no perception of personal space, because he kept tromping over the boundaries into mine. "The sooner she looks at the clock, the sooner we can move on to more important areas in here."

Cooper pulled a pair of neoprene gloves from his inner jacket pocket, tugging them on. "Which one?" he asked me.

I pointed at the one with the wolves.

With a slow, steady hand, Cooper lifted the clock off the wall. I shined the light on it. "Turn it around."

He obeyed without comment, shifting the clock with care, keeping it level. I flicked the clasp holding the back panel in place. Inside there was no battery, just the mechanical workings, the cuckoo sleeve and mechanism, and what looked like German writing, which I guessed was the clock's name or its maker's signature. No hidden treasure, no skeleton keys, nothing but clock guts.

Cooper clasped the panel closed. "See," he said, hanging it

back on the wall, "you wind these kinds of clocks."

"Show me how." I knew how, but I wanted Cooper to wind it up. I was curious if it had wound down or was broken.

"I don't think it's a good—" Cooper started.

Hawke nudged me aside with his hip. "Like this." He showed me, pulling one chain at a time.

"Careful, Hawke," Cooper said, his face tight with what looked like disapproval.

When Hawke finished, the clock sat there, quiet and still as before.

"Did you wind it all of the way?" I asked.

"I think so," Hawke said.

Cooper leaned closer, frowning at it. "I don't think any of us should mess with it anymore. We don't want to break it."

"It appears to be broken already." I looked over the rest of the clocks, counting five others that weren't moving either. Were they broken, too, or just wound down?

"So the clock is broken," Hawke crossed his arms over his barrel chest. "Big deal. That doesn't tell us who killed the victim or why. We need to be looking for something in the bedroom, I'm betting."

"Now who has OCD?" I asked, stepping back from the wall. I wanted to try winding the other clocks, but knew better than to suggest it with Detective Impatient-pants sulking in the wings.

How long did a wound clock take to unwind? If Cooper was right, they would each slow to a stop before long since Ms. Wolff wasn't around to keep them moving.

"Why the interest in the clocks, Parker?" Cooper asked.

I didn't know why. Maybe I was fascinated by them, by how many there were, by the reasoning behind none of them being quite the right time. I'd love to spend some time with a ladder and flashlight, looking over the workmanship and theme of each one, but I knew there was no way either detective would be having any of that today.

"It's just odd," I ended up telling him.

"Everything in this town is just odd," Hawke said, trudging back toward the window. He pulled the curtains aside and frowned. "Always has been. I've never understood why you came back here, Cooper. You were on your way to becoming something big down in Rapid, following in my footsteps."

"That's not important right now," Cooper said. I could hear how clenched his teeth were. Hawke's attempt to bolster Cooper seemed to have pissed him off instead. "Parker, are we done with the clocks?"

For now. "Sure."

I walked over to the chalk outline on the floor, skirting it to take a closer look at the old fashioned phone. "Why did you guys take a picture of the phone?" I asked Cooper.

"No reason. It's standard procedure."

I shined his flashlight on it, bathing it in a bright halogen glow. It reminded me of one I'd seen Bogie use in *The Big Sleep*, with its square base, pyramid-shaped body and curved hand piece. An industrial cord wrapped in black braided fabric ran out the back and down the wall, disappearing behind the end table. "Is there any way to confirm this is the phone she called me from?"

"It's not the phone she used," Cooper said.

"You're certain?"

He nodded. "It's just for looks. The plug in doesn't fit the outlet in the wall."

I pointed at the pen in Cooper's breast pocket. "Can I borrow that?"

"You're not going to stomp on it, too, are you?"

"Just give me the damned pen."

Cooper obliged.

I pulled my sleeve down over my hand, using it as a glove so that I could pick up the handset. It felt solid, heavy in my hand. I held it close to my ear without touching it. Sure enough, there was no dial tone. I used the pen to spin the rotary dial. It spun back to start position, moving slow like the one my grandmother had owned back when I was a kid.

I handed Cooper back his pen. "So she kept it for decoration only, you think?"

"That's my guess," Cooper stuffed the pen back into his

pocket.

Detective Hawke shifted over by the window. "So we have authentic German wall clocks and a genuine antique phone. We're really cooking on finding clues now. If this is your usual modus operandi, it's no wonder it's taking you so long to solve these murders."

I ignored Hawke, turning my back on him. "She liked antiques," I told Cooper.

He nodded.

"And not the cheap ones. Do you have any idea what Ms. Wolff did for money?" Because Social Security checks did not cover the cost of these pieces.

"From what I can tell so far, she never had a taxpaying job."

Never? "Was she a widow?"

"There's no marriage license on record for her."

"She must have come from money then."

"I'm still working those details out."

What did that mean? That he couldn't find anything about Ms. Wolff in any official records?

I thought about asking him to clarify, but something in the way he kept shooting gunslinger glares at his partner made me hold my tongue. I wanted to know the lowdown on the history between Cooper and Hawke.

"Let's move to her bedroom," I said. That should make Hawke happy.

"Finally!" The other detective rubbed his hands together. "Now we'll get to the bottom of things."

I followed Cooper through the doorway. The bedroom was about ten square feet smaller than the living room. A twin-sized bed split the room in half, with two doors on the opposite wall. One doorway led to the bathroom, the other door to the closet I had seen in the photos Harvey and I looked at in Cooper's house yesterday. The bedroom walls looked gray in the dimness. I flicked on the overhead light, but the room still appeared shrouded.

Detective Hawke skidded to a halt inside the bedroom door, whistling through his teeth as he looked around. "You're kidding me. More clocks in here, too? This dame had a real hang-up."

Freesia, the owner of the Galena House, hadn't been telling tall tales when she talked about how many clocks Ms. Wolff had. The wall on my right was covered with them. How did the woman sleep with all of the ticking?

My focus zeroed in on the dresser. I skirted the bed, wanting to see Layne's picture with my own eyes, yet dreading it at the same time. Sure enough, there it was stuck in the mirror frame, the photo I'd taken of Layne.

In it he held up his glass dinosaur egg sculpture in front of his smiling face, Aunt Zoe's workshop in the background. I could see the reflection of my own arm and the camera flash in the old family heirloom mirror hung on the wall behind Layne. The snapshot of me that Aunt Zoe always kept stuffed in the mirror's corner was just visible in Layne's picture.

The photo within a photo scene reminded me of standing in a house of mirrors, how my reflection went on and on. Did the irony of a snapshot stuck in a mirror that was showing in the background of another snapshot stuck in Ms. Wolff's dresser mirror mean anything?

Even though Cooper had told me the photo of Layne was here in her bedroom, seeing it made my hands clammy. Pictures tucked into a bedroom mirror seemed like such a personal thing. Why was it *my* son? Why was his picture the only one on her dresser? How had she gotten that photo?

Did this have anything to do with Rex being in town? Was Ms. Wolff somehow related to Rex? I didn't remember him talking about having relatives in the hills, but then again we really didn't waste a lot of time talking back then.

"Are you okay?" Cooper asked, coming up beside me without bumping into me like his clod-footed partner.

"I don't know," I answered honestly. "I can't make sense of it."

"That's unfortunate, because I was hoping this was a clue to why she called you. It seems too odd to be happenstance."

"Can I have that picture back?" I asked.

"We'll want to keep it in evidence for some time after we

finish with the crime scene details."

"Can you make a copy of it?"

"I'll see what I can do," Cooper said.

"Hey, Coop, did your camera guy get a shot of this?" Detective Hawke pointed into the closet.

"The heads?" Cooper asked.

Hawke nodded. "She must have twenty of them lining that shelf. Has anyone cut one open?"

"Why?" I asked.

"Coop and I once worked on a drug trafficking case where they kept the goods hidden inside mannequin heads similar to these. We got a nice commendation when we solved that one, didn't we, buddy?"

"Yes, you sure did," Cooper answered, his lips barely moving. His whole face seemed to have hardened into a veneer. "But those are not mannequin heads in the closet, they're styrofoam heads."

"Same thing." Hawke waved off Cooper's distinction and stepped inside the closet.

"Drugs?" I asked Cooper. "You think an old woman like Ms. Wolff would be mixed up with a drug cartel?"

Hawke poked his head out of the closet. "We've seen weirder things happen down in Rapid, haven't we, Coop?"

Cooper didn't reply.

"Is that where he lives?" I asked Cooper.

"Yep," Hawke called out before Cooper could reply. "I'm here only for as long as it takes to fix Coop's messes."

I heard Cooper swear under his breath and looked up in time to see him shake his head and turn away. He moved over to another antique dresser on the other side of the room.

"So you two used to work together?" I asked loud enough for either man to answer.

"We were partners for a few years." A thump came from the closet along with Hawke's voice. Two more thumps followed. "Two of the best detectives in western South Dakota, ain't that right, Coop?"

Cooper grunted, sounding a lot like his uncle when Harvey

ate and used caveman vernacular for our dinner conversations. Something had happened down in Rapid, something that made Cooper leave and move back home. Did it have anything to do with getting involved with a witness, as Hawke had accused him of doing earlier? Or had something else gone down that had driven him out of Rapid?

I shifted my concentration back onto the task at hand. Cooper's ancient history could be saved for this evening at the dinner table with Harvey. Following in Cooper's footsteps, I pointed the flashlight on the dresser drawer he'd opened.

"She had nice dressers, they match the headboard." I admired the construction of the drawer, noting the handcrafted details. Then I shined the flashlight inside of it, running my finger over a soft cotton nightgown. "Didn't you go through all of these drawers already?" I couldn't imagine Cooper being any less thorough than a proctologist.

"Yes, but you haven't." He reached in and pointed his gloved finger at something in the back of the drawer. "What do you make of that?"

I leaned closer, aiming the light beam on the back panel of wood. Weird looking scrolls, wavy dashes, and dots were written on the wood in black ink—not the ball point pen kind, but rather the ink that comes from an inkwell. "You think those markings have some kind of meaning?"

"I have no idea. They're only on the back of this drawer, not the others." He shut the top drawer and pulled out the second, having me shine the flashlight in it, too. Sure enough, the wood was unmarked.

Two more loud thumps came from the closet.

"What's he doing in there?"

"Looking for a trap door. Hawke assumes all closets come with trap doors."

"How long have you known him?"

"Too long."

"Does he have something to do with why you left?"

Cooper shut the drawer hard enough to rattle the crystal hair brush lying bristles up on the matching mirror. The hairs sticking out of the bristles looked thick, coarse and wiry, reminding me of my hair. "That's not relevant to our purpose here."

"A simple yes or no would suffice."

"Nor is it any of your business, Parker." He waved his hand around the room. "Do you see anything else that connects you to Ms. Wolff in one form or another?"

Detective Hawke stepped out of the walk-in closet, a scarf dragging behind him. "There's no trap door in that one."

"I believe I told you that in the car on the way over here."

I snagged the scarf from Hawke and folded it. "May I look in there?"

"Have at it," Hawke said. "You won't find anything besides old dresses that stink like mothballs and boxes full of fancy hats."

I stepped through the closet doorway and paused, taking my time looking up, down, and everywhere in between. The overhead light was bright enough that I didn't need Cooper's flashlight, so I switched it off, careful not to get zapped.

Moving to the wrap-around racks full of clothes, I started pushing back hangers, checking out clothing tags. The dresses and outfits were dated, but most were still in tiptop shape, looking as if Ms. Wolff had purchased them in decades past and stored them in here. By the fifteenth or so tag I checked, I noticed something that made me pause and double-check a few, then I moved forward through several more.

"What is it?" Cooper asked from the doorway, where he stood watching. I figured he probably was observing my search techniques critically, itching to tell me how I was doing things wrong.

"The sizes are different."

"Maybe she gained or lost weight and kept her old clothes."

"Maybe," I said, continuing.

The sizes continued to fluctuate in grouped increments, getting larger and larger. Some of the more dated pieces had no tags at all and looked hand sewn. She must have been a clothes hoarder. By the time I'd gone through the lion's share of her outfits, I'd learned something else. I thought about keeping it to myself, but I had told Doc and Harvey that I'd let the law solve this mystery and I had sort of meant it. With Rex showing up in town, I had enough on my shoulders.

"I don't think these were all her clothes," I told Cooper.

"Why?"

"They not only vary in sizes but style as well."

"Maybe she liked to change it up periodically."

Hawke's head appeared over Cooper's shoulder. "I thought all you women like to buy whole new wardrobes on a whim?"

"How many women have you lived with Detective Hawke?"

"A couple."

"Not including your mother or any sisters?"

"Enough to know women like to shop," he said, his cheeks darkening.

"What's your point, Parker?" Cooper asked. "That Ms. Wolff liked to play dress up?"

Possibly. Or maybe she'd supplied the opera house in Lead with several outfits from her closet for their historic plays, which could connect her with Jane and Jane's murder, which kind of led to me—Jane's employee. It could be one of those six degrees from Kevin Bacon deals, only starring me.

"Or she had another woman living with her at one time," I threw out my original idea. Or several.

Cooper moved his jaw back and forth, seesawing on that. "Duly noted. What else do you notice in here?"

I turned the flashlight back on and shined the light on the racks of shoes. "The shoes range in size, too." Style as well, some reminding me of what flappers used to wear back in the 1920s, others from an even earlier era, the leather stiffer, hardened with age.

I looked up at the hat boxes. "I assume you went through those."

"Of course."

"Are they actual hats?"

He nodded.

"Do the brands on the hat tag match the box brand?"

"We didn't note that detail."

I turned to Hawke. "Will you get me a chair from the

kitchen?"

"I could lift you up," Hawke offered, cracking his knuckles, his eyes sizing me up. "What do you weigh? A buck fifty? Sixty?"

If he had been closer, I'd have stomped on his other foot just for bringing up the subject of my weight. "Or you could get me a chair from the kitchen. I'm a bit prickly to the touch."

"You look soft in all the right places to me."

"As soft as a porcupine," Cooper said. "Go get her a chair, Hawke."

"That wasn't a very nice thing to say about me," I jested while we waited.

"It's not my job to supply you with compliments."

"You do a great job of delivering insults."

"Those are on the house." Cooper stepped aside to make room for Hawke and the chair.

I climbed up, careful to balance. "Can I touch a lid without screwing up anything?"

"Be my guest."

I lifted and peeked, reaching inside. Sure enough, the hat matched the box. I looked into several of the hat boxes, the results the same each time.

"Well?" Cooper asked.

"They match."

"Does that mean anything to this case?"

"It means she could afford to buy expensive hats and took as much care with them as she did her pricey clocks."

I sighed and placed my hands on my hips, peering down at the closet contents from my aerial stand. Who was this woman? Where had she come from? Where had all of her money come from? Why did she hone in on me and my kid? Why did she have so many foam heads and yet kept her hats in boxes? Did she collect the heads like she did the clocks?

"Are we done here?" Hawke asked. "Because I'm as hungry as a bear in spring and you said something about getting lunch when we finished."

Cooper's eyebrows lifted. "Are we done, Parker?"

"I guess."

I climbed down and slipped past the two detectives back into the bedroom. I was stumped. I returned to the mirror that held Layne's picture. What was the connection here? Why my son, damn it?

My gaze drifted, taking in the books on the long bookshelf over by the window. My feet followed. Freesia had mentioned Ms. Wolff had a collection of historical books on Deadwood. I ran my fingers over the spines. Layne had an obsession with Deadwood's history. He'd spent many hours at the Deadwood library over the summer, boning up on the town's past. Was that the answer? Had he met Ms. Wolff there, struck up a conversation on history, and … then what? Given her a picture of him holding the glass dinosaur egg?

No, that didn't fit this puzzle.

I glanced back. Cooper waited in the doorway, his shoulder resting on the jamb. He gave the appearance of being relaxed, but his steely gaze missed nothing.

"Did you guys go through these books?" I asked.

"We dusted them for prints."

That wasn't exactly what I meant. There could be something stashed inside them or a clue within the pages. I needed more time in here to go through it all. I was missing something; I could feel it in my gut.

"Look who I found lurking inside the front door," Detective Hawke said, dragging Freesia into the bedroom by her wrist. "She claims to own the building."

"She does," Cooper said, pulling Freesia's arm free from Hawke's grip. "Sorry about that, Freesia. Hawke is new."

Once again, I noticed how courteous and kind Cooper was with Freesia, whereas I received teeth gnashings regularly.

"I'm not 'new,' just not local."

"Hi, Freesia," I said, glad to see her again. "Are these the books you were telling Harvey and me about the other day?"

Freesia's smile brightened the room, her yellow T-shirt and white capri pants even more so. "Yeah, those are the ones." She joined me, smelling like fresh wildflowers, and pointed out two in particular. "This one has my great, great-uncle mentioned in it, and this one was a favorite of hers. I often found it out in her living room when I'd stop by."

Hawke shouldered his way between us, and grabbed Ms. Wolff's so-called favorite from the shelf. "I'll take this one and go through it." He pulled the other book and held it out for Cooper. "You can look through that one."

Cooper shook his head. "I don't have time for light reading. Give it to Parker."

Hawke and I both hesitated, me in surprise that Cooper would let me take something from the scene of the crime, Hawke for whatever reason—probably because I was female and blonde. He gave me the book with a shrug. "It's your funeral, Coop."

I held the book close to my chest and nodded my thanks to Cooper. There was one guy I knew who could find the needle in this haystack—Doc. He knew Deadwood inside and out. His library of local history books was three times the size of Ms. Wolff's. I'd be handing this little number off to him later tonight.

But that wasn't enough. There was something more here.

Could it be that I was feeling Ms. Wolff's ghost following us around? Nah, I was still a dud when it came to the paranormal. Nothing there had changed, at least not that I could tell in spite of what Cornelius believed.

Somehow I needed to get Doc inside this apartment. He was better at seeing things hidden in plain sight than I was. He could also see if Ms. Wolff was still hanging around, trying to dust her clocks.

However, while Cooper was being extra generous today, I had a feeling this was the limit on his sharing. There was no way I could explain to the detective why I thought Doc needed to come in here. I was pretty certain that Cooper would find the idea of Doc being a medium amusing at best.

"Ms. Parker," Freesia said, peeking over her shoulder at the detectives waiting in the doorway. She lowered her voice, "I need to talk to you when you have a moment."

"If it's about the case," Cooper said, his hearing working very well, "you need to let me know as well."

"Both of us," Hawke added.

Freesia's cheeks darkened. "It's ... it's not about Ms. Wolff. It's about this place."

"What about it?" I asked, wondering if she was going to tell me that it was haunted. Knowing the story from years back about the shrunken heads, I wouldn't blink twice if she mentioned there were wispy, headless forms floating around.

"I think I want to put it on the market." She cast a nervous glance over her shoulder again. "As soon as the police will allow it."

And there it was—the golden opportunity to drag Doc in here when nobody else was looking.

I hooked my arm in hers. "Let's talk outside, shall we?"

Chapter Nine

Thursday, October 4th

I was afraid to open my eyes.

After yesterday's debacle the idea of facing what today might dish up and leave behind steaming on a plate made me whimper and wiggle deeper under my soft cotton sheet.

The smell of bacon and eggs wasn't going to lure me out either. Nope. I had problems that not even bacon was going to solve.

I curled into a ball, flitting through yesterday's events on fast-forward, trying to make sense of it all—Rex, Ms. Wolff's closet, Detective Hawke and Cooper's history, Layne's picture, clocks upon clocks. The little snow globe I lived in had been shaken up again, just when it had seemed like the last flake had fallen and life might settle down.

My cell phone rang from its perch on the nightstand. I peeked out from under the covers and saw Natalie's name on the screen.

She was exactly who I needed right now. I grabbed the phone. "I'm so glad you called back."

I'd phoned her late last night, wanting her shoulder to whine on but had gotten her voice mail instead. I'd kept my message short and didn't mention Rex's name in case anyone else happened to replay my message at a later date—something my daughter had done in the past with my phone.

"Sorry I didn't get back with you last night." Natalie sounded a bit froggy. Neither of us was good at early mornings. "I was at the bar late. You wouldn't believe the crazy shit going on down here."

She wasn't going to believe the crazy shit going on up here

either. I crawled out of bed and closed my bedroom door, wedging my sweat pants into the crack at the bottom to be safe. "As fond as I always am to hear about your family and their adventures, I need to hog the spotlight for a moment."

"Shoot, babe."

"I had a new client come into the office yesterday."

I tiptoed to my closet and slipped inside, closing the door behind me. Darkness shrouded me. My clothes deadened all sound except my breathing. It was no wonder Addy's chicken, Elvis, loved roosting in here whenever she could.

"Oh, yeah? Was this one as cracked as Cornelius and his tall hat?"

I wished. I'd take ten bizarre oddballs like Cornelius over Rex any day.

"No." I leaned my head against the wall. "It was Rex Conner."

"Who!"

"You heard me. Don't make me say his name again. I'm afraid it will conjure the devil himself to appear in the flesh right here in my bedroom." It was bad enough I was going to have to face him in broad daylight and pretend everything was hunky dory.

"He walked right into your office?" she asked.

"Yep."

"Holy fucknuts, Vi." Natalie let out a hard, cold sounding laugh. "That piece of shit really has a huge set of testicles on him, doesn't he?"

"They aren't that huge."

"Gross! Do you have to remind me that you allowed the asshole to copulate with you?"

"Hey, let's not waste time tallying up who's been with the most losers again. We already know you win, hands down."

"We need an arbitrator to determine the final count, and you know it." Natalie sighed. "Damn. When I saw Rex at the Piggly Wiggly last month, I'd hoped it was a one-time happenstance."

"Me, too. I was on pins and needles for a week, but then nothing ever came of it and neither of us saw him again. I wished him long gone for another decade. Turns out I should have sacrificed a certain chicken to the gods to make it so."

"What are you going to do?" Natalie asked.

"Drive him around town today."

"What?"

"He wants to look at places to rent." Or buy, but I crossed my fingers that by not saying those words aloud, it would keep it from happening.

"No way."

"Yes."

"Don't you have a restraining order out against him?"

"No. He relinquished all rights to the kids, but that's it. He didn't want anything to do with us, so my lawyer said there was no need for the restraining order. Plus he was never violent, so I wasn't too worried about his coming around."

"Maybe you could tie him up, drive him over to that big coal mine in Wyoming, and dump him out in an ore car headed to China."

"That's an idea." More of a pipedream, really.

"Fuck," she said, repeating my word *de jour* for yesterday.

"Yeah. That about sums it up."

"Did he ask about the kids?"

"No, thank God. We both acted like strangers. Nobody at work knows who he really is." Not yet anyway. But after the odd looks Mona was shooting me while I tried to get him to leave without another appointment, I was pretty sure I'd be getting some questions from her sooner rather than later.

"Will you be alone with him today?"

"Yes."

"Are you carrying anything?"

"Just the extra pounds between my shoulders and knees that I always keep handy."

"That was only funny the first time you said it years ago. How many times do I have to tell you that?"

"Many more to come. I'm a slow learner."

"You need to get Harvey's shotgun," she said, sounding serious.

"What? Why? You think I should drag him out into the hills and shoot him or something?"

"For protection, you dodo. What if he's come back to hurt you?"

"Why would he do that?"

"Maybe he joined some weird cult and one of their directives for him is to remove all ties to his past life via bludgeoning or skinning you or something even worse."

What could be worse than being skinned? I stood there listening to my breath for a moment. "Have you been wearing a hat while you're working in the sun down there, Nat?"

"Shut up. I'm serious, Vi. It's weird that he came back. He didn't ask a single thing about the kids when I looked him up that one time while tracking down the bitch from hell."

Natalie's favorite nickname for my vile little sister reminded me of another thing to worry about. "Oh, God, I forgot that my sister is in town, too."

"I thought she was staying down in Rapid at your parents."

"That's what I mean. It's too close. Her internal Rex radar is going to pick up on him being in the state, I'll bet. When she finds out he came to see me first, she'll go for my throat."

"Maybe that's a good thing."

"I disagree. I like my throat."

"I mean maybe she'll lure him away from you again like she did before and they'll run off into the sunset to commit their foul deeds together for eternity."

"Well, one can certainly hope." I shoved some of my shoes out of the way and lowered to the floor, leaning my back against the wall.

"Have you told Doc that Rex is in town?" Natalie asked.

"Huh-uh."

"Why not? You think he'll get all weird and jealous about him?"

"No." I hoped not anyway. That didn't seem like it was Doc's style, although I wouldn't mind a little jealousy coming from him every now and then. I certainly had plenty for both of us. "I haven't told him because I'm not sure how to do it."

"The truth would probably be the best thing to start with," she said. I wondered if there was a hidden barb in there for me after I had lied to her about my feelings for Doc from the get-go. "You have told Doc about Rex, right?"

I grimaced in the darkness. "Sort of."

"What does 'sort of' mean?"

"He knows the kids' father is alive and that Rex wrote them off when they were born. He also knows about Susan seducing Rex and their sordid relationship. But I'm afraid if I tell him that Rex is not only here in Deadwood, but that the jerkoff has also finagled me into showing him around town, things might kind of blow up."

"Like Doc will be pissed at you?" Natalie's tone spelled out her doubt on that.

"Like he'll bail on me."

"Why would he do that?"

"Nat, my kids haven't exactly been angels to him since finding out we're dating."

"So they're being brats. I'm sure he understands this is temporary."

"Does he? He's been a bachelor for a long, long time. Maybe his tolerance for kid crap is low or almost dried up already. What will happen when I say, 'Oh, and by the way, their father is now in town and inquiring about me'? I'm sure that's a sticky ball of drama he'd rather not touch." Hell, I sure didn't want to touch it, and here I was with my hands stuck to the damned thing.

I had to deal with it. Doc didn't. He could walk away and not look back without any entanglements to slow him down.

"Hmmmm." Natalie's voice grew louder in my ear, like she'd shifted her phone closer. "My gut says that you need to talk to Doc pronto about this."

"What about what *my* gut thinks?"

"Your gut's wrong. It usually is, especially when it comes to this emotional type of crap. We should go with my gut. It's a much smarter gut."

"Says the woman who is on sabbatical from men currently."

"My sabbatical has nothing to do with my gut. That's all my

screwed up heart's fault. It gets confused too easily, mistaking lust for love, and winds up face down in a gutter."

Mine did, too, which is why I was trying to keep my heart gagged and locked in the basement whenever Doc came near.

"My gut on the other hand," she continued, "knows what it's talking about, and it's one hundred percent sure you need to tell Doc that the father of your children is not only back in town but looking to snag some action from you as well."

I sighed. It was all I could do at the moment with how tight my throat felt thanks to this new noose closing around it.

Natalie snickered. "Jeez, this really feels like soap opera material here. I'm looking around for Luke and Laura or Nikki and Victor. Who was it Susan Lucci played?" She started humming the theme to *As the World Turns.*

"You have your soaps all screwed up, Nat." I pinched the bridge of my nose. "What makes you think Rex wants 'action' from me?" I hadn't even told her about his ambiguous question regarding my availability.

"Because through it all—the lies, the affair, the rejection of your kids, your sister's psychosis—Rex always wanted you. Even after I threatened to remove his dick with a pair of pliers if he didn't cough up information on Susan, he asked if you'd lost the baby weight yet and wondered if you were seeing anyone."

"No, he didn't."

"Yes, he did."

I let that sink in. "Why didn't you tell me that back then?"

"Because he was a disgusting warthog who treated you like dog shit. Besides, would it have mattered?"

"No." Except I might have enjoyed that tidbit as a token I could hold in my mind over Susan after she'd seduced him away from me.

I had been done with Rex as soon as I had caught him in bed with my sister. Unfortunately, I wasn't done with Susan. She could still get under my skin, dang it. Maybe hypnosis would fix that weakness in my force field.

"Exactly," Natalie said. "But now this has relevance. He's obviously trying to get back into your life for whatever reason—

sex or the kids or both."

"Too bad. The door is firmly shut, deadbolted, barred, and barricaded." I was thinking about building a brick wall for extra precaution while I was at it.

"Good. That's why you should come clean with Doc. He needs to know where you stand *before* he finds out that your ex is in town from someone else and he comes to the conclusion that you're hiding it from him for some reason."

I was, but the reason had everything to do with my future with Doc and nothing to do with any old feelings for Rex. Natalie was right, though. If Doc found out from anyone else about Rex, he'd at least want his house key back. At least. And I liked having that key. Some days I stared at it for several minutes and smiled—how pathetic was that?

"Fine, fine. I'll tell him." While I was at it, I might as well fill him in about how months ago Rex had been trying to find out information on me from the dead guy Harvey had found on his ranch.

"Today, Vi. You need to tell him today before you spend time alone with Rex."

"Fine, I'll stop by his office and break the news."

"Good. Wear something sexy that he likes when you tell him; it may help soften the blow."

"If only it were that simple." I'd go in my birthday suit if it meant him staying by my side come what may on the Rex front. I thought about my stretch marks and changed my mind. Maybe a negligée would be better.

"Doc may surprise you. He isn't like those other boring cretins from your past."

I knew that. He was the first one who saw ghosts. Not to mention his many talents with his hands.

The sound of Layne yelling Addy's name and pounding on a door disrupted my visit to the closet of solace. I opened the door, blinking in the morning brightness. "You need to hurry up and come home, Nat."

"I know, I'm missing Oktoberfest this weekend up there, which really sucks. It's one of my favorite festivals in the hills."

"I was referring more to helping me out with Rex and the other stuff going on."

The pounding and screaming coming from the outer hall stopped. Either the kids had worked out their differences, or an alien ship had beamed one or both of them up. Either solution worked for me.

"How's the dead woman mystery coming along? Has Detective Cooper figured it all out yet?"

"No and now he has help."

"What do you mean?"

"They gave him a partner. Some detective named Stone Hawke who Cooper used to work with down in Rapid."

"You're making that name up. It sounds like some testosterone-filled hero from an action movie."

I chuckled at her echo of my first impression. "I know, right?"

"What's the story on the dead woman?"

Unfortunately, Cooper had sworn me to silence after we'd left the apartment yesterday. I was too paranoid that the detective had bugged my cell phone somehow when he had it earlier this week to blab anything case-related to Natalie. If she were hiding in the closet with me this morning instead of hanging out in Arizona, I would have spilled it all and made her promise to tell no one.

"No answers yet," I said, which was the truth.

"What's this Stone Hawke guy like?"

"He annoys me."

"More than Cooper does?"

"Cooper is frustrating, Hawke is just plain irritating."

I heard someone holler in the background on her end of the call. There was a rustling noise and then a "be right there" in Nat's slightly muffled voice.

"Vi, I gotta go. Gramps needs me to run to Yuccaville for some supplies."

"Okay. Thanks for talking me down off the ledge."

"Anytime, babe. Walk softly around Rex and carry a sharp stick at all times until I get home."

"And then what?"

"And then we'll tag team on his sorry ass and send him away limping ... if he's lucky."

"Good. Be careful down there. Watch out for snakes and scorpions."

"I'm more concerned about Aunt Deborah—her bite is more poisonous than a black widow's."

"She was always nice to me."

"That's because you're not related to her." She made a loud kissing noise in the earpiece. "Stay out of jail, Vi," she hung up.

"I'll try," I told my reflection in the mirror.

I glanced at the clock. If I was going to dazzle Doc today to soften the blow when I hit him with the whole Rex crap, I needed to get to work on taming the bramble of curls on my head pronto.

Two hours later, I walked through Doc's unlocked back door wearing a pink cashmere sweater dress that hugged me in all Doc's favorite places, raspberry red lip gloss, an extra coat of eyeliner and mascara, and my purple boots. Coffee scented steam leaked from the lids of the two mochas I'd picked up on the way to sweeten him up a bit before I dumped my bad news all over him.

"Doc?" I called as I hip bumped the door closed and dropped my purse on the floor. His 1969 Camaro SS was sitting in the parking lot, so he had to be here. But was he alone? I'd walked in to find Detective Cooper here more than once, so I knew better than to start blurting out anything that could incriminate me.

Doc stepped out from the bathroom, hair damp and wavy, shaving cream on part of his jaw, shirt off, khakis zipped but unbuttoned ... my gaze stumbled at that point, getting tangled up around his bellybutton.

Whoa!

Something detonated in my chest, discharging a blast of heat through me that almost melted my eyeballs. Shit, I wondered if I'd just blown a fuse in my heart. I needed to put down the danged mochas before I popped the tops right off from squeezing so hard.

Doc surveyed my outfit. A smile spread up to his dark eyes, making them seem to sparkle. "Morning, Boots."

I held up the coffee. "I got you a mocha."

"A siren bearing coffee? Damn, it looks like I'll be crashing into the rocks today."

Crossing my fingers he meant that as a good thing, I followed him back into the bathroom. I leaned against the doorframe, listening to him scrape the razor up his neck as I did my best not to openly ogle.

I couldn't help it. I still periodically pinched myself to see if this was all real. A girl like me didn't get to win guys like Doc. We usually got the Rexes and Rays of the world, drinking our way along until there was enough numbness to forget we'd ever hoped for more.

"Why do you shave here in your office instead of over at the gym?" I asked to change the subject in my mind.

Doc had a routine of hitting the Rec Center first thing in the morning, like Jerry and Benjamin, whereas I had a routine of hitting the snooze button over and over, sometimes throwing the damned alarm clock across the room.

He made two final swipes and then rinsed the razor. "It's too busy there in the morning. I take a quick shower and then get out." He raised his brows at me in the mirror as he toweled off the remnants of shaving cream. "To what do I owe the pleasure of you standing in my bathroom doorway first thing, wearing a dress that makes me want to get all sweaty again?"

"I need to talk to you."

"If you wanted me to be able to converse, you shouldn't have worn those boots with that dress."

I contemplated skipping the whole Rex subject and focusing on running my fingers over all the parts of his skin. I should probably make sure everything was still where it had been the last time I'd explored.

"Do you have any clients scheduled for the next half hour?" I asked.

"No." He grabbed a blue shirt that hung from a hook on the

wall. "Is your headache gone?"

He was referring to the reason I'd given last night to get out of talking to him on the phone after he'd returned home from his card game over at Cooper's. The whole mess with Rex had me tied up tight. I'd feared Doc would hear the tension in my voice, know something was wrong, and I'd spill everything over the phone. The story about Rex needed to be face to face.

"Not quite." I had an appointment with my headache this afternoon.

He slipped his arms into the sleeves of his shirt, leaving it hanging open. He reached for his drink. "I missed you last night."

My heart frolicked about, kicking up its heels, rolling around in dandelions. I leaned my head against the door. "What? Cooper and Reid don't cut it when it comes to snuggling on the couch?"

"Your skin is softer than theirs." Doc took a drink of coffee, groaning in appreciation. "Good coffee and a hot babe in boots. This must be a dream." He put the drink on the counter and reached for me, pulling me into his arms.

"My drink," I said, trying not to spill it on either of us.

He took it and set it on the counter next to his. Then he got busy checking out my dress, feeling this, that, and all things in between until I was pressing into him. His palms idled on my hips. "I really like this dress."

"Good." I stood on my toes and kissed him, tasting the mocha on his tongue. "I want you to take it off me sometime."

"Twist my arm." He kissed me back, his hands busy playing Lewis and Clark again, exploring my frontier and then some through the sweater fabric. "You need to spend the night with me again soon."

I slid my hands inside his shirt, trailing over his bare shoulders. Goose bumps rose under my touch. "Like a slumber party?"

"I foresee little slumbering." He leaned back against the counter and settled me between his legs. "Now tell me, Violet. What's on your mind? Does it have something to do with yesterday's excitement?"

My eyes widened, my gaze falling to his Adam's apple. Oh crud. Did he know about Rex already? How? "What do you mean?"

"Your visit to Ms. Wolff's place with Cooper. Did you find something?"

Oh, that. I could meet his eyes again. "What did Cooper tell you?"

"He mentioned that you gave his partner some trouble."

That was putting a *nice* spin on it. Cooper must have been practicing speaking to the press. "Detective Hawke rubbed me wrong."

"Apparently, you're not the only one. Cooper was grinning when he told Reid and me how you threatened to stomp on the man's testicles, and Cooper rarely makes any facial expressions during poker."

"You mean the great Stone Hawke wasn't there with you guys last night?"

"No, Harvey was the fourth."

"Oh. I thought Harvey was out with one of his lady friends since he didn't spend the night on Aunt Zoe's couch."

"He crashed on mine instead." Doc wound one of my curls around his finger. "Did you miss his snoring?"

"I missed his cooking at breakfast." Although Aunt Zoe had made a mean bacon and mushroom omelet in his place.

Doc's brown eyes searched mine. "What did you see in Ms. Wolff's apartment yesterday?"

"Cooper didn't say anything about our walkthrough?"

"Just that he made you swear to keep quiet, and then he specifically told Harvey not to badger you for details."

Cooper had warned me to keep my lips sealed when in his uncle's company or he'd shut me out of the investigation on Ms. Wolff's death entirely, even if my son was somehow involved. "But he didn't tell *you* not to ask me about it?"

Doc shook his head.

"I wonder why not."

"We're sleeping together."

"You and Cooper?" I asked with a grin.

"I tried to seduce him, but he threatened to handcuff me."

"I know those handcuffs well."

"My little jailbird." Doc chuckled and kissed my knuckles. "Cooper probably figures that since I get to see you naked, you're going to tell me about what you saw in that apartment."

"You haven't seen me naked in over a week."

"And I've been counting the hours as they tick slowly by."

Hours ticking by reminded me of the German Black Forest clocks, so I started my play-by-play of yesterday with them. Doc handed me my coffee partway through, drinking along with me as I told him all that happened, everything I remembered noticing that gave me pause, and some of my speculation and concerns about Layne.

"Where's the book Cooper let you take home?" he asked.

"By your back door in my purse."

"Do you mind if I take a look at it?"

"That's why I brought it."

"I'll scan through it and let you know what I find." He finished his coffee and tossed it in the trash. "Are we still on for dinner at your aunt's house tonight?"

"If you're good with pizza again." Aunt Zoe needed to be at her glass gallery on Main Street to prep some shipment so she was going to be late. Since Harvey hadn't mentioned he was coming over for certain, that left me in charge of dinner. Pizza was one of the few things I could cook without burning—usually.

"Sure, but let me bring it this time."

"On one condition." When he nodded, I continued, "You come with me to Ms. Wolff's apartment."

Both of his eyebrows inched up. "To what end? You think she's still in there?"

"I was thinking more along the lines of you finding whatever it was that I missed."

"What makes you think you missed something?"

"I don't know, my feminine instinct maybe." Since Natalie said my gut was often wrong, it couldn't be that. "There's something in there, I know it, but I couldn't see it."

"Do you think Cooper will allow me in there?"

"Cooper doesn't need to know."

He crossed his arms over his chest. "Is this going to get us thrown in jail?"

"Would that be a problem?"

"It could hinder."

"I'll have a legal way of entering the apartment within a week." At his inquisitive stare, I explained. "The owner of the Galena House is considering putting it on the market. She wants me to go through the place with her this weekend so I can give her an idea of what I think she may be able to list it for."

His gaze narrowed. "Won't they still have Ms. Wolff's apartment blocked off?"

I held my index finger to my lips, leaning closer to him. "Cooper uses strips of tape," I whispered, winking. "I think I can figure out how to get past tape."

"Oh, really?" Doc grabbed my finger and held it. "Violet Parker, if you ever give up on the realty business, maybe you could go into the cat burglar field."

I wiggled my eyebrows at him. "So will you sneak in with me if I can arrange it?"

"You know I will." His attention headed south. "Now about this dress and those boots."

As much as I wanted to lean into him and see how far he was willing to go this morning before we had to get to work, I had to deal with the Rex situation. My pulse pounded in my head as I stood on the edge of the truth about my ex being in town, fretting about what his presence might do to whatever was going on between Doc and me.

"Doc," I said, licking my suddenly dry lips. "There's something else you need to know." I lifted his chin so his focus was on me, not my dress.

"What?"

I opened my mouth, then closed it, then opened to try again, hesitating.

"Violet, what? Are your kids okay?'"

"Yes, for now."

He frowned. "What's that mean?"

I took a deep breath, clasping my hands together. "I have a problem. A mega problem."

He waited as I stepped back and rubbed my arms, then clasped and unclasped my hands.

"I don't know how to say this."

"Just let it roll."

Okay. "Rex is in town."

Doc sat on that for a moment, long enough for me to wonder if he remembered who Rex was.

"You mean your ex-boyfriend?"

I nodded. Good, he remembered.

"Layne and Addy's father?"

I nodded again.

"The man you said you haven't seen since before they were born."

I kept nodding like one of those bobblehead dolls, my muscles tight from the neck down.

"How did you find out he's in town?" Doc asked, his expression unreadable.

"He came into Calamity Jane's."

"When?"

"Yesterday."

Doc cocked his head to the side. "Before or after you went to Ms. Wolff's apartment?"

"Before."

"That explains Cooper's question."

"What question?"

"He asked me if you were experiencing more stress than usual lately due to Ms. Wolff having Layne's picture, or if there was something else going on with you."

That wasn't surprising. During lunch yesterday, Cooper had kept staring at me when he thought I wasn't looking. He must have picked up on the volcano still spewing lava inside of me. But Hawke had gone on and on with tales of his cases ad nauseam. Every time Cooper tried to broach what had me shoving salad pieces to and fro on my plate, Hawke would interrupt. At first I thought it was a power play, but then I realized it was Detective Hawke's way. It went along with his lack of recognition of personal space.

"I was pretty pissed off when I showed up, which is why Detective Hawke and I will not be exchanging Valentine's Day cards next year."

"That explains why you went off on Detective Hawke."

"Partly. But if he hadn't been a jerk out of the gate, I wouldn't have broken his pen."

Doc rubbed his jaw. "Seeing Rex had to be quite a shock for you."

Backing into the zappy end of a cattle prod would have surprised me less. "You could say that."

"How did Rex find you?"

I considered telling him about the text messages Cooper had found from Rex on that decapitated guy's phone, but I decided to keep to recent events. "He saw my billboard."

"Of course." Doc grabbed my arm and turned me around so my back was to him. "Does he want to see his kids?"

"He didn't even mention them. Nor did I." His hands warmed my shoulders.

"What did he want?"

"To look at some rental places."

"He's sticking around?" He began kneading the tight muscles around the base of my neck, working out some knots I had cinched there.

"According to him, yes." I let my head loll forward under his touch. "I tried to tell him there was nothing to rent, but Jerry made a point of saying there were places available."

"Does anyone at work know who he is?"

"No. I don't want them to either. I can't have anything getting back to my kids."

"What are you afraid of?"

The unemployment line, running into another albino, something happening to my kids, losing Doc—the list was quite long. I wasn't sure he had time for me to start scrolling down it, so I summed it up for him. "Everything, damn it."

"Are you afraid he wants to be in their lives now?"

"Yes."

"Would that be so bad?" he pressed with both his words and fingertips.

"That son of a bitch left me high and dry. He had his chance when they were in the womb and again when they were born, but he rejected them both times. I won't let him reject them a third time." Especially now when they were so vulnerable when it came to needing a father in their lives.

I'd thought off and on over the last decade about Rex and his actions, trying to understand how he could walk away from his kids without a single fight. Even prior to the kids being in the picture, he'd been oblivious to how I'd felt about him sleeping with my sister. The way he had come back afterward, before he had known I was pregnant, and couldn't comprehend why I had been so upset he'd had sex several times with Susan. I finally surmised that he didn't realize how his actions hurt others. He had no empathy in him to get it.

I rested fully back against Doc's length, taking his hands from my shoulders and wrapping them around me. "I don't want to confuse my kids when it comes to him, Doc."

"He's their father."

"He's a sperm donor and he signed a paper stating that he agreed to be only that."

Doc spun me around, lifting my chin so I could meet his gaze. "So why's he here then?"

"I don't know. His job."

"Maybe, but why is he here looking you up?"

I chewed on my lower lip.

"Violet, did he ask you out?"

"Well, not really. But he made it so I have to go out showing him places today."

Doc's jaw tightened. "Alone?"

"I think so."

His whole face hardened to match his jaw. "He wants you back."

"No." I still didn't believe that. Rex was messing with me for kicks. I could see the fun he was having yesterday on his face.

"Trust me, Violet." Doc ran his finger down the fabric on my shoulder. "He didn't look you up just to see how you've changed in ten years, not after all that happened in the past with him and your sister. He may be here for his job, but he came knocking to pick up where you two left off."

Doc and Natalie must be reading from the same play book. "You mean with me slamming the door in his face?"

"Okay, before that." He pulled the collar of my dress to the side and kissed my bared skin. "Please tell me you aren't going to wear this dress today when you're with him." His lips trailed along my shoulder, heading toward my neck.

I leaned my head to the side, giving his mouth an all access pass.

"Or the boots." He breathed against my neck, making me quiver. "Especially the boots." His lips grazed my ear. "You'll drive me to drink if you do."

I pulled his mouth to mine and kissed him until he groaned. "This outfit was supposed to keep you from dropping me like a hot potato after I told you about my Rex problem. I'm going home at lunch to change."

"Into what?"

"A snowmobile suit."

He chuckled. "Make it one of those camouflage ones that hunters wear so he can't see you." His hands spanned my waist. "I'm worried about you now."

"Doc, trust me, I can't stand the guy. I want him to leave the state—no, make that the planet."

"That's not what I mean." He tucked me under his chin, stroking my back. Much more of that and I'd quit my day job and become his full-time lap cat. "I'm worried about what the stress of him being here is going to do to you. You already have trouble sleeping with all of the nightmares. Now you have a whole new problem to keep you awake at night."

Like last night. I needed to start bringing Layne's collection of archaeology books he got from my brother, Quint, to bed if this was going to keep up. I might as well put all of those hours spent staring at my ceiling to good use.

Closing my eyes, I breathed in the scent of Doc's shaving cream still lingering on his skin. "Are you upset with me?"

"Why would I be upset?" He kissed my forehead. "By the way, in case you haven't figured it out, this is me *not* dropping you like a hot potato."

That made me smile up at him. "Hey, maybe we could set up Rex and Tiffany, kill two birds with one stone."

"You want to go on another double date?"

"God, no." The one time Doc and I had been suckered into that situation had been once too many.

"Good." Doc laced my fingers in his. "Violet, I want to meet Rex."

"What? Why?" Doc wasn't the sort to play the overbearing, jealous boyfriend, so why would he want to see my ex?

"Partly out of curiosity."

I could relate to that. "And what's the other part?"

"To figure out exactly what his intentions are when it comes to you and your kids."

Chapter Ten

I had Addy's chicken for lunch. Unfortunately, she wasn't fried or baked or roasted, but rather alive and clucking down near my boots as I sat on Aunt Zoe's back porch steps.

The sunshine played peek-a-boo with me as Elvis the chicken and I shared my peanut butter sandwich. She acted as my fellow barstool buddy, gobbling up the pieces of crust I threw her way, while I griped about my irritating ex. In the end, we washed the sandwich and all of our regrets from our naïve younger years down with some of Aunt Zoe's sweet lemonade. Who knew chickens had regrets and liked lemonade? I learned something new every day.

New things like Detective Hawke now had my cell phone number and liked to leave multiple messages spaced two minutes apart if I didn't drop my sandwich and answer his calls at once— all four of them. I was still so annoyed by some of his comments from yesterday that I refused to even listen to his voicemails.

And other new things like what a Papa Legba voodoo spirit wanga bag was.

At first I'd thought Cornelius' phone had auto-corrected his text message when it came through with those peculiar words, so I'd laid my peanut butter sandwich down and texted back: *A Papa what?*

Elvis seemed as clueless as I was when I read it to her.

Cornelius replied with an internet link to show me an example of a Papa Legba wanga bag.

To which I'd followed up with: *Why do I need to know this?*

His answer was: *Papa Legba stands at the spiritual crossroads.*

With all of the weird stuff that had happened to me since I'd moved to Deadwood, I was beginning to feel as if I were standing at the spiritual crossroads myself. Or rather the end of the stage line, which Deadwood had been back in Wild Bill's time. Like many of the pioneers of the Black Hills, maybe ghosts had also stepped off the stagecoach here and never left.

Cornelius had continued: *Papa Legba will help to make our séance successful.*

I wasn't sure I wanted the outcome to be a success. What would that entail? After the way Doc had reacted last time, I was afraid too much success might seriously injure him.

Cornelius' final text had left me scratching my head. *Wanga bag coming your way. DO NOT BUY ANY FROG'S TOES! See you Sunday at sunset.*

After that, I'd enabled the Do Not Disturb feature on my cell phone, pocketing it for the rest of my lunch with Elvis. Neither of us was in the mood to have our feathers ruffled any further.

When I arrived back at work, Mona told me that Rex had called and needed to postpone our search for rentals until tomorrow afternoon. Before I could even bend my knees to jump for joy, Jerry charged through the front door, holding it open for two people to follow: a man and a woman. Both were dressed from head to toe in black, including sunglasses. For a moment, I wondered if they were secret agents who'd come in search of alien beings. When they took off their sunglasses, they reminded me more of Sonny and Cher—minus the moustache, the butt-length hair, and the wild seventies outfits.

"Everybody huddle up." Jerry's loud voice cut off the discussion Mona and Ben were having about the importance of staging a house based on a home's expected buyer type.

In Jerry speak, huddling up meant he wanted our attention. I wadded up the piece of paper with Rex's phone number on it and tossed it in my trashcan, wondering what Jerry was up to now.

"I'd like to introduce you all to Dickie Dowdin, the producer of *Paranormal Realty*," Jerry waved his hand toward the man, "the reality television show I told you all about on Sunday."

Oh, shit, right. Today was the day we were supposed to meet the reality television crew who will be making our lives hell for the next several weeks. I stifled a groan and dropped into my chair.

"Dickie's here today with his assistant," Jerry continued, "and we'll be having a two-on-one with each of you this afternoon in my office so he can get to know you better."

"Actually," Dickie spoke up, resting his hand on the shoulder of his black-haired assistant, who stood several inches taller than him, "it will be a three-on-one, since Honey will be present, too."

Honey? Dickie the Producer made it sound like things were going to get sticky in Jerry's office. I glanced over at Ray, not surprised to see a doofus-like grin on his too tanned face. I could only imagine the porno soundtrack that was playing in his skull with that Honey three-on-one bit, what with his love of juvenile insults and jokes. *Bom-chicka-bom-bom.*

No, stop the music. That was a bad idea—I'd just eaten.

I backed my brain out of that red-light alley and focused on the producer's assistant, Honey. Given her long hair, smoky accented eyes, and dark red lipstick, she didn't look as sweet and pure as her name. With those long legs and so much black covering her, a Gothic name like Raven would have suited her better. She stood next to Dickie and nodded at each of us in turn. Her chin reminded me of an old-fashioned typewriter, especially when she reached the end of the line and her chin whipped back to her boss, as if someone had hit the return bar.

Jerry jammed his hands into the pockets of his navy dress slacks, rocking back on his heels. "This afternoon's team-ups will help Dickie and Honey decide how they want to spread themselves over our snug little team both on and off-camera."

Oh, dear Lord, had Jerry really just said that? Or was my brain now stuck on an X-rated station while sitting on a stained, musty couch next to Ray?

Honey's cheeks darkened as she grimaced at Jerry, clearly catching his accidental innuendo.

Ray coughed into his fist, trying to hide his snickers.

Mona shot him a glare and then moved her laser beam to Jerry, her eyes widening with a stark shut-up scowl.

I opened my desk drawer, burying my face in it while pretending to dig for something while the awkward moment sat there in the middle of the office like a leather-clad, chained up sex-slave with a ball-gag jammed in his mouth.

Jerry seriously needed to stop eating, drinking, and sleeping sports; and I needed to stop flipping through the movie channels at one in the morning when the extra R-rated shows were hogging the stations.

"I'm looking forward to hearing your plans for the television show," Ben said, being his usual wonderful, true-blue, polite self. His comment shooed the invisible sex masochist from the room and turned the channel back to normal programming.

Honey flashed him a smile, blinking her dark eyelashes a few extra times. She either had an instant liking for my co-worker, which was normal for most people when it came to Ben, or she was using her lashes to fan her still pink cheeks.

"Thank you," Dickie said, his expression smooth as yogurt. He sounded sincere, his teeth showing when he smiled at us, but I didn't trust him. No doubt years of being in the biz had trained him to play his audience. I wouldn't be shocked if he pulled out a mic from behind his back and started singing, *I got you, babe* to Honey to distract us into compliance. "We're going to enjoy spending the next few weeks with all of you, learning about your jobs and this area of the country."

I glanced around at my coworkers, imagining them on camera. Of the four of us, Mona and Ben would perform the best. Mona had been on stage before, acting in several plays up at the Historic Homestake Opera House in Lead. Ben just had a natural smoothness with people that won him quick smiles and return business. Honey was still sending happy faces in his direction. I'd be content to act as their understudies for this. Rather relieved actually.

Jerry pointed at me. "Violet, you're on point first."

"Me? What? Why?"

"Because you have an appointment this afternoon with Mr. Conner. When's he going to be here?"

"Actually, he rescheduled to tomorrow." So somebody else could go first.

Jerry clapped his hands. "Great. That's even better. It gives me an idea."

Oh, hell, not another one.

He turned to Dickie. "At lunch you mentioned that you'd like to do a ride along, if possible. How about tomorrow? Violet can take you and Honey with her and her new client, give you both a feel for our day-to-day operations here."

I could what? With my ex in the car? No way. Absolutely not. The last thing I needed was a reality television producer and his assistant listening in on my conversations with the estranged father of my children. That was a sure-fire recipe for a disaster of mushroom cloud proportions.

"No!" I said, not meaning to blurt it out with so much defiance.

All eyes turned my way. Jerry's were the widest. I guess he hadn't expected me to disagree with his playbook.

"Do you have a schedule conflict, Violet?"

I scrambled to pick up my fumble. "More like a vehicle conflict. My pickup won't fit four."

The wrinkles on his forehead smoothed out. "That's no problem. You can borrow my Hummer."

He wanted me to drive that tank on Deadwood's narrow streets with a carful of people who stressed me out just by existing in my realm? The chance of careening over the edge of a road to my death would be high in a friggin' rickshaw with this crew. No thanks. "I'm not comfortable with the size of your vehicle."

Nor was I comfortable with the size of his marketing ideas. They were all of the "Think big—MEGA BIG" mentality, shouted out by that guy who did the monster truck commercials. I on the other hand was of the "Be realistic, jackass" mindset.

"We could use our rental," Honey offered, her smile as sweet as … *"Don't say honey,"* a voice said in my head.

"How do you feel about using their rental car, Violet?" Jerry asked.

"I'm not sure my insurance will cover me." After my Bronco had gotten torched, my insurance agent had stopped smiling at me in the Piggly Wiggly when our carts passed. In fact, he now avoided me to the point of detouring down the tampon aisle to escape me.

"You can use my Subaru, Violet," Ben spoke up. "It's narrow with four-wheel drive and completely paid for. Don't worry about your insurance. I've seen you drive. You're safe."

Doh! Ben wasn't helping. "Are you sure you don't mind?" I asked, trying to hit him with ESP waves telling him to mind, dang it.

"Not at all."

"That's good teamwork, Ben," Coach Jerry said. "So there we are. You two can come tomorrow and Violet will take you out on the road, show you how we treat our clients, and give you a taste of Deadwood."

I sat there in the middle of Shit Creek, sputtering, not a paddle to be found.

"Sounds like a plan," Dickie said.

"I hope you don't mind us infringing," Honey blinked at me, her smile super sweet, like hon ... that's it, I needed a timeout. My brain seemed to be short-circuiting.

"It's not a problem," I said.

Only it was. A very large problem. And on top of it all, I now had to change my plans.

The scheme Elvis the Chicken and I had come up with at lunch involved driving Rex to a location where we could sit inside the Picklemobile with the windows rolled up. I'd find out exactly what the hell he was doing back in town, and what his intentions toward my children were. Then I'd tell him to stay away from me and mine, threaten to file for a restraining order—employing the lawn clippers I'd shoved under the seat, if necessary—and strongly suggest he use another real estate company. I'd brought one of Tiffany's cards along just in case.

Now I would have to actually dig up a few places to show Rex and do some prep work, damn it. This all cut into the time I'd wanted to spend scouring the internet for more information on German Black Forest cuckoo clocks and makers of fine hats.

"Violet," Jerry said, "give us a few minutes to get set up in my office. I'll holler when we're ready." He offered Dickie and

Honey some coffee before leading them down the back hall.

I groaned and covered my eyes with my palms, resting my elbows on the desktop. I should have stayed under the covers.

"Vi," Mona said, "are you feeling okay?"

Not at all. I peeked out at her. "The verdict is still out."

Ben placed today's rental properties report on my desk. "This TV show is going to be a positive thing, Violet. You'll shine on camera."

That was a good reminder to add extra makeup on the days I had the cameras following me so it wasn't my nose, chin, and forehead that were shining instead of my skills.

Ray snorted. "I don't know why you're getting your panties in a twist, Blondie. It's not like you have to actually make sales happen. If that were the case you'd have been out of a job long ago." He kicked his boots up on his desk, lacing his fingers behind his head. "Hell, this show is right up your alley. It's all about kooks and spooks. With your frizzy hair and criminal record, you're exactly what they need to make their show go viral."

I flipped him off with both birds.

"Stay tuned for more Violet 'Spooky' Parker after these messages," he poked some more.

"Ray," Mona said, "insulting Violet won't make up for your inadequacies."

"What are you talking about, Red?" He crossed his arms over his chest. "And don't play your shrink games on me."

She looked over at him with one arched brow. "I ran into one of your ex-girlfriends the other night at Charles' Club. She shared a few details about what's been going on with you lately while we waited for our drinks." Her gaze dipped downward. "It makes sense now why you keep harassing Violet."

What did? What had his ex said? I leaned forward, my focus bouncing between Mona and Ray. Was she messing with him for my sake, or was she serious?

Ray's whole body went rigid, his boots hitting the floor. Whether or not Mona was toying with him, she'd apparently pierced his hull. "She's lying."

"You don't even know what she said."

"I don't need to. I dumped her, and now she's pissed. I can only imagine the line of crap she fed you."

Mona shrugged, sliding her rhinestone reading glasses onto her nose. "If you say so, Ray."

"Keep out of my private affairs, Red." Ray grabbed his keys and slammed his drawer shut. "Or I'll start raking through yours."

"Where you going, Ray?" Ben asked. "Jerry told us to stick around."

"Out. If Jerry asks, tell him I'll be back in time for my interview." With a parting scowl at Mona, Ray slammed out the front door.

Mona watched him leave, and then gave me a quick wink. "You'll do great, Vi. I have faith in you. You're a natural."

"Violet," Jerry poked his head out his doorway. "We're ready for you in here.

I stood and smoothed my tunic and dress pants. Ray was probably right. I was overreacting, and I blamed Rex. If he weren't in the picture, tomorrow would be no big deal. The key was to keep things bland and boring with Rex. I could do that.

"Thanks." I patted Mona's shoulder on the way to Jerry's office. "Coffee's on me tomorrow for that one."

Inside Jerry's office, the three of them sat behind his desk, reminding me of a panel of beauty pageant judges. Too bad I'd walked into the swimsuit competition part of the show.

"Close the door behind you, please," Jerry said. He slid on a pair of black rimmed reading glasses, picked up a notepad, and clicked his pen a few times.

My eye started to tic.

I shut the door.

* * *

Several hours later, I sat in Aunt Zoe's kitchen with pizza remains scattered on plates around the table, my mouth still tasting like pepperoni. Addy and Layne were in the backyard sitting on the swing set. They kept shooting dirty looks my way like I'd eaten all of their cotton candy.

"I've ruined their lives again," I told Aunt Zoe as she collected the kids' plates.

I'd ordered them into the backyard moments ago, forgetting to tell them to take their plates to the sink in the midst of the whining and bitching as they stomped outside.

"It's not your fault you can't take them to Oktoberfest. You have to work." She dropped a kiss on the top of my head. "Don't beat yourself up too much. You're just getting started on messing up their worlds. Wait until they hit the teen years."

Doc squeezed my leg under the table. The warmth of his palm through my yoga pants eased some of the stress left over from the day's messes. "I can take them tomorrow afternoon."

I sat back, stunned. After the cacophony he'd just witnessed when I told my kids they couldn't go to the festival tomorrow without me, I was surprised he wanted to be in the same town right now. "Don't you have any appointments?"

"Just one." He pointed across the table at Harvey. "He's sitting right there. I bet he'd be willing to reschedule."

"Hell, I might as well go with you," Harvey wiped his mouth and hands with his napkin. "We can jaw about my uncle's estate while we're strollin' around, checkin' out the kids' projects they were bawlin' about." Harvey shot me a questioning look. "Unless you want me to ride along with you and those TV people?"

I hadn't told Harvey or Aunt Zoe about the Rex factor yet. Only Doc knew the whole truth as to why I was hyperventilating on the inside about tomorrow afternoon's appointment. The fewer who knew about Rex being in town, the less chance there was of someone slipping about his paternal role in front of my kids.

Aunt Zoe hadn't actually met Rex way back when. She knew all about him but wouldn't be able to pick him out in a crowd. Harvey didn't need to know about the kids' dad at this point. Part of me was worried he'd come up with some crazy reason to shoot Rex's ass full of buckshot, and the other part hoped he did.

"Thanks, Harvey, but I don't think my boss would appreciate

me bringing my bodyguard along. He's pretty stressed about this whole TV thing going well."

In spite of Jerry's cheerleader attitude this afternoon in his office, I'd caught glimmers of his anxiety in the way he'd kept fidgeting and frowning at his desktop during the meeting. His normal air of confidence had been absent. When Ben had told me Jerry was off his shooting game earlier that morning, I started to do some mental math.

In spite of Ben being hired, Calamity Jane Realty hadn't had a big upswing of sales since Jane had died. When I started adding things up, a suspicion crept up. Could Jerry be taking such outlandish marketing gambles because the company was having money troubles? Maybe Jerry had been trying so hard to build Ben's and my careers with these stupid billboard ads and the television show so we could keep our jobs.

Aunt Zoe returned to the table. "Violet, what are you going to do about this television crew invading your privacy?"

"As far as I can see, I have no choice but to go along with it. I like my job. I don't want to lose it."

"At what cost to your reputation?" she pressed.

I guffawed. "My reputation is in shambles already. You know that."

"Jane would never have put you in this position."

"True." I polished off the last bite of my crust. "But maybe it's a matter of Jane not having been willing to take risks."

"What do you mean?" Aunt Zoe crossed her arms over her chest, looking miffed. "Jane took plenty of risks. She hired you based on a recommendation alone."

"Yes, and I'm thankful to both of you for taking a chance on me. But Jane made it no secret that she couldn't afford to hire two employees when she took me on. That's the whole reason Ray was so bent on getting me fired—it was always Ben or me when Jane was alive. Now with Jerry at the helm, it's Ben *and* me. That addition to the headcount had to come at a cost to the company's bottom line."

I glanced at Harvey then Doc. Both were eyeing me— Harvey stroking his beard, Doc fiddling with his fork.

"I don't begrudge Ben his job," I continued, wanting to persuade them to see this from my newfound perspective so they wouldn't think I was a nincompoop for going along with Jerry's ideas. "He's a much better co-worker than Ray."

"That's cuz he's sweet on you," Harvey said.

Doc slanted Harvey a nod of agreement.

"He might have been at one time, but now he's always professional."

"Sure he is. The boy still thinks he has a chance of gettin' in your bloomers." Harvey's two gold teeth showed through his whiskers. "That dog's still on the hunt; he's just bein' sly about gettin' you up in the tree. Am I right, Doc?"

Doc grunted, letting his fork rest on the table.

I wasn't going to argue with either of them about Ben's intentions. They weren't important considering I was howling at the moon each night about the man whose hand was now draped over the back of my chair, playing with my hair.

I waved Harvey's smirk away and focused back on Aunt Zoe. "For now the cost to keep both Ben and me rather than make us fight for one position might mean I have to shed a few pounds of pride and dignity."

"That billboard is more than just a few," she muttered.

"The way I see it at this junction in my career, if Jerry asks me to wear a velvet sweat suit and dance to the oldies in public because he believes it will help my sales, I'll have to start practicing the Twist and maybe the Charleston, too."

"Velvet, huh?" Doc said, his eyes twinkling.

He had a fantasy involving me wearing one of those velvet belly dancer tops. It included him taking it off of me with his teeth. He never clarified what was going to happen after that, but based on previous experiences when his teeth were involved, I had a good idea and it made me tingle all over imagining the scene.

"Fine," Aunt Zoe said, sounding like it was anything but. "I understand you need to do what's necessary in order to provide for the kids, but I reserve the right to pop your boss in the nose for plastering my niece on a billboard like that. You're not a piece of meat, Violet Lynn. You deserve to be treated with respect, not dressed up in leather and displayed on high like a trollop."

"I wasn't wearing leather."

Her lips thinned. "I was making a point."

Harvey snickered. "Doc doesn't mind the leather, do ya?"

"Leather chafes me in places. I prefer velvet."

That got a bigger chuckle out of Harvey. He pushed to his feet. "Be right back. I need to hit the head."

After he left, I took Aunt Zoe's hand and held it to my cheek for a moment. "I appreciate you wanting to protect me, but don't hurt this hand punching Jerry." I had a theory that he was made of a block of granite covered in skin. "You need it to create more gorgeous glass pieces."

She opened her palm and cupped my jaw. "I'm worried about you." Her tone was warm but serious.

"I'm okay," I sort of lied. Although sitting here in her kitchen surrounded by some of the people closest to me, I felt better than I had all day. Except when it came to those two kids who were still shooting me with laser glares. Letting them down always made me feel low, like toenail fungus level.

Her blue eyes bored into mine. I tried to hide my worries behind a big goofy grin that I hoped reached all the way up to my eyes.

"What aren't you telling me, Violet Lynn?"

That the bogeyman was in town, making me want to lock my kids in their bedrooms until I could make him go away again. "Nothing."

She scanned my face, up and down, left to right. "Is it something to do with Ms. Wolff and Layne?"

"No. Last night I told you everything I saw in her apartment with Detective Cooper and Hawke." That was the truth. Even though Cooper had made me promise not to say a thing, I'd shared it all with Aunt Zoe and then made her pinky swear to secrecy. I'd hoped that her eyes would light up with answers to some of my many questions about Ms. Wolff, but she'd frowned and shook her head through it all.

She released my chin and sat back, her gaze still boring into me. "You and I need to have a long talk one of these days about what it is you are trying to protect me from."

"What do you mean?"

Aunt Zoe tapped her index finger on the table. "I think you underestimate what I can do to help you better understand some of your problems."

"What problems?" I tried to keep a straight face.

She snorted, shooting a look out at the kids. "Now is not the time or place. But how about telling me why a 'Detective Hawke' called here this afternoon looking for you."

I hadn't filled her in about that Neanderthal. Crudmongers, that detective was persistent. I cringed just thinking about him.

"He mentioned something about a book," she added, her eyebrows inching up, her unspoken question shining clearly in her stare as it bounced between Doc and me.

"He's probably referring to a book I got from Ms. Wolff's bedroom," I answered, clarifying it wasn't about *the* book. "I'll call him back later tonight."

If it were an emergency, Cooper would have shown up at my door demanding my presence "or else." Since it was only Detective Hawke who was calling, I was going to answer on my terms when I was darn well ready.

I turned to Doc. "Did you have a chance to read through any of that history book from Ms. Wolff's place?"

"I skimmed it this afternoon in between clients. When I get home tonight, I plan to take a closer look."

Fudge, that meant he wasn't going to be staying late. I really had been looking forward to exploring more under his shirt after the kids had gone to bed, especially after the way his fingers kept stroking my neck. "I appreciate your help."

"It'll cost you," he returned. His eyes were dark, foreshadowing wicked deeds.

For him, the moon.

I focused back on Aunt Zoe. "It's not like the other book," the one made of flesh that starred a demon who haunted my nightmares. "This is just a book on the history of Deadwood."

"Sort of," Doc said.

"What do you mean?" I asked.

"From what I could tell after a quick skim this afternoon, it's more like a personal account of what occurred here during the gold rush years and after."

"Personal how?" Aunt Zoe rested her elbows on the table, leaning into the conversation.

Rubbing his jaw, Doc shrugged. "It's as if the author knows all of the characters firsthand, telling tales from the viewpoint of the participants."

"Are there pictures in it?" Aunt Zoe asked.

"A few. They were pretty grainy."

Aunt Zoe's phone started ringing.

"You want to get that?" she asked me. "It's probably a certain detective calling for you. He mentioned calling again this evening."

I shook my head. "Let the machine get it. I'll call him later." The new detective was going to have to learn that I wasn't going to be bossed around so easily.

It rang again.

Doc stood and stretched. "I should probably head out so I can get started on that book."

Nodding, I pushed back my chair. "I'll walk you out."

We passed Harvey at the archway between the dining room and kitchen.

"Where are you two headin'?"

"I'm taking off," Doc said.

Harvey glanced at the phone on Aunt Zoe's kitchen wall. "Is someone gonna get that?"

"No. It's probably Hawke again. I'll call when I'm ready."

He let us pass.

"I'll leave the door unlocked," Doc called over his shoulder.

"Why are you telling Harvey that?" I asked as Doc held open the front door for me.

"He's crashing at my place again."

"You don't mind?"

"There's plenty of room for company," he said.

I'd noticed. I'd also wished a few times for an invitation to fill his house with all of my stuff when I felt less able to take on the world alone. I did my best to squelch that wish whenever it popped up. Daydreaming about playing house with Doc would put my heart on the edge of a cliff. I preferred it to stay about ten feet back on safer ground.

Doc closed the door behind us. "Cooper mentioned at the poker game that he's concerned about Harvey staying alone at the ranch with everything going on. That in turn concerns me, so I told Harvey I wouldn't mind him using my couch instead of your aunt's after he mentioned sometimes feeling like a third wheel here."

I hadn't realized Harvey felt that way. I hoped it wasn't something I'd done. He might snore like a chainsaw and keep me up past my bedtime talking some nights, but I'd gotten used to him being there. Hell, I'd come to rely on his help with my kids.

Doc took my hand and led me down the porch steps. "Come on. I have something for you."

"What?" I asked when we reached his car.

He opened the door, reached down inside, and then put something cold and cylindrical in my hand. "This."

I held it up in the moonlight. "What is it? A flashlight?"

"And a taser." He showed me how to turn it on.

I'd seen one exactly like it yesterday. "Did you steal it from Cooper?"

"He had an extra, so I traded for it."

Great, Cooper and I now had matching flash-tasers. We could take turns tasering each other instead of using barbed insults. "Traded what?"

"It doesn't matter." He closed his door quietly. "There's something else I wanted to tell you while we're alone."

My silly heart was all ears suddenly. "What?"

He glanced back at the house, then said in a lowered voice, "I want to see Rex before you leave with him tomorrow afternoon."

That wasn't on my list of things I wanted him to say to me while we were alone. "Why?"

"Because I'm taking Layne and Addy to the Oktoberfest and

I want to keep an eye out for him in case he leaves your office and decides to head to the festivities."

"Doc, you don't need to do that."

"I know."

"It's not a good idea." I wanted to hug him for offering, but my knees shook at what my kids might tell him when I wasn't there.

"What are you afraid of?" he asked.

He must never have seen *The Parent Trap*. I hesitated, not sure how to explain without making my kids sound like little hell spawns, which they weren't.

Aunt Zoe and I had put our heads together last weekend, discussing the change in the two of them since I'd told them about Doc. I fretted I was putting my needs over theirs, but she thought they were reacting out of fear, afraid of losing me to him. He was a threat. They didn't get that I wasn't going anywhere without them.

"I won't let anything happen to your children," he assured.

I squeezed his hand. "I know you won't."

"Good. Then I'll pick them up here after they get home from school."

"Okay." I'd have a talk with the kids tonight and threaten to lock up indefinitely all they held dear if they gave Doc a single problem tomorrow. "I'll let Aunt Zoe know."

"What about Rex?"

"I'll figure out something so that you can see him before we head out. Just be around your office at two." That was the magic hour when the black hole was going to open up and the sucking sensation would begin.

"I'll be there." He tugged me closer, sliding his hands along both sides of my face. He tipped my mouth so it lined up with his. "Make sure you take your taser with you tomorrow, Boots."

"You want me to zap Rex in front of the TV people?" That would make for some exciting television.

"I'd like you to zap him period." He brushed his lips over mine, a feathery tease. "Aim low."

I laughed quietly, teasing back with my mouth. He let me

play. "Speaking of exes," I said, coming up for air, "have you heard from Tiffany today?"

"She stopped by."

Urchhh! I pulled away, gaping up at him. "What? Why?" I punched him playfully on the shoulder. "And why am I just hearing about this now?"

He captured my wrist, lacing our fingers. "She wanted to talk about the account I'm still managing for her."

"Oh." I called bullshit on that being the only reason, but I wasn't going to say anything and sound like a jealous girlfriend.

"And to find out how long you and I have been an item."

Aha! The green monster woke up with a start and lit a brush fire in my throat. "She just out and out asked, did she?"

"Not in so many words."

Damn that woman. "What did you say about us?"

What would I have said about us to Tiffany, I wonder? Probably that Doc and I were so obsessed with each other that we were going to start wearing matching clothes that showed off our identical tattoos.

He towed me back into his arms and swung me around so my butt was pressed against his car. "I told her the truth."

"Which is what?" I asked. When Doc just stared down at me, I kept rambling. "I want to make sure Tiffany and I are on the same page when she lunges for a handful of my hair."

"She's not going to bother you, Violet."

"I believe you're mistaking her for someone sane." I rested my thumbs on his belt. "You know she intends to win at all costs." He was the one who'd told me how competitive she was, even in the bedroom.

"There's nothing to win, though," he said.

"Quit being obtuse. She lost you to me and now she wants to win you back." When his eyes narrowed at that last bit, a fire whistle blared in my head. I panicked and added, "At least that's what *she's* thinking. I'm not saying that I own you or have any kind of possession of your thoughts ... or stuff."

Did that even make sense? I shut up before my foot could wiggle any further into my mouth.

"Tiffany's motivation and actions don't matter, Violet. My mind is made up."

"Made up in what way?" About us? If so, inquiring minds would like to know if he's on the same out of control mining cart that I seemed to be.

He pressed closer, his body heating mine. "You know."

"No, I don't." I raised both eyebrows. "Is it so hard for you to say?"

"That depends on what you want to hear."

That he was gaga for me. That he thought about me night and day. That he daydreamed about spending more of his waking hours with me while I was clothed as well as naked. That he wanted to start making pancakes and bacon for me and the kids every morning and tuck us in at night. Was that too much to ask?

I generalized it for him. "Some affirmation would be nice."

He nestled into me, my soft parts yielding to his hardness. The car's metal chilled me through my clothes, making me shiver and burrow deeper into his jacket. The heady scent of him changed my shivers to quivers. His mouth toured across my shoulder, up my neck, around my ear, and along my jaw until I was panting. An ache I called "Doc-itis" throbbed throughout, making me want to wrap my limbs around him and cling.

He ended his tour with a tender, slow taste of my lips. "Is that affirmation enough?"

Nope, I wanted more. A lot more. "So you're a show not tell type of guy?"

"You could say that." He rubbed against me, showing me plenty.

That would have to be good enough then. "Okay, as long as you keep your 'showing' monogamous."

"Every night I lie in bed and think about showing you all sorts of things." He kissed me again, this time using his tongue to help convince me. "Only you, Boots."

It wasn't a declaration of love, but I'd take it. Plus he was willing to spend time with my kids. That had to count for something, especially with the way they were acting out around him.

"Good." My fingers trailed down his front, heading south of his waistband.

He stopped me before I could reach pay dirt. "The same goes for you," he whispered, moving my hand back to his chest. "Monogamous showing."

"Deal." I scraped through his shirt with my nails, making him groan.

"Violet?" Harvey called through the screen door.

Doc stepped back.

I growled. Was it too much to ask for a few more minutes alone with Doc? "Yeah?"

"You'd better get in here." The porch light flickered on.

I shielded my eyes. "Is something wrong with the kids?"

"No, it's your aunt."

"What about her?"

"She's upstairs breakin' things from the sound of it."

"What? Why?"

"She got a message." Harvey glanced behind him and then stepped aside as Aunt Zoe crashed open the screen door.

"What's wrong?" I asked as she flew down the porch steps.

"Here," she handed me her keys. "Harvey, watch the kids."

"On it," he said, leaning against the porch post.

"What am I doing with these?" I asked, holding up her keys.

"Driving. I'm too pissed to be behind the wheel."

I looked back at Doc. "I gotta go."

He nudged me toward Aunt Zoe's pickup, which was parked next to his. Her passenger door slammed loud enough to make Mr. Stinklestine's Chihuahua start yammering.

I climbed in beside her, settling in behind the wheel. "Where are we going?"

"To get that stinking, no good, lousy, rotten sheep herder."

My world was currently littered with no good lousy sheep herders, so she was going to have to be more specific or we'd be out all night.

I turned the key and shifted into reverse. "Which particular sheep herder are we talking about?"

"Reid Martin."

Chapter Eleven

"Here I go down that wrong road again," Aunt Zoe said as we bumped along a gravel road that kept twisting its way upward through the trees and rocks.

"What? I thought you said to take a right back there before the cattle guard." I tapped the brakes as we jiggled around a washboard curve. I hit the high beams, but they only spotlighted the trees not the road, so I clicked back to low.

"I did. You're fine. I'm talking about Reid." She sighed, leaning her head against the head rest. "And Crystal Gayle."

I shot her a frown. "The country western singer?"

"Yes, don't you remember that song?" Aunt Zoe sang the chorus of *Wrong Road Again*.

"Now I do." I sped up along a straight stretch, keeping my tires out of the deep grooves someone had probably made during last spring's snowmelt.

Aunt Zoe continued to hum the tune while I focused on driving, watching for deer, coyotes, or anything else that felt like scaring the crap out of me on a dark night in the forest.

"What did Reid say in his message?" I interrupted her humming.

When we'd left Deadwood, she'd been busy giving me directions in between her long-winded rants. This was the first I'd had a chance to get much of a word in edgewise, let alone ask any questions.

"That he's stuck up here and can't reach Cooper." She called Reid yet another not so nice name under her breath.

"Wasn't there someone else he could call?" Someone who wasn't using his picture for target practice?

"No. I'm the only other one who knows where to find him

up here, especially at night." She pointed at a gravel road spurring off to the left up ahead. "Take that one."

I was so turned around at this point that I understood why only she could find him. "Did he say what he was doing way out here?"

"No, but I suspect it involves a bottle of whiskey."

Reid came up here to drink? Alone? If so, Mona might be right about him being broken. Reid didn't seem like the kind to go off on binges like this. I knew he was pining over Aunt Zoe, but this was Shakespearean teenager tragedy stuff, not something I'd expect of Deadwood's well-respected fire captain.

"I don't get it," I thought aloud, wondering why Reid was so messed up about Aunt Zoe all of a sudden. What had changed?

"It's our spot," she explained.

"Your spot?" I glanced over at her, seeing lines creasing her forehead in the dashboard lights.

"Where we used to go to …" she flapped her hand in front of her, "you know, have a little fun out under the stars."

"Oh." That spot. I focused on the pitted road, keeping my mind from going *there* with Reid and my aunt. "How much further is it?"

"Another half mile or so."

We bounced along in silence for a couple ticks of the odometer. "You think he's there alone?" I asked, trying to prepare mentally for the shit storm that would hit when we reached this spot of theirs.

"For his sake, I hope so."

Me, too. I also hoped for Reid's sake her shotgun wasn't tucked behind the seat.

She pointed out the windshield. "You can see his pickup up ahead on the right."

The headlights reflected off the chrome back bumper of his red dually truck. I pulled in next to it and cut the engine, leaving the headlights on.

"Where is he?"

"Just through the trees. You can see the path."

It was more of a deer trail, actually.

She grabbed a flashlight from the glove box, opened the door, and stepped down. "You coming?"

I hesitated. "You sure you want me to?"

"If he's drinking, I'm going to need your help. He's not a little guy."

No, he sure wasn't, but I'd much rather have stayed alone in the dark pickup in a spooky forest than witness the hellfire Aunt Zoe was about to blast at Reid.

Pocketing the keys, I shut off the lights and followed her into the cool evening air. A fresh, pine-scented breeze blew through the needles overhead. Their whispers grew louder while twigs crunched under our feet. Up ahead, I caught glimpses of firelight through the trees.

When we stepped into the clearing I paused, realizing two things at once.

First, Reid probably wasn't drunk—not yet, anyway. The bottle of wine sitting on a nearby tree stump—along with two glasses—hadn't been opened yet, neither had the picnic basket on the ground on the other side of the fire.

Second, his phone message had been intended as a party invitation for Aunt Zoe alone, not the two of us.

"Oh, shit," I heard Aunt Zoe say under her breath from where she'd stopped in front of me.

A rustling sound in a young stand of straggly trees to our left turned out to be Reid crashing through it with an armload of branches and bark. Feeling like a monster truck-sized third wheel, my gut sank even deeper. I'd have much preferred Bigfoot. We could have run off together to go scare campers carrying cheap video cameras and left Reid and Aunt Zoe alone to reminisce about old times at their favorite spot.

"Hi, Zo," he said, shielding his eyes.

Aunt Zoe lowered the flashlight.

To Reid's credit, his smile for Aunt Zoe only slipped for a moment when he saw me there next to her. "You brought Sparky along."

"I thought I was going to need her help." Aunt Zoe jammed her hands on her hips. "But you're not drunk."

"No," he dropped the kindling next to the fire, taking his gloves off and shoving them in his back pocket. "I'm done with the heavy drinking. It doesn't work."

What did that mean? Alcohol wasn't getting him drunk anymore or it wasn't making him forget a certain hard-headed aunt of mine?

"You acted drunk on the phone," she accused.

He shrugged. "I was pretending. You won't take my calls, so I had to figure out some way to get you to talk to me."

"So you lied and played on my sympathy?"

"I didn't outright lie about anything. You just assumed the worst about me." His gaze moved to me. "Did you really bring Sparky to help?"

"Why else would I drag her away from her children on a weeknight?"

"Because you were afraid to be alone with me."

Aunt Zoe's chin shot up. "You don't scare me, Reid Martin."

"You say that," he pulled a wine opener out of the pocket of his jean jacket and grabbed the bottle from the stump. "But we both know you still have feelings for me."

There was a steely confidence in Reid's tone that might have chafed my hide if I had been in my aunt's shoes. I took a step backward, wanting to inch my way into the trees where I could take cover.

"The only feelings I have these days when it comes to you are heartburn and indigestion." Without taking her eyes off Reid, she said, "Violet, stay put."

Her tight tone took me back to my childhood. I froze. "Yes, Aunt Zoe," I responded, just like the old days.

Reid chuckled, low and smooth. He pulled the cork and grabbed a glass, filling it half full with red wine. "I don't believe you. There's still fire in your eyes."

Aunt Zoe grabbed my forearm and stalked over to Reid, dragging me along with her as if she figured I'd make a run for it given the chance. She was right.

"Fire in my eyes?" She pointed at her face. "This isn't the heat that used to burn for you. That cooled long ago. This is fury, plain and simple."

Reid handed me the glass of wine. I took it without thinking.

"That's what I'm talking about." He picked up the other glass and poured wine into it. "If you didn't care anymore, you wouldn't be threatening to fill me with holes every time I came near."

"Damn it," she muttered. "I should've brought my shotgun."

I looked down at the glass in my hand. Why was I holding wine? This wasn't my party. I gave it to Aunt Zoe, who took it probably for the same reason I had—because it was handed to her. Or maybe she planned on throwing it in Reid's face.

I glanced toward the deer trail. Maybe I should high tail it back to the pickup and deal with the ass chewing she'd give me later for abandoning her.

"See, you still care," Reid said, handing me the other glass of wine, which I took again, feeling like I was guest-starring in a Three Stooges comedy. "I had to reach the bottom of several bottles of whiskey to figure that out, but I came around. Now you need to come around, too."

I fidgeted, wishing a sinkhole would open under my feet.

"I'm not coming around to anything when it comes to you." She thrust the glass of wine back to him, sloshing it over the side onto her hand, which she wiped off on her jeans. "You had your chance years ago and passed it up. There is no second time around for us."

Not sure what to do or where to look, I stared into the bottom of the glass as I took a sip of the dark liquid. The wine had a deep tone with a hint of fruity sweetness. "What kind of wine is this?" I blurted out.

"Zo's favorite," Reid said. "It's a Gamay."

"That's a Gamay?" she asked, still huffing.

Reid gave her a crooked smile. "It's what we always drank up here."

She grabbed the bottle and tipped it, gulping down a good-sized swallow. "This doesn't mean I'm giving in to you," she said, taking another smaller drink. "It's just a shame to waste perfectly good wine on a starry night."

"I couldn't agree more," Reid said, holding out his glass in a mock *cheers* and then downing some wine. "Sweet on the tongue. Reminds me of you." He winked at Aunt Zoe.

I looked up at the sky, searching for a UFO to flag down. Anal probing would be only slightly less comfortable than standing right here right now.

"This isn't happening, Reid," Aunt Zoe said, setting the bottle on the stump. "We're leaving now."

Toot toot! That was my cue. I handed the glass back to Reid.

"Don't you want to see what's in the basket?" he asked, setting both glasses down on the stump.

Well, I sure did now, but I didn't know if Aunt Zoe was going to fall for his parlor trick.

"Unless it's a killer Chihuahua that I can sic on you," she said, "I'm not interested."

Reid crossed his arms over his chest, his eyes narrowing as he stared at her. "You never were good at bluffing."

"We're leaving now," Aunt Zoe said through stiff lips, but her feet stayed planted.

"No, you're staying and opening the basket," he told her.

"How about I go warm up the pickup," I offered, taking a step toward the trees.

"Don't even think about it, Violet Lynn."

"Got it." I focused on the fire and began whistling quietly to myself.

"What's in the basket, Reid?" Aunt Zoe asked.

"Come and see." He walked over to the basket and opened one side of the lid.

Aunt Zoe tapped her foot a few times and then growled. "You're such a pain in the ass." She joined him.

The firelight bathed them in an orange glow, the darkness behind them black velvet sprinkled with starry diamonds. I took a sip from the closest wine glass, not caring which had been mine, as I waited to see what was in the basket.

"What is it?" Aunt Zoe squatted down, reaching inside. She pulled out a small box.

A jewelry box? I gasped, which earned a wrinkled brow from

both of them.

"Sorry," I said, staring into the bottom of my glass again.

"No, Reid," I heard Aunt Zoe say. I peeked up to see her holding the box out to Reid.

"You're jumping to conclusions, Zo. Open it."

She wiggled off the lid, frowning down at whatever was inside.

I took a step closer. What was it? Diamonds? Rubies? Sapphires? What?

"You're kidding," she said and chuckled. "I can't believe you still have this."

What was in the box? I opened my mouth to ask but then poured more wine in it instead of catching another glare.

"You always were such a sentimental sucker," she said.

"Hey, now," Reid said. "Don't be making fun in front of Sparky."

Aunt Zoe put the lid back on.

What was in the box, damn it?

"Zo, I need to talk to you for a moment." He glanced my way. "Alone."

Thank, God! "I'll be in the truck."

"Hold up, Violet." Aunt Zoe stopped me before I'd made it two steps. "Reid, if you have something to say, spit it out."

"Fine," Reid said, not sounding like he meant it. He pointed at the box. "That's for you to keep."

"I can't."

"You can. Listen," Reid paused, frowning over at me.

Sorry, I mouthed, wishing I weren't standing there eavesdropping on this private conversation. I considered zipping my coat closed over my head to escape.

He turned back to my aunt. "I want you back."

"No."

Ouch! She hadn't even taken a moment to think about it.

"Shut up and let me finish," he said, undeterred. "I want you back in my life, morning, noon, and night. I was an idiot to let you go before, and I've regretted it every day since you kicked me out. Please stop torturing me and let me in again."

Holy crap! I held my breath as I waited for Aunt Zoe's response.

She stared down at the box in her hand, her shoulders rising and lowering several times, and then she held it out to him. "Would you hold this for a minute?"

He took the box. "What do you say?"

For the first time since he'd stepped out of the trees, he sounded uncertain. My heart clenched for him.

"I say that I owe you this." She pulled back and punched him, landing a right jab to his left cheek.

My jaw hit the forest floor, followed by my glass of wine, which broke into pieces.

Reid took a step backwards. His boot heel caught on a root, and he stumbled back several more steps before falling out of sight into the darkness. In the silence that followed, I heard the cracking of breaking branches, a thump, and then a yelp from somewhere below.

"Oh, shit!" Aunt Zoe ran to where he'd disappeared. "Reid? Are you okay? I'm so sorry! Reid?"

I picked up my jaw and ran over, shining the flashlight down over a small outcrop in the rocks. Reid lay about seven feet below on a bed of pine needles and bent over yearlings. He blinked as I willed him to move.

Aunt Zoe latched onto my arm in a death grip. "Please be okay, Reid," she whispered. "I wanted to hurt you back a little, not kill you."

"Reid?" I called down, taking stock of his limbs, making sure nothing was bent in an odd way. "Is anything broken?"

He squinted in the bright light and sat up with a grunt. "Just my pride." He stood slowly, wincing. "And maybe my left ass cheek."

A strangled garble sound came out of Aunt Zoe's throat.

"Can you walk?" I asked.

"Probably with a limp."

"How about climbing?"

He bent sideways, stretching his lower back. "I think so, if you don't mind giving me a hand at the top."

"I could've killed him, Violet," Aunt Zoe said, her voice shaking. She stalked toward the fire, her right hand clenching and unclenching. I hoped she hadn't broken any bones. Her hands were her livelihood.

I waited for Reid, latching onto him and tugging a few seconds later.

He came up limping as he'd predicted, still holding the little box. He gingerly touched his face below his left eye. "Damn, Zo. Your punches get harder the older you get."

"I'm sorry." Aunt Zoe was still flexing her hand, staring blindly into the fire. "But it's your fault."

"You punching me was *my* fault?"

"You broke my heart, you son of a bitch. It took a long, long time to heal it, and now you lure me up here to tell me you've regretted what you did all of this time. When I think of the years of feeling empty inside … years, Reid …" she shook her head, lifting her gaze to his. "You're lucky I didn't bust that wine bottle over your thick skull."

He limped closer to her, rubbing his lower back as he went. "I'm sorry. I was confused from the whole divorce mess back then, not thinking straight."

"How do I know you won't get confused again?"

"I won't." He stood across the fire from her. Wise man, I thought. "Things are different this time."

She stared at him, her eyes glistening in the firelight. "You're right. They are. I'm the one who can't do it this time." She looked over at me. "Violet, give me the keys, please."

I obeyed without question, giving her the flashlight, too. "Are you okay?"

She shook her head. "I need a big favor."

"Sure. What?"

"Take him home. I don't think he should drive tonight after that fall."

"I'm fine. I don't need a nursemaid."

"This isn't open for discussion."

"But," I started, looking back and forth between them. "What about …" it was obvious that she still cared for him. After the way he'd just poured his heart out for her, how could she walk away from him?

I tried to help Reid out. "I don't even know where the hell I am."

"Reid will get you back to town. Harvey can come and pick you up when you get Reid home." She kissed me on the forehead. "Sorry to leave this on you, kiddo."

"I ... uh, okay." I frowned my apology to Reid.

"I'll take that," she said and retrieved the little box from Reid, pocketing it. Then she headed for the trees.

I called out, "Where are you going?"

"Somewhere to think." She held her right hand up, flexing her fingers. "And to ice my hand. Your face is getting harder the older you get, Reid. Sorry I almost killed you."

I watched her disappear into the trees and then turned to Reid. The night had gone from awkward to downright squirmy.

"I'm sorry, too." I didn't know what else to say to him.

"Aren't we all, Sparky. But I had to give it one last shot before throwing in the towel." He held up the bottle of wine. "Come share a drink with me under the stars."

How could I turn him down after he and his heart had been belted off a cliff by my aunt? I joined him in front of the fire, sipping from the other glass since mine was in pieces at my feet. "It's a nice night, not too breezy."

"Yep," he took a drink from the bottle.

I heard some coyotes yipping in the distance and took a step closer to Reid, shooting him a quick smile. "A bit spooky, though."

He nodded. "Especially after some of the bogeymen you've faced."

"And bogey-women," I said, thinking of a certain raven-haired bitch and her demon book.

"Are you talking about Ms. Wolff?" he asked.

I shot a cautious glance his way. That was supposed to be top secret. I hadn't said a thing to anyone about Ms. Wolff's death, and I'd bet my pathetic savings that Doc had not let out a peep either. Was Cooper sharing secrets? Or had Harvey leaked?

"What do you know about Ms. Wolff?"

"She's dead." He didn't mince words. Hell, after the night he was having, he probably wasn't in the mood for niceties.

"Did Cooper talk to you about it?"

He shook his head. "I ran into Coop's ex-partner at the store last night."

"Detective Hawke?"

Reid scowled. "Yep, that asshole."

"And he spilled his guts about the whole case?"

"I would call it showing off rather than spilling." Reid drained the bottle. "He was trying to impress me."

"How long have you known him?" I dumped the remains of my wine behind me on the ground when he wasn't looking. If I was going to be driving, I didn't need any more wine.

"Too long. It's a small world here in western South Dakota. I first met him working on an arson case a few years before Cooper came back to Deadwood. He was full of bluster, no substance, and not much has changed over the years except his title."

"What's the story behind Cooper and him?" I pressed as much out of curiosity as the desire to keep from returning to the subject of my aunt's rejection.

"They were partners for a few years down in Rapid, working their way up through the ranks together. Then shit started to go sour." He kicked some dirt on the fire, smothering the flames, leaving only glowing embers. "A girl died, leaving behind a mess involving a local politician, some drugs, and a lack of solid evidence. During the investigation, Coop got screwed."

I remembered Hawke's question about Cooper sleeping with another witness. "You mean screwed as in jerked around or screwed as in having sex with a witness?"

Reid stared at me in the faint light of the dying embers for a few coyote howls. "Who told you about that?"

"Hawke mentioned it."

"The stupid buffoon needs to keep his mouth shut."

"Did Cooper getting involved with the witness muck up the case?" That would explain why Hawke was higher up the chain.

Squatting, he picked up the broken glass and put the shards in the picnic basket. I joined him, careful not to get cut.

"Coop didn't screw any witness on that particular case," he said. "Hawke was referring to another one, and the female in question happened to have been a local girl who was dating Coop for several weeks before the shit hit the fan. Technically, he wasn't screwing a 'witness' at the start. It turned out that his girlfriend was a liar who used her body to get what she wanted. In this case, it was her hands on some evidence that would keep her off the suspect list, where she belonged right next to her fellow conspirator and other boyfriend."

"Oh, jeez, that had to sting."

I remembered Natalie telling me how Cooper had given her the brush off one night after they'd done some heavy flirting in the Purple Door Saloon. When she asked him back to her place, he'd told her he didn't get involved with locals and that was the end of that. After hearing about this, his distance made more sense.

"Hawke made it sound more basic," I told Reid. "Like Cooper was a fool who couldn't keep it in his pants."

"I'm not surprised. Unfortunately, Coop's superior took Hawke's view of the whole thing. He believed Hawke's version of the story about who solved the case—as in Hawke himself—and promoted that shitbird over Coop." He stood, brushing his hands off on his jeans.

I did the same. "Talk about getting screwed."

"Yeah. That was the final straw for Coop. After that, he came back home, returned to his roots." Reid grabbed the bottle and my empty glass, tucking everything away in the picnic basket. "Coop told me most of this one night years ago when he was pretty wasted. Said he'd been afraid he might shoot Hawke if he didn't leave Rapid."

"But now Hawke's back." Was Cooper's trigger finger twitching lately?

"He's not just back, he's been pulled in to supervise and advise Cooper."

Damn. Talk about salt in the wound. And here I was pissing

and moaning about Rex and Tiffany. At least I didn't have to report to either of them.

Reid kicked more dirt on the fire, grabbed the basket, and then flicked on a flashlight. "You ready?"

"Sure."

"Let's go home." He led the way.

While we crunched through the trees, my thoughts replayed the angry glares and terse comments Cooper had given Hawke while we were in Ms. Wolff's apartment. It was no wonder he'd been so tense, stuck dealing with Hawke and me—two of his least favorite people in the world. Maybe I should try to be a little nicer to Cooper while his ex-partner was in town. If he was fighting the urge to shoot someone, let it be Hawke instead of me.

"Sparky, you understand that what I told you tonight isn't public knowledge."

"My lips are sealed."

I saw his pickup ahead in the clearing. He held his keys out to me when we reached it.

"You okay to drive?" he asked. "Not tipsy or anything?"

"Not even a little." Between the cool, fresh air and the eye openers flying at me tonight, I felt stone cold sober.

I took his keys and climbed behind the wheel of his big rig. It smelled like the pine tree air freshener hanging from the mirror. Fake pine scent, really? In the Black Hills where all I had to do was take a sniff out the window?

I settled behind the wheel, getting acquainted with his rig, the lights, gear shift, and emergency brake. I preferred not to drive tanks through the woods at night, but I knew the road conditions from the drive up and was only worrying my lower lip about deer or other critters jumping out in front of me. And maybe a ghost … or a one-armed, spikey-haired pixie freak bent on revenge.

Reid grunted as he climbed up, moving slowly as he placed the picnic basket in the back seat and shut his door. "You know which way to go?"

"Not really. You'll have to direct me most of the way back down to the main road."

"Will do." He shifted, taking the weight off his left side.

I backed up slowly, the size of the truck making me more cautious. We rode along in silence, interrupted only by his directions.

I thought about what I had to face tomorrow with Rex and swallowed my groan.

"What do you think happened to Ms. Wolff?" Reid asked out of the blue.

"Me?"

He chuckled. "I don't see anyone else in here with us."

Why would he care what I thought? He was the Fire Captain, I was just a Realtor. I shrugged. "I think someone murdered her."

"Yeah, but why? She was such a sweet little thing.'

"You knew her?"

"Sure. There'd been some false alarms at the Galena House apartments over the last few years. Plus we went in once a year and checked out the fire extinguishers and tested the alarms. She always made sure we had a handful of those German cookies of hers when we left."

Freesia had mentioned those cookies, which reminded me that I needed to take Freesia a listing agreement and discuss her options. "I never actually met Ms. Wolff," I told him. "Only talked to her that once on the phone."

"Slow down a little," he said, "we're turning right just around this curve."

After we made the turn, I asked, "What do you think of all of those cuckoo clocks?"

He snorted. "Those are bizarre. I figured she collected them like how some people fill a glass case with thimbles or silver spoons they'd picked up in different states."

"They creep me out a little," I admitted, thinking about the one with the wolves on the hunt.

"You know what really gave me the willies?" he asked.

I had trouble imagining much of anything giving Reid a scare after the things he'd probably encountered in his job over the years. "What's that?"

"All of those wigs." He made a shuddering sound. "She told

me once they were made of real hair. I'd take a wall of clocks any day to those wigs."

Was he thinking of the hat boxes? "What wigs? You mean the hats?"

"No, I mean the wigs on those styrofoam heads in her closet. She'd have me go in there and test one of her smoke alarms every time I made my annual ..."

My brain blocked out his voice, needing to focus for a moment. What did he mean there were wigs in her closet? "When were you there last?" I interrupted.

"Let me see, we had inspections in that area of town a couple of months ago."

"And you saw wigs in her closet then?"

"Sure. Same as always."

"How many wigs?"

"Too many. Maybe twenty or more, and none were the same or even close."

Where had the wigs gone? Had she sent them all off for cleaning? Is there such a thing as a wig cleaner? Or had someone taken them after they killed her?

"Sometimes when I was in there," Reid continued, "I'd imagine her talking to the heads, maybe when she felt lonely. I figured if I ever went in there and she'd drawn faces on those styrofoam heads, I was going to talk to Coop about calling in the men with the straitjackets to haul her away."

"Did you ever see her without a wig?"

"I'm not sure, maybe. I remember once someone had pulled the fire alarm in the middle of the night, thinking they'd smelled smoke. When we arrived, all of the occupants were standing outside in their robes and slippers. Ms. Wolff looked more frail than usual that night, which I'd attributed to her being shocked by the fire alarm. But maybe her seeming feeble to me was more because of her hair."

"What about it?"

"It was the first time I'd ever seen her with white hair."

I hit the brakes, making Reid reach for the dashboard. Dirt billowed around us, floating through the headlight's beams.

"What is it?" he asked. "Did you see a deer?"

"She had white hair?"

He did a doubletake. "Uh, yes."

"Like old lady white hair—thinner, curly maybe?" I was thinking of the women I'd often see in the hair salon I used to go to in Rapid that had been located a block away from a retirement community.

"No it was plenty thick and straight as a board. It hung down to the middle of her back." He let go of the dashboard. "It seemed to almost glow in the moonlight."

Thick white hair. Could it be ... ? Panic pulsed through my legs. The urge to take flight made my feet tingle.

"Sparky," Reid grabbed my arm, squeezing. "Are you okay?"

Hell, no. If I was right, there was a distinct possibility I was going to need CPR soon. Good thing I had a firefighter sitting next to me.

"What is it?" he asked again.

"It's nothing." I followed his earlier prompt. "I thought I saw a deer." I hit the gas again, bumping along.

Holy grim reaper! What if Ms. Wolff was another one of those albino-looking beings? Had she known Caly and the creepy tall Donald Duck-looking twins from the Mudder Brothers? Did they have something to do with why she'd contacted me? Was that why she'd called me an executioner, because of what I'd done to the creep in the Mudder Brothers' basement? What had she heard about me? Did she have Layne's picture because she planned to hurt him? Or use him to get to me?

The trip back to the main road passed in a blur of dirt and trees and frets. My brain whirled with more questions, the final one being did I dare to tell Cooper my theory about Ms. Wolff and her white hair and take a chance of him shooting me for even mentioning the word *albino*? Or did I keep this to myself and dig deeper at the risk of winding up with another shriveled skull—this time my own?

Chapter Twelve

Friday, October 5th

Morning showed up swinging a basket full of bright sunshine. I could hear the birds crowing about it through my closed window, but I remained under the covers unconvinced it was worth getting up to see. The way my luck had been going, today would end with yet another ex-someone showing up to stir a little more craziness into my world.

I still couldn't believe I had to help Rex the Rat find somewhere to live on the same continent. The Universe had a really warped sense of humor. Maybe he'd be interested in a recently vacated apartment with walls full of cuckoo clocks.

Oh, Ms. Wolff. Why did she have to drag me into her troubles? I had plenty of my own keeping me busy without all of the questions she'd spawned. True to my word, I'd sat on my big theory about her and her white hair after returning to civilization last night, keeping it all to myself.

When Harvey had picked me up from Reid's, he'd been full of questions about the two fighting lovebirds. It'd been easy enough to keep his focus on their sad state of "no affair" rather than what had me jumping at shadows.

I knew Doc had planned on reading Ms. Wolff's book, so I'd texted him a brief *Sleep tight* message, not wanting to interrupt him. I sure hoped he'd find some answers for me in that book.

Aunt Zoe had been in her glass shop until the wee hours of the night. I'd seen her moving around in there with her thick, heat-resistant gloves on when I peeked out the back door before heading up to bed.

That left Cooper. I wasn't going to give Detective Hawke the time of day after learning what I had about him from Reid. One prickly detective in my life was plenty. In spite of how much Cooper made me curse and swear, Doc had convinced me that Cooper's actions were out of concern for my health and welfare. I had a feeling Detective Hawke's agenda was all about Stone Hawke.

As I lay there on my bed listening to the sound of Miss Geary's garage door opening, I pondered different ways Cooper might react to my theory. The best being he'd shower me with praise and hand me my own Citizen Detective badge to wear. The worst involved him putting a bullet in my foot to slow me down before chasing after me with an orange jumpsuit in my size.

The sound of a banshee scream stopped all of my thoughts in their tracks.

"What in the hell was that?" I asked the ceiling.

The crash of breaking glass resonated from the street below my window.

I sat up, threw off the covers, and rushed to the window in time to see Miss Geary swing a fire poker at a headlight of the familiar black Jaguar that was idling in her drive. Broken glass and plastic pieces littered the concrete around her red feather high-heeled slippers, sparkling in the sunlight. While I gaped out my window, she pulled back to swing again.

The driver's side door opened. A pair of legs came into view covered in black trousers, then a brown leather bomber jacket. I didn't catch a look at his face, but his blonde hair was slicked back like he'd recently gotten out of the shower.

I heard the driver yell, "Stop it, Beatrice!"

She ignored him and swung the poker at the grill. More pieces of car scattered across her drive. She tried to pull the poker free as the driver closed the distance, but it was snared.

The driver grabbed Miss Geary and hauled her away from the car while she waved her arms around like an angry orangutan. Then he stalked back and yanked the fire poker free of his grill, throwing it into the flower bed. He glared down at the damage.

A bolt of recognition zapped me, making me almost keel over. My hand flew to my mouth and I took a step backward.

Rex!

What in the hell was he doing over at Miss Geary's? Had he found out where I lived and come looking for me? For my kids?

I turned back to the scene below. Miss Geary was shaking her fist at Rex, shouting for him to get off her property before she called the cops.

Rex pointed at her and said something back that I couldn't hear, partly due to the window, mostly due to my panic. Then he slid behind the steering wheel and slammed his door, tires screeching in his wake.

The birds and I were too shocked to make a peep.

The garage door closed, shutting Miss Geary and her feather slippers inside.

A few seconds of silence passed.

The birds started chatting away again.

I still had the wind knocked out of me, so I walked back until my hamstrings hit the mattress and sat down.

Why was Rex ... the black Jaguar ... Miss Geary's younger stallion ... *holy shit!*

I raced over to the window again, remembering how many times Aunt Zoe and I had seen that damned car parked in Miss Geary's drive. It was the same car, right? What were the chances of Miss Geary finding two younger stallions with black Jaguars to keep in her stable? No, it was the same.

It'd been Rex over there all of this time.

I had a feeling his presence in Miss Geary's bed had more to do with spying on me and my kids than enjoying her tarts.

The kids! My heart raced.

He'd seen my kids, I was sure of it. Oh, fuck!

I fell back against the wall, my gaze darting in panic. Had they seen him? Talked to him? Did they have a clue who he really was?

That no good son of a bitch! What should I do? What could I do?

I ran to the bedroom door.

Wait. Neither Addy nor Layne had said a thing to me about a "man" over at Miss Geary's.

I pulled my hand away from the doorknob. I had to calm down, act normal, and pretend I hadn't learned the bogeyman had been sleeping across the street for the last month.

Okay, I could do this. I returned to my bed and sank onto it, burying my face in my shaking hands. Why was he back? He was supposed to be gone for good.

I took stock of my situation. So Rex had been watching us from across the street all of this time. Now what?

The solution was simple—I was going to have to kill him.

I'd just have to figure out how to do it without Detective Cooper figuring out I was the murderer. Maybe I should wear a white wig while I did it.

My phone rang. I looked over. Speak of the devil.

I took a calming breath, then another since the first didn't seem to take before picking it up. "It's a little early, Cooper."

"This is Detective Hawke." The voice matched the name.

"Why are you calling me from Cooper's phone?"

"That's not important. I need to talk to you about the Mudder Brothers' investigation."

"Does Cooper know you called me from his phone?"

"I left multiple messages for you yesterday. Why didn't you call me back?"

I didn't like the tone he was using. It felt a bit too much like I was being scolded. "I was busy."

"I need you to come down to the station, Violet."

I didn't like his casual use of my name either. We weren't chummy enough to be on a first name basis. I dug my heels in. "Do you have a warrant for my arrest, Detective Hawke?"

"A warrant?" I could hear the surprise in his question. "I ... uh ... no, of course not. I just need to ask you some questions about the events that took place on the night of August twenty-third."

"Ask Detective Cooper about it when you give him his phone back. He knows the story well." Without further ado, I hung up.

The phone rang again, showing Cooper's name. I sent it to voicemail.

I didn't have time to deal with Detective Hawke and the Mudder Brothers mess today. I had to torture and then slay the man who had fathered my children. The question was how to pull it off with Sonny and Cher along for the ride?

* * *

I managed to get dressed, feed the kids, and drop them off at school without biting anyone. That seemed like quite an accomplishment since my teeth hadn't stopped gnashing since Rex had peeled off down the road. As I pulled out of Aunt Zoe's drive, I wondered if Miss Geary's teeth were still gnashing, too.

Detective Hawke was waiting for me in the parking lot behind Calamity Jane's. Damn, he was as persistent as a honey badger.

"Violet, I need to talk to you." He didn't even wait for me to step out of the Picklemobile.

"Where's Detective Cooper?" I had to push him backward to get out.

"Over at Ms. Wolff's apartment."

Had Reid talked to Cooper? Maybe he had mentioned my fascination with Ms. Wolff's wigs. "What's he doing there?"

"Police business."

Oh, so it was going to be like that. I slammed the door and detoured around Detective Hawke.

He tried to attach himself to my side as I strode across the lot toward the back door. By that I meant he kept bumping into me with his shoulder as if we were joined by a rubber band.

"What were you doing at Mudder Brothers Funeral Parlor the night George Mudder was killed?"

"Have I made it back into the top ten suspects' list for George again?"

"No." Bump.

"Then what does it matter?"

"I find it curious that you happened to be there the night everything went down." Bump, bump.

Did he not realize his shoulder was trying to hockey check

me? "Curious? I find it unlucky."

"You seem to wind up in a lot of unlucky places. I've read your file. It's extensive."

"Do you mean extensive in a good way or bad way?" I had a feeling that if it was full of Cooper's handwriting, it was the latter.

"Let's not get distracted with unnecessary details here." Bump.

He pulled a notepad out of his jacket. I'd seen Cooper with a similar notepad too many times to count. They must hand them out with their badges.

I stopped outside Calamity Jane's door. I didn't want to walk in with a detective badgering me and give Jerry a coronary on the day his precious television crew would be following me around.

Hawke clicked his pen, then gave me the stink eye. "You're not going to assault my pen again, are you?"

Maybe. "Just ask me your damned questions."

"What do you know about the contents of the crate in the storage room that night?" Detective Hawke was standing way too close, especially considering the saccharine sweet, minty brand of cologne he'd flea-dipped in this morning.

I frowned up at him, backing against the door to try to get him out of my personal space. "What do you mean?"

"I was reading through the reports for the case and your coworker, Ray Underhill, mentioned in his that you had been harassing him lately about his activities with George Mudder."

"Ray said that?" What a stinking turd. I feigned surprise. "I wonder what he was referring to by that. We have a friendly competition going on here at work with a little bit of taunting here and there. Maybe I struck a nerve and didn't realize it. He is the type to bottle up his feelings." A voice snickered in my head at that doozy of a lie.

"I haven't met with Mr. Underhill, but I plan to set up a meeting with him soon."

Great. Without a doubt, Ray would do whatever he could to get me even more under Hawke's microscope. I needed to move my queen before that horse's ass tried to pull a checkmate on me. The problem was I was running a tad short of patience and tact at the moment.

"Here are a couple of things to write on your handy notepad there. First, I was visiting George Mudder with my friend that night in order to find the name of a woman who'd died in the late 1800s. Mudder Brothers' books on deaths are more complete than the library's records."

He made a few chicken scratches on his paper.

"Did you find out the name?"

"No."

"Why were you looking for information on this dead woman?"

"There's a rumor that the hotel my client is buying is haunted and she's one of the ghosts."

"You mean one of the guests."

"No, I mean ghosts. I wanted to find out more about her for my client. He enjoys the ghost stories." Especially the ones he conjures up.

Hawke wrote a few more things down and then looked up at me. "What was the other thing you wanted to tell me regarding that night?"

"I saw Ray's penis."

Detective Hawke wrote the letter P and then his gaze shot back to mine. "What did you just say?"

"You heard me. It was cold and Ray was naked and terrified. You can imagine the state of his penis in those circumstances."

Hawke wasn't writing any of it down. I tapped his pad. "You need to make note of that."

"Why in the world would I need to note that, Violet?"

"Because it's half of the reason Ray is going to lie to you and try to set me up as the number one suspect in the Mudder case."

"What's the other half?"

"He's afraid of me."

Detective Hawke's head cocked to the side. "Afraid of your temper, you mean?"

"You think I have a temper?"

"Well, you did stomp on my pen, threaten to do the same to my testicles, and then later clomped on my foot. I think you have a tendency toward violence, Violet."

Violent Violet—a new nickname. That would make Cooper smile. Me, not so much. "I disagree. I think that I have a tendency toward standing up for myself in the face of egotistical assholes and dangerous killers." I tapped his pad once more. "Shrunken penis. Remember that."

With a wave goodbye, I stepped inside Calamity Jane Realty and closed the door on Detective Hawke's frown.

Jerry called out to me as I walked by his office.

I backed up. "Yes?"

He eyed my black slacks and silver sweater. "Nice. Very classy. I like your hair pulled back and twisted like that."

"Thank you." I'd dressed the way Jerry had specifically requested yesterday, so I wasn't sure why he was making a big deal of it.

"After you put your stuff down, please come back here. I've made up a game plan for your route today."

"You mean you've picked out what places I should show Mr. Conner?" Besides the bottom of a mine shaft?

He nodded. "I want to make sure our guests get a good taste of Deadwood today." He pulled some notecards out of his briefcase. "I've written a few scripts here, too."

He had to be freaking kidding me. "Jerry, why don't you take Mr. Conner and the other two out today instead of me?"

"No way. This is going to be your day to glow, Violet."

Glow? With Rex sitting within slapping distance while I had to keep my hands to myself, it might turn out to be my day to actually combust.

Unclenching my jaw, I focused on Jerry's efforts at growing my career. "Okay, let me put my stuff down and we'll go over everything."

"Thanks, Violet." His tone was genuine. In return for that, I'd give today my best shot, but I made no guarantees.

By the time Dickie and Honey strolled into the office after lunch dressed in black, same as yesterday, I had my route memorized and knew my lines by heart. At Jerry's request, I'd added a dab more mascara and powdered my nose. He'd given me a thumbs up and a "go work your magic." I was considering some voodoo, starting with a doll that resembled Rex. I just needed to borrow Mona's brooch with its sharp pin.

Jerry welcomed our special guests with a smile that bridged his earlobes. He nudged me forward. "Violet's ready to go. We're waiting for her client to arrive."

Honey unzipped the black backpack she was carrying and pulled out a hand-held video camera. "Do you mind if we film today, Violet?"

"Film?" I looked at Jerry, my eyes wide. I did not want to be on film with Rex. The camera would see everything, including the murder in my eyes, giving Cooper the evidence he'd need to lock me up for good when Rex went missing. On top of that, if any of today's events made it to the television screen, my kids might see it. "I'm not sure today is a good day for me to be recorded."

Honey's forehead made a deep V.

Jerry stepped forward. "What Violet means is that she isn't prepared to be taped."

"Oh," Honey's face smoothed. "It's not for the show. This is just me getting some stuff on film so I can start putting the script together. I'll use it for my own work. I won't let anyone else see it."

I didn't like this recording business still, but to buck her now would seem childish. "Okay, but I don't think you should record my client. He hasn't signed off on anything. I wouldn't want to make him uncomfortable."

That was a big honking lie. I wanted to do all kinds of things to make him miserable and then some.

"No problem. I'll keep the camera focused on the scenery so neither of you end up on film."

"Thank you." Now we needed Rex to show up and we could get this disaster … I meant day … started.

I excused myself, slipping into the restroom. My pep talk in the mirror was short and sweet. "You can do this. Don't kill Rex in front of the camera."

When I stepped back into the front room, Jerry was introducing Rex to Honey and Dickie, explaining the situation.

Still wearing his brown leather bomber jacket over a white collared shirt, black trousers, and dark leather shoes, Rex looked like he'd come from the set of *Top Gun*. Even his blonde hair had that windblown look.

As I listened to Jerry, I crossed my fingers behind my back, willing Rex to opt out of having company while we were checking out places.

The sleazy voyeur looked at me with a leer that made me want to smash a cream pie all over his face. "I'm sure the four of us will have an interesting day together."

I collected my purse from my drawer. Pulling out my cell phone, I pretended to check my messages. I sent Doc a quick text: *Be out by your car in one minute.*

I didn't wait to see if he replied because Jerry stepped closer. "Make this opening kickoff count, Violet," he said for my ears only.

I nodded.

He patted me on the shoulder and gave me an "atta girl."

I wondered what he'd do if I slapped him on the ass and said, "Yes, coach!"

After a few more pleasantries, we all headed out the back door. Ben's Subaru sparkled in the sunshine. I knew from an earlier conversation with Ben that yesterday Jerry had given him cash to get it detailed for today's show and tell.

Halfway there, I glanced over and saw Doc pretending to get something out of the trunk of his Camaro.

"Mr. Conner," I called out, wanting to make sure Doc didn't confuse Rex for Dickie, who was talking to Jerry as he walked us to the car.

Rex looked over at me, his eyebrows raised above his aviator sunglasses.

I scrambled for something to say. "Nice shades." Sheesh, that wasn't very smooth. Wait, maybe it wasn't so bad. Doc needed to see Rex without his glasses on. "Can I see them for a moment?"

"Right now?" Rex asked.

"Yes."

"Why?"

Just take off the damned glasses, creep. "I'm considering buying a new pair and I like the looks of those."

"They're expensive," he said, handing them to me.

What did that mean? Had his spying included my bank account? I was tempted to snap back something about how a lack of child support for the last decade hadn't helped but closed my lips, pretending to check out the glasses.

"Try them on," Rex urged.

"Nah, I wouldn't want to scratch them since they're so pricey." I handed them back, pretty sure Doc had seen enough. I know I had after the first ten seconds Rex had walked back into my life.

One more peek at Doc won me a heart-warming smile, along with an eyeful of Doc in his jeans and dark green Henley. I crossed my fingers that vision would hold me over throughout my afternoon in Purgatory.

Jerry saw us off like a proud father watching his kids head off for college. I watched him waving in my rearview mirror.

The first house on Jerry's route was Lilly Devine's place. This morning I'd learned that the owner was having trouble selling it, so he was willing to rent. Mona had been the one to tell Jerry it had a reputation for being haunted, so going there was a three-pointer—Jerry's words, not mine.

I figured it was going to be a waste of time on both accounts. Rex's tastes had always been more upscale than the Devine house's décor; and while Dickie claimed to have psychic powers, I was of the school of thought that believed he could talk to dead people when I heard it with my own two ears.

I stayed on script as we toured the house, making sure to give Dickie and Honey plenty of time to film the particular bedroom where Lilly's boyfriend supposedly had killed her.

After spending some time walking through this house with Doc a couple of months ago, I had a different theory than what the police had suspected at the time of Lilly's death. In my version of how the events took place, the murder occurred in the basement and the boyfriend dragged her body up to the bedroom. Why? Either for some twisted necrophilic fetish or to make finding her body more dramatic.

While Honey taped, Dickie spouted ideas for some scripts they could do while filming the house. Rex watched from his post holding up the bedroom door frame, his smile bemused. I had a feeling he believed in ghosts about as much as he did in being a good provider for his offspring.

I excused myself from the show prep and headed to the kitchen. Leaning against the sink, I watched the trees sway in the breeze outside the kitchen window. Every now and then a tiny branch took flight across the yard. What I wouldn't do to take wing after one and escape.

I closed my eyes, practicing some yoga *ohms* in my head.

Remaining civil to Rex was draining my batteries. There were two voices playing in my head at all times—Violet the happy-go-lucky Realtor who enjoyed spinning in circles in a grass-covered field in the Swiss Alps, and Violet the raging mother who wished she'd brought a pocketful of threepenny nails to pulverize between her molars. I could only hold the latter in check for so long.

Maybe Detective Hawke was right about me. I was prone to violence. Rex sure seemed to bring out the beast, making me tug and pull at my chain, practically choking on my collar as I lunged for his throat time and again.

I ohmed that snarling dog vision away and focused on one of the good things in my life at the moment—Doc.

Tonight after the kids were tucked in their beds safe and sound I was going to sit down next to him on the couch and tell him my theory on Ms. Wolff being an albino. If anyone was going to buy into it, he would.

Then the two of us could put our heads together—and maybe some other body parts—after all, it'd been a while since I'd gotten to enjoy all of his anatomy. After I'd finished reacquainting myself with his skin and more, we could try to come up with a way to convey my theory to Cooper that wouldn't make him want to use me as a punching bag.

"Violet," Rex said from behind me.

My shoulders tightened at the sound of his voice. "Yes?" I said in my Swiss Alps version voice, since I didn't know if he were alone or not.

"I bet I can guess what you're thinking."

Memories flooded through my thoughts. We'd played this guessing game often while dating. He had always been certain he'd known what was on my mind and had usually been wrong. "What am I thinking?" I played along, opening my eyes in time to see another small piece of tree branch sail past. I highly doubted he'd guess that my thoughts were focused on a dead woman with a shrunken skull.

"You're wondering if I came to the Black Hills to get back together with you."

"Hmm." Not even close. I glanced over my shoulder at him to make sure we were not being filmed.

"I'll admit," his smile was predatory as his gaze traveled down my backside. "I do still find you attractive, in spite of the evidence in your hips that you gave birth."

I gripped the sink, feeling the anger start to bubble in my stomach. I wasn't going to plant my boot in his mouth. Calamity Jane needed today to go well. I had to take one or more for the team.

"I've thought about you often over the years," he continued, "wondering what could have happened if you hadn't gotten pregnant."

Oh, did he mean with *his* freaking kids! My esophagus burned. He'd wondered what could have been? Hell, I wondered what could have happened if the bastard had paid me child support.

"We could've really had some fun, you and I."

"What about Susan?" I let that slip out and then clamped my lips together, the traitors.

"She was a distraction that got out of hand."

I whirled. "Why's that? Because my sister was stupid enough to fall in love with you?"

He waved her feelings off like they were child's play. "There is no such thing as love, only degrees of lust."

I sure hoped Doc didn't agree with Rex on that score.

"Since I'm stuck working here for the next several months and you're still single, I've come to the conclusion we should continue where we left off."

If that was his idea of a romantic proposition, he needed to back the truck up and start with some roses, maybe chocolate, and then shove both up his ass and leave me alone.

"You want to get back together?" I asked, confirming I'd heard him correctly.

"Only on a physical level, of course. No strings. Neither of us need that."

"What about the offspring you produced?"

"What offspring?" One blonde eyebrow cocked upward. "I distinctly remember signing a paper relinquishing any claim to *your* children."

"Yes, you did." I closed in on him, smelling notes of cedar and cardamom in his cologne, as well as the leather from his jacket. I stood on my tiptoes and whispered in his ear. "So why in the fuck are you spying on us from my neighbor's house?"

He scoffed. "You assume that's the reason I was staying with Beatrice?"

"It's a little too much of a coincidence that you just happened to be bunking across the street."

"I suppose it might seem that way." He shoved his hands in the pockets of his jacket. "She means nothing, I assure you."

That probably explained why Miss Geary had attacked his car with a fire poker this morning.

"I wasn't really spying," he continued. "I was curious. I wanted to watch you go about your daily life."

"Violet?" Honey called from the other room.

"I'm in the kitchen," I returned, all sweet and helpful. Then I poked Rex in the shoulder, glaring holes through to the back of his skull. "We're not some goddamned ant farm for you to watch through the glass."

Honey breezed into the kitchen, video camera at her side. Dickie followed, reciting something under his breath.

"Are you two done in the bedroom?" I winced inwardly at

how that sounded.

Honey chuckled, obviously catching my *faux pas*. "Yes. Dickie felt the brush of fingers on the back of his neck."

"There's a definite presence in that room," Dickie took out a handkerchief to wipe his brow. "My EMF meter was all over the place."

So was my ASS meter, thanks to Rex.

"We'd like to come back here again," Honey said, "and try to capture some stuff on film. That room is hot with paranormal activity."

Maybe Lilly Devine's ghost was moving about the place, like Prudence had in the Carhart house.

"Are there any other rooms in this place we should film?" Honey held up her camera.

I really wanted to get this tour over and done with so I could wave Rex goodbye, but I had an idea about the basement. It was time to see if Dickie really was the medium he claimed to be on his show.

"I wanted to show Rex the space downstairs. It's the nicest part of the house." Holding open the door that led downstairs, I ushered them in front of me. "Dickie, would you mind hitting the light switch there on your left?"

The fluorescent lights down below flickered and buzzed. Rex held the door for me to follow Honey. The basement was the same as I remembered from the last time I had been down there—tan carpet with white paint on the walls. Bright and normal looking.

When I had been here before, Doc had refused to even walk down the stairs. The scent of whatever was down here had been so strong he'd paled at the top step. Being the dud that I was, I could have slept down here if I hadn't known any better. Unfortunately, I did, and after too many scary ghost movies in my lifetime, I had to wonder if Lilly Devine was standing right at my shoulder, covered in blood, staring at me.

I hid my unease behind a polite smile, watching Dickie for any signs that he was picking up something else lurking down here. He walked around, his EMF meter out in front of him.

Rex looked around the basement. "This place has potential, but I don't really want to put the work into it since I'll likely be gone by next summer."

I wondered if there were something I could do to speed up his departure.

"Are you sensing anything, Dickie?" Honey asked as she slowly spun in a circle with the camera rolling, careful to avoid Rex and me, as promised.

He shook his head. "She must stay in the bedroom where she was killed."

Based on my last visit, I disagreed, but I kept that to myself. "If you guys are finished here, we can move to the next place on the list."

While they filed up the stairs. I took one last look around. As before, the basement seemed fine, but I didn't. Without my ghost bloodhound by my side, I felt blind, skittish.

The next stop was a new listing located on the south end of Main Street on the way to Central City. I hadn't visited it before today, so I was as curious as the rest of my company.

Close to three thousand square feet, it was a Depression-era house with aluminum siding available for rent or sale since the owner had recently passed away. The décor was 1970s ornate with a gold velvet couch, white carpet, two chandeliers, and rich red curtains. Liberace could have lived there. The bedrooms came furnished with the latest fashions from that decade. Powder blue walls and lots of shag carpet. Even the kitchen was carpeted in a short loopy golden brown nap, reminding me of my grandmother's house when I was growing up.

"What's the story on this place?" Dickie asked me after our tour.

We stood in the kitchen while Honey went from room to room filming.

I leaned against the speckled Formica counter top, scanning my notes. "It's affordable and recently vacated." That was all I had on the cue cards. My script had been focused on the original antiques located throughout the house.

"Did the last owner die in here, too?" he asked.

"No, she was in the hospital. She'd lived here since the middle of last century, though."

Rex turned up his nose. "It looks like it."

"Dickie," Honey yelled from upstairs. "Come up here and tell me what you think of this."

He excused himself.

I was curious to see what she was talking about, but I was more interested in taking advantage of my moment alone with Rex. I waited until I heard Dickie's footfalls cross overhead before turning on Rex. "You need to find another Realtor."

"But I want you, Violet."

I fingered Tiffany's business card in my coat pocket. "You don't always get what you want."

"Is that a challenge?"

"Did you really think you could walk back into my life and plant yourself in my bed, Rex?"

He strolled closer, his eyelids lowered, his expression flirty. "I still remember exactly how you like to be touched."

I shuddered, repulsed by his attempt to turn me on. A plane ticket to South America with his name on it would really light my fire. "For you, it would require something longer than a ten foot pole."

"There was a time when you couldn't keep your hands off of me."

"People change," I said, backing into the corner between the sink and stove. "Young girl crushes die a horrible death."

"I see the way you look at me, Violet." He encroached on my space, much like Detective Hawke had earlier.

"Good. Then you've noticed the disgust and loathing hovering in this area." I circled my face.

"I've noticed the passion boiling inside of you when you stare at me." He leaned toward me, his mouth way too close.

I reared back, gripping a cupboard door to keep my balance. "Trust me, that's not passion."

He tipped up my chin. "The attraction is still there."

This was turning into a B-rated Mexican soap opera, all *pasión caliente* and bad acting. I'd stomached about enough. "Rex, stop it."

"It's raging between us, Violet, burn—"

I slammed the cupboard door into his face, a trick I'd learned from an old Tom and Jerry cartoon. However, unlike Tom the cat, Rex's face wasn't as flat as a pancake when I pulled the door away. But his nose was bleeding.

I pointed at it. "Oops. You've got a little blood there." A couple of drips splattered onto his white shirt. Or maybe a lot.

He pinched his nose and looked up to the ceiling, cursing. "God damn it, Violet! What's wrong with you?"

"No means no, jerk," I said, pulling a towel out of one of the drawers. I hoped the house's selling agent hadn't taken a towel inventory.

"Holy crap," Honey said from the doorway. "What happened to him?"

Rex glared at me, continuing to hold his nose.

I shrugged. "I think it might have been the ghost of the old woman who lived here."

Honey started to raise her camera to film it, but I shook my hand at her, reminding her of our agreement.

"You need some ice," she told Rex. Setting her camera down, she went to the freezer. "There are no ice trays in here."

Been there, done that, I thought. What was it about the senior citizens around here being anti-ice tray?

"Is it broken?" Honey asked, reaching toward Rex, who pulled away.

"Don't touch it."

"What happened?" Dickie asked, joining our bloody party.

"The cupboard might be haunted," I told him, keeping a straight face. "It swung right open and slammed Mr. Conner in the nose. Maybe the ghost doesn't like men."

Dickie scratched his neck. "I did feel a bit nauseated upstairs a moment ago."

"I felt nauseated a moment ago, too," I said. "Right before that cupboard door swung open. How crazy is that?"

Rex grumbled through the towel.

"We should get him to the hospital," Honey suggested.

"I'm fine. It's not broken," he shot me a snarl and then winced from wrinkling his nose. "It just hurts like hell."

"Maybe we should drop you off back at your car," she said.

That reminded me of Miss Geary going at it with a fire poker and gave me another idea.

"That's probably for the best," Rex conceded. "I'll have to reschedule with you, Violet."

"I'll see if I can fit you in another time." As in *never*.

I ushered everyone out the front door. "If you guys will give me a second, I need to make sure the upstairs toilet is turned off. Some ghosts have reputations for making toilets run and waste water."

I closed the door behind them. Taking the stairs two at a time, I pulled out my phone. I hit the call button after looking out the window to make sure all three were in the car below.

"What do you want, Parker?" Cooper's voice was as terse and sandpapery as ever.

"I need a favor."

"You have the wrong number."

"No, don't hang up."

He waited.

"I need a favor, please."

"What?"

"There's a black sports car parked behind Calamity Jane Realty. Both headlights are busted out."

"What are you trying to do, get a badge for crime fighter of the week?"

I ignored his sarcasm because I really wanted him to deliver on this favor. "Will you send one of your men over there and ticket the driver for broken headlights?"

Silence again from Cooper's end. Then I heard his chair creak. "Let me get this straight. You are calling Deadwood's only paid detective with a request to ticket some driver with broken headlights."

"Yep, that's about right."

He laughed, a genuine, gut-busting laugh. Had I been sitting across from him, I probably would have fallen over backwards in my chair in shock.

When he stopped laughing, he said, "You're a funny woman, Violet Parker."

"I'm serious. Will you please do me this one favor?"

"No. I don't do personal favors, especially for the woman who probably bashed out the headlights of a perfectly good '69 Camaro."

"It's not Doc's car and I'm not the one who did the bashing."

"Who did?"

"That's not important," I said. "The point is they are broken and I feel it's unsafe for him to be driving around Deadwood."

"Bullshit, Parker. Who owns the car?"

"Some guy."

"I'm not sending out anyone unless you come clean."

I covered the mouthpiece and swore at Cooper, then put the phone back to my ear. "Fine."

"I heard what you called me."

"I don't know what you're talking about. There must have been some interference."

"It was your voice," his chair creaked again, "and I do not fornicate with monkeys."

Oops, he had heard me. "Are we going to do this or not?"

"Give me a name, Parker."

"Rex Conner."

This time the pause was filled with the sound of his breathing. I wondered if he remembered where he'd heard that name before.

"The same Rex Conner that inspired you to throw up all over my tie back in August?" he asked.

Yep, he remembered. "That's him."

"What is the father of your children doing in town?"

"Harassing me." I glanced down at the Subaru. I really needed to get down there before one of them came looking for me.

"Would you like to file a report on why you bashed out his headlights?"

"No. I didn't do it, damn it." I sighed. "You know what, never mind, Cooper. I gotta go."

"Violet," the terseness in his voice stopped me from hanging up.

"What?"

"Is there something you need to tell me about Rex Conner?"

"Yes. He's an even bigger asshole than you are!" I hung up then, blaspheming both men all of the way downstairs.

"Everything okay?" Dickie asked when I crawled in the Subaru.

"Just dandy." I backed out of the drive and headed back to Calamity Jane's to drop off Rex. Halfway there, my phone rang. I used the earpiece Doc had bought me. "Hi, Jerry."

"Violet, I had an idea. Scrap that last place on the list and take them up to the Carhart house."

"What?" That was the last place I wanted to go. I was allergic to the ghost in that house. She used people like puppets to talk to me, making me break out in panic. "Jerry, that place is on the sale pending board."

Zeke and Zelda Britton were in the process of obtaining financing to buy it.

"I know, but take them there anyway. Ray informed me it's definitely haunted and you have a history with the entity there. Maybe this ghost friend of yours will make an appearance for Dickie and Honey."

Ray! That meddling son of a bitch. "Fine, but I have to drop off Mr. Conner first."

"Why? Did he choose one of the first two places?"

"No. He had a little accident and needs to ice his nose."

"Damn." There were a couple of seconds of silence, then, "Well, in the meantime, let's focus on Dickie and Honey. Get out there and wow them, Violet."

"Will do." I hung up as I was pulling into the parking lot.

"You've got to be kidding me," I heard Rex mutter.

Up ahead, a familiar sedan sat blocking Rex's Jaguar, a red flashing bubble perched on the roof.

I eased to a stop in front of Cooper's car. Rex was out the

door before I shifted into park.

"Sit tight for a minute," I told Dickie and Honey, "and we'll head to another house I think you'll really like."

I stepped outside in time to hear Rex say, "Hello," in a nasally voice.

Cooper eyed him from head to toe, hovering on the bloody towel before his gaze slid to me. He shook his head. "Unbelievable."

"What?" I feigned innocence.

"What's the problem, officer?" Rex dabbed at his nose.

"Are you the owner of this car?"

Rex nodded.

"I was cruising by and noticed you're missing both headlights."

"I had a little accident this morning," Rex explained. "I'll get them fixed in the next day or two. They have to special order the headlights."

Cooper nodded. "Right. There aren't many Jaguars up here in the hills." He flipped open his notepad. "According to your tags, you're Rex Conner."

"That's me."

Cooper tapped his notepad. "Well, Mr. Conner, I'm going to need you to come over to the station with me."

"For broken headlights?"

"No, regarding a recent murder case."

"Murder? What are you talking about? You must have the wrong guy."

"Is this your phone number?" Cooper asked, showing Rex a number on the paper.

Rex nodded. "That's my cell phone."

"Right." Cooper pocketed the notebook. "Mr. Conner, your number was listed in the phone of a murder victim found on August thirteenth."

"What?"

"Would you like me to drive you back to wherever you're staying so you can get a new shirt, or would you rather come straight over to the station with me now?"

"This is insane. I'm a well-known scientist." Rex rearranged the towel he still held to his nose, frowning down at the blood-stained cloth.

"And I'm a small town detective. Now that we're done with the meet and greet session, let's go."

"Fine. My bags are in the trunk. I'll grab a shirt and we can go to the police station."

"We could swing by the ER if you'd like. It's right down the road."

"No." He touched his nose gingerly. "It's just bruised." Rex glared at me over the towel. "In spite of someone's attempt to turn it inside out."

"Lucky you." Cooper hit me with a steely glance as he held open his passenger door. "Mine ended up broken."

Chapter Thirteen

All the way up the hill into Lead I dodged and weaved. Unfortunately it wasn't because of any other traffic, but rather a butt load of questions from Honey and Dickie about the blood-splattered history of the Carhart house. I made sure to skip over my bit part in the various tragedies that had been acted out there.

What I really needed was silence. I wanted to prepare for how I was going to make sure Prudence the ghost didn't actually join our party today while Dickie did his best to lure her out. Unlike Lilly Devine's place, I had a feeling it wouldn't matter at the Carhart house that Dickie wasn't as much of a medium as he said he was. His being open-minded about the possibility of paranormal activity would be all Prudence needed to get her toe in the door.

"What a lovely place," Honey said after I pulled into the Carhart driveway and cut the Subaru's engine. "Is it as pretty on the inside as out?"

I smiled at her in the rearview mirror. "It's a beautiful house," I answered with my old mantra.

I stared through the front windshield at the buttercream colored Gothic-Revival style house with its steeply pitched roof and even steeper cross gables. The Carhart family had meticulously maintained the place over the last few decades. I admired the house's elegant lines and point-arched windows that were emphasized by a fresh coat of chocolate-colored trim paint. In spite of all that had happened in there, the place had a nineteenth century charm that still shined through.

I looked up at the attic window. There was nobody standing there looking out, but I knew that Prudence waited inside; I just couldn't see her. Thinking about that gave me a rash of chills. I dropped my hands from the steering wheel before Honey noticed my goosebumps.

"If you two are ready, I'll take you on a tour of the house." The lockbox still hung from the front door, and I knew the code by heart. Wanda was staying with her sister until closer to the final move-out date. She'd left most of the furnishings in the place for now, according to what she had told me on the phone a week ago.

"I can't wait to see the inside," Honey said, shoving open the door.

I could. The plush shag rugs, birch floors, stained glass, and impressive staircase had lost their appeal.

"You say this place is haunted?" Dickie asked as we climbed the porch steps.

"That's the rumor," I told him, punching in the code. I held open the door and followed them inside. The place smelled like caramel mixed with vanilla today. My sweet tooth panged in my mouth. "I have a favor to ask of you two."

"Sure," Honey said, digging her video camera out.

I wasn't sure how to make this request without creating more questions, so I spit it out. "Don't touch me while we're in here."

I shut the door and locked it.

They both turned, frowning at me in unison.

Jinx, I thought.

"I'm sorry," Honey said, "if I made you uncomfortable in either of the other places. I didn't mean to."

"You didn't," I said with a smile, trying to smooth things over. "It's an odd request that I have while we're in this particular house." When they both continued to frown at me without moving, I added, "I like my personal space buffer."

"Does this have something to do with a ghost?" Dickie asked.

Definitely! "What do you mean?"

"I mean have you found that if you maintain a certain amount of space around you that you have more brushes with the ghost?"

It was the opposite actually, but he didn't need to know it.

"Yes, that's it."

He nodded. "I understand. I need a certain amount of space in order to make sure the interactions are pure."

I gave them wide berth in the foyer and led them into the living room. "Notice the wrought iron vent grates and the original molding from when the house was built."

Honey ooooohed.

Dickie whistled through his teeth. "Nice chandeliers."

"Wow," Honey walked around touching things, seeming to forget she had a camera clutched in one of her hands. "This place is beautiful."

I told everyone so.

After touring them through the dining room and kitchen, I instructed them to head upstairs and I'd catch up in a minute, claiming the need to check my emails. As soon as I heard them talking upstairs, I scurried into the kitchen over by the stove, facing the slatted pantry doors.

"Prudence," I whispered to the ceiling, feeling sort of like Samantha on *Bewitched* calling for her mother. "I need you to keep quiet today and not play any of your parlor tricks with my guests." I started to walk away and then returned to my spot by the stove, looking up at the ceiling again. "Don't bug me about finding the timekeeper either. I've no idea where you might have lost a watch. The 'librarian' you requested will be here soon."

Zelda Britton, who was in the process of purchasing this place with her husband, was a librarian. If Prudence's previous request for such a person meant something else, she would have to be mad at herself for being overly cryptic when giving me orders from beyond.

I found Dickie upstairs in Wanda's bedroom, checking out her walk-in closet. The bare light bulb overhead flickered as I entered the small, elongated rectangular room

"You looking for a new dress?" I joked.

He chuckled. "Gingham is my favorite, you know."

"I'm sure your fans would adore you in a nice red pattern."

I thought I heard the floor creak out in the bedroom, but when I peeked out the closet doorway, nobody was there. I narrowed my eyes, hoping Prudence was going to be a good girl today.

Dickie touched the sleeve of one of Wanda's black and yellow gingham dresses. "Really? I always thought black was more my color."

I'd noticed that. I led the way out of the closet.

He looked around the room with its antique headboard and dressers and soft beige tones. "It's hard to believe all of that violence you told us about happened in this house. It feels so serene, so calm."

I thought of my last encounter with Prudence here and held in a snort. "The owner has taken wonderful care of it over the years in spite of the violence."

That made me wonder if Prudence had been whispering in Wanda Carhart's ear all of these years on the decorating. To look at Wanda and her *Little House on the Prairie* outfits, one wouldn't think of her as knowing how to deck out a house, yet this place deserved to be the cover model for an antique homes magazine. The woman had trouble keeping ice cube trays in the fridge, for Pete's sake.

We strolled out into the hall.

"Is that the attic?" Dickie pointed at the door in the ceiling. At my nod, he asked, "May we go up there?"

I hesitated. I thought of the attic as Prudence's lair and wasn't sure she'd like me allowing these strangers to trudge around up there. On the other hand, there were some interesting antiques up there and I was pretty certain Honey would enjoy getting some of it on film. In the end, my boss's wishes for me to make Dickie and Honey happy won out over Prudence's wishes. After all, it was a minor blip in her world.

"Sure." I grabbed the broomstick handle with a hook on the end and handed it to Dickie, careful not to get too close. "Just be careful on the ladder. It's a little rickety."

"Honey?" Dickie called as he pulled open the attic door.

I unfolded the attached ladder for him.

"Honey, where are you?" he called again.

"Maybe she's in one of the other two bedrooms." I brushed

off my hands. "I'll go check while you head up."

I made sure Dickie made it up the ladder okay and then headed off in search of Honey. She was nowhere to be found. I even returned to Wanda's room and checked the closet, but found it empty as well.

"You okay up there?" I called to Dickie as I passed by the attic ladder.

I heard a sneeze, and then, "Yeah. There's lots of interesting furniture up here. Tell Honey to hurry up before my lungs fill with dust."

If I could find her, I'd happily deliver the message. I was anxious to get the hell out of the house before my lungs filled with panic.

"Honey?" I called, walking down the stairs.

The front living room was empty, as was the dining room. "Honey?"

I stepped into the kitchen and found Honey standing with her back to me next to the stove, almost exactly where I'd stood fifteen minutes before.

"There you are," I said, walking around in front of her. She had the camera held arm's length in front of her at an awkward angle, eyelevel yet tipping to the left. The red record light was blinking, so I tried to keep out of the shot. "Oops, sorry about that, Ho—"

Then I looked into her face and choked on the rest of her name. Her eyes were rolled back, white. Her jaw hung slack with a line of drool running down one side of her mouth.

"Honey?" I whispered and reached out toward her. Then I remembered where I was and pulled back, afraid of who would start talking if I touched her.

"Honey," I said in a stronger voice. "Can you hear me?"

The drool stretched down to her collarbone.

I looked around, saw a jar of wooden spoons next to the stove, and grabbed one. I poked her in the ribs. "Honey," I said, "come back."

The camera tipped further. I reached for it, afraid she'd let go in her trance. Extracting it from her hand, I placed it on the counter, and hit the Stop button on top of it. It dinged twice.

A gasp from Honey dragged my focus back to her face. Her eyelids fluttered, her mouth opening and closing.

Crap, what was going on in her head? I suspected this was Prudence's doing, but what if Honey was diabetic or epileptic? I dropped the spoon and grabbed her by the shoulders, squeezing, throwing my Prudence aversion aside. "Honey, open your eyes," I said in a calm, firm voice.

Her eyelids continued to flutter, but her mouth stopped its

dying fish routine.

"Honey, if you can hear me," I thought of something that might pull her back from wherever, "Dickie needs you up in the attic to film some antiques."

Her eyes closed. She started to lean backwards, pulling me forward until I stumbled on the toes of her boots, but then I caught the counter and braced myself. She seemed to snap back upright, almost head butting my chin.

She coughed and gasped a couple of times before meeting my gaze. "Why are you looking at me like that? What?"

"Do you remember anything that happened in the last few minutes?"

She touched her jaw, and then frowned down at her hand. "Yuk, is there something on my chin?"

"You were drooling."

"Oh, gross! I'm sorry."

"Don't be. Do you have any medical conditions that would cause you to have a seizure?"

She leaned back against the counter, shaking her head.

I put my arm around her shoulders. "Let's get you into the sitting room and settled on the couch. I'll bring you something to drink."

She let me lead her out of the kitchen. "How long was I out?"

"I don't know." I pointed at the leather sofa, moving her toward it. "I walked in the kitchen a few minutes ago and found you looking catatonic, holding the ..." Wait a second. I remembered the way the camera was pointing. She'd been filming herself. "Out of curiosity, when prepping for a show like this, do you ever film yourself talking into the camera?"

"No." Honey dropped into the couch cushions, her frown deepening. "I was in the kitchen."

"I know." I thought we'd established that already.

"No, you don't understand," she leaned back into the cushions, covering her eyes with the heels of her hands. "The last thing I remember is filming that upstairs bedroom that looks out over that huge pit next door."

"You don't remember coming down here?"

"No. I remember hearing you coming up the stairs as I focused on a weird drawing on the wall and that's it. Then I woke up in the kitchen, drooling like a zombie."

I'd seen plenty of zombies last month. She wasn't anything close to them or I would have run screaming out the door.

"Was I filming when you found me?"

"I'm not sure," I sort of fibbed. I wasn't one hundred percent sure what had been going on when I walked in, and until I got a peek at the video, I wasn't sure I wanted her to know what I thought I had seen.

"Where's my camera?"

"In the kitchen. I'll bring it when I get you some water." She took a shaky breath. "Maybe we should drive you to the hospital, make sure you're okay and didn't have some kind of seizure." Although I feared the "seizure" had been done by Prudence, not anything chemically or physically within Honey herself.

"Thanks, but I feel fine, Violet, just a little tired."

"Tired?" I chewed on my lower lip. "That's not good. It could be a sign of another episode coming on."

"We can wait a few minutes longer," Honey said, her breathing growing steadier. "I used to have panic attacks at my old job. I've learned a few tricks to level out my blood pressure."

I stood at the edge of the white shag carpet, kneading my hands together. "I'll go get some water. You relax there for a few minutes."

Hustling into the kitchen, I went straight for the camera and took it into the pantry, closing the door behind me. Light filtered in through the slats. In the semi-gloom, I hit the Rewind button, counted to ten, and then hit Play. I adjusted the volume so only I could hear it.

I watched the video as Honey focused on the pit through the window, mentioning the depth I'd told her and how long it had sat abandoned.

My phone vibrated in my pocket. I pulled it out, seeing Jerry's name and a *How's it going?* text. Now was not the time, Jerry, I thought and started to shove my phone in my pants again but then had an idea. I hit the button to record a video on my phone and held it close to the camera's screen as Honey exited the bedroom.

The view on the screen was upside down now, though, and bumping as Honey walked along the upstairs hallway and down the stairs. She must not have realized she'd left it on. I leaned closer, trying to hear if she was commenting on anything, but there was nothing but a slight static as it bumped into her thigh with each step.

On the screen she made a straight shot for the kitchen, the staircase disappearing as Honey turned the corner at the threshold. I could see the upside down green refrigerator, including the apple magnet Wanda had left there with a note apologizing for the lack of ice trays.

Then the screen shifted violently as Honey lifted it, turning it around to focus on her chest and mouth.

"Where have you been, Violet?" When Honey spoke my name in the video, I almost peed my pants right there in Wanda's pantry.

For one thing, Honey's mouth moved like someone else was pulling strings to open and close her lower jaw. I'd seen that done before in this very house, and there was no getting used to the lightning bolt of fear that shot through me each time it happened.

But what had my heart cowering against my ribs in panic was the lilting sound of Prudence's voice instead of Honey's huskier tones.

I leaned closer to the video as the camera lens jerked up a few more inches. I might have screamed had I not seen Honey with her eyes rolled up so only the whites showed when I first walked into the kitchen.

Honey's jaw unhinged and moved up and down a couple of times before Prudence's words came out, as if she were trying to get the hang of the controls in Honey's head.

"We have no time for these games, Violet. Every night they grow stronger. You must stop these attempts to avoid me and pay attention to my instructions. I have waited too long. Your life, among many, will depend upon what I share."

I could hear my voice in the camera calling Honey's name in the background.

A drop of drool leaked from the corner of Honey's mouth as Prudence worked the strings a few more times in silence.

"I speak not of a timepiece," she finally said through Honey's mouth again, "but the keeper of time. I must confer with Miss Hoont." Honey's head fell to the side, like Prudence had dropped a string. Her mouth still moved jerkily open and close. "We must act quickly. If the librarian does not arrive soon, bring me one who can bridge the channel."

I heard my voice coming closer in the video, calling for Honey.

The camera shifted close to Honey's rolled back eyes. "Return the teeth to me!" Prudence's voice was a loud, sharp whisper at this point. Then the camera pulled back to arm's length.

"There you are," I heard my voice say on the camera and then a flash of my silver sweater and hair passed to the side of Honey.

"Violet?" Honey called from the sitting room. "Where are you?"

Shit! I hit the Stop button, my breath as loud as a locomotive in the closet-sized pantry. Why couldn't Prudence leave me alone just this once? What did she mean by bringing her the one who opens channels? Why couldn't she speak in layperson terms for me?

"Coming, Honey," I yelled out the pantry door.

I held the camera in the slatted light and hit the Rewind button again. When I hit Play, we were back up in the bedroom with Honey talking in the background in her normal voice. I put the lens cap on the camera and hit the Record button. On my phone, I stopped the video recording and pocketed it. While Honey's camera recorded the backside of a black lens cap over top of Prudence's message, I closed the doors and hustled over to the sink, running water.

I peeked out the kitchen doorway. "Sorry, I got a text from Jerry that distracted me and then I couldn't find the glasses. Your water is on the way."

"Thanks," Honey was standing staring out the window where I'd once watched two women fight and then kiss and make up. "Sorry to yell like that. I thought I saw this curtain move on its own and I kind of freaked out."

"There's a register below it," I pointed out.

"Oh, whew!" Honey said. "For a moment there, I thought the ghost had paid me a visit."

The ghost had, but nobody needed to know that but me.

Dickie came down the stairs. "Where have you been, Honey? I needed you in the attic."

While Honey explained her odd behavior, I slipped back into the kitchen, took my time getting the water, and brought two glasses to them.

"Have you seen Honey's camera, Violet?" Dickie asked as I handed his water to him.

The urge to apologize for the lack of ice cubes made it to the tip of my tongue before I bit it back, along with a bubble of hysterical giggles. Dear Lord, I was turning into Wanda Carhart.

"It's in the kitchen. I'll go get it."

Again, I took my time, banging cupboard doors, before sneaking into the pantry and checking how far I'd recorded over. The blackness from the lens cap filled the screen as I fast-forwarded through it. I breathed a sigh of relief when at the end of the blackness there was nothing else.

I shut it off and carried it out into the sitting room. "I had to put a few things away Ms. Carhart had left out. Here's your camera. It was over by the flour canister."

"How bizarre. I don't remember even setting it down."

"Dickie, don't you think we should take Honey to the clinic to have a doctor look at her? See if she had some kind of seizure?" I wanted to get the hell out of this house now before Prudence made an even bolder attempt to talk to me.

"Maybe Violet's right, Honey." He stood, rubbing his forearm and wincing.

I glanced down and notice a large bluish-green lump on it. "Is that a bruise?" I asked, stepping closer.

He frowned down at it. "Yeah. I got it when I was up in the attic."

"Did you run into something?" Like a ghost obsessed with time and teeth?

"No." He glanced up the stairs. "That's what's so weird. I didn't touch anything. I was staring down at a crib that looked like something from the late nineteenth century and reached down to touch what looked like a snip of blond hair. My fingers had almost touched it when something seemed to hit my forearm. Then I heard Honey call for me, so I went over to the ladder, but nobody was there. After that I noticed the bruise on my arm."

I had a feeling I knew who'd bruised him. "Did anything else happen in the attic?"

"Yes," he frowned up the stairs then turned back to me. "It kind of freaked me out."

That surprised me since Dickie claimed to be on a chatting basis with ghosts. "What's that?"

"I was heading back over to the crib when it felt like someone reached into my mouth and yanked on my tooth."

"What do you mean?" Honey asked.

Dickie opened his mouth and pointed at one of his canines. "See this one? I could swear it felt like someone reached in there with a pair of pliers and tugged."

I took a step backward. "You're kidding me."

"As a matter of fact," Dickie said, "I think the sucker is loose now."

Return the teeth to me! I heard Prudence's voice echo in my head. Had she tried to take one of Dickie's teeth? I covered my mouth with my hand, afraid I might scream if I didn't block it.

What did Prudence want with those damned teeth? I gulped, worrying about what she might do to Zelda if I didn't bring the box of teeth back.

More importantly, how in the hell was I going to get them back from Cooper?

Chapter Fourteen

One dark and spooky Halloween night long ago, a man wearing a hockey mask wielding a revving chainsaw had chased me out of a haunted house. I'd screamed so loud while running for my life that my voice had been hoarse for two days.

Prudence had now one-upped that night's chase on the scare-the-shit-out-of-me scale.

I managed to keep my tremors in check during the drive back down to Calamity Jane's. Dickie and Honey were both wiggling in their seats with excitement, full of hot air on how they could include the Carhart house in their show. I wasn't going to be the one to inform them that the Carhart house was sort of off limits to them. That was Jerry's job.

My job was to show them a good time. As far as I was concerned, I'd delivered and then some thanks to Prudence.

By the time I replied to a few emails and wrapped up for the day it was nearing dinner time. Jerry practically patted me on the head as I left. I half expected him to scratch me behind the ears and offer me a Scooby snack for doing my job so well with the television folks.

I rolled home in the Picklemobile, refraining from chewing on my knuckles about what Prudence's messages meant until I could see Doc and show the video to him. He would help me make sense of it all.

At least I hoped so.

There were three vehicles in the drive when I arrived at Aunt Zoe's—Harvey's pickup, Doc's Camaro, and Jeff Wymonds' truck with its extra big tires. The last one made me pause. What was Jeff doing here and how was Doc feeling about it?

I collected my wits along with my purse. The cold crisp

October evening and the memories of Honey's puppet performance at the Carhart house had me shivering while I scurried up the walk. The screen door creaked open as I hit the top step.

Doc stood there in the same clothes he'd been wearing when I had seen him in the parking lot behind Calamity Jane's.

"Hi," I stopped in front of him, eyeing him up and down, making sure my kids hadn't done any visible damage. "It looks like Addy and Layne didn't leave any bruises or claw marks on you." I hoped he hadn't been waiting for me so that he could tag me and then run for his life and never look back.

"No injuries." His grin spread up to his dark eyes. "They aren't as rough on me as their mother, the bruiser."

I made a fist and threw a pretend punch.

He caught my hand and used it to tug me closer. "How'd it go today?" he asked, fingering one of my loose curls.

I wasn't sure if he meant with Rex, the television folks, or Prudence, so I started with the one unsettling me the most. "Prudence wants her teeth back."

His brow creased. "That's going to be tough to deliver unless you have a plan on how we can break into the evidence room at the Deadwood Police Station."

"Well, one idea did come to mind."

"Uh oh."

"I was thinking you could distract Cooper while I sneaked in and grabbed the goods."

"I don't think Cooper's coworkers would let you through the front door these days without hitting the silent alarm." He pulled me toward him, lowering his lips. "Kiss me 'hello,' Boots."

I obliged without hesitation. He tasted citrusy and safe, like Aunt Zoe's lemonade and home-sweet-home. I went up on my tip-toes and dove in for seconds, thirsty for more after the day I'd had. As I burrowed into his warmth, he wrapped me in his arms, enveloping me in his subtle yet spicy cologne, along with a hint of tomato sauce. He must have been cooking dinner when I pulled into the drive.

Our "hello" tongue tango deepened into a "come to bed

with me" rhumba. The temptation to sneak him into the hall coat closet and forget about reality for a few sighing breaths flared.

A crash in the kitchen doused the flame. I groaned and detached from Doc's embrace.

"Harvey's making lasagna," Doc explained, towing me inside and closing the door behind us.

That explained the tomato I'd smelled. The thought of Harvey's lasagna had drool pooling in my mouth.

"By the way," Doc said, "we have company."

I wasn't sure by his even expression if this was a major problem or a minor annoyance. "I noticed. What's Jeff doing here?"

"We ran into Kelly and him down on Main Street and Addy invited them here for dinner."

"Wasn't that polite of her," I said with a dose of sarcasm, kicking off my heels. I'd be sure to give her ear a tug for dragging Jeff here when she knew Doc was staying for dinner.

"It's not a big deal." Doc winked at me. "He can look all he wants, so long as he doesn't touch."

I didn't even like Jeff looking after his many comments about wanting to see me barefoot and pregnant. He made me worry about getting knocked up by telekinesis alone somehow.

"Cooper called me looking for you," Doc said.

Was he sure it was Cooper, or had it been Hawke pretending to be Cooper again? I hadn't been sure myself a short time ago when I'd seen the number on my cell phone screen, nor had I wanted to talk to either man right then, so I'd kicked the call to voicemail to deal with later. "Did he leave a message?"

"Yes. He wants you to come to the station tomorrow morning."

I cursed under my breath. "Did he say why?"

Did it have anything to do with his tea and crumpets with Rex this afternoon?

"Something about a potential assault charge."

"You're kidding." I crossed my arms over my chest and set my chin. "I didn't hit the son of a bitch that hard." Hell, he'd only bled a little and out of only one nostril.

Doc's chuckle stopped short. "Yeah, I *was* kidding. Cooper mentioned that he needed to confirm some details on one of your 'unsolved messes'—that's what he called it."

My chin lowered a few notches. "Oh. Okay."

His dark eyes squeezed into a squint. "What do you mean you didn't hit him that hard? Did you head butt Cooper again?"

"No." I lowered my voice, glancing around to make sure no other ears were present. "Mr. Conner had a little accident this afternoon."

"Really?" The lines on Doc's forehead flipped from vertical to horizontal. "What happened?"

I didn't want Doc to think I was trying to make him jealous, so I kept it brief. "He stepped too far into my personal comfort zone."

"And?"

"And he accidentally ran his face into a cupboard door and got a bloody nose."

"I see." Doc's jaw tightened. "And so it begins."

What did he mean by that?

I didn't have time to find out because right then Jeff Wymonds strolled out from the kitchen, wiping his hands on a dishtowel and tossing it over his shoulder. It flew through the air, hit the wall, and fell to the floor. Sometimes I understood why his wife had left him for another woman.

"Violet Parker," he said, "I hear you're thinking about selling the Galena House."

My mouth fell open. "How did you hear that?"

Freesia had dropped off the listing agreement this afternoon while I was at the Carhart house.

"I've told you before, it's a small town."

"Not that small."

Jeff looked at Doc. "Do you mind if I have a minute alone with our Realtor?"

"Nope," Doc started to walk around me.

"Doc, wait." I stopped him, plucking my cell phone from my purse and handing it to him. "Check out the recording I made today."

His gaze moved to my phone and back to me, one eyebrow lifting. "Okay" he said, his tone suspicious.

"Alone," I added.

Jeff snickered. "You should be careful making X-rated videos of yourself on your phone, Violet Parker. That could easily get into the wrong hands."

I shot Jeff a 'no shit, bozo' glare. To Doc, I clarified, "It's not of me."

"Bummer, dude," Jeff consoled Doc.

"I'll go take a look now." Doc gave my arm a squeeze and left with my phone.

Jeff watched Doc disappear into the kitchen, then turned back to me. "Harvey tells me that you and Doc Nyce hooked up."

I wasn't sure exactly what he meant by that. "We're dating, if that's what you mean."

"Are you seeing anyone else?"

Where was this heading? "No, just Doc." One man was enough for me.

"Whew!" Jeff wiped his brow, his smile wide with what seemed to be relief.

"Were you worried about me seeing someone else besides Doc?"

Just a few weeks ago, Jeff had smelled beef jerky on my lips and had latched onto my face in what he called a kiss. The way his tongue had shoved aside my uvula, it had felt more like he was trying to plant one of those sharp-toothed alien babies in my stomach.

"Yeah, me." He took my hand, obviously mistaking my befuddled expression for something else. "I didn't know how to let you down easy."

"Let me down where?" Had I missed the first few pages of this chapter in the Jeff and Violet story?

"I'm seeing someone." He grinned sheepishly. "Well, not officially, but we're screwing around every chance we get."

"Oh, that's ... uh ... wonderful."

Hallmark needed to make a card that said: *I'm positively thrilled you're getting laid!*

"I was going to keep waiting for you, Violet Parker, but my plow was getting rusty and needed a good greasing."

I tried not to let my grimace show too much. "Well, I'm glad you've found someone to grease it for you."

"If you change your mind about your client-with-benefits buddy," he nudged his chin toward the kitchen.

"Doc's my boyfriend," I clarified in case Jeff thought he might come around looking for a *greasing* from me in the future. "We're pretty serious." I was pretty serious about Doc, anyway, so it wasn't a total embellishment.

"If you say so, Violet Parker." Jeff mock-punched me in the shoulder. "But if you find yourself in need of a good stud," he winked, "you know who to call."

I sighed. "Jeff, you just told me you were seeing someone else. Don't you think it's disrespectful to proposition me while you're sleeping with her?"

"I'm not talking about me." He pointed his thumb at his chest. "This stud is busy in the barn. I have a good buddy who's got a reputation for helping lonely women de-stress," he made an intimate gesture, "if you know what I mean."

Eww. "Gotcha."

"His plow is super-sized." He held out his hands like he was telling a big fish story and waggled his blond eyebrows.

I wrinkled my nose. "I'd rather not talk about farm animals or equipment any more tonight." I had teeth to get back from a prickly detective.

"Okey dokey, but let me add that my wife left her favorite dildo behind if you'd rather borrow that."

A used dildo? My, oh my, how sweet of him to offer.

I forced a change of subject. "Who told you I was selling the Galena House?"

"Freesia Tender did. I ran into her at the store yesterday. She'd seen your For Sale sign in my front yard and wanted to know how things were going for us."

"What did you tell her?"

"I told her that the garage roof explosion was my fault not

yours, and that you were a good Realtor who had your shit together."

"Thank you for that … I think."

"I also told her that you didn't believe in ghosts and liked to get really friendly with your clients."

My neck warmed. "Well, you didn't need to go that far."

"Don't worry. I told her that you're only into men so she was safe."

Wow. The heat spread to my cheeks. I was surprised Freesia went ahead and signed the listing agreement after talking to Jeff. I tried to come up with something nice in return, recognizing his attempt to help underneath his blunders. "I appreciate the reference, Jeff."

"Sure thing." He nodded toward the kitchen. "I hope you don't mind if Kelly and I stay for dinner. She's having fun with Addy and Layne, and old man Harvey's lasagna is legendary in this town."

"Not at all." Especially since Jeff's plow was now being greased in somebody else's barn.

"I promised your boyfriend I'd keep my hands off of you."

Jeff said that as if he and I shared a history involving more than one slobbery, tongue jab at my tonsils. "And how did Doc take that?"

Jeff guffawed. "He told me—"

"Violet," Harvey said from the kitchen archway. "I need your help in here."

Damn. I sort of wanted to hear Doc's response to Jeff's promise to keep his hands to himself.

I led the way into the kitchen.

"'Bout time you got home, girl." Harvey handed me a basket full of pieces of French bread. He pointed at the butter dish sitting on the counter. "Get these ready for the oven and pour something to wet our whistles."

Jeff slid past me without trying to cop a feel for once and went out the back door where the three kids were playing in the yard. Doc must have slipped off to watch my Honey-the-Puppet video.

"How many of us are there?" I asked Harvey.

"Seven with the three kids. Your aunt's buns are bustlin' tonight what with the Oktoberfest bringin' tourists with overflowin' billfolds to the beer troughs down on Main Street."

Earlier this week Aunt Zoe had showed me the new glass beer mugs she'd created for the event. My fingers were crossed she sold out.

"Thanks for making dinner." I patted the old buzzard on the back as I moved past him toward the fridge.

"Welcome. You owe me two meals out now, you know. I'll be 'spectin' an extra round of desserts for feedin' your buddy, Wymonds, too."

"Put it on my tab."

"You can bet your momma's bloomers I will. Watch that lasagna."

"Watch it do what?" I asked, opening the fridge. "Burn?" I pulled out several bottles of beer and a pitcher of lemonade.

When I turned around, Harvey was gone and Doc was standing there instead. His grim expression said he and I were on the same page when it came to Prudence now. He took the pitcher from me, setting it on the table.

I placed the bottles next to it. "I'll grab some glasses."

He caught my arm, pulled out a chair, and pointed at it. "I'll get the glasses, you have a seat."

I nodded, relieved to plant my butt on a chair. I stretched my neck from side to side, working on getting rid of some of today's tension.

Doc came back, set a glass next to each plate, and then moved behind me. His hands went to work on the tight bow strings that were keeping my head from falling off and rolling across the floor.

"Are you okay?" he asked.

"I don't know." I felt detached from it all, like Prudence manipulating Honey had happened to somebody else, someone on a television show I'd been watching.

He squeezed and released several times, inciting grunts and moans from me. "That video was sort of creepy."

More like a shitload-full of creepy. "You should have seen it in person. I almost swallowed my tongue when I saw Honey standing there with just the whites of her eyes showing." I groaned in pain as his fingers strummed a string of tight muscles that seemed to shoot arrows into my brain. "To add to the freakiness, Dickie swore that while he was up in the attic someone tried to yank out one of his canine teeth."

"Christ. She really meant that last bit about wanting her teeth back, didn't she?"

I murmured in agreement as he worked on a muscle running behind my shoulder blade.

"Has Prudence ever made a point of contacting you from the kitchen before?" Doc asked.

"No, but I think I know why she chose that location this time around."

He squeezed and released again. "Oh, yeah?"

"When I first arrived today, I ushered Dickie and Honey upstairs to get them out of the way. Then I went into the kitchen where they couldn't hear me, stood in that very spot, and talked to Prudence aloud."

Doc's fingers paused. "Really?"

"That surprises you?" He should know the level of my insanity by now, I'd think.

"It wasn't that long ago when you thought I was nuts for believing in ghosts. Now you're—"

"I know, I know. But that was before Prudence, Kyrkozz, and you convinced me otherwise. Plus now I know you better, and I believe in you." I thought of the wicked things he'd done to me in the shower last time we had a chance to spend time in there. "And we've seen each other wet and naked several times."

That didn't really have anything to do with the subject of ghosts, but I wanted to change it to something that would warm the day's chills completely out of my system. Thinking about Doc in the shower was just the ticket.

He chuckled. "Not nearly enough."

I tapped his hands. "Don't stop yet."

"Tell you what," he leaned down and spoke in my ear,

"spend another night in my bed and I'll do a lot more." His lips grazed my neck.

Pleasure washed downward, leaving a trail of goosebumps on my arms as it rippled and flowed. I glanced toward the back door, making sure we didn't have any faces pressed against the glass. "Like what in particular?"

Before he could answer, I heard the front door shut.

I sat up, pulling away from his touch, trying not to look like we'd been up to any hanky panky.

Harvey paused in the kitchen archway, his gaze bouncing back and forth between us. He snorted, then walked over and dropped an envelope on the table in front of me. "Look what I found."

"What's that?"

"Open it and see."

I did, peeking inside, pulling out a cut and folded piece of yellowed newspaper. I unfolded the paper, my eyes scanning the lines of text.

"Where'd you get this?" I held out the decades old article about the severed heads found in the Galena House.

Harvey slipped on a pair of oven mitts. "My pappy was a doozy of a hoarder when it came to magazines and newspapers—oh, and whiskey bottles, lapper that he was." He opened the oven and pulled out a casserole dish of cheesy goodness that had my saliva glands kicking into high gear.

He set the dish on the stove top and leaned against the counter, hooking the big thumbs of the oven mitts in his suspenders. "Mama stopped crowin' at him to throw stuff away early on and started keepin' it all organized. She stored everything in date order until she passed. I tossed all those whisky bottles before the grass had even grown over my pappy's grave, but I couldn't bring myself to burn the history in those papers and magazines. Not after my mama spent so much time playin' librarian with them."

I looked at the paper again, reading the short article. The *Black Hills Trailblazer* hadn't wasted much print on it, unfortunately. There was a brief mention about a fourth body found all in one piece, nothing shriveled on it, though, just a regular murder. The grainy picture next to it was of the Galena House. The place looked pretty much the same, although the porch didn't look so rickety. I guess I'd hoped to see a picture of the shrunken heads, as gruesome as that would be.

"Thanks," I told Harvey as I handed the article to Doc, who'd settled into the chair next to me. "Now we have a definite date when the previous decapitations occurred and some details." What there were anyway.

While Doc read through the article, the back door opened and Jeff strolled in. He sniffed the air over the casserole dish and groaned, licking his chops.

Harvey snapped him with a dishtowel. "You're breathin' all over my masterpiece, ya lunk-head."

"I can't help it. I could smell that clear in the backyard and I haven't eaten since that big brat I had at the festival."

Doc handed the article back to me, shaking his head as if he'd read something he didn't like.

Harvey snapped Jeff again. "Go wash up."

Jeff started past the table and then paused. "What's that?" he asked, peering down at the article in my hand.

"Nothing," I said, folding the article. "Just an old article on the Galena House that Harvey brought to me since I'm going to be selling it."

Jeff pointed his index finger at me. "That reminds me of something Freesia told me." He looked back at Harvey. "Do you remember old Ms. Wolff, Harvey?"

Harvey busied himself with cutting the lasagna. "Sorta."

"She made some of the best homemade cookies," Jeff said, rubbing his stomach. "What did she say they were called? Oh yeah, peppernut cookies."

"When did you have her cookies?" I asked, surprised Jeff had known her.

"She used to set up a booth during Oktoberfest down near the Badlands section of Main Street when I was a kid. She and her girlfriend would sell all of these old-fashioned German sweets for dirt cheap."

"Girlfriend?" I asked. Jeff's wife had left him for another woman and now he had a chip on his shoulder when it came to females being friends.

"I never saw them kissing or anything like that, but they went all over town together."

"That's right," Harvey chimed in. "I'd done forgotten about their booth." He grinned at me. "I usually stayed close to the beer and brats during the festivities. That's where ya find the loose women looking for some German style lovin'."

I didn't even want to know what was involved in German style loving, so I moved the subject right along. "Who was this other woman?"

"Miss Zuckermann," Jeff answered. "She always made these hard fruit candies that had some natural herb extract in them. My mom loved them and would send us to buy a couple of bags worth. She'd hide them up in her closet so they'd last through the year." His nose wrinkled. "They always tasted like medicine to me."

"Are you talking about the same Zuckermann who owns the Candy Corral on Main Street?" Doc asked.

"Yep, that's her." Jeff said. "I noticed she closed up shop early today, skipping the festival for once. I figured she's all upset about her old girlfriend keeling over."

Somebody was sharing whispers about Ms. Wolff's death. It must have been Freesia.

Jeff knocked twice on the table. "I better go wash up so Harvey will let me eat." He headed through the archway into the dining room.

I looked at Harvey. "Maybe you and I need to go pay Miss Zuckermann a visit to give our condolences."

And maybe while we were there, Harvey could smooth talk her into sharing how well she knew Ms. Wolff and if she knew anyone who might have had a big enough grudge against her to come callin' with an axe in hand.

Doc nudged my thigh with his knee, his eyes warning. "You sure that's a good idea? Maybe you two should leave the comforting to Detective Cooper."

I guffawed. "He's about as comforting as hugging a ball of rusty barbed-wire."

Harvey set the lasagna on the table in front of us. "I'd bet my left nut that Coop's already been there to do his comforting."

I crossed my arms over my chest. "Why do you always bet your left nut and not your right?"

"It's smaller, hairier, and looks like a peach pit, not near as purty as my right one. I never bet my prize-winnin' ball."

I groaned.

"You had to ask," Doc said, chuckling.

"I should know better by now."

Harvey hollered out the back door for the kids to come in and wash their hands. Then he joined us at the table. "That article reminded me of something I want Coop to look into."

"What's that?" I asked, wondering how much sway Harvey had with his nephew these days now that he was associated with me.

"If the Deadwood police ever figured out what weapon was used to cut off those three heads way back when." Harvey spooned a scoop of lasagna onto one of the empty plates. "Remember," he said to me, "Mudder Brothers has quite a collection of sharp tools down in their basement."

I nodded, thinking of a certain pair of long, deadly scissors I'd used once myself that were now locked up in the Evidence room along with Prudence's teeth. "I thought Eddie Mudder made it through the suspect hoops, though."

"For his brother's death, sure. But this ain't his brother."

"Was Eddie even born when those heads were found?" Doc asked.

"No, but his wild-eyed daddy was. They carted him off in a padded wagon when I was still learning to shave and greasing my hair back."

"Let me get this straight." I wanted to make sure all three of us were on the same page, because Harvey sometimes skipped forward several chapters without telling me. "You think Eddie's dad killed the other three and now Eddie is following in his dad's footsteps?"

He shrugged and dished up another plate. "It's an idea I had

He shrugged and dished up another plate. "It's an idea I had when I saw some old obituaries in the newspapers while searchin' for this article. Eddie's dad used to be the embalmer at the funeral home back before it belonged to George and Eddie." He handed me a plate of lasagna.

I hadn't realized the Mudder boys were playing their part in a family tradition.

Harvey raised his bushy eyebrows. "Who'd know better how to deform a skull than someone who dabbles with corpses for a livin'?"

I picked at my lasagna, my appetite waning as I pictured Eddie in his rubber apron elbow deep in his work. Tomato sauce and blood were a bit too similar at the moment.

Handing a full plate to Doc, Harvey added, "After the Mudder Brothers fun you two had that night, I told Coop to ask Eddie about the creepy tools we saw in their basement."

"Wasn't there a scythe in there, too?" Doc asked me.

I nodded, staring at Harvey with my fork hesitating above the steaming cheese. "Did Coop ask him?"

Harvey grunted in acknowledgment.

Addy, Kelly, and then Layne came stumbling inside the back door, laughing and bumping into each other. Addy's chicken followed them inside using the cat door Aunt Zoe had installed last week for the damned bird.

"Addy, put that chicken in the basement." I thumbed toward the dining room. "Then go wash your hands—all of you."

After the three had tromped off, Harvey leaned forward. "Turns out George and Eddie weren't the collectors. Those tools have been in the family for a *looooong* time."

Chapter Fifteen

Saturday, October 6th

I dreamed that all of my teeth were being yanked out one-by-one.

Gasping awake, my nightmare continued when I realized there were fingers in my mouth gripping my bottom incisors. Then I realized they were my fingers and spit them out, wiping my hands off on my camisole, which was damp with sweat.

"Damn you, Prudence, and your obsession with teeth," I grumbled and rolled out of bed.

I checked the time via my cell phone. It was super early, as in dark o'clock still. Outside my window, the street was shadow-filled and empty. I opened my window, breathing in the fresh, cool air. The birds hadn't even started their pre-dawn chatter yet. I shivered as a breeze blew over my sweaty camisole and I shut the window.

Crud. I could really use someone to talk to right now, somebody who could help me forget about my problems long enough to catch a little more shuteye. I hesitated in front of my bedroom door, thinking of Aunt Zoe sleeping two doors down. I hated to wake her up, though. She'd looked so tired when she'd come in late after the first night of Oktoberfest. I wondered how much of it was due to a lack of sleep since that fight with Reid. Lately, she and I'd been wearing matching red-rimmed eyes in the mornings. She didn't talk about why, and I hadn't asked ... yet.

I slumped onto the bed, wondering if Natalie were awake yet down in Arizona. Probably not since she was with her cousins who liked to hang out at the bar into the wee hours.

I pulled up Doc's number, hesitated, and then hit the Call button.

It rang five times. "Violet?" his voice sounded rough.

"Were you sleeping?" What a dumb question. I'd already heard the answer in his voice.

"Are you okay?" he asked back.

"Yes." I touched my teeth. One seemed to wiggle a smidgeon. "I think."

"What time is it?"

"Early."

"Are your kids okay?"

"Yeah." I scrubbed some sleep from my eye. "I just ..." *needed to hear your voice*, "I had a nightmare."

There was a pause from his end. "Kyrkozz, Wolfgang, or Caly?"

"It was Prudence this time." I actually couldn't remember the details, only her face leaning over mine and the feeling of my teeth being tugged on. "She'd come to collect my canines."

"You want me to come over?"

"No, you might wake up Aunt Zoe and the kids."

"You could come over here."

"Harvey's on your couch again." Last night, the old goat had informed me that was where he'd be in case I needed my bodyguard. "He sleeps like a new mother."

I knew from experience that Harvey woke at the mere swish of a sock brushing over the carpet. There was no sneaking past him in the middle of the night for a leftover steak, a few spoonfuls of ice cream, or the bottle of tequila I kept above the fridge.

"I noticed that about him. What can I do to help?"

"Talk to me."

"Okay." I heard his bed creak and imagined snuggling up to him on his soft sheets. "Do you want to talk about Prudence and her weird messages?"

"Not really."

"Then tell me something about you," he said.

Besides the fact that I'd fallen head over heels for him and lately had begun to daydream about a gold ring, a layered cake, and a long white dress?

"Something from your past that I don't know," he added.

"You go first." That gave me time to come up with something other than my usual boring tales of family drama, unwed pregnancy, and shitty jobs. What I didn't know about him could keep us chatting for weeks.

He cleared his throat. "Let's see ... I worked in a garage during college."

"You mean as a mechanic?"

"Yes. My grandfather taught me all about engines while I was growing up. He considered the hours we spent in his shop as part of my vocational education while he was homeschooling me. He's the one who got me hooked on Detroit muscle and steel."

"You enjoyed it?"

"Very much. Tinkering with engines is relaxing, and the times spent with my grandfather are some of my favorite memories."

My throat constricted a little for him, knowing what I did about his childhood.

"By the time I finished college," he continued, "the owner of the garage had become a good friend. Actually, he was more like an uncle to me. He helped me fix up my car."

"You mean your Camaro SS?"

"Yep."

He'd had that car since college and it still looked that good? Maybe he shouldn't let my kids ride in it anymore. Their ability to cause mass destruction with only their fingers was legendary.

"Have you stayed in contact with the garage owner?"

"He's dead."

I plucked at a loose string edging my pillowcase. "I'm sorry."

"I haven't tried to look him up since I heard the news."

Did Doc mean the guy's ghost? "Can you do that?"

His chuckle sounded husky with sleep yet. "I was kidding, Violet. Your turn now."

I leaned back against my headboard, weeding through my past. There were a lot of thistles and dandelions growing there, quite a few brambles, too, but none had the emotional level of what Doc had shared. I didn't want him to feel shortchanged because I wanted him to keep telling me more, to open the Book of Doc even wider.

Then I remembered something that might appeal to him. "I have an irrational fear of rune casting."

"Did you say rune casting?"

"Yes, as in the casting of runes to figure out the path one is taking and the likely outcome. My grandma-great is to blame. Casting her runes was part of her daily routine."

"Was she into tarot card reading, too?"

"Nope, just runes. She carried them in a little pouch made of some kind of soft leather—I think it was deer skin, maybe rabbit. They were made of bone, worn smooth on the edges with small cracks throughout." I could still envision them as clearly as when I was a child watching her yellowed fingernails as they clacked against them. "She said they'd 'sing' to her."

I remembered her telling me that one day when I found her kneeling on her attic floor next to the runes. The memory of her tired, lined face in the morning sunlight appeared in my mind, fresh as when it had happened. Her watery eyes had locked on me, widening, then returned to the stones that were spread on a black piece of cloth she also carried folded in her pouch. She picked the stones up as I stood there and put them back in her pouch, muttered something under her breath, and cast them again. Her frown dragged her wrinkles downward when her focus landed on me again.

"Why do you fear them?" Doc pulled me back to present day. "I didn't think runes were used for fortune telling. That they were more of a prediction, and you could change the outcome if you veered your current path."

"How do you know about runes?"

"I read a lot."

"I noticed." Just like Layne. If my son could ever get past his worry about another man stealing his place in my heart, I had a feeling he and Doc would be as thick as thieves.

"Especially about topics having to do with the supernatural, mysterious, paranormal, or magical," Doc said.

Of course he did, with his history. I should have figured he'd know as much about runes as I did. Probably more.

"So what happened that caused you to fear them?" he prodded. "Was it something to do with your path back then?"

"No, my path was always boring according to her reading of the runes—I'd continue to go to school, learn as much as I could, and be a good girl." That was what she told me, anyway, when I was younger and would ask her to cast the runes for me.

I closed my eyes, thinking back again to that morning in her attic. I could still smell the old varnish and stale air. Dust particles had danced in the sun, orbiting the crown of her head, reminding me of Saturn's rings, which we'd recently learned about in school. "She scared me off runes when it came to her path," I told Doc.

"What do you mean?"

"She told me one day when I'd walked in on her reading the runes that every time I was in the room with her while she cast them, the same rune would appear in a negative position."

"*Merkstave.*"

"Yeah, I think some people call it that." It had been a while since I thought about my father's and Aunt Zoe's grandmother. She'd always seemed so very, very old with her craggy face and dull silver hair.

"Did she say which rune or what its position meant?" Doc pressed.

"She showed me once. The rune reminded me of an old telephone pole, or a capital Y with a third line going up through the center. Sort of like a fork. I can't remember the name of it."

"And what was her take on the meaning of it showing up in Merkstave?"

"She said it showed hidden danger surrounding me. Once she even mentioned that she'd catch a whiff of death in the air for a second or two right when the rune stone was cast. She took both signs as warnings."

"Warnings about what?"

"Me. I was a threat to her."

"You were a kid."

"I know, but she always watched me closely with a guarded look in her eyes. After a while, I started to feel uneasy around her and began making excuses not to visit her or my grandmother when I knew Grandma-great would be there."

One time, my mother begged me to go, resorting to bribery, telling me that my dad's family was accusing her of keeping me from them. I knew she would never understand my reasoning, so I didn't try to explain my steadfastness. To this day, she still groused about my stubbornness and how I took after my father and his family.

"I never told my dad or Aunt Zoe this, but I was relieved when she died. She had grown so creepy as her arthritis crippled her. I can still see her hands, gnarled and claw-like as she cast the runes." I shuddered at the memory and burrowed under the blanket.

"Whatever happened to her pouch of rune stones?"

"I don't know. I haven't seen them since. I figured Grandma buried them with her mother." I tried to remember if Aunt Zoe had ever mentioned the rune stones but nothing popped into my memory. However, something recent resurfaced. "I guess I shouldn't have been so surprised to find out Grandma-great taught Aunt Zoe how to read and write Latin." I lowered my voice to a whisper. "Maybe she was some kind of sorceress."

"So you've never had anyone else cast rune stones in your company?"

"Nope. In college, some of the girls would play with tarot cards, palm reading, or rune stones. I'd always leave. I'd had enough of that hocus pocus stuff as a kid."

"Is that why you hooked up with Rex back then?" he asked. "Because he was a scientist—all black and white logic and the practical application of theories?"

"Maybe. I remember thinking how steady and down-to-earth he was." I laughed with a good dose of sarcasm at reality. "But then my crazy world caught up with us and I rubbed off on him." I pursed my lips, contemplating Rex's actions back then from a different perspective. "You know, now that I think about it, I shouldn't have been surprised he ran away from me and my babies. He was used to a much more staid, non-dramatic life. Then I blew in like a prairie dust-devil and probably scared the hell out of him."

Doc chuckled. "You certainly discombobulated me from the moment you threw yourself at my feet."

"Hey! No low blows before sunrise."

"I meant that in a good way."

"Yeah, right. And I didn't throw myself at your feet. I fell." Over his damned boxes of books.

"Like an angel from heaven." The mirth in his voice came through the line clear as could be, along with his chuckles.

"More like a klutzy girl from next door."

I smiled at the memory of our first meeting. I'd taken one look at those books and figured conversations with Doc would be boring as hell. Boy, had I been wrong there.

"No, not klutzy. Stunning and sexy. You knocked the wind out of me."

"Now you're kissing up so that I'll bring my purple boots over to your bedroom again sometime soon."

"It's the truth, I swear." His laughter warmed me inside and out. "You still spin me all around, Violet, but I'm not running anywhere." His tone had a serious note in it that made me feel all sparkly inside. "I like feeling flummoxed when it comes to you."

You say that now, I thought, *but what about when you get tired of me and my* ... I shook my head and jammed that worry into a closet way back in my brain, slamming the door and leaning against it for good measure.

I opted for humor rather than throwing myself at his feet and begging him never to leave me. "Good, because I'd hate to have to hunt you down and drag you back here if you decided to run off, but I will. I know where Aunt Zoe keeps the log chains and padlocks."

"What? No rack or iron maiden for me?"

"No way. I like to stare at your body too much to mar it. It'd be a life of sexual slavery for you, Mr. Nyce."

"I'm your huckleberry, but only if I get to pick your dominatrix outfits. I've put some serious thought into this many a long, lonely night." His voice had a huskiness that made my nether regions pulse and tickle.

I grinned at the ceiling. "I don't know if you can handle my whip. Are you sure you're up to it?"

"Sure. Stop by my office this afternoon and I'll give you a demonstration."

There was nothing I'd like more except I had a feeling reality wasn't going to allow that to happen. "That may be tough. I promised Addy and Layne I'd take them to the wiener dog races at the festival." I yawned in silence, blinking away a sudden heaviness in my eyelids.

"You're not going in to work?"

"Jerry rewarded my good behavior with the television people by granting me a Saturday off." I was hoping to make it a foursome with Doc as part of our little family group, but he'd told me last night he had several client appointments throughout the day.

"What about your ex?" Doc asked. "Doesn't he want to see more places today?"

"Nothing was mentioned about another appointment before Cooper led him away."

"Exactly why did Cooper lead him away? You left that detail out yesterday."

Oh, fudgesicles. I'd forgotten that Doc didn't know that Cooper had already learned all about Rex a couple of months ago. I wasn't sure how this information was going to go over for Doc, but I hoped it didn't end up with him grinding his teeth at me for keeping secrets. Who knew Rex wasn't going to just blow away in the breeze again and instead actually show up on my doorstep?

Or rather across the street from my doorstep, the asshole.

I took a big breath and let 'er rip. "Actually, Cooper's part in this started back when Harvey found the headless dead guy who was palming my business card. You remember when I told you about Cooper informing me that the dead guy had a message about Aunt Zoe and me on his cell phone? And then I threw up on Cooper's tie?" I didn't wait for a response from Doc. "It turned out the message came from Rex's cell phone. After Cooper tracked it down, he asked me who Rex was. When I told him the bastard was the father of my children, I asked Cooper to keep that to himself, which he did." Cooper might inspire a lot of cursing and stomping from me, but he was trustworthy. I'd appreciated that particular personality trait of his in this case. "Yesterday afternoon, when I called to tip Cooper about Rex being in town, he met us in the parking lot behind Calamity Jane's and insisted the jerk go to the station to answer some questions. You and I both know how good Cooper is at strong-arming to get his way."

Whew! There, I had spread everything out on the table. I chewed on my knuckles, waiting to see how Doc reacted.

"Is there anything else you haven't told me regarding Rex intruding into your life since you moved to Deadwood?" I couldn't read anything into his tone, which seemed as steady and level as always.

I hesitated, yawning again while pondering his question. I wanted to make sure I hadn't forgotten something before I told him there was nothing else. Then I remembered an important tidbit. "Maybe."

"What else, Violet?" There was an obvious growl in his voice.

Ah ha! There was the frustration I'd been wincing about while waiting for it to surface. I was glad to know he was human after all when it came to dealing with an ex. If the situation were reversed, I'd have been wheezing days ago from the jealousy ogre clamping down on my lungs.

"Just one more thing, I swear," I told him.

"I'm all ears."

"I recently found out that the owner of the black Jaguar sharing Miss Geary's garage lately is Rex. He's her young stallion."

"Did he tell you that?"

"No. I saw their breakup yesterday morning before heading to work. Miss Geary has a wicked swing."

A long bout of silence came from his end.

Had I lost the connection? "Doc?"

"Do you mean to tell me that son of a bitch has been spying

on you and your kids from your neighbor's front door?"

"Yes, and her bedroom window. But now that he's done sowing his wild oats in her field," *oh lordy, Jeff Wymonds was rubbing off on me,* "Rex needs a place to rent, so he came to me."

"Ahh, fuck. This just keeps getting better."

I grimaced at the static of irritation scratching his voice. Doc wasn't one for much swearing, at least not in front of me. His lack of filter this morning said a lot.

"Doc, I'm sorry about all of this Rex crap."

Why did Rex have to come back now, when I'd finally started getting my life together and had found someone who was ten times the man Rex ever was?

"Don't apologize for that piece of shit, Violet. You're not responsible for his actions."

If I could wish Rex away with an eyelash, I'd pluck every one and go around with bald lids to make sure he stayed gone for good this time.

"So is this spying game of his the reason you slammed a cupboard door into his face?"

"Mostly." We didn't need to get into the details of Rex wanting to warm my sheets again.

Doc grunted.

I wasn't sure what that meant in regards to my admission. I needed to get a caveman dictionary. I thought about asking him to define his grunt, but didn't want to push him at the moment. My unwarranted anxiety about Doc washing his hands of me and my multitude of ever-growing problems kept me in check, as usual.

"Are you sure you didn't break Rex's nose?" Doc asked.

"Yeah." I knew the difference thanks to my fun times with Cooper. "Rex would have howled a lot more if it was broken."

"That's too bad."

I smiled, relaxing back into the soft bed now that my admission about Rex hadn't resulted in more than some minor bumps. "I'll try harder next time."

"Use an oak cupboard door. That should do the trick. Or just taser him."

My chuckle stretched into a yawn that I couldn't quite stifle.

"Are you getting sleepy, Boots?"

"Uh-huh." I shifted lower in the bed, letting my chin loll to the side. "You have a way of sedating me, like a really good drug."

"This has nothing to do with good drugs, woman. I've got you under my spell. You're doomed."

I snuggled into my pillow, imagining his arm wrapped around me, pulling me back into his warmth. "I like it when you doom me. I'd like it even more if you could come over here right now and doom me some more."

"How about I tell you exactly how I'd ruin you once and for all," Doc said, "starting with those lovely, smooth legs of yours?"

Yawning again, I pulled the covers up to my chin. "I thought you told me once you weren't a leg man."

The sandman began to work his magic, making my eyes hard to keep open.

"Yeah, but we weren't talking about *your* legs then, Boots. They're in a class all their own, along with the rest of your soft, curvy parts. Now close your eyes, listen, and go to sleep."

I did as he told me in that exact order. When I opened my eyes next, the sun was awake and waiting outside the window. My phone lay quiet and dark beside me. Doc must have hung up after I crashed.

I stood and stretched, trying to remember how far up my legs Doc had made it before I fell asleep. He was past my knee, wasn't he? Had I dreamed him saying he wanted to lick ice cream off of my thighs? I must have because it was peanut butter fudge, my favorite, not his.

I took my time getting up and moving. I hadn't had a day off in a while, so I wanted to savor this one. Detective Cooper's text message saying he wanted to reschedule our meeting to a future date made me dance a little jig on the way to the bathroom.

The kids got tired of waiting for me while I showered, shaved, primped, and styled. The Oktoberfest Weiner Dog races in Deadwood were no Del Mar horse track event, but I wanted to be dressed to impress in case Doc was able to wrap up his

appointments early and join us at the festivities. One never knew
when a certain red-haired, evil ex-flame would suddenly appear
and try to show up all the other fair maidens in town with her
perky breasts, flat stomach, and voluptuous everything else.

Applying one last coat of mascara, I practiced my glare in the
bathroom mirror. "Back off, bitch. He's mine."

"Who are you talking to?" Addy asked from the doorway,
where she stood watching me with Elvis at her feet.

"Myself."

"Aunt Susan says that only crazy people talk to themselves."

My sister's name set off alarms in my head. I whipped
around. "You haven't been talking to Susan, have you? You
know how I feel about that." As much as I'd have liked to handle
my dislike for all things Susan with maturity and pretend
everything was fine and dandy between us in front of my
children, the instinct to shield them from the forces of evil won
out.

"Aunt Susan told me that a long, long time ago. It might
have been back in August when we were staying with Grandma
and Grandpa for a few days."

August was not exactly ancient history. Funny how time
worked in a kid's brain.

"I'm not crazy." Although I wasn't as positive as I sounded
about my sanity after some of the peculiar stuff I'd witnessed
since moving to Deadwood. "Some people talk to themselves
because they need to vent."

Addy's chicken tipped her head to the side and clucked at me
and then strutted away.

I took that as an insult. "Adelynn," I pointed my tube of
mascara at her, "you know that chicken is not supposed to be
upstairs."

"Ah, come on, Mom. Give Elvis a break. It's National
Chicken Week, you know." She said it as if it were one of the
eight major U.S. holidays.

"There is no such thing as National Chicken Week. You
think I was born yesterday?" Maybe I should look that up online
later to make sure of that. I tossed the tube of mascara into my

makeup bag. "Let's go eat breakfast. Aunt Zoe and Layne are waiting."

I followed her downstairs, walking while she bounced and chattered about selling wiener dog sweat suits at next year's Oktoberfest.

"Yesterday, Kelly signed her dad up for the wife carrying contest when he wasn't looking," Addy informed me as we joined Aunt Zoe and Layne at the kitchen table where a cup of coffee waited for me, along with eggs, bacon, and toast.

"You're too good to me." I kissed Aunt Zoe on the forehead and dropped into my chair, reaching for the coffee.

"It's part of the deal we made when you were eight—I take care of you when you're young and you take care of me when I'm old."

The coffee was sweetened just right. "The deal still stands." I held out my finger for a pinky swear.

"Mom, will you do me a big favor?" Addy asked when we'd returned to eating and drinking.

"Sure." I took a sip of coffee.

"Will you be Kelly's dad's wife and help him win the trophy for us?"

The gulp of coffee I'd been swallowing went down all wrong and then burned its way back up and out through my nose. I grabbed the napkin Aunt Zoe held out and swiped at the drips coming out my nostrils, nailing Addy with a watery-eyed squint. "I am not going to be Jeff's anything, Adelynn Renee."

"It's only for pretend. Sheesh, Mom, lighten up."

"I'll lighten up when you quit trying to marry me off to that man." I sneezed out a couple more coffee drips into the napkin, and then picked up my fork and dug into my eggs. "He has a new girlfriend, anyway. She can be his contest wife."

"Mr. Wymonds has a girlfriend?" Layne asked, his eyes shining with obvious glee.

I felt the same way about Jeff taking his "plow" elsewhere and smiled back at him. "Yep. He told me about her last night."

"And you're not sad, right?" Layne asked.

"Not at all."

"Good."

"No, it's not good, Layne." Addy pinched her brother's arm, which resulted in a return shove. "Just because she's not going to marry Kelly's dad doesn't mean she won't get married to someone else someday, you know."

Layne sneered at Addy. "Doc said he isn't going to marry her, remember?"

Doc said what now?

I lowered my fork, my frown careening into Aunt Zoe's matching one. Why would Doc say that? Had he even given me a chance?

Then I realized that my kids must have harassed him about marrying me and my humiliation from his rejection flared even higher thanks to a sharp slap of mortification. My cheeks burned clear to my ears. I glanced downward while I picked up both halves of my heart and shoved them back into the hole in my chest cavity.

Placing my fork on the table next to my spoon, I wiped my mouth with my napkin. "What did you two say to Doc yesterday?"

They both started defending themselves at once, pointing food covered forks at each other, doing their best to shout louder than the other. I decided right there and then to start their punishment by grounding them at least until they were dead, maybe even through the end of time.

"That's enough!" I interrupted, out-yelling both of them. "Go outside." I needed a few moments to corral the hurt tearing through me at Doc's response, a short breather before I could act rationally when it came to my bratty spawn. When they just looked at me, I barked, "Now!"

"But we're not done," Addy pointed at her half-full plate.

"Take your plates and go eat on the back porch."

Addy stood and collected her food and silverware. "Do we still get to go to the wiener dog races later?" she asked as she backed through the screen door.

I picked up my coffee cup. "I don't know."

"You're the one who stuck us with Doc yesterday," Layne

said as he followed her. He paused on the threshold, one blonde eyebrow raised in challenge. "Don't be mad at us because he doesn't want to marry you. Besides, I thought you said you were just really good friends."

I set my coffee cup down and leveled my glare on him. "Doc is my boyfriend, Layne. Whether or not he wants to marry me is not even up for discussion at the moment."

"We don't need or want a dad." His chin jutted. "We've lived this long without one and we're doing just fine." He slammed the door closed behind him.

I gaped at the door for a few seconds before turning to Aunt Zoe. "This is some fucked-up shit I'm in."

She burst out laughing.

"It's not funny," I told her.

Several snorts of laughter were her response, which in turn made me start to giggle in spite of my current maelstrom.

When we stopped laughing, she swiped at the tears in her eyes. "I'm sorry, sweetheart. I didn't sleep well last night and that whole blow up caught me completely off guard."

"You and me both." I picked up a piece of bacon, not sure I was up to eating it now thanks to the angst churning in my gut. "I thought we were making some progress with those two accepting Doc. Now I'm thinking it's only gotten worse."

"I disagree. This is progress. They know Doc is in the picture and not going anywhere. They're having to adjust is all, which is usually not an easy thing."

I groaned and sat back, clutching my stomach. "Why on earth did they have to ask him about marrying me?"

"Because they love you. They're afraid of losing you and at the same time they want some kind of affirmation from Doc that he's not going to leave you ... and them. Plus, in their heads, marriage is the next logical step. Keep in mind that they grew up watching Disney movies. They don't know that sometimes you can love someone with everything you have and never get your happily ever after."

I did a doubletake. "Are we talking about Doc or Reid?"

Her blue eyes flashed in pain. "There's nothing to talk about when it comes to Reid."

"Really? Because you've been playing that super sad Linda Ronstadt song over and over. What's it called? *Long, Long Time,* isn't it?"

"I don't know what you're talking about."

"I heard it coming out from under your door last night when I was getting ready for bed."

"This topic is off limits this morning." She wrinkled her nose at me. "And you need to stop listening under my door."

"Okay, okay. You want me to go eat outside, too?"

She spared me a small smile and returned to her breakfast.

I on the other hand returned to my wallow. "How do you know they weren't trying to scare Doc off?"

"Did you mention anything in front of them about Doc's aversion to marriage when it came to his ex-girlfriend?"

"No, only you know about that." I might have told Natalie, too. I couldn't remember.

"Then they have no clue that bringing up marriage would scare him, right?" At my nod, she continued. "Violet, they're kids. They're putting out feelers."

"Do you think I should bring it up with Doc?"

Aunt Zoe shrugged. "How bad do you want to know why he said he wouldn't marry you?"

I considered trying to play it cool and lie that I didn't care.

She smirked at me. "Let me rephrase that. How awkward of a conversation do you want to have with Doc about marriage?"

I shuddered visibly at the thought. "Face-to-face rejection is not really my thing."

"What is your thing?"

"I'm still figuring that out." I tossed the uneaten piece of bacon onto my plate. "Apparently, it's not getting married."

Not that I wanted to rush down the aisle anytime soon, but having the option would be nice when it came to Doc.

Aunt Zoe scoffed. "You and me both, kiddo."

Chapter Sixteen

Sunday, October 7th

Twenty-four hours later, I was still obsessing.

Never mind that I sat in Bighorn Billy's Diner with Ray, Mona, and Ben while Jerry led our weekly meeting; or that I should be listening to my boss's game plan for the next week since he'd mentioned something about me playing "point guard" with Dickie and Honey.

I stabbed at my salad with my fork, wondering why I gave such a damn that wedding bells weren't in the future for Doc and me.

It wasn't like I didn't have bigger problems, what with Rex leaving multiple messages for me at work about going out to see more houses. His badgering wasn't going unnoticed by Mona, who was asking a lot of questions now, wondering if Rex and I had met before he'd walked in our office looking for a Realtor.

Then there was Detective Hawke, who had tried to get a hold of me on my cell phone several times this morning. I doubted he appreciated being sent to voicemail call after call.

I shoved a forkful of salad in my mouth, chewing the hell out of it. Marriage was probably overrated anyway. And I surely didn't need a man to make me feel more like a woman. Hell, I felt plenty female every month when my period came: cramps, hormone rages, and all.

I tried to focus on the good things happening in my life, like yesterday with my kids. We had made up after our spat and not only had shared lots of laughs at the wiener dog races, but they'd also gotten up early today and served me a breakfast of Pop Tarts, grapes, and orange juice in bed. And last night Doc had called, flirting and laughing with me as if he hadn't told my kids he wasn't going to marry me.

The salad tasted dry and stale. I grabbed the ranch dressing and coated the chopped leaves in my bowl and then some, making ranch dressing soup with a sprinkling of lettuce.

Who said I even wanted a husband? I'd been raising my kids on my own since they were born. Did I really want to put up with someone else coming into my home and directing me on how to lead my life? How to raise my kids? Layne was right on that level—we'd been fine for a long time on our own. If any man thought that I was going to cook him dinner each night or have his breakfast ready for him when he got up in the morning, he was in for an unhappy reality.

Shaking my head at the image of me in a June Cleaver apron, I snorted and plucked out a crouton floating in the ranch dressing. I may have fallen in love with Doc, the big bozo, but if no vows were exchanged it wouldn't be the end of the world. We could still have fun under the sheets and enjoy each other's company until it grew stale—like my salad.

I crunched on the crouton. So there was no reason to be obsessed with Doc's matrimonial allergy. It was time to quit spinning my wheels in this stupid rut, shift into four-wheel drive, and get the heck …

"Violet?" Jerry's voice penetrated my inner rant.

I looked up from fishing lettuce pieces from my soupy salad to find four pairs of eyes locked on me.

Shit, what had I missed. "Yeah?"

"What do you think of Ray's suggestion?"

If it came from the mouth of that horse's ass, I'd bet old man Harvey's left nut that I was going to hate it. Or was it Harvey's right nut? I shrugged. "I think we should discuss it more," I said with as much absolute vagueness as I could muster.

Ray smirked. "I told you she wasn't paying attention."

I fantasized about jamming croutons up Ray's nose.

"Did you even hear what we've been talking about for the last five minutes, Violet?" Jerry asked, frowning down at my bowl of ranch dressing.

"No." My face warmed. "Sorry. I have some stuff going on

at home that's distracting me."

"Ray suggested you take Dickie and Honey out to Willis Harvey's ranch," Ben supplied, winking in response to the *Thanks* I mouthed for helping me out while his uncle circled overhead with his sharp beak snapping.

Go to Harvey's, huh? I glanced at Ray. What a friggin' stupid-assed suggestion. I turned to Jerry with a polite smile. "I'm not so sure that's a good idea."

Jerry's big forehead got all crinkly. "Ray seems to think the excitement that's gone on out at Mr. Harvey's ranch would score us a three-pointer on the publicity factor. I think he may be onto something. Try to look at it from a marketing perspective, Violet."

Ray played chicken with my glare, neither one of us looking away until Mona waved her hand between us.

I set my fork down. "Marketing-wise, I still think this is a bad idea." At Jerry's raised brows, I explained, "First, I'm not even sure that the police have removed all the barriers and crime scene tape from the property. Second, we'd be exploiting a poor old man who might not want negative attention."

A guffaw came from the dick-weed across the table. "Come on, Blondie, who are you trying to fool? Old man Harvey would love to have his mug on television. He'd probably figure out some way to use his celebrity status to score some new action down at the Prairie Dog Palace."

Ray pretty much nailed that one, but I wasn't going to let him know it. I mocked a shocked expression, open mouth and all. "Really, Ray, that's a bit crude for a work meeting." I looked at Jerry. "Are you going to let him speak like that in front of Mona?"

Jerry pointed at Ray. "Knock off the inappropriate language at the lunch table, Ray."

My nemesis cleared his throat, glancing at Mona. "Sorry about that, Red. I forgot where I was."

"And don't call me Blondie," I added.

That earned me a curled lip but no apology.

Jerry sat back, pushing his cleared plate away. "Violet, why don't you ask Mr. Harvey how he feels about entertaining some visitors from the television industry?"

Sighing, I caved to my boss with a nod.

"Mention that there's a chance he'll be on TV, that might make him more amenable," Jerry added.

Harvey was going to eat this up. "Will do."

Zoning in and out for the remainder of the meeting while fishing for lettuce, I piped up when prodded about the statuses of Jeff's and Cooper's houses. A nod was enough of a reply for Jerry when he asked if we were still waiting for the final paperwork on Cornelius's hotel purchase.

My phone buzzed in my pocket several times during the meeting, but Jerry had made it clear a couple of weeks ago that cell phones were supposed to be muted and not answered during company meetings. If it was Detective Hawke calling for the umpteenth time, I didn't want to talk to him anyway. Dealing with one pain-in-the-ass cop was bad enough, I didn't need two law dogs nipping at my heels day and night.

When lunch finally wrapped up, I zipped out of there like Speedy Gonzales, wanting some fresh air and space to get my head back in the game. Big, puffy clouds floated overhead like cottony bundles of flotsam, letting the jet stream swirl them across the sky. A cool breeze made me button up my cable-knit sweater.

Enough with this Doc and marriage shit, I told myself. If he didn't want to play house for the long term, that was fine and dandy. Aunt Zoe was a great role model—strong, independent, in charge of her own destiny.

I adjusted my collar. Although this whole deal with Reid seemed to have made her stumble a bit lately. My chest constricted thinking back on the way Reid had looked that night in the forest. Truth be told, I liked Reid and sort of wanted him to win her over, even if it meant she was no longer my role model for singledom, and my kids and I had to find a new home. With the commission from Cornelius's purchase of the hotel, I'd be able to afford a deposit on an apartment up in Lead and several months' rent until I had more sales.

Doc said he isn't going to marry her, remember? Layne's voice replayed in my thoughts.

"So screw him," I grumbled, climbing in the Picklemobile.

Actually, that was what had gotten me in trouble with Doc in the first place.

My cell phone buzzed as I pulled into my parking spot at Calamity Jane's. Doc's Camaro was gone, I noticed, shifting into park. He must be out at the client appointment he had told me about last night. Good. I could probably use a little more cartwheeling at my internal pep rally before I could resist kicking him in the shin.

I pulled out my phone as the Picklemobile let out her final sputter and bang, relieved to see the name on the screen.

"Hello, Cornelius."

"Who is this?" he asked.

"You called me, who do you think I am?"

"This is intriguing. Let's see, are you alive or dead?"

I pondered that for a moment. "On the inside or outside?"

"Inside. It's common knowledge that all dead cells float to the surface and flake off, so your outside is in a constant state of death and decay."

Gross! That wasn't true, was it? "My blood is still red."

"What about your heart?"

"It's hard and thorny."

"Ah ha! This must be Violet Parker then."

"Now wait a second," I said, not liking how his game had ended. "I was kidding around about my heart."

"I know," he chuckled. "That's how I knew it was you, Violet. Now what do you need from me?"

"You're the one who called me."

"Did you not request me to set up a séance with you?"

"Are you back in town?"

"I don't understand the question."

"Never mind," I said, getting out of the Picklemobile. "What do I need to bring to the séance?"

"Elk."

"A live one?" Since it was Cornelius, I thought I'd better

make sure.

"Of course not," he said as if I were the ridiculous one in this conversation. "I don't have this suite set up for butchering. Just bring three elk steaks."

"You're not going to do anything weird with elk blood are you?"

He laughed. "Most of the blood rituals I know involve chicken, not elk."

"Then why do I need to bring the elk?"

"I've been wanting to try it. Someone told me it has an interesting taste."

Layne would tell him it tastes like poop. Just to make sure Cornelius and I were on the same page, I asked, "You want the steaks cooked then, right? Not tartare?"

"Violet, you ask the most absurd questions."

Said the kettle! "So are we on for tonight still?"

"Absolutely not. I'm in no mood to talk with the dead after the trip up here from Nevada. I need to cleanse and realign my chakras first."

"You're serious?"

"Why wouldn't I be?'

"Okay, how long will it take you to get your chakras washed up and put back into place?"

"Wednesday evening."

"That's three days away," I complained, wanting to get this séance over and in my rearview mirror.

"That's odd. And here I thought it was still yesterday."

I squeezed my forehead. "Fine, Wednesday it is. I'll bring the steaks."

"Perfect. Grab some chicken feet, too."

"To eat?"

"Oh, Violet," he said as if I were a big disappointment to him. "Chicken feet are for good luck and protection."

I hung up and cursed at my phone before stuffing it back into my purse. I'd bring him some chicken feet all right, along with the damned chicken still attached. If only Addy weren't so gaga about Elvis.

Wednesday, huh? I crossed the parking lot, heading for Calamity Jane Realty's back door. I hope that day worked for Doc, because I wasn't going to go through the pain of rescheduling it with Cornelius.

Mona and Ben were working at their desks when I got to mine. I wondered if Ray had snagged Jerry and was filling his head with poison about me.

Sheesh, my insecurities were taking over. I dropped into my chair. I needed to step back and reassess what was going on in my life. As my mother often said, not everything was about me.

I looked over at Mona. "Where are Ray and Jerry?"

"They stayed back at the diner. Ray wanted to talk to Jerry about you."

"What?!"

She grinned. "I'm kidding. Jerry wanted to work on yearly goals for Ray and brainstorm some new marketing ideas."

I wondered how that was going over with Ray? The jerk had been untethered when Jane had been in charge. He made a point of doing what he needed to do when necessary to make sales happen. How would he feel about someone coming in and telling him how to make his money?

"I need to run out and do a couple of home previews for a client of mine," Ben said, jingling his keys. "See you two later."

An hour passed in peaceful silence with only the sounds of Mona's fingernails clacking on her keyboard and the periodic hum of the printer as I took care of some paperwork.

Then a dark cloud floated into the room.

"Hello, Miss Parker," Rex said, shutting the front door.

I groaned inwardly and fixed a smile on my face, playing nice. "Mr. Conner, what brings you here this afternoon?"

His return smile looked wintery. "Didn't you receive any of my messages?"

"Messages?" I feigned confusion.

Mona's clacking stopped.

"I still need a place to live."

"Oh, those messages." With Mona being the one who had told me about his phone calls, I couldn't pretend otherwise when she sat right next to me listening to our conversation. "I've been busy with other clients and haven't had time to get back with you."

His smile remained chiseled in place. "Do you have time this afternoon to show me more?"

More of what? From the glint in his eyes, I had a feeling we weren't talking only about places to live. "No, not really."

"How about tomorrow?"

"Unfortunately I have appointments all day long."

Rex's face hardened visibly. "Maybe I can stop over tomorrow night at your aunt's place and see if you can spare me a few moments then."

My chest tightened in one constrictive spasm, making me cough. I stood up, needing to escape and catch my breath while I figured out how to keep Rex at arm's length. "Excuse me," I wheezed, "I need to step outside and," I banged on my chest, "cough this out."

I raced past him out the front door, leaning against Doc's front windows as I coughed out the mixture of rage and fear clogging my esophagus.

"Violet, stop playing games." Rex said, joining me.

Since Doc's blinds were closed, I could see Rex's reflection in the glass. I whirled on him, circling with claws extended. "How dare you threaten to come to my front door."

He raised a haughty blonde eyebrow. "If you're not going to play by the rules, then I'm not either."

"What rules? This is no game." We were talking about my children's state of mind here. Didn't he get that?

"Then I guess you need to return my calls and do as I request, don't you?"

I cocked my head to the side. "Are you blackmailing me?"

"I'm trying to decide if I should return to Beatrice Geary's bed and wave goodnight to you from across the street every evening." His gaze traveled down to where my sweater was unbuttoned at my chest. "Of course, if you'd play nicely with me, I'd stay away from Beatrice and let you keep me entertained as far away from your children as you'd like while I'm in town."

This wasn't happening, nor was it going to start happening in this lifetime. My ears rang from the blood pounding through them. "Go fuck yourself, Rex."

He tsk-tsked me, waving his index finger in front of my nose. "You're making a mistake, darling."

I smacked his hand away. "No, I'm making sense, whereas you're off your meds." Gripping my sweater collar tight at my throat, I leaned toward him. "Stay away from my kids."

"Or what?" He laughed at me, leaning his shoulder against Doc's front window. "You always were so adorable when you got all feisty." He reached out to stroke my cheek. When I recoiled from his touch, his lips thinned. "It's too bad you didn't put as much effort into stopping us from propagating those children as you do keeping me away from them."

Tires screeched on the busy street behind me. Rex frowned over my shoulder, but I kept the egotistical shithead locked in my laser beam. "I'm not joking, Rex."

He focused back on me, his gaze cold and calculating. "Neither am I, Violet." Bending closer, inches from my face, he spoke with a menacing quiet. "I get what I want."

A car door slammed.

A horn honked as a diesel pickup gunned past us.

"You rotten bastard." My breath rasped, my windpipe tight with rage. "If you come near my children, I will go straight for your throat." I meant that with every fiber of my being. I'd plead temporary insanity at the murder trial.

Rex's attention strayed over my head. "This is a private conversation between the lady and me," he said, sounding curt yet polished. "You can move along."

A hand gripped my shoulder. "No can do," Doc said. "This is my office."

Relief rushed through my limbs knowing Doc had my back.

"You're parked in the middle of the street." Rex said.

"I know." Doc pulled me backward, stepping in front of me to face off with Rex. "How about you move along and stop bothering Violet." It was more of an order than a request.

Standing up straighter, Rex tried to meet Doc eye-to-eye. He fell about two inches short. "Who are you? Her bodyguard?"

"No, that job's already filled." Doc crossed his arms over his chest, making a nice solid wall for me to peek around. "Trust me, you don't want to meet the man who watches over Violet. Or his shotgun."

Rex's chin came up. "Is that a threat?"

"Simply a warning," Doc said. "Harvey will take great pleasure filling your ass full of lead if he finds out you're harassing Violet."

"Harvey, huh?" Rex looked down at me. "Is that who's keeping your bed warm these days?"

"Wrong again." Doc's voice had a steely hardness that I hadn't heard before.

I moved up next to Doc and aimed my thumb in his direction. "That's his job."

Rex assessed Doc with a cool onceover. "Of course. You're the one who drives the old Camaro."

"And you're the one who drives the new Jaguar." Doc put his arm around my shoulder. "Now that we've talked cars, how about you get in yours."

"Is there a problem here, gentlemen?" Cooper asked from behind me.

Rex's glare swung from me to Doc and back again, before his face morphed and that perfectly polished smile returned. "No, Detective. We were just getting to know each other."

Cooper positioned himself so he could step between Doc and Rex if needed. "Sounds like warm and chummy stuff." He glanced at Doc. "Nyce, I'm going to need you to move your car. It's illegally parked."

Doc grunted. "I'd be happy to as soon as Mr. Conner takes his leave."

Stepping back, Rex gave a nod to Cooper, then turned to me. "I'll give you a call, Miss Parker."

"I'll be busy."

"Maybe your boss won't." With that threat, he walked off down the sidewalk toward downtown Deadwood.

Doc looked down at me, his eyes assessing. "You okay?"

I nodded, biting my lower lip. I had a feeling Rex was far from done fucking up my world, though.

"Give me your keys, Nyce," Cooper said, holding out his hand. "I'll park it around back."

Doc obliged without hesitation. "How'd you get over here so fast? That's some lightning fast police work."

The detective nudged his chin at the station across the street. "I'd just parked when I heard you lock 'em up."

"Sorry about that. Violet looked like she could use a referee."

"If I'd only had a bat, you could have played umpire."

"More fun times with Violet, I see," Cooper said, chuckling. He held up Doc's keys. "I've been wanting to give that big block under your hood a try." He pointed his index finger at me as he backed away. "Stay out of trouble, Parker."

I stuck my tongue out at him, watching as he slid behind the wheel and rumbled off. I caught Doc's hand and squeezed it, wishing we were standing somewhere other than next to a busy street in front of the whole wide world. "Thanks."

His smile warmed away my morning's self-doubts. "I figured I'd better step in or I'd be talking to you through jail bars again."

"Rex threatened to come to Aunt Zoe's if I didn't start taking his phone calls."

Doc cursed under his breath. "He's not going to just go away, is he?" At my head shake, he looked in the direction Rex had taken, his jaw tight.

"I'm sorry."

"I told you not to apologize for him." He trailed his thumb along my jawline. "You sure you're okay?"

"Yes," I hit Doc with a hard stare. "But I'll kill that son of a bitch if he comes near my kids."

"I don't doubt you." Doc pulled me into his arms, resting his chin on my head. "Somehow I need to keep it from coming to that."

Chapter Seventeen

"This is a bad idea," I whispered, tiptoeing through the thick shadows cloaking the side of the Galena House.

"That's my line usually," Doc whispered back, tugging me along behind him.

We moved silently through the grass, skirting a couple of bushes. The sound of the wind in the pines overhead drowned out any noises we made as we sneaked up to Ms. Wolff's apartment window. I could smell rain in the air. Lightning flashed in the distance; thunder rumbled along after it. The sensation of impending doom made my feet feel like I was wearing concrete-filled shoes instead of boots. My knees trembled for reasons other than the cold October night air.

When we reached the living room window, Doc pulled me back against the side of the house next to him. A car cruised by slowly out front.

I held my breath until it moved up the street. Standing on my toes, I spoke close to his ear. "Maybe we should abort for tonight and try again another day."

I felt more than saw his gaze on me. "What has you so nervous tonight?"

"Are you kidding? It's a dark, stormy night and we're sneaking around a house that was the recent site of a murder. Need I say more?"

"Back in August you were lurking around a funeral home in the dark, peeking in the windows of a garage-turned-morgue without a care."

Not totally without a care. I was pretty jumpy that night, too. "That was different."

"How so?"

"I hadn't had any run-ins yet with freaky, snake-eyed people who turn into smoke when stabbed. My only worry that night was getting busted by Cooper and thrown in jail."

"Nobody knows we're here, Violet. Not even your freaky friends." He leaned out and looked toward the street. "All clear." Doc turned around and lifted up the window Freesia had left unlocked.

Earlier in the afternoon, Harvey and I had called on Freesia under the guise of me being her Realtor and Harvey being my assistant. The Realtor part was true, the assistant was a stretch, but Harvey had promised to dress appropriately for the visit and he had—in a green suit jacket and orange polyester dress pants. My comment that he looked like a pumpkin earned me a hard pinch on the arm.

While Freesia toured us around the Galena House showing me the finer points of her family's hand-me-down so I could write up an enticing sales description, Harvey followed along giving his usual two-cent commentary. Thankfully he kept it to the NC-17 rated version without too much detail.

At the end of the tour, I hesitated, trying to come up with a way to convince Freesia into turning the other cheek at some point so I could sneak Doc into Ms. Wolff's apartment for some scratch-and-sniff reconnaissance. I almost choked on my tongue when Harvey asked her outright if we could go through Ms. Wolff's apartment under the cover of darkness, to look for clues about her killer since we'd been the two who had discovered her body.

Freesia hesitated, explaining that she was concerned we'd be caught by the police, who visited multiple times some days and cruised by periodically at night with their spotlights roving. She didn't want us to get busted and end up in hot water with Detective Cooper. The butthead had even mentioned my name to her, stressing that she not let me in without his approval.

Harvey twisted his beard on that for a few moments and then held up his finger. "How about this?" he said to Freesia. "After we leave, you go inside and unlock the living room window and leave it that way all night. Come morning, you go back in and lock the window."

Freesia smiled. "I can do that." She'd lowered her voice and added, "Just be careful about touching stuff. Detective Cooper and Detective Hawke have been in there so many times they'd probably notice if anything has been moved."

Harvey and I promised to keep our hands in our pockets and walked out on the front porch in time to run into Hawke.

"Parker, I need to talk to you," he said as a greeting.

His use of my last name reminded me of Cooper, which made my hackles all uppity.

"Gotta run," I said, racing past him down the front steps. "Give Detective Cooper my love," I added over my shoulder.

"You can't keep avoiding me," he hollered after me.

Until he had a warrant to drag me in for questioning, I sure could.

Harvey and I had hopped into the Picklemobile and sputtered down the road, calling Doc along the way to fill him in on our plan.

"Violet," Doc whispered, nudging me back to the present. "Come on, we don't have all night." He laced his fingers together holding his palms out for me to use as a step. "Climb up."

I glanced toward the trees, half expecting to see Cooper crashing through them like Bigfoot's kissing cousin. "Maybe we should go play some slots at one of the casinos, test our luck there instead of here."

He stood up. "This was your idea, remember?"

"I know. I know."

"Don't go chickening out on me now."

"I'm trying not to."

"Would you feel better about doing this if your bodyguard was here with us?"

"No. He might accidentally shoot one of us in the ass."

"There's always that risk with Harvey." Doc bent over and laced his fingers again. "Come on, Tiger, up and in."

Sighing, I did as he asked, using his hands as a step. He lifted me up and into the open window.

Even darker shadows waited inside the apartment window. I

tried to be careful not to make many sounds as I pulled myself inside, keeping my grunts and curses under my breath. I had one leg over the sill when my sweaty palm slipped off the ledge and I tumbled onto the living room floor with a muffled thump-thump-thump. By the time I'd untangled my limbs and figured out what had happened, Doc had already hoisted himself inside with more grace than I could muster even in my prime.

He smiled down at me in the shadows. "Nice landing, Maxwell Smart. I hope you remembered to mute your shoe phone."

"Showoff," I whispered, taking the hand he offered to help me to my feet.

While I made sure my arms and legs were still bending the right way, he leaned out the window, crooking his neck to check the front of the house again.

"Still clear," he closed the window and turned toward me.

"What about ghosts?"

He sniffed, and then inhaled slowly. "That's weird."

"What?"

He sniffed again, but shook his head. "Never mind." He walked over to the wall and clicked on his flashlight. "Holy shit, look at all of these clocks."

"I told you she had a fetish." I didn't relish looking at all of Ms. Wolff's freaky clocks in the dark, but we didn't have much choice since the Deadwood Police Department still wasn't allowing anyone other than cops into the apartment.

Tiptoeing across the floor, I winced with each step. The boards under the carpet seemed excessively squeaky tonight.

He shined his flashlight around. "She really was obsessed."

I pointed at the clock with the wolves on the attack. "This one wasn't working when I was here with Cooper."

He focused the beam on it. "This isn't your normal Black Forest clock design."

"I know. It's super creepy, right?"

"Yeah." His light beam moved up over the ticking clocks. "All of them are eccentric and macabre. The times are set differently, as Harvey and you said. I wonder why."

"You think Harvey's right? That she liked clocks, not necessarily caring about the actual time?"

Doc moved his light beam over several more, his profile thick with shadows. "How come so many of them are still working?" he said more to himself than me.

"What do you mean?"

His frown lines looked extra deep thanks to the shadows. "Didn't you say there were no batteries in the back of the one Cooper took off the wall?"

"Yes."

"If they're on a winding mechanism, I'd expect the clocks to come to a stop. But all of these clocks are ticking away and it's been a week since Ms. Wolff died."

"Maybe Cooper has a cop in charge of winding duty."

"Maybe, but I doubt it. There's no way Cooper would want any of his guys messing with potential evidence."

"You think there's something in these clocks that helps explain what happened to Ms. Wolff?"

"Hard to tell." Doc reached high, pulling one off the wall that was striking the top of the hour. "Check out this one."

I grimaced, glancing over my shoulder, feeling as if Cooper were going to pop onto the scene and chew Doc out. "Be careful."

He aimed his light on the spinning part as it circled slowly, spotlighting a bear-like beast with long fangs chasing down a little girl who was on the ground backing away.

I shivered at the scene. "These clocks and this place are really eerie in the dark." I moved closer to Doc. "Is there anything in here with us?" I whispered.

"It's standing right next to you."

I almost leapt into his arms right there and then, clock be damned. "What? Where?"

He chuckled as he lifted the nasty beast clock and hung it back in place. "I was kidding, Violet."

"Not funny." I punched him in the arm.

"Sorry." I could hear the grin in his voice. "I find it interesting that you're so skittish after all you've been through."

"It's all that I've been through that has taught me to be so skittish."

Doc gave the wall of clocks one last head shake. "Show me where you found her body?"

I led him over near the old-fashioned phone and pointed at the floor. "Right there, and the head had rolled under that end table."

Doc bent down and peered under the table. He sniffed and stared down at his hands for several seconds.

"What is it?" My gaze darted to the dark corners. "Do you sense something coming?"

"It's already here."

"I told you that's not funny."

"I'm serious this time." He stared over his shoulder toward the shadowed hallway that led toward the front door. "But for some reason it's keeping its distance from me. That's a first for me. Usually they seek me out."

"Can you actually see it?"

"No, not even the blur I can sometimes pick up. But I keep catching hints of it. Something tells me it's hiding over by the door."

Hiding? Was it scared? Was it trying to sneak up on us? "You think it's Ms. Wolff?"

"No."

"Why not?"

"Because the tones I'm picking up aren't typical for an older ghost, especially not a woman. It's more pungent, musty." He inhaled again. "Like fermenting sauerkraut."

Was it me? I'd been sweating bullets since we'd parked up the road, drips rolling down my back before we'd even gotten out of Doc's car. I sniffed my armpits. Nope, my antiperspirant was still doing its job. Damn, I'd sooner it have been me than the alternative.

"Who else would be in here with us?" I squinted into the dark hallway, trying to catch a movement even though I was a dud in the ghost-detection mine field.

He stood and shined his flashlight into the hall. "Who

knows? It's an old house."

I wondered if it were one of the previous murder victims. I imagined the Headless Horseman holding a shriveled pumpkin head. The boom of thunder outside made me gasp and jerk.

I rubbed shoulders with Doc—well, my shoulder, his elbow due to his height. "Maybe we should try this again on a less dark and stormy night."

He squeezed my hand. "Show me the bedroom, wimpy."

"Why not? It's where we usually end up."

"I beg to differ, Boots. You have only recently moved to my bed after gracing my office and stairwell a few times first."

I kept him close to me as we made our way into Ms. Wolff's bedroom. I motioned him over to the closet and slowly opened the door, afraid something would reach out, grab me, and pull me back in with it. No monsters waited for me inside.

"There are the styrofoam heads," I pointed my light up at them.

"What's in the hat boxes?"

"Just hats." I ran my fingers along the dresses and shirts and sweaters hanging along the walls. "Notice how many dresses she had and all of the different styles."

"What about them?"

"Don't you think it's weird?"

"Should I?"

"Yes. This isn't normal." I shined my light at the shoes lining the floor, running the beam along the toes. For a moment, I thought I saw something moving in one, my pulse skipping a beat, but then realized it was a dust bunny.

"Where's the picture of Layne?" Doc asked.

I led the way to the dresser. "There." I pointed at Layne's photo, which was still jammed into the edge of the mirror where Cooper had insisted I leave it. "It's unnerving."

"No, the wall of clocks are unnerving. This here is spine-chilling." Doc stood staring in the mirror for much longer than I figured he would. Then he bent his knees and lowered himself to my eyelevel, still looking at the mirror.

"What are you doing?" I asked him.

"Checking to see if I can figure out what Ms. Wolff saw when she looked in this mirror."

I bumped him aside and centered myself in front of it. "She saw that dresser over there, the bed, and the door."

Doc walked over to the doorway. "How much of me can you see?"

"From mid-thigh to your chin."

"Look at Layne's picture."

I did. "Okay."

"What's reflected in the mirror when you look next to where his picture is placed?"

"The dresser."

"All of it?"

"No, just the top three drawers. The bed blocks the rest."

Doc moved over and opened the third drawer down, then the second, then the first, sorting through each as he went. "Just clothes," he said and sounded unhappy about it.

Then I remembered Cooper standing in the same spot and something he'd pointed out.

"Open the top drawer again," I told Doc. "No, all of the way and look at the back of the drawer."

He did, shining his flashlight in the drawer. "What's that?"

He'd found the weird writing. "Now step aside," I said, "but keep your flashlight beam on it."

He moved. When he adjusted his beam of light, I gasped.

"What do you see?" he asked me.

I leaned closer to the mirror, squinting to read the words. "Maybe it's a message."

"What's it say?"

"I don't know. It looks like German or maybe some Slavic language." His flashlight beam bobbed. I turned and saw him holding his phone with one hand while shining the light with the other.

"There," he said, double-checking the picture before stuffing his phone back into his pocket. "I can upload it to my laptop, reverse the image, try to figure out what it says."

I turned back to the mirror, frowning down at the picture of my son. "Do you think Ms. Wolff set all this up on purpose?"

He came up behind me, meeting my eyes in the mirror. "I don't know. Are you sure you'd never met her before?"

"I don't remember her face, but I've seen a lot of people since moving up here." I stepped back, leaning against him. "Why would she leave me a message?"

Had she known someone was coming for her? She had told me she didn't have long when she phoned that fateful day. Had she had enough time to plant this clue and write her message between the time she called and my arrival? Or had she set that up before she called, figuring on it being insurance if I didn't get to her before they did.

Maybe the message wasn't even for me. Maybe she put Layne's picture there to remind herself where she'd left her note. If that was so, why use Layne's picture?

Doc wrapped his arms around me. "I don't know. Until we figure out what the message says, we're guessing at best."

I glanced over at the bookshelf. "Did you find anything in the book Cooper gave me to read?"

"All kinds of interesting historical information on Deadwood, but nothing in particular, and not a mention about Ms. Wolff."

He'd beat me to my next question, so I moved on to the final one. "So what now?"

"Let's get out of here before someone sees my car parked down the street and Cooper shows up at the door spitting nails at us. We'll figure out what this message says after I can play with it on the computer and maybe have more answers." He kissed the top of my head and then snagged my hand and pulled me out of the bedroom and across the living room.

He didn't have to pull hard. This place felt like death tonight, all dried up and hollow, bones rattling. I wanted to get back to the land of the living.

"Oh, and one more thing," he said after opening the window.

"What's that?"

"About the séance—"

"You don't want to do it anymore?" I interrupted, my fingers crossed behind my back.

"I want to change the setting for it."

"What do you mean?"

"Instead of having it in Cornelius's hotel room, I want to see if we can find a way to have it here."

"Here?" I looked over at the wall of creepy clocks ticking away, the floor where Ms. Wolff's body had lain in a gnarled heap, the shadow-filled corners. "Why here?"

Doc shined his flashlight toward the dark hallway. "Because our ghostly visitor is still hiding over there and I want to know why."

* * *

Monday, October 8th

"You look like something old Red hacked up," Harvey said to me as he settled into the passenger seat of Jerry's Hummer. Old Red was his lazy yellow dog out at the ranch who only moved to get closer to his food dish these days.

"Good morning to you, too, buzzard-breath." I shifted the Hummer into reverse and backed out of Doc's driveway. The beast drove like a tank.

Since I was picking up Dickie and Honey and taking them out to Harvey's ranch, Jerry had insisted I use his fancy rig. He'd also sent me home to change after seeing my sensible brown boots and capri corduroy pants. I thought I looked nice but practical, since we might be traipsing around in the mud at Harvey's ranch after last night's storm. Jerry thought I needed more pink and white and a lot less brown, as in none. He also suggested a silky neck scarf to add a Grace Kelly flare to my ensemble. I was surprised he even knew who Grace was since she hadn't played any professional sports.

"You catch any shuteye last night?" Harvey said, leaning close to look me over. His hair was damp and wavy. I could smell Doc's sandalwood-scented soap on him.

"Not really."

I'd tossed and turned about the message on the back of Ms. Wolff's dresser drawer. Until Doc could decipher it and we figured out if the message was for me or for someone else, I doubted I'd be slumbering peacefully anytime soon. The shy ghost hiding in her apartment hadn't helped with my sheep-counting woes either. The topper of my middle-of-the-night anxieties, of course, was the séance Doc swore he was dead serious about having in her apartment. My problems with Rex didn't stand a chance of elbowing to the front of my worry line-up against last night's excitement.

"Your peepers look like they're covered with red spider webs. And look at those dark bags underneath." He pinched my cheek.

I batted his hand away. "What'd you do that for?"

"Your cheeks are pale."

"I'm a natural blonde. Pale skin comes as part of the package deal."

"You look like one of those zombies hanging out at the Opera House last month before you went and screwed up their play."

I hadn't screwed up anything. It wasn't my fault that a bitchy white-haired sprite with a fetish for spikey stuff had gone on a killing spree and taken out part of the cast.

"You are doing wonders for my ego, old man."

"Well, the scarf sure looks purty. Is that warm and fuzzy enough for ya, or do you need me to write ya a love poem?"

"I'm allergic to poetry." After my coworker, Ben, had played Shakespeare this past summer and had tried to woo me with a slew of Roses are Red sonnets and flower bouquets, I'd changed my standards when it came to romance. These days, a thick steak and a cold bottle of beer were good enough.

Rolling to a stop in front of the hotel where Dickie and Honey were staying, I snapped one of Harvey's suspenders. "Promise you'll be polite in front of my guests."

"Of course I'll be polite. My mamma didn't raise me to be an addle-headed coot."

"And that you won't talk about sex, guns, and prostitutes or your history with loose women and kissing cousins."

He crossed his arms over his chest. "Shucks, girl. All that leaves us to chew on all day is a bunch of fiddle faddle."

"*And* that you'll keep quiet about all of the body parts and weird discoveries going on at your place."

His chin jutted. "I thought these folks wanted to hear the juicy stuff. That's what makes good TV."

"When it comes to your ranch, I want to be in control of what juicy stuff they hear."

"You can never tell which way a pickle's gonna squirt." He waggled his fingers at Honey as she approached with her cell phone in one hand and her camera bag over her shoulder

"Just try to be good," I whispered through a big smile and rolled down my window. "Hi, Honey."

"Morning." She glanced back at the hotel. "Dickie will be here shortly."

"This is Willis Harvey."

Harvey leaned forward. "You can call me Bill."

I did a doubletake. *Bill?* I mouthed.

Harvey winked at me.

"Nice to meet you, Bill. Thank you for letting us take a look around your ranch today. I hear you might have a ghost for us to see."

"Maybe more than one. I'll introduce you to Bessie, too."

I smacked Harvey's leg.

"Who's Bessie?" Honey asked.

"My guardian angel."

Here we go again. I was thankful that Dickie was walking out the hotel lobby doors so that we could get one step closer to the end of today.

After introductions were made, we cruised on up Strawberry Hill and south on State Route 385. Several twists and curves up a winding gravel road and we bumped into Harvey's ranch.

"Home sweet nightmare," Harvey muttered.

Shooting him with a pointed glare, I stopped in front of his porch and killed the engine. "How about we start inside and finish with your old family cemetery?"

"Is the cemetery close by?" Dickie asked as he joined Harvey and me on the front porch.

"Just two whoops and a holler past my old barn there." Harvey pointed toward the barn, behind which we'd found part of a human scalp with the ear still attached back in July. But Dickie didn't need to know that detail.

"Let's say 'Hello' to your pappy's ghost, shall we, Bill?" I said to Harvey, pulling open the screen door.

Harvey led the way.

An hour later, we'd traversed his house and the barn and inside his attic. Luckily the only excitement had been in the barn when a rat had raced across the top of Honey's boots, making her scream and high-step for a few seconds. Other than critters, Harvey's place was nice and quiet on the ectoplasmic front.

"Let's drive back to the family cemetery now." I stepped out onto the front porch, holding open the screen door for everyone to follow. I had a feeling that the sooner we could get back to town and away from this place, the sooner my tension headache would break.

Dickie and Honey were wrapping up, videotaping Harvey's commentary about the history of his family's ranch.

I heard a suckling-snorting sound behind me and looked around to find Red, Harvey's fat yellow dog, splayed out on the porch while chewing on what looked like a dirty, old boot.

"Hey, Red," I let go of the screen door and walked over to the old dog. "Can't you find something better to chew on?"

Red spared me a few pants and then returned to tugging on the leather uppers. The eyelets and hooks looked like tarnished brass. They were probably pricey boots before Red got ahold of them.

The screen door creaked open. "What're you buggin' old Red about?" Harvey asked me.

I pointed at the boot. "He's eating one of your boots."

Harvey shuffled over. "That ain't my boot." He bent over with a grunt and tugged it free of Red's jaws. When he held it up, a dollop of slobber dripped from it, splatting on the porch right next to my taupe-colored, open-toed suede bootie.

I grimaced at the saliva-coated leather and the dirty sock jammed partway in it. "I supposed that isn't your sock either."

The screen door creaked as Dickie and Honey joined us on the porch.

Red whined up at us, licking his chops.

"This here?" Harvey reached into the slobbery mess and pulled out the sock with his fingertips. "Nope. Wool makes me itch all over."

"I know all about your issues with wool." Too much.

"What's in there?" Honey asked.

I frowned as she approached, wishing I'd ignored Red and his chew toy. "You mean the boot?"

"No, the sock." She pointed at the toe. "There's something in it."

"Probably a dead mouse," I said, hoping to scare her back a step. It worked.

Harvey tipped the sock upside down and shook it out on the porch. A collection of bones rattled onto the boards, along with chunks of what looked like light tan turkey jerky.

The three of us bent over to get a closer look.

"Is that ..." I gasped and stood upright so fast that stars floated through my vision.

"They look like metatarsals and phalanges," Honey whispered, a mixture of awe and disgust in her tone. She gaped up at me. "You don't think ..."

"Yep," Harvey said. "I do think so."

"What is it?" Dickie asked, horning in on our circle.

"The partial remains of a foot," Honey answered. She reached for her camera. "We need to get this on film."

"Oh, shit," I muttered, kneading my forehead with my palms.

Dickie pulled a pair of reading glasses from his shirt pocket. He lowered onto one knee and peered even closer. "Look at the dried pieces of skin. These must be really old."

I frowned at Harvey. "Cooper's head is going to explode when you call him."

"Me?" Harvey dropped the sock and wiped his hands on his

jeans. "I ain't callin' Coop. I did it last time. It's your turn."

"No, I called him last time."

"But ya blamed me."

"Who's Cooper?" Dickie asked.

"Deadwood's detective." I pointed at Harvey. "And *Bill's* nephew, which is why he's calling."

"I'd love to get an on-camera interview with Mr. Cooper," Honey told Dickie. "I have release forms in my camera bag."

Staring down at the bones, Harvey shook his head. "What we got us here is a hair in the butter."

"More like the whole damned scalp." I grabbed my phone.

Chapter Eighteen

"Parker," Detective Cooper said when he joined Harvey and me in the kitchen an hour later, "would it be too much to ask for you to go one month without finding a body?"

"It's only a foot." I met Cooper's glare head on. "And it's not even fresh."

"You're splitting hairs."

"Besides, I didn't find this one, the dog did. I just called it in for him since his English isn't so good." I sipped on the cup of black coffee Harvey had made while we waited for Cooper and several members of the sheriff's department to finish studying the boot and the bones. "Maybe you should make Ol' Red your partner. He has a better track record at sniffing out clues than you. Harvey could get him one of those Sherlock Holmes hats." I chuckled at the image of Cooper and Red in my head.

"Are you done?" Cooper asked.

"Almost." I grinned at Harvey. "Dickie and Honey could start an all new television series about Cooper and Red's crime-solving adventures."

Harvey's gold teeth glinted. "They could call it *The Canine and the Cop.*"

"I love it. Ol' Red gets top billing."

Cooper scrubbed his hand down his face. "I think I'll throw you both in jail this time, and let Red eat the key." He took the cup of water and ibuprofen his uncle was holding out for him. "Thanks." He gulped them down and then grimaced across the room at where Dickie and Honey were talking with one of the deputies. "What's the story with those two?"

"They're here to film your great grandpappy's ghost," Harvey answered.

"My boss has me showing them around," I added. "They have a reality TV show called *Paranormal Realty*. They're in town to scout out filming locations and plan their show."

Cooper squinted from me to Harvey and back. "You two are going to be on television together?"

"I hope not," I said.

Harvey hooked his thumbs in his suspenders. "Your uncle's gonna be a big star, boy."

"The world won't know what hit it." Cooper pulled a key from his pocket and handed it to me.

"What's this?"

Harvey nudged me with his elbow. "I think you're going steady now."

"The key to my garage."

"Why do I need to get into your garage?"

Harvey nudged me again. "Maybe he's keeping his case board there and saving you the hassle of breaking and entering this time."

"I didn't break and enter last time." I had a key then, too.

"No, but you did trespass," Cooper said.

"Now you're splitting hairs." I held up the key and raised my eyebrows.

"I've cleaned up the garage so you can let buyers see it when you show the house."

"What about your motorcycle?"

"Reid's storing it for me for the winter."

I closed my fist around the key. "How's Reid doing?" I hadn't seen the poor guy since Aunt Zoe had clocked him.

"He's limping along."

I worried my lower lip. When I'd mentioned Reid's name to Aunt Zoe yesterday as a litmus test, there'd definitely still been an abundance of acid.

"Coop," Detective Hawke said, stepping inside the front door and coming our way.

I caught the scowl that flitted over Cooper's face before he fit his stony mask back into place.

"What?" Cooper's back seemed to stiffen as he waited for

Hawke.

"The sheriff needs you outside."

Cooper cursed under his breath. Head down, he strode out the door.

"Parker," Detective Hawke turned his burly brow my way. "There's nowhere to run and hide today, Chicken Little."

I crossed my arms over my chest, bracing for whatever Hawke had been wanting to badger me about for the last few days. "All right, let's get this over with."

"Relax, Parker. I'm not a proctologist."

He'd sure been a pain in my ass since our first meeting.

The detective pulled a pen from his blazer pocket. A pad of paper came next, which he flipped open. He clicked his pen, shooting me a wincing glance. "How's your temper today?"

I kept a poker face. "That depends on what your pen writes down on that pad of paper."

"Don't take your frustrations out on my pen, Parker."

"If you're that concerned about it, maybe you should deputize it and threaten to arrest me if I lay a hand on it."

Harvey snickered and handed me a couple of ibuprofen. "You're probably gonna need these by the time he's done."

I needed them an hour ago. I chased the pills with a drink of water and then lifted my chin. "I'm waiting, Detective."

"According to your statement on the Hessler case, you were romantically involved with Wolfgang Hessler."

I frowned as the gears ground in my head. "What … wait … Wolfgang … why are … who said …" I stopped, my tongue untangling, and skipped beyond the first five W's that had tumbled from my lips. "Let's get something straight. I was not romantically involved with that man."

"Did you not write in your official statement that you'd gone on a date with Hessler?"

"Yes, we did go out to The Wild Pasque once, but that hardly constitutes romantic involvement."

"And did you not also state that you were on a dinner date with him again the evening he took you to his house and tried to light you on fire?" Hawke flipped his notebook back several pages and read, "He said he had to kill me because he loved me." One thick eyebrow was raised when he looked up at me. "Those were your words, weren't they?"

I sputtered again. Harvey slapped me on the back. "Yes," I said when I'd pulled myself back together.

"So have we fully established that you were romantically involved now?"

"No, you've established that I was romantically involved with Wolfgang by misconstruing the events that took place during the two dates I had with a psychotic murderer. I would disagree and say that since he and I exchanged only three kisses during our brief client-Realtor relationship, and one was forced upon me while I was tied up and on the verge of being barbecued, this was more a case of me selecting the wrong recipient for some misguided flirting."

Hawke scribbled something in chicken scratch while shaking his head. "You're a real piece of work, Parker. It's no wonder Coop keeps a bottle of whiskey in his desk drawer these days."

"Leave me out of Cooper's problems."

"Fine. How long have you been friends with Wanda Carhart?"

"Friends?" I looked over at Harvey, who mocked zipping his lips.

"I wouldn't exactly call them friends," Harvey stepped in on my behalf. "It's not like they get together for beer and chit-chat about who knocked up who and whether the baby-daddy knows about it."

Hawke smirked at Harvey. "Are you her lawyer now?"

Harvey harrumphed. "Maybe I am."

My phone rang. I glanced down at the screen and saw Natalie's name. Whew! Perfect timing.

"It's my boss," I deadpanned to Hawke. "I need to take this or I could get in big trouble at work."

I turned my back on his suspicious gaze and answered the call. "Hi, boss, what can I do for you?"

"Did you just call me boss or hoss, as in Hoss Cartwright from Virginia City?" Natalie asked, her voice sounding tired.

Why in the hell would I call her Hoss? She knew I was more partial to Marshal Matt Dillon, all tall and handsome with that sexy, commanding voice of his, not Bonanza's Cartwright men and their drama. Dressing up like Miss Kitty was one of my favorite Halloween costumes. Maybe I could convince Doc to put on a cowboy hat and U.S. Marshal badge this year for trick-or-treating with the kids and me. He was almost as big as James Arness.

Where was I? Oh, right. Putting on an act. "Yes, I'm still stuck out here at Harvey's place."

"What're you doing at your bodyguard's creepy ranch?"

I glanced over at the detective, who was watching me like a … well, a Hawke. "No, I'm not alone, but I can find a private place." I tilted my phone away from my lips. "I need to step outside, Detective. How about we continue your version of the Spanish Inquisition another time?"

"Violet, what the hell's going on?" Natalie asked in my ear.

"Just a minute, please," I said into the phone and then palmed it. I didn't wait for Hawke's answer. I rushed past Dickie and Honey and out the door. Edging around the crime scene tape, I weaved through the sheriff's crew.

Privacy awaited me over by the clothesline between the barn and house. I leaned against one of the poles and soaked up the bright October sunshine flickering in between puffy marshmallow clouds. The cool fall wind toyed with the end of my scarf. I should've grabbed my jacket on the way out.

"Hey, Nat. Sorry about that. I'm in a bit of a pickle here."

"Why are you at Harvey's place talking to Detective Cooper?"

The odor of exhaust coming from one of the sheriff's cars idling by the barn tickled the back of my throat. "Actually that was Detective Hawke. Cooper is busy talking to the sheriff."

"Detective Hawke? You mean Cooper's new partner?"

"Actually, I found out he's an *old* partner. The scuttlebutt is that they used to work together down in Rapid City, but then Hawke screwed him over and Cooper transferred up here to Deadwood."

"So Cooper really must not be thrilled about any of this."

"He's swearing more than usual these days."

"Why is the sheriff out at Harvey's anyway?"

I caught the end of my scarf, tucking it into my neckline. "Harvey's dog found a boot."

"This is the same dog that found that guy's head?"

"The one and only."

"Damn, that dog has a nose for trouble."

I practically heard that punch line clunk on the ground. "That was lame, Nat. Try again."

"How about this: Sounds like old Red is good at sniffing out trouble."

"No, that was worse. You should just move on."

"Fine, but Cooper needs to partner with that dog."

I laughed. The breeze whipped up, carrying it away. "Great minds think alike."

"What's the big deal about this boot?" Natalie asked.

"There was still a foot in it."

There was a long pause from her end, and then, "Holy shitballs of fire."

"Well, actually, it was a few chunks of dried flesh and the bones, so not like a whole foot, still juicy, ankle and all." I shuddered at the thought of that, turning my back to the mayhem buzzing around the front porch.

"What are you, Violet? Some kind of human magnet for missing body parts?"

"I'm beginning to wonder if I'm cursed."

"Maybe some old gypsy woman has it out for you."

Either one of those would help make sense of my run of bad juju since coming to Deadwood. "Of course, the TV people that Jerry has following me around had to be here to see it."

"What did Jerry say about this when you told him?"

"I haven't yet. I figured I'd wait to see what the sheriff said before I crossed that bridge."

"What's Cooper think? Is it another murder?"

"Cooper's not saying anything, as usual. Harvey heard one of the deputies complain about probably having to spend the day scouring the graveyard behind Harvey's place to see if the boot came from there." I frowned up into the trees that climbed the hillside next to Harvey's house, peering into their shadowed underbellies. Was something up there watching us hop around like vultures picking at a fresh kill down here?

"I would think a freshly dug grave would be easy to spot."

I rubbed over the goosebumps on my arms. "I asked Cooper if it might have come from that cave nest where they found those remains and other nasty stuff months ago."

"What did Deadwood's favorite detective say?"

"The butthead told me that was police business."

"Of course," Natalie said, snorting. "I think that's one of the five responses they programmed him to say back when he was at the police academy."

I chuckled. Nat had been bit by Cooper's sharp teeth a couple of times herself. Weeks ago over a six pack of beer, we had concocted a theory—Cooper was half-robot, created by the evil emperor to destroy all cute and furry creatures when he wasn't blowing up rebel bases.

"So where are you?" I asked her.

"Sitting on my back deck."

"When did you get home?"

"About an hour ago."

"How was Arizona?"

"Fun, lots of laughs, kind of crazy. My cousins are nuts."

"You sure didn't fall far from that family tree."

"Take a train, peanut brain," she said, throwing one of our childhood insults back at me. "So what have I missed here?"

"Let's see," I decided to skip the stuff about Ms. Wolff for the time being and get right to the heart of my frustrations. "Rex is fucking with my world through my job. He tried to make a move on me while I was showing him a house and I hit him in the face with a cupboard door."

"That no good, piece of—"

"Parker," Cooper barked from behind me.

I jumped and whirled. His expression was all tornadoes and hurricanes as he stormed up to me. Great, what had I done now?

"What?" I held the phone slightly away from my ear.

"You need to leave now."

His demand was my wish. I could hear Natalie still ranting through the line.

Cooper frowned at my phone. He must have heard her voice, too. He pointed at it. "That's not Nyce, is it?"

"It's Natalie."

He rubbed his hand over his jawline as if my response required thought. "She still down in Arizona?"

"No, she's back home."

"She is?" He nodded repeatedly, like a bobble-headed version of himself answering his own question. His gaze locked on my phone. As I watched, the weather on his face changed from stormy to partly cloudy to a chance of sunbreaks.

Then he looked up at me and the supercell formed again, swirling and dark, making his eyes narrow. "Tell her you'll call her when you're back in Deadwood," he ordered, mistaking me for one of his subordinates. "I want those TV people out of here before someone gets stupid about being on camera and leaks something important."

I glared at his stiff shoulders as he strode away, raising the phone to my ear again. Natalie was winding up her anti-Rex tirade, working on the T's in her swear word vocabulary.

"Nat," I interrupted. "Cooper's kicking me out of here."

She sniffed. "Well, you'd better leave then before he gets out the handcuffs again."

Just the reminder of being cuffed and hauled into jail made me feel like kicking something, preferably something on Cooper's body. "That still fries my patootie." I started back toward the house. "Come to dinner tonight? Harvey mentioned something about grilled ham and cheese sandwiches."

"Yum! I'll bring the beer."

I had a feeling that after today, I was going to need something stronger. "Make it tequila."

* * *

Tuesday, October 9th

The Galena House looked benign in the late morning sunshine when I pulled up in front of it and shut off the Picklemobile. It was still in need of a little TLC and a whole lot of paint, but it reminded me much less of the House on Haunted Hill when thunder and lightning were not part of the backdrop.

"This pickup has an odd smell to it," Cornelius said from the passenger seat. He sniffed a couple of times. "Like someone let a jar of petroleum jelly go rancid under the seat."

I hadn't smelled rancid petroleum jelly so I wasn't sure which particular smell he was referring to—the one coming from the glove box, the seat cushions, or the vents. I was used to all of the truck's unique odors, just as I'd grown accustomed to most of Cornelius's eccentricities.

"Think of riding in the Picklemobile as a unique life experience. If that doesn't help, roll down your window."

"I don't like it," Cornelius said.

"Listen, until you get your rental fixed, this is what we have." Cornelius had somehow managed to inadvertently disable his rental car's electrical system again. I was beginning to think he should add "Electromagnetic Anomaly" to his business card in addition to Ghost Whisperer.

"I meant I don't like the house."

I sighed. It was that or hit my head against the driver's side window a few times and forehead bruises were hard to hide.

I'd told Doc last night that moving the location of the séance was not going to sit well with Cornelius. He was set up in his hotel suite with all his gadgets and sensors. Leaving his outfitted ghost lab would put a monkey wrench in his ability to record all aspects of ghosts and ghostly chatter.

"Why don't you like it?" I asked.

"There's bad energy here. Look," he said, pointing out the window at the house. "You can see it radiating from the roof."

I peered at the roof for a moment. "Are you talking about the smoke coming from the chimney?"

"I'm talking about the blackness billowing up and out. It speaks of deep set decay in the heart of the house."

Someone's creative mind needed to be reined in and put back in its barn stall. "It's more of a light gray, don't you think?"

"There's a cancer in that place, Violet, spreading from the inside out. It doesn't smell right."

"I thought you said it was the pickup that stunk."

"Nor does it feel right," he continued as if I hadn't interrupted. "If I go into a séance feeling this way, things will turn sour. I know this from experience. Did I ever tell you about my cousin and what happened to her?"

I knew a little about his cousin's freaky death and Cornelius's role as a suspect in it. All that aside, it wasn't like Cornelius to be so negative and resistant to anything paranormal. Usually he jumped at the chance to chat with new ghosts.

"Did you drink your daily protein shake yet?" I asked.

"No. And my morning carrot was soft."

I wasn't sure if he was referring to an actual orange vegetable or a physical problem south of his belt buckle, nor did I want to risk clarification. I pulled out a protein bar I'd packed for my own lunch and unwrapped it. "Here, eat this." He stared at it as if I'd pulled it out from the Picklemobile's glove box. I shoved it under his nose and insisted.

"I'm allergic to blueberries," he said.

"Those are chocolate chips. Eat it."

He took a bite and nodded his acceptance.

"Okay," I said, "let's go meet the owner. She should be waiting for us." Before he could open his door I grabbed his arm, his wool jacket scratchy to the touch. "Here's the thing. She doesn't know about your ability."

"Which one?"

The one that allowed him to shoot webs from his hands, what did he think I meant? "Your ability to talk to ghosts."

"Oh, that?" he said, as if it were his least important ability.

"Yes, that. So let's keep that secret of yours between us."

"Of course." He shoved open the door. "I always try to lie low and blend in."

I looked at his stovepipe hat, black wool coat, pointy goatee, and the walking stick he was unfolding as he stepped out onto the street. "Right. You're a regular chameleon."

We walked to the front porch, the clack-clack of his walking stick on the sidewalk echoing down the street in an otherwise quiet moment.

Freesia opened the front door, greeting us with a smile. "Good to see you again, Violet." Her gaze climbed all of the way up to the top of Cornelius's hat. The curves in her cheeks deepened as her smile grew wider, making her eyes sparkle. "And who is this tall drink of water?" she asked, her voice growing huskier than normal, breathier. She batted her long eyelashes at him.

I did a doubletake. Was she flirting with Cornelius? Could that even be possible? Had the magnetic poles switched places?

"This is Cornelius Curion," I told her. "He's a client of mine." I turned to him, checking to see if he'd noticed he had an admirer. The bonehead was frowning down at his glasses, trying to wipe a dirt smudge away with wool. I cleared my throat. "Cornelius, this is Freesia Tender. She owns the Galena House.'

Freesia held out her hand.

Cornelius looked up at it and reared back a step. "I don't shake hands. It can send my aura into a maelstrom."

Her cheeks warmed at his rebuff. She pulled back her hand and shoved it into the pocket of her capri pants. "Your aura, huh? You must be into the spiritual world."

"Yes. I'm a ghost whi—"

I elbowed him in the solar plexus, aiming to knock him off course. Instead I knocked the wind out of him. He gasped and coughed and gasped some more.

When he caught his breath, he grimaced at me. "That was unpleasant."

"Oops," I replied.

"What were you saying?" Freesia asked. "You're a ghost what?"

I glared at him.

"That's all," he said. "I'm a ghost."

She touched his chest, scraping her nail down the wool of his coat. "You feel like a real man to me."

Oh, Lord, was this really happening? Had Freesia been brainwashed by an evil presence in the building? Was she looking for the 'keymaster'? Was the Stay Puft Marshmallow Man going to come strolling down the street next?

Cornelius appeared oblivious to Freesia's flirting, looking away to cough into his hand a couple more times. Then he took off his round-framed glasses and put them in the inside breast pocket of his coat. "Freesia," he said, peering down the hall behind her at who knew what. "Did you know that your name is the same as a fragrant, delicate flower that is easily damaged by the elements?"

"So I've been told."

"Are you?" he asked, his gaze focusing back on her.

"Am I what?"

"Easily damaged?"

"Oh, no, darlin'. I'm hardy as a dandelion."

Cornelius frowned. "You're referring to the weed, right? Not a dapper lion or an herbal tea?"

Okay. We'd reached the end of the stage line. It was time for everyone to get off and move along. "Freesia," I took her by the elbow and turned her toward the stairs. "Do you mind showing Cornelius and me around the building?"

"Sure. Would you like the same tour as the one you had yesterday with Mr. Harvey?"

"That's fine."

"I'd like to view the attic," Cornelius said. "And the basement."

I frowned at him but said nothing. I thought he was concerned about the evil billowing from the heart of this place. If so, why would he want to scope out the scariest parts of the house?

Freesia had a sexy hip-swing going as she climbed the stairs in front of us. "You're welcome to take a peek," she glanced back and winked at Cornelius. "I can show you my apartment, too, if you'd like."

"That won't be necessary," I said, raining on her flirt fest.

"Maybe another time," she directed at Cornelius.

Criminy. She must have been sniffing glue before we arrived. "Is that the door to the attic?" I asked, moving us right along, wanting to get this over with so the world could return to its normal programming.

It was the door, luckily. We climbed upstairs and looked around at a couple of large rooms packed full of old furniture, stacks of books and boxes, and huge conglomerations of dust bunnies. Down in the basement, the musty smell came complimentary with the dirt floor. Old shelves lined the concrete walls, broken furniture was scattered here and there along with rusted paint cans and some paint-peeling doors.

Back on the first floor, we paused outside of Ms. Wolff's door. The tape was still there, X-ing off the doorway. I frowned at it, thinking about Layne's picture tucked into the mirror inside.

"Sorry, I still can't let you in, Violet," Freesia said.

"Why not?" Cornelius asked.

Freesia looked at me. "He doesn't know?"

I shook my head.

"I don't know what?"

I opened my mouth to tell Cornelius about Ms. Wolff, but he covered my mouth with his hand. "No, don't tell me, I'd rather find out later."

"Find out later?" Freesia asked. She turned to me. "Are you thinking of sneaking inside again tonight?"

Cornelius gasped. "I can't believe you came here at night without me?" He sounded hurt, which was ironic considering a short time ago he didn't even like the place.

I shrugged at him. It wasn't like we were ghost hunting partners. "Sort of." I kept my answer evasive to protect Freesia in case Cooper came around asking questions.

"Did you find something?" he pressed.

"Sort of," I said again.

"Is that why you want to have a séance in there tomorrow night?"

Lucky for him, I hit him with a glare instead of my foot.

Freesia's eyes widened. "You want to have a séance in Ms. Wolff's apartment?"

I hemmed, hawed, and then looked at my toes. "Sort of."

Both Cornelius and Freesia were silent.

I looked up, expecting to meet resistance. "Listen, we don't have to do it. It was an idea. I thought it could help the cops." I grabbed Freesia's arm. "But I didn't plan to tell them about it, just kind of sneak in, try to talk to some ghosts—with any hope, Ms. Wolff—and then leave."

"Are you both mediums or something?" Freesia asked.

"Or something," I mumbled.

"I talk to ghosts," Cornelius explained. "Violet acts as a conduit for me."

I winced in anticipation of her blatant disbelief.

"How cool! I used to have fun in college with my girlfriends playing with a Ouija board. I swear that thing would move on its own sometimes." Freesia's smile had a conspiratorial feel to it. She leaned in closer. "I'll tell you what. If you let me join you guys, I'll sneak you into Ms. Wolff's place tomorrow night."

"There's one more of us," I said. "My boyfriend." I risked a glance at Cornelius to see his reaction to me adding another attendee.

He nodded. "Safety in numbers."

I'd heard that before.

"If I can come, he can come." Freesia sidled up next to Cornelius, flirting with her body and smile this time. "We can make it a double date. I'll bring some wine."

"No!" Cornelius said.

I gaped at him. Damn it, he was going to blow this opportunity. If Freesia wanted some flirting in return for a night in Ms. Wolff's apartment, he was going to have to suck it up and take one for the team.

"Wine dilutes the channel." Cornelius pulled his glasses from his pocket. "Make it mead." He turned to me. "And don't bother with the elk steaks. I already tried them." The way his nose wrinkled told me he felt the same about eating elk as my son.

"Are you saying you're game?" I asked him, unsure if I wanted the séance to happen or not. If we got caught in Ms. Wolff's apartment with candles and recording devices, Cooper would be all too happy to throw me in jail.

"Yes." Cornelius put his glasses on and gave me that weird crooked lip thing he did in place of a smile.

"What changed your mind?"

"The ghosts. They have something they want to tell me."

Chapter Nineteen

Bighorn Billy's parking lot bustled with post-lunch patrons ogling a group of mint 1940s era Mercurys. The fall sunshine reflected off the cars' flawless paint jobs, lighting up the excited faces of their admirers. Unfortunately, none of them were fit for time travel. I really could have used a way to zip back in time and figure out why Ms. Wolff had left that picture of Layne on her mirror and who had murdered her before Harvey and I got to her place.

Inside the diner, Dean Martin crooned about bedding down with his rifle and pony in a purple lit canyon. I recognized the song from *Rio Bravo* and puffed out my chest like the Duke facing down a mob of outlaws ... or in this case, one particular bristly detective sitting alone in the back corner booth. As I stood inside the door, wondering if coming here was a mistake, Detective Cooper nailed me with his cop squint and waved me over. If I turned tail and ran, would he chase me down and tackle me? Could I call that police brutality?

I blew out a breath. Dang, I might as well get this over with. Amidst the scent of burgers, coffee, and all things grilled and deep fried, I joined him at the booth, dropping into the opposite seat.

"I'm surprised you agreed to come here," was his greeting.

I shrugged off my jacket. "You did use the word 'please' for once." His invitation to meet and chat was so polite and non-curse filled that at first I thought he'd called the wrong number. I glanced at him. "You're not dying are you?"

"Don't get your hopes up, Parker."

After I settled into the booth and the waitress stopped by to take our drink orders, I picked up the menu. "Did you order another salad for me?"

Cooper had a bad habit of ordering diet food for me if I ran late. He claimed he was watching out for my figure, but I suspected something more along the lines of payback for the heartburn I seemed to cause him most days.

"Not this time," he said. "I thought I'd wait for you."

I looked up from the menu. "Wait a second, who are you really? Are you Detective Cooper's non-evil twin?"

"No. I'm still evil, but I'm tired of chasing ghosts."

That was something we had in common. I lowered the menu. Taking a closer look at him, I noticed a patch of stubble on his jaw he'd missed with the razor, the tired lines around his eyes, and the tufts of hair pulled this way and that.

"Your eyes are red," I said, focusing back on the menu.

"Yours are, too."

"It's called nightmares about dead people coming back to life. What's your excuse?" Next we'd start trading scar stories.

"Nightmares about live people turning up dead."

The waitress brought our drinks and took our order. After she left he leaned back in the seat and watched me.

I wasn't in the mood to have a staring contest. "Why am I here, Detective? Is this about the sale of your house?" I doubted it, but a Realtor could hope.

"Detective Hawke has a theory about you."

"Uh-oh, this can't be good."

His lips twisted in a wry grin, confirming my fear. "He thinks you're a witch."

I leaned forward. "Come again?"

"Not the wart-nosed, green-skinned, black pointy hat kind—more of a sorcerer of sorts who dabbles in black magic, voodoo, or other kinds of pagan rituals."

"He thinks I'm a witch?" I was still having trouble processing that part of his theory.

"I understand his confusion considering your crazy hair." Cooper sipped his coffee. "But I told him I disagreed."

"Gee, thanks." I wrinkled my nose at him. "What is Detective Hawke basing this theory on? Let me guess, he found my flying broomstick. Or was it my jar of frog hearts?"

"He's gone through all of the case files and your statements and believes there is a reason you have been involved in some manner with all of the deaths."

"That's insane. It's coincidence."

"Is it?" Cooper's gaze searched mine.

"What do you think?"

He shrugged. "I think you need to stay away from the Galena House."

That came out of left field. "What?"

"One of the patrol units called in late this morning and told me he saw you and an Abe Lincoln look-alike leaving the Galena House."

My cheeks heated. His implicit accusation burned all of the way down, firing up my resentment toward him and his men. "Freesia Tender hired me as her Realtor."

"I know that, but there is no reason for Cornelius Curion to be in that house with you."

"He is a client of mine," I bit out the words.

"He's already buying The Old Prospector Hotel."

"True, but maybe he's interested in more than one property in Deadwood, have you considered that?"

"Is he?"

Rather than lie, I dodged his question, taking a card from his deck. "That's privileged Realtor-client information."

The waitress appeared with our side salads and forced our conversation to go nonverbal for a moment. Cooper tried to intimidate me with his squint. I lifted my chin in response.

After she left, he picked up his fork and aimed it at me. "Stay out of Ms. Wolff's apartment without a police escort, Parker. We've left that place taped off for a reason."

"What reason?"

"That's none of your business."

"As Freesia's Realtor, it is my business. I need to know how soon the apartment will be cleared so that I can take interested buyers through the house without wincing when we walk by your police tape."

He chomped on a bite of salad. "I'll remove the tape when I'm done collecting evidence."

"What's left to collect? You've dusted for prints and taken pictures of everything, and you're undoubtedly having Ms. Wolff's body autopsied. Is there something else you are trying to find there? Does it have to do with those shrunken heads from decades ago that you're trying to tie together with Ms. Wolff's demise?"

His fork lowered, his nostrils flaring. "Nothing of concern to you. Just an answer or two."

I didn't give up that easily. "Like who killed Ms. Wolff and if it's related to the previous murders?"

"Like why she called you instead of the cops if she knew someone was going to kill her."

Holy crap. Cooper was actually confiding in me. I lowered my eyes, not wanting to appear to be too much of an eager beaver. I poked at my salad with my fork. "It makes no sense."

"I'd also like to know what she wanted to tell you that was so damned important."

"Me, too." If Cooper didn't interfere with the séance planned for tomorrow night, maybe Doc would have some kind of answer for both of us. Although I wasn't sure how I could share anything learned without Cooper going ballistic. "I'd like to know if my son is somehow involved and now in danger."

"Me, too, Violet." He lowered his fork, his steely eyes locked onto mine. "Trust me, that's a top priority."

"Thanks," I said, really meaning it.

"Has Conner bothered you since that whole scene on the sidewalk in front of Nyce's office?"

"No. Why? Can you arrest him for being an asshole?"

He shrugged. "If he becomes a problem, we can discuss a restraining order."

"Well, well, don't you two look as cozy as bugs in a rug back here in the corner," a voice I loathed intruded on our conversation. "I hope I'm not interrupting your little liaison."

I slapped a smile on my cheeks and directed it up at Tiffany Sugarbell. She looked extra voluptuous today in her black seersucker dress and white silk jacket. A pearl pendant necklace rested perfectly at the top of her cleavage, reminding me of an upside down exclamation mark.

"What brings you to Deadwood, Tiffany?" I pretended I didn't want to flick her perfectly upturned nose.

"I have a one-on-one with an old flame."

With Doc, you tramp? She was trolling for a reaction from me, but I wasn't going to get snagged in her net this time. Been there and done that too many times since falling for him. It was time to cling blindly to some trust.

She leaned closer, palms down on the end of our table. "I promise not to tell Doc that I caught you two back here all alone," she said with a glint in her green eyes, "sharing whispers and googly-eyed stares."

Cooper and I exchanged sidelong glances. He raised one blond eyebrow at me; I rolled both of my eyes in return. Someone had been reading too many romance novels lately and it wasn't me—I hadn't been reading enough thanks to the utter chaos going on in my world. Maybe I should skip the books and make Doc reenact some hot sex with me.

"Ms. Sugarbell," Cooper said, turning his cop stare her way. "Is there something you need from us this afternoon?"

She stuck out her lower lip, all flirty and pouty. "Ah, Coopster, don't be such a frowny face."

My lips trembled from holding back my grin. "Come on, *Coopster*," I couldn't resist, "turn that frown upside down."

"Shut it, Parker," he snapped.

"So, Violet," Tiffany turned her high-wattage smile on me. Her fangs looked recently sharpened and shined.

I winced in preparation for her bite.

"I saw your billboard out on Interstate 90."

Many, many responses passed through my brain, most badmouthing my boss. I settled on the safest. "You did?"

"That's an interesting brand you're putting out." Her laughter couldn't sound any more canned if I'd opened her lips with a can opener. "Get it, 'putting out'?"

Here came the claws. I'd been waiting for this since she'd

caught Doc kissing me in the parking lot.

"Yep," I said, going with safe-mode again. I stabbed a grape tomato, wishing it was her ass.

Cooper shot me a mischievous look over the rim of his coffee mug. "What are you putting out, Parker? It's certainly not fires. You keep starting those. Do I need to arrest you for something else?"

"The next time you handcuff me," I played along, "use the fur-lined ones, please. Last time you left me bruised." I wasn't kidding. The cuffs he'd made me wear on the way to jail had left my wrists dotted with black and blue spots.

"I'm surprised Doc likes to share you, Violet," Tiffany said. "He was rather possessive when we were together."

More phony baloney crap. "I'm not much for being caged."

Cooper snorted. "Your feathers were pretty ruffled that time I tossed you behind bars."

I thought about kicking him under the table, but figured he'd use it as an excuse to lock me up and keep me away from the Galena House. "No comment."

"I ran into Ray Underhill the other day," Tiffany told me. "He mentioned the strategy you've been using to lure clients."

If I were a betting woman, I'd put all of my money on Ray telling her I was prostituting myself. I hoped that was all he'd told her. *Don't let her see you sweat!* I clasped my hands together on the table, trying to appear casual and chit-chatty. "Oh, yeah? What did my good buddy Ray have to tell you? I hope he didn't give away all of my secrets."

"It was enlightening. I can see that I'm going to need to up my game now in the realty business." She rubbed her hands together. "I do love some good competition."

Oh, I knew all about her competitive nature. Too much, actually. There were some things about Doc and Tiffany that I would like to untack from my brain and blow out my nose.

"Especially when it involves using feminine wiles," she said with an exaggerated wink.

"Parker has wiles?" Cooper asked, and then took a bite of his sandwich. His eyes roved back and forth between Tiffany and me as he chewed.

Tiffany touched his shoulder, tipping her head back and letting out a big, breast-bouncing laugh that stressed the seams of her dress. "Oh, Coopster. You're so cute. That must be one of the reasons Violet agreed to sell your place."

Cooper was cute? Sure, if you thought sharks, electric eels, and water moccasins were adorable. I peeked over at Cooper to see if he'd fallen for her eye-catching boobie-trap. He was watching me with a small grin at the corner of his lips, clearly enjoying the show. The bastard.

"Cooper's no different from any of my clients."

"Oh, Jeff Wymonds filled me in on your Realtor-client policies. You really know how to close a deal."

Undoubtedly, Jeff's conversation with her did not help my professional status in any way, shape, or form.

"Anyway," Tiffany said, her expression hardening. So much for the nicey-nices, I guessed. "I stopped by to say 'hello' and see if there is anything else needed by my client to make the sale of the hotel go smoothly for Mr. Curion."

"Nope, we're good."

"That's what he told me last night when we went out to dinner."

She what? With Cornelius? Why didn't he tell me?

"Don't worry, Violet. It was a spur of the moment thing. I happened to be in the hotel lobby when he came downstairs looking for somewhere to go grab an elk steak. Instead of giving him directions, I drove him there. That man has some interesting ideas."

And a broken down rental car. She didn't know the half of Cornelius' lore. Actually, maybe she did after having dinner with the infamous ghost hunter. I hoped he'd kept his big mouth shut about the séance—about all of our séances for that matter—and waxed on about his dislike for elk over the after dinner wine.

"Mr. Curion really gets around," Cooper said.

"He did mention he's considering looking for another property to purchase."

"See," I told Cooper, silently thanking Tiffany for

inadvertently helping justify my actions with Cornelius at the Galena House.

He grunted and took another bite.

"Of course I left him one of my cards in case he needed a more experienced Realtor for his next purchase."

I lowered my hands under the table to hide my balled up fists. The red-haired bitch was moving in on my client. That made me wonder how things with Jeff had gone. Was she playing the puffed out breasts and pouty lip game then like she was here with Cooper? Wait a second, was Tiffany the "field" Jeff was plowing these days? Heat crawled up out of my collar.

"It was good to see you again, Tiffany," I said, blowing her off as kindly as possible. I wasn't in the mood to circle and take swipes at each other any longer. "If you don't mind, Detective Cooper and I have a few more things to discuss about his house before he needs to get back to work."

"His house? If you say so." She leaned down and whispered something in Cooper's ear.

He stared across the table at me as he listened, his face its usual stony mask. I was pretty sure she wasn't conspiring with him to get me a surprise "we love you, Violet" gift.

"You two have fun now." She waved her fingers at us. "I'll be in touch, Violet. Give Doc my love."

She could take her catty love and go flush it down the men's urinal. I watched her sashay all of the way out the door. When I turned back Cooper offered me a French fry. "She sure is something, isn't she?" he said, his poker face on.

"Oh, she's something all right." I took the fry and crammed it in my mouth, thinking of all of the adjectives I'd use for Tiffany.

"Uncle Willis would've loved hearing that conversation."

"What did she whisper to you?"

"That's police business."

"You can shove your police business where the sun doesn't shine."

"Now, now, Parker, there's no need to ..." he trailed off, his gaze locking onto something behind me, his eyes widening. Then he sat up straighter and finished with, "get all pissy."

"I'm not getting pissy," I growled.

"Hi, guys," Natalie said as she dropped into the booth seat beside me. She glanced at me and did a doubletake. "What's got your face all puckered up like that?"

I scooted over, making room for her. She looked much more comfortable in her blue jeans and red flannel shirt than I felt in my dress pants and cashmere sweater.

"Nyce's ex-girlfriend," Cooper said.

"I thought I saw that red-taloned bitch filing her teeth on her way across the parking lot." Natalie grabbed my arm, looking it over. "Did she break the skin this time?"

"No, but she did leave a few indentations right here." I touched my back.

Natalie chuckled, stealing a tomato from me and popping it in her mouth. She turned toward my booth companion. "Hello, Detective Cooper. Are you keeping this girl out of trouble?" She pointed her thumb in my direction.

Cooper hesitated long enough to make me wonder if he had a French fry lodged in his gullet. I frowned across at him, noticing that his cheeks had a slightly red hue to them, but there were no signs of choking.

"Are you okay?" I asked him.

He shook off whatever had given him pause. "Sure. I just remembered something I need to do back at work."

"I see you're still all work and no play, Detective," Natalie said, softening it with a grin. She shoulder bumped me. "I think I've come up with a solution on how to cover that stupid tattoo."

"Which one?"

"The one on my hip with shithead's name in it."

"A big, solid black heart would do it."

"That's lame. I was thinking more along the lines of a sun. I saw some cool sun sculptures down in Arizona. They gave me the idea."

Cooper pushed his plate away and dropped some cash in the middle of the table. "I need to go, Parker. This should cover the bill."

"I hope I didn't interrupt any official police business," Natalie said.

"We were finished." His gaze slid to mine, warning me. "For now."

"Do you mind if I finish your fries?" Natalie asked.

"They're all yours." Cooper slid out of the booth.

"Thanks, I'm famished." She pulled his plate her way. "I hope your Cooper cooties don't fight with my cooties."

"They'll probably try to arrest them," I muttered.

Cooper shoved his arms into his jacket. "I'm sure our cooties would get along fine, Natalie."

I pointed at Cooper. "Tell Detective Hawke he better watch out or I'll put a hex on him."

"A hex?" Natalie asked.

"Be careful feeding that fire, Parker. It could flare up in your face." He took a few steps away, but then came back, his focus on Natalie. "Do something different than a sun."

Natalie chomped on his French fries. "You have a better idea, Detective?"

Cooper pulled a notepad and pen from his jacket pocket. He wrote something down, and then tore the paper off and handed it to her. "Go see her. You'll love her original work."

Pocketing the paper, she thanked him. His skin darkened under his rigid expression. After a nod, he strode out the door.

"Was it just me," Natalie said when the coast was clear, "or was Cooper off his meds today?"

"Maybe he's upped his dosage." I bit into my burger. With Tiffany and Cooper no longer antagonizing me, my appetite had returned and then some. "He even warned me about Detective Hawke, totally unprompted."

"No way. If he's sharing police business with you, he must really loathe that ex-partner of his."

"Maybe," I said, shrugging. I took another bite of my burger, wondering if Jerry noticed how long I'd been gone.

"What are you up to tonight?" Nat asked.

I swallowed. "Wild and crazy sex probably."

"With anyone in particular or only in your dreams?"

"I have the kids tonight and Harvey's on Doc's couch."

"Your dreams it is then."

I wished I had been able to sleep well enough to get a few dreams in lately. I'd almost dozed off at work earlier. "I'm hanging out at home. Why? You want to come over again?"

She bit off the end of a French fry. "I was thinking of paying someone a visit and wondered if you wanted to come along for shits and giggles."

"Oh, yeah?" I wiped my hands on my napkin. "Who?"

"Rex Conner."

Chapter Twenty

Wednesday, October 10th

It was a beautiful day to talk to dead people.

At least that was what Doc told me when I answered my cell phone way too early in the morning.

"I disagree," I told him, yawning. After all of the tossing and turning I'd done instead of getting decent sleep, my outlook had a lot less rosiness to it. I squinted at the clock. "Why are you calling me so early?"

"I have to head down to Rapid City this morning and wanted to talk to you before I hit the road."

I snuggled under the covers, wishing he were lying there next to me. "Mmmm. I missed you last night."

"I bet you say that to all the boys who call you at dawn." The beep-beep-beep of his coffeemaker reached my ears.

"Only you." I yawned again, changing my earlier wish to include fresh coffee along with Doc in my bed. Some bacon, too. "I tell the others to call back at a decent hour."

He chuckled. "How late did Natalie stay?"

"I think she's still here. I left her downstairs snoring on the couch sometime after midnight."

"I take it you talked her out of hunting down your ex and castrating him."

"Yeah, but it took quite a bit of tequila. Her loathing for him goes clear back to my second date with the ass."

"What happened on your second date?"

"He stood me up. When he finally called me later in the week, he said he'd been too busy working on a project in the lab to remember about our date."

"His loss."

"Nat never gave him a second chance."

"But you did."

"I'm a sucker for smart guys."

"You're not allowed to attend any Mensa conventions."

His words made me smile, helping me forget about all of the crap in my world for a few blinks. "I hadn't told Nat about the showdown in front of your office until last night." I stretched. "She's all primed to go ape shit on Rex now. He'd better hope he doesn't cross her path anytime soon."

"I sort of hope he does. I'd be happy to spring for Natalie's bail."

"I'll make sure she has your number for her one collect call. So what's the plan for tonight?"

"Sneak into the apartment, lure the shy ghost out of hiding, and leave before the cops catch us."

"You make it sound like a slam dunk," I said.

"You've been hanging around your boss too much. Next you'll start slapping me on the butt and telling me I need to take it to the hole more often."

"Sounds kinky, and you should."

"Okay, then I will."

"You could start right now," I teased. "You have a house key. Come on over and I'll practice my ball handling."

We'd traded keys not long ago. It wasn't a promise ring or his letterman jacket, but it would make stalking much easier and reduce the chance of me breaking another one of his windows.

He sucked air through his teeth. "Such a vixen, Boots."

"Or maybe I could sneak over to your place tonight while Aunt Zoe watches the kids and you could practice hitting the boards harder."

He went quiet. "Have you been saving these up or what?"

"No, they're just popping into my head. My brain must be stuck on the sports channel, damn it."

"We'll have to change that station to porn, sweetheart. Too much of this men's locker room chatter and I might end up on the bench. Unless you want to cheerlead naked for me."

Jump up and down in front of him while naked? Hell, no.

Not even drunk on a bet. I wanted him to fall head over heels in love with me, not keel over dead from laughter.

"I'll practice my porn movie star lines." I made a few kissy sounds in the phone. "Ya big stud," I added in a breathy voice.

"That's more like it."

I heard what sounded like an automatic garage door opening.

"What time am I picking you up this evening?" he asked.

"For basketball themed sex or the séance?"

"We'll start with the séance."

"How about five-thirty? Cornelius said something about sunset at six-twenty and twilight being at six-forty-something. He wants us to be set and up and rolling before both."

"He's not filming this, right?"

"I told him only audio devices and that none of it was allowed to be published in any shape or form."

"And he agreed?"

"Well at first he pouted, but then he consented."

Doc's keys jangled in the background. "Good. It will just be the three of us then."

"Uh ... make that four." I'd neglected to tell him about Freesia, not knowing how to drop that bomb. Turned out all I had to do was let it go.

"Violet," he sounded a little tense.

"I couldn't help it. I had to make a deal in order to get us into the apartment."

"Who's the fourth?"

"Freesia Tender. She owns the Galena House."

"Is she psychic?"

"No, but she was an instant fan of Cornelius and likes to dabble with ghosts."

"Violet," his tone was more resigned this time, less tense.

"I didn't want her there, Doc, but she figured out we are going back in and wants to be part of it. She knows the risks with the cops."

"But does she know the risks with the dead?"

Did I? I grimaced, thinking of how Cornelius's cousin had died. "She either joins us or the gig's off."

"Sounds like we have no choice."

"We do have a choice—we could skip the séance and watch a scary movie from your bed instead."

"As much as I like the bed option, I want to know if and how Layne and you fit into Ms. Wolff's demise."

"Yeah, me, too."

"After we're done at the Galena House, I'm going to drag you to my place, tear off your clothes, and play some one-on-one with you."

One-on-one—basketball lingo. "Ha! I got you."

"Yes, you do, Boots. I'll pick you up at five-twenty."

"Should I wear somber black and serious gray this time or stick with jeans and a T-shirt?"

"My only concern will be the color of your underwear."

"That'll be a mystery for you to solve." I changed into my husky porn-star voice. "See you later, ya big stud."

Chuckling, he hung up.

I thought about trying to fall back to sleep, but my eyes were now wide open and my brain busy worrying about what was waiting for us in that apartment. Was it a Prudence-like ghost who would use Doc to talk to the rest of us? Or was it a more malevolent presence, waiting to pounce and send Doc reeling as soon as he opened himself up to it. How was I going to handle smoothing things over with Cornelius and Freesia if Doc had severe tremors or was knocked unconscious? And how would I bring him back if things went sour and he was stuck on the "other side"?

Rather than let those thoughts fester, I got up. I considered going out for a run and then laughed all of the way to the shower at the mere notion of me jogging.

Later that afternoon, I was wishing I'd tried harder to fall back to sleep. My eyes burned, my brain felt like I was on a ten-second delay, my teeth were clenched when I wasn't paying attention, and my tongue kept getting stuck to the roof of my mouth for no reason. The shitload of stress in my life was really ganging up on me.

It was Ben's turn to babysit the TV folks, so I was free to go about my business. Rex hadn't bothered me since Doc faced off with him on the street, but I had a feeling we were far from finished with the dramatics. Hell, I'd written him off a decade ago and he'd returned, so there was no way he was giving up that easy.

At four-thirty, I headed home and changed into jeans and a T-shirt, leaving my hair loose—how Doc liked it best. My stomach jangled with nerves, but I managed to swallow a few bites of leftover roast and carrots before Doc showed up in Aunt Zoe's drive with Harvey in tow.

Harvey walked in the door with a large pizza as I was stuffing my cell phone in my purse. The kids jumped up and down, barely managing to spare me a kiss goodbye on their race to the kitchen.

"Addy," I called after her, "you get to bed early tonight. You need some rest so that cold doesn't get any worse."

Aunt Zoe smiled up at me from the couch when I kissed her on the cheek. "Don't come home tonight, sweetheart. A night with Doc might help you relax," she winked at me, "and maybe you can get some sleep afterward, too."

I placed my hand on my chest, faking shock and dismay. "Aunt Zoe, what are you insinuating? You know I'm holding onto my virginity until marriage."

"Violet, dear, that's not your virginity you're clutching when Doc's around, it's your heart. Your virginity ran off with that heavy metal drummer you were dating after high school. What was their band called? *The Screw Ups*?"

"*The Nail Heads*," I corrected, "and I'll have you know I never slept with him." I did have a few standards, and his interest in "nailing" multiple groupies at once turned me off.

"I like *The Screw Ups*. It has a better ring to it." She patted my arm. "Go have a good time with Doc."

Zipping my black hoody up to my chin, I pulled the hood over my loose curls, slipped on my boots, and headed out the door. I was looking forward to an evening with Doc period, with or without ghosts.

He stood leaning against his Camaro waiting for me, looking good in a dark blue jacket and jeans.

"Remind me," he said, holding open the passenger door for me. "Are we tagging some train boxcars before or after the séance?" His smile made his eyes crinkle in the corners. "I'll need to stop by the hardware store to pick up some spray paint."

"When we're running through the forest from Cooper and Hawke, you'll appreciate my outfit choice."

"I always appreciate those boots." He shut the door behind me, crossed in front of the car, and slid behind the steering wheel. Before he started the car, he grabbed me by my hoody strings and tugged me over, giving me a kiss. "Your lips taste like raspberries tonight."

"Wait until you try the rest of me."

His gaze traveled over my face, his eyes darkening. "Damn." He let go of my coat and started the car. "First, let's go meet a ghost." He shifted into reverse.

We parked several blocks away and walked to the Galena House to avoid the cops. I wasn't just being paranoid about Cooper. Earlier today when I'd called to fill Freesia in on the séance details, she'd told me the police were cruising by her place about once an hour. Undoubtedly I had Cooper to thank for such vigilance, the big buttinski.

Cornelius had planned to take a taxi there with his equipment since his rental was still making the mechanic scratch his head. True to his word, he did just that, arriving at the same time as us.

After a quick check for cops, we each grabbed a piece of Cornelius's equipment the taxi driver had unloaded from the trunk. Freesia waited at the door, hurrying us.

"I've been keeping watch from the attic. A cop car is heading this way."

We made it behind the closed front door as the Deadwood police cruiser rolled up. My heart thumped while I waited for Freesia to tell us he was coming up the walk.

"Okay, we're clear," she said, rubbing her hands together.

I blew out a sigh. I had a feeling that if Cooper caught us here, he'd revert to the former version of himself around me—the one with the pulsing vein in his forehead and snarling upper lip. With Rex in town, I needed Cooper and his police pals on my side in case I got mad enough to follow through on Nat's castration plan.

"You must be Freesia," Doc said, holding out his hand. "I'm Doc Nyce, Violet's ..." he hesitated, looking at me with a raised eyebrow.

"Boyfriend," I finished. "I told you about him yesterday."

Freesia shook Doc's hand, looking him up and down. She grinned at me. "You forgot to mention a few things."

"How do I open this?" Cornelius asked in front of Ms. Wolff's taped-off door. "It seems to be stuck."

"I thought I unlocked that," Freesia said, joining him.

I looked over at Doc. "You ready for this?" I whispered.

"As ready as I'll ever be." He took the piece of equipment I was holding, doubling his load and leaving me unencumbered. "Try not to give me a black eye this time, Tiger. It makes a guy look bad when his girlfriend keeps beating him up."

I faked a few Rocky punches while he bobbed and weaved. "You're a lot easier to hit when you're busy playing with ghosts."

"There, got it," Freesia said from down the hall. "You two coming?"

"Here we go," I said under my breath and led the way.

Nothing had changed inside Ms. Wolff's apartment except the amount of dust coating the surfaces. The ghoulish clocks still ticked, the mannequin heads still sat empty, and Layne's picture was still stuck in the mirror. I liked this place less and less each time I visited.

I joined Doc, who stood watching Cornelius open his cases. The infamous ghost whisperer pulled out gadgets and spread doohickeys around on the carpet while Freesia asked questions about his expensive toys.

"I forgot to bring the chicken feet for good luck," I told Cornelius.

He patted his coat pocket. "Not to worry, I always carry an extra one on me at all times."

He carried around a dried chicken's foot? Layne would think that was the coolest thing ever and probably want his own to carry. I could imagine fishing it out of my son's pocket while doing laundry. Yuck.

"Did you figure out what the writing on the inside of the drawer means?" I asked for Doc's ears only. I'd bugged him with that same question each day since he'd taken the picture of the backward scrawls.

"No. It's similar to the Latin I can find online, but different enough that I can't make sense of it."

"You think it's based on Latin?"

"Maybe. Or Latin could be based on it for all we know. I need to contact an expert in linguistics, but that might raise complicated questions depending on what the message says. I'm not sure how careful we should be about this."

Me, either. That was the problem. I wondered if there were a way I could involve Cooper and his long arm of the law without raising his suspicions on how I'd "somehow" figured out the mirror trick with the writing. Maybe I could tell him I'd had an idea about the drawer, and then convince him to bring me back here. With him here in the apartment, I could pretend to discover the writing in the mirror trick.

I watched as Cornelius took out four almost L-shaped metal objects and placed them on the living room floor, forming the L's into outward facing corners of a big square, spaced about six feet apart. Next he placed a compass above the inside corner of each L. Not a circle compass that spun based on the magnetic poles but rather the drafting tool an architect or engineer used to draw circles. I took a step closer, realizing the L was actually one of those square tools also used by engineers.

"Is this part of the Wanga bag deal you were telling me about?" I asked him.

"No. We changed venues. I didn't feel this was the right place to incorporate that spiritual element. Besides, it's on backorder."

"Then what are you doing?" I asked Cornelius.

"This is the symbol of the Freemasons," Doc spoke up.

Of course. "That's where I've seen it."

"There's often a capital G in between the square and the compass." Freesia kneeled down and drew the letter G on the carpet with her finger. "My family has belonged to the Freemasons for generations."

"Is there a reason you're making four Freemason symbols on the carpet?" I asked Cornelius.

"Yes," he said, lining them up more exactly.

When he didn't say more, I growled. "Why?"

"Violet, your aura is going to turn black again."

I was going to strangle him with my aura one of these days and make his match mine. "Please explain, Cornelius." I used my nice Realtor voice.

"When we were here last, I noticed the Freemason symbol in the concrete at the base of the porch," he explained. "In my experience, it helps the flow of energy if the ghost feels at ease with its surroundings. Based on all of the work done over time in Deadwood by Freemasons, there is a chance a ghost here tonight might have been a member of the Freemasons or married to one."

I shot Doc a questioning glance.

He shrugged in response and continued to watch Cornelius make his preparations.

Next Cornelius dug in his wool coat pocket and pulled out four triangular shaped stones the size of his palm. He put one at each of the corners.

"What are those?" Freesia asked.

"They represent the four elements symbolic to the Lakota Indian culture—earth, fire, air, and water. Since the Black Hills is sacred ground to the Native Americans, and there is a chance that we may come across an even older ghost than one of the town builders, I want to cover both possibilities."

I looked to Doc again, but he was staring toward the hallway as he had the other night, a frown on his face. I watched him closely for a moment, noticing the flare of his nostrils. He was picking up a scent of something; I could see it in the stiffness of his body.

"What a coincidence. There are four of us," Freesia said, squatting down to take a closer look at one of the stones.

"No coincidence," Cornelius said, adjusting the compass and

square nearest to him. "Violet chose you for a reason."

"I did?" My memory of this was me telling him I'd rather Freesia not know about our history with ghosts.

"Of course." Cornelius unclasped one of the equipment cases Doc had carried in from the taxi. "As a conduit, you are continually working to open channels. You may not have realized it, but subconsciously you were seeking a fourth for our séance in order to create the stronger union needed to widen the channel."

I was beginning to think he had me confused with that old oracle lady on *The Matrix*. Next he'd be handing me a spoon and telling me to bend it with my mind alone.

"If you say so," I said. "But why four rather than five?"

Doc walked over into the shadowed hallway, moving slowly. Was something wrong or was he being cautious?

"The number four has great significance." Cornelius pulled out his recorder that captured sounds at multiple frequencies and set it right outside of the square. "There are four cardinal directions, four seasons, four sides of a square, four ages of man, and four cosmic elements. The list goes on, but I really don't need to tell you. You obviously know this."

Or not so obviously.

"So are we going to form a circle inside of this square you've made?" Freesia asked.

"No." Cornelius opened the last of his equipment cases and pulled out several odd-looking meters—some I recognized from before—and a video camera. "We'll each sit at a corner, within the square but facing outward."

Freesia watched him with her dark eyes glittering in the glow of the battery powered camping lanterns Cornelius had brought along. "Does facing outward have some meaning rather than facing inward?"

"Not especially," he answered. "I've found that people focus better when sitting in a square formation if they have their backs to each other."

I pointed at the video camera he was checking. "We're not recording tonight, remember?"

"That is incorrect." He unfolded a tripod. "I agreed not to

film the four of us. I'll set this up in the bedroom."

"Filming what?"

"The mirror."

The one with Layne's picture. "Why that mirror?"

"Mirrors are sometimes windows to other worlds or dimensions."

I followed him through the doorway, watching as he set up the tripod. "I always thought that was something Hollywood had made up to add suspense."

"Mirrors capture souls, Violet." He said it as if I were an idiot to think they were used only to look at oneself. "Since this was the victim's bedroom, there is a good chance that if she's still with us in spirit, she will show herself in here where she was probably most comfortable."

Cornelius left me alone with the recorder and mirror.

I stared at the blinking red light on the camera. Had Ms. Wolff been standing next to me while I looked into her bedroom mirror days ago? The hair on the back of my neck prickled. I shuddered and tried to shake off the heebie jeebies that were crawling up my spine.

Doc's warm hand on my back had a calming effect. When my gaze darted up to his, he smiled and tweaked my chin. "She's not here," he whispered in my ear.

My pulse slowed back to its regular rhythm. I followed him out to Cornelius's square, which now had a candle placed on a plate in the center of it.

Cornelius checked his watch, and then peered out the window. "It's almost time. Each of you take a corner."

Doc took the one facing the hallway. I didn't want to face the bedroom or the wall of gruesome clocks, so I sat on Doc's left, looking at the spot where Harvey and I'd found Ms. Wolff's gnarled up body. Freesia sat kitty corner, the clocks in her sight.

"Should I be holding something?" Freesia asked.

"No." Cornelius took his place diagonal from Doc, facing the bedroom. "I recommend the yoga Namaste position with crossed legs. You'll need to focus on opening your thoughts, stepping outside of your conscious mind."

Yada, yada, yada, I thought, yawning. I sat on the carpet cross-legged, wondering if anyone would notice if I grabbed a couch cushion so my butt wouldn't go numb. I began some deep breathing techniques, playing along.

"It's time," Cornelius turned off the lanterns, leaving us lit by only the flickering candlelight. It smelled like vanilla, or maybe sweeter, like cookie dough. Was there a scent that worked better than others for luring the dead? I preferred fresh baked apple pie.

I checked on Doc. He had one arm resting on his raised knee, his other leg stretched out in front of him. He gave me a thumbs-up. I blew him a kiss back.

"Violet," Cornelius's voice seemed extra loud in the ticking apartment. "Open the channel."

Right. This was the part where I pulled paranormal shit out of my ass.

I cleared my throat. Here went nothing. "If there is someone here, please tell me your name." After pausing for a few breaths, I spoke again. "If someone is in this apartment with us, please step forward and tell me why you are here."

Cornelius began to hum, as he had in our past séances. The clocks ticked rhythmically along with him, lulling me into calmer waters.

Closing my eyes, I tried another avenue. "My name is Violet Parker. I've come here to talk to you. Please tell me your name." I knew as sure as Tom the cat would never catch Jerry the mouse that nobody was going to answer me, but if it distracted Cornelius long enough for Doc to touch base with the ghost in the hallway, then my work here tonight was done.

I let Cornelius hum for a bit longer, patting down another yawn, and then spoke. "Are you a woman or man?"

A look in Doc's direction showed him with his head resting on his raised knee now, his back curved into a C shape. I stretched mine, resisting the urge to curl up and take a nap for a few minutes. My lack of sleep was catching up again now that I was sitting still.

"How did you die?" I played the *Changeling* movie over in my head, remembering that medium's questions and the spine-chilling effect when the child's voice responded. It was probably best not to go any further there.

"Were you young when you were killed?"

My thoughts shifted, beginning to swim, one floating past another as I drifted in the current, waves lapping, lapping, lapping …

I sank deep down into dreamland, then thrashed my way back to the surface.

I jerked awake, finding myself standing in front of the bedroom mirror in Ms. Wolff's bedroom. What was I doing in here? I must have sleepwalked. I hadn't done that in years. I looked for the picture of my son. Only it wasn't there.

Crap, had I taken the picture in my sleep, my subconscious wanting to protect him? I checked my pockets. Nope. I wasn't supposed to move it for some reason. Why was that? My brain felt foggy, my thoughts fuzzy notions.

I scrubbed my hands down my face and then looked at my reflection in the mirror. Something wasn't quite right. I could see Cornelius's camera, the red light blinking. The door was closed, the bed was made, the dresser was in the same place as usual.

I turned around to look at the scene and see if I could figure out why something felt off. The scene before me made me scratch my head. There was a completely different bed in front of me. Not just a different bed spread, but the whole thing was bigger with a headboard. I looked over at the camera to make sure it was recording so we could get this odd bed thing on film, but there was no camera there. No tripod. Nothing.

I looked back in the mirror. There the camera sat on its tripod, the red light blinking. When I turned away from the mirror, it was gone again, and the bed changed. The wall was different, too. The paint seemed darker. The dresser was gone as well.

What in the hell was going on?

I walked around the bed and stood where the tripod should be. I checked the mirror; it was right next to me in the reflection. Had Cornelius changed the mirror as a practical joke? No, Cornelius wouldn't know a practical joke if it squirted him in the face. Something was off kilter. Was it me? My pulse picked up speed; I could feel it fluttering in my neck.

I started toward the closet. This wasn't making any sense. The sound of a loud thump on the other side of the bedroom door made me stop. Had Cooper found us?

I slowly turned the bedroom doorknob, making only the slightest squeak. I peeked out through the gap and pulled back out of sight, my heart sprinting as fast as it could go.

The albino's twin! Shit! Shit! Shit!

I stared across the bed at my wide-eyed reflection in the mirror. The video camera reflected there blinked its red eye.

Ohhhhh. I slapped myself across the forehead. Duh. Now I got it. This was a dream. That explained the mirror trick. Cornelius's earlier explanation about mirrors had left an impression on my dream architect.

Okay. Only a dream. Been there, done that. Might as well see it through until I woke up.

I looked out through the crack again, bolder this time now that I knew it wasn't real.

The albino's twin hadn't come for me after all. I was looking at my brain's recreation of my Mudder Brothers' nemesis. Out in the living room, the Donald-Duck looking fiend stood tall and frightening as ever, his face clenched in a manic smile, his eyes bulging more than usual as he raised a medieval looking ax over his head.

I looked down and grimaced. Great, another decapitation replay. One could never get enough of those.

Before I could turn away, the ugly duck swung the ax, severing the white-haired head from the body. The head bounced onto the floor, rolled a foot or two, and then stilled. I gagged. Sometimes my brain was such an asshole.

A bright light flashed, temporarily blinded me, heat making me step back. When my eyes readjusted and I looked back at the macabre scene before me, the head was gone ... sort of. In its place was a shrunken, smoking raisin version of it lying there on the scarred plank floor. Another white flash made me shield my eyes and wince. This time a gnarled, shriveled body was all that remained. I covered my nose as a familiar odor wafted through the crack in the door. It was the same smell Harvey and I had noticed in Ms. Wolff's apartment the day we'd found her.

The ugly duckling kicked the shriveled head, knocking it into two others just like it. All three rocked and rolled a little, then came to a stop.

Three shriveled heads? Oh, now I got it. This dream was about that old article Harvey had showed me. The mysterious shriveled heads piece. My brain had come up with an answer to the mystery. I wondered how Cooper would feel if I said to him, "Listen, I had this dream about those heads. I think I know who the killer is and how he did it."

The detective would probably laugh his own head off.

Movement in the hallway across the way caught my eye. A skinny man with hair greased back and a black leather jacket peeked around the corner. His gaze landed on the shriveled remains of the three victims, his eyes widening to the size of silver dollars. His gasp of surprise resounded across the room, catching the ax-happy-albino's attention.

I shook my head at the greaser's mistake. What a newbie. He might look like James Dean with his cuff-rolled jeans and black boots, but he wasn't nearly as cool as the iconic rebel.

Before the newbie could turn to run, the albino grabbed him inhumanly fast, lifting him by the neck. The greaser flailed, kicking in the air, trying to scream, but the albino's chokehold left no chance. He stilled, his face turning blue-ish purple.

"What have we here? A nosey field mouse?" The albino spoke in that Slavic accent he'd had in the Mudder Brothers' basement. My memory seemed to be flawless when I was sleeping.

"Put him down!" I demanded, halfway across the living room before I realized my feet had taken action. The stench of the gnarled bodies still hovered, making me gag a little.

The albino turned his head in my direction. His eyes were reptilian, his nose and mouth pushed out into what looked like a short snout. For a moment, he looked more like a white fanged beast than an ugly duckling, then he blinked back to normal dark pupils.

James Dean's wide eyes met mine. He made a gurgling sound in his throat, his tongue lolling partway out.

"By whose order?"

What did he mean by whose order? Me and my can of whoop ass, that was who. "Put him down!" I said again, louder, treating him as I would a disobedient child.

"As you wish." He threw James Dean across the room with jaw-dropping force. The greaser slammed into the wall headfirst with a loud, sickening thud, leaving a trail of blood down the wall as he slid to the floor, landing in a tangled heap.

I rushed over to the greaser, squatting next to him.

He was still alive, but his neck was twisted around at a horrible angle. His eyelashes fluttered. He coughed, blood splattering. His mouth moved like he was trying to speak. His breath sounded gurgled, labored. Under the scent of blood, I could smell the pomade he'd used to slick back his hair.

Damn it. How many people had to die in my nightmares? How many times was I going to have to face off with monsters before I could return to happy dreams full of rainbows, chocolate, and poppy fields?

Sighing, I stood, facing my nemesis. "All right, you ugly son of a bitch, let's do this."

The albino hefted his medieval ax. "Do what, human?"

"Do I really have to spell it out for you?" I'd replayed this scene in different variations more times than I could count over the last few months. Usually the nasty bastard came at me with his barbed, shiny hook. The ax was a new touch, along with the shrunken heads, but the scene was the same otherwise. "Let's get on with the usual fight-for-my-life crap. Lose the ax, though. Try leveling the playing field for once."

"The ax?" The albino looked down at the blade in his hands and then back at me. "You speak of this?"

"Yes, that weird battle ax thing you're holding." I must have conjured that up thanks to the old *Conan the Barbarian* movie I'd watched the other night with Natalie.

"It is a scythe," he clarified.

I rolled my eyes. "Are you seriously going to stand here and argue with me about the name of that stupid thing?"

He swung it back and forth between us, his lips pulling back in a snarl. "You have made a grave mistake, wench."

"This isn't my first rodeo, dickhead. Put the ax down and fight like a man."

"But I am not a man." The albino hefted the ax back and forth between his hands.

"Do you always pick on things smaller than you?" I asked, moving sideways, keeping space between us. Was I going to live through this nightmare, or die from his blade and wake up sweating and clutching my throat like so many other times?

"It is in my nature to hunt smaller prey."

"Fine, you big bully. Take a swing and let's get this dance started."

"Violet!" the guttural sound of my name coming from the dying man was new, a different dreamland special effect. One that gave me pause.

"What?" I called out, keeping my focus on the ax.

The greaser coughed again; it sounded thick with blood.

The albino lifted the ax. "As you command, wench."

He swung, I dodged, darting around the side of him, faster in my dreams than I ever had been in real life. I ended up closer to the greaser, who was battling a rally of coughs.

"Let go of the ghost, buddy," I told him. "This might get ugly here soon. Trust me, I've had these nightmares before."

"Boots," the greaser gasped. "Run, damn it! Run!"

I heard his death rattle, and then silence. I glanced down into the wide, glassy eyes of the greaser. Blood dripped down his chin. His chest no longer hitched.

Did he call me *Boots*?

The albino closed the distance between us. A mark on his left cheek caught my attention. Was that a birthmark shaped like a horseshoe or a dirt smudge? Something tried to surface from my memories. Something about Cooper. I struggled to dredge up why that mark even mattered.

He raised the ax again

"Wait!" I held up my hand.

He didn't, swinging a slicing blow at my neck.

I slammed back against the wall the greaser had dented, the blade slicing through my hoody right above my left breast.

I felt a burning sting. Pulling my hoody and T-shirt aside, I touched where the blade had cut me. It was shallow, but deep enough for blood to well and trickle down. Uh oh.

Boots? Only Doc ever called me Boots. That had never happened before in any of my nightmares.

"What will it be, wench?" the albino hefted the ax, his eyes morphed into snake-slits again.

A flash of the last time I'd fallen asleep around Cornelius whizzed through my thoughts. We had been up at Mount Moriah that time. There'd been spittle in my hand when I'd woken up. Did that mean this was somehow …

"Shall I remove your head or heart?" the ugly beast asked.

… the real deal?

The cut on my chest throbbed. That was different, too.

My breath caught. I might really be fucked this time.

"Wait!" I held up my hands between us, forming them into a T. "I'd like to take a ten-minute timeout, please."

He laughed, all heart-stopping and evil sounding. Vincent Price must have taken lessons from him. He raised the ax, his face contorting into a maniacal clown grin, his body bowing with strength and force. "Your time is no more, wench."

The blade sliced through the air.

Chapter Twenty-One

And missed ... barely, burrowing into the wall next to me.

I'd dodged his blade at the last second somehow. I didn't waste time figuring it out. There was no way I was going to give him another chance to cleave me in two.

While the creep struggled to tug his blade free of the wall, I scrambled around him. But I wasn't fast enough. He caught me by the hood and yanked me backward off my feet.

I landed flat on my butt with an "oof!"

He let go of me to double fist the ax handle and swing, giving me the split second I needed to roll out of the arc of his blade. The floor boards vibrated from the force of his blow. Jesus! The ugly bastard was a damned juggernaut.

I shoved to my feet and ran for the dining room, putting the table between us. Food sat on three plates, half-eaten, with forks and spoons at the ready, reminding me of the unsettling ghost story about Roanoke, Virginia. Serving dishes filled with mashed potatoes, meatballs, and green beans were centered on the table. I hurdled a tipped over chair.

The ax-happy-asshole stretched his neck and stalked after me, dragging his blade along the floor. Behind him on the wall above the splayed greaser's body, I saw three letters drawn with red paint: *M I R.*

Where had those come from? I didn't have much time to ponder the letters' origin before the albino came up with a quick way to get around the table—chop it in half.

His ax fell, sending wood splintering every which way.

Before he lifted his weapon again, I grabbed a chair and slammed it down onto his back.

He stumbled forward into the wall, giving me the time I

needed to race around the table mess.

His arm was too long, though. He snagged me again, catching me by the hair this time, and yanked me onto the broken table. I rolled down one of the broken halves onto the floor, landing facedown amidst green beans and potatoes. I pushed up onto my palms, my fingers squishing meatballs under my palms, the scent of tomato sauce thick around me. I'd missed landing on a serving fork by inches.

"No more games," he said in his thick Slavic accent.

"Damned straight!" I grabbed the fork.

He raised that blasted ax again.

I gripped the fork and lunged at him, slamming the sharp fork tines into his thigh with a war cry that would have made Red Cloud proud.

The ax swooped sideways, missing his mark—me. His bulbous eyes widened, his expression looking surprised as he looked down at where I'd jammed the fork into his leg.

I glanced down, too, frowning at the line of black smoke rising from his thigh.

He roared in pain, sending me crab-crawling backward through the potatoes and splintered wood.

As I pushed to my feet, he reached down and jerked the fork out of his leg, pressing his hand over the smoking wound.

"What have you done?" His snake eyes measured me from head to foot. "What are you?"

I didn't have time to stand around and explain the birds and bees to him. I glanced toward the window next to the dead greaser, doing a doubletake on the wall above him. Three more letters had been scrawled in what I realized was blood, spelling *M I R R O R*.

Mirror? What did that mean? Who was writing it?

A growl-filled groan from my nemesis made me whirl.

The smoke had stopped, but he was still clutching his thigh. His lip curled as he stared at me. "Who sent you?"

I thought of Cornelius and Doc, of the séance, but said nothing to him and backed toward the bedroom door, which was wide open, beckoning.

The albino grabbed the ax handle, using it as a crutch to limp toward me. "Who are you, wench?" he took another hobbled step, his face tight with pain or fury or both. I wasn't going to ask for clarification.

"Your nightmare," I told the albino and dashed toward the bedroom door, slamming the thick oak door behind me. A skeleton key was in the lock. I turned it and twisted the knob, making sure it was locked.

Stepping away from the door, I listened for the sound of his footsteps. My breath raced in and out, my heart thumping hard and fast.

The knob twisted on its own.

Crikey, that juggernaut was a persistent son of a bitch.

I needed a weapon. If the fork hurt him, maybe I could stab him with a piece of broken glass.

Turning toward the dresser mirror, I squeaked in surprise at the sight of Freesia standing there in the reflection. The video camera blinked red behind her. She summoned me with her hand, hurrying me.

The *mirror.*

The message scrawled in blood on the wall.

Oh, yeah, the mirror. But how did I …

A boom hit the other side of the bedroom door, rattling it in its doorframe.

I nearly jumped out of my skin. I raced around the bed, skidding to a halt in front of the mirror.

How was I going to …

BOOM! The door shook again.

"Go away!" I yelled. "I'm a little busy in here right now."

Damn it, if that freaky-eyed asshole would just give me a moment to think.

I frowned into the mirror, trying to concentrate on Freesia's face, her brown eyes, her arm and hand.

A splintered crashing sound resounded behind me. His ax had punctured the wood, I knew it. I dared not look around and let the terror I could feel welling inside of me take over and render me helpless.

Freesia's hand.

I closed my eyes and thought of the demon's tongue I'd grabbed onto in the darkness of my mind at Wild Bill's gravesite. I remembered Cornelius's meditation teachings, the candle flame on which he'd told me to concentrate. I let my mind reach into the shadows.

Freesia's hand.

A crash sounded behind me, muted as my mind turned inward. I imagined a wall of bulletproof glass behind me, blocking the juggernaut, and focused on that flame, on reaching further into the darkness and beyond.

Freesia's hand.

I grabbed her palm, clutching it tight. She pulled hard, dragging me all of the way into the blackness. I could feel myself falling, falling, falling.

And then I landed on something hard.

Pain shot out from my elbow, making my fingers tingle. I groaned and rolled off of my arm.

Then I remembered my attacker and sat up, my gaze darting all around the bedroom, searching for him and his sinister ax. Freesia lay on the floor next to me, her eyes wide, her mouth slack-jawed. I could hear her panting.

"Holy shit," she said. She looked across at Cornelius, who was squinting into Ms. Wolff's bedroom mirror. "Did you see that? Hot damn! That was way more intense than the Ouija board games we played in college."

"Shhhh," Cornelius said, leaning his ear close to the mirror. His wool coat almost brushing Layne's picture.

"Where's Doc?" I asked. "Why are we in the bedroom?"

"We moved in here to help you get back out," Freesia whispered.

"He's still in there," Cornelius said, leaning his head on the mirror. He began his rhythmic hum.

"Who's in there?" *The killer?*

Clutching my throbbing elbow, I spun on my hip. They must have moved Cornelius's square into the bedroom while I was out of it. Ms. Wolff's twin bed had been pushed back, making more room between it and the dresser. Doc lay flat on his back in the opposite corner, near the end of the bed. His eyes were closed but movement fluttered underneath them, like butterflies under a sheet.

Oh, no. I crawled over to him, feeling his cheek, his neck, his hand. His skin felt cold and clammy.

Still humming, Cornelius knocked on the mirror.

Knock. Knock. Knock.

I frowned over at Freesia. "How long has Doc been out?"

Cornelius lifted his head from the mirror, catching his breath and humming some more. Then he knocked three times on the mirror again.

"I don't know," Freesia said, joining me at Doc's side. "We moved into the bedroom when we realized you had left the square and sleepwalked in here. We found you standing in front of the dresser mirror."

The humming stopped.

"How long ago was that?" I pressed.

Cornelius turned toward me, his face paler than normal, his cornflower blue eyes filled with a mixture of apprehension and sadness. "Violet," he started, his frown scaring me, "I fear we've lost—"

Something pounded on the mirror, making it vibrate. Layne's picture slipped out of the edge and floated onto the dresser top.

Freesia yelped in surprise.

I met Cornelius's wide gaze. "Who was that?"

"He's stuck inside," he answered.

"What do you mean stuck?"

"Your friend went back in to show you the way out. When you came through, you blocked the way back."

"I did what?"

"Closed the portal, if you will. Would you like me to explain the physics of it?"

"Not at this very moment. What do you mean by stuck?"

"I mean he cannot return."

"Can't you open the mirror again?" Freesia asked.

Cornelius shook his head. "That is too dangerous for Violet.

She's inexperienced in the ways of psychic travel."

"No." I looked down at Doc's fluttering lids, felt his pulse strong under my finger. "He's not stuck in there."

"I told him there was great risk involved in going back," Cornelius said, pulling on his goatee. "But he insisted."

It must have been Doc who wrote the "mirror" message for me on the wall somehow.

Another bang vibrated the mirror.

"How long has Doc been out?" I asked Freesia again.

Her eyes grew watery. "I don't … I don't know. Maybe ten minutes."

"There's still time," I said, straddling Doc's waist. How was I going to get him out?

"Time for what?" Freesia asked.

"Cornelius," I called, adjusting Doc's arms so that I wasn't kneeling on them. "Do your humming trick."

Cornelius cleared his throat, lowering onto the edge of the bed, and started making the rhythmic noises in his throat. His eyes closed, he tipped his chin up. The humming grew louder. I had no idea if that would make a difference or not, but short of calling in the cavalry, I was taking all of the help I could get.

I trailed my fingers down Doc's chest, swallowing the panic that was threatening to shove screaming up and out from my chest. I could get him back. I'd done it before. I just needed to figure out how.

"Doc," I said in a commanding voice, "wake up."

That didn't work. His eyes continued to move behind his lids, but his body lay still underneath me.

I shook his shoulders. "Doc, wake up. Come back to me."

Still nothing changed.

"What if you kissed him?" Freesia asked.

"That won't work." I had no delusions about my powers as Princess Charming. I'd tried kissing him awake before in Prudence's attic and it hadn't done a thing. I leaned over his face, running my hands down his cheeks. "Doc, come on, you have to wake up. I need you here."

Nothing, damn it.

I turned his head to the side.

"What are you doing?" Freesia asked.

"I have an idea." I place my lips close to his ear. "Dane Nyce, you get your ass back to me right now. I'm going to start counting. You have until I reach ten."

I glanced over at Freesia. She was chewing on her knuckles, her eyes rimmed with worry lines. Cornelius continued to hum from the bed in a fully focused rhythm.

"One," I said in Doc's ear. "Two. Three."

Something hit the mirror again. Freesia screeched and watched the glass as if waiting for someone to fall through it.

"Four. Five."

Doc's right arm twitched, but his eyes remained closed, the rest of his body motionless.

"Six. Seven."

The whole dresser vibrated from a blow to the mirror, the drawer handles rattling against the wood. I wasn't sure who or what was behind it—Doc or the juggernaut or something else.

"Eight."

Come on, Doc. I need you to wake up.

"Nine."

I checked the mirror, pausing to see if it was bowing or splintering or rippling. Nope, none of the above.

"Ten."

Everything went quiet around me, including Cornelius. I stared down at Doc, willing him to open his brown eyes and look up at me.

But he didn't.

"What are you going to do?" Freesia whispered.

An idea hit me. "Bite him."

"That's unorthodox." Cornelius said. "Yet brilliant."

I bit into the soft, fleshy part of his earlobe.

Doc groaned.

I held the bite and tugged on his lobe. "Open your eyes, Doc," I spoke through clenched teeth.

His eyes flashed open as if by the touch of a magic wand. "Oww!" He jerked free of my bite.

I sat up and smiled down at him, relief coursing through me, making my eyes a little misty.

His face scrunching in pain, his dark eyes focused on me. "What did you do to me?"

"I brought you back." I bared my choppers. "By the skin of my teeth."

Cornelius stepped around us, heading toward the video camera. "She used pain to withdraw you from a potentially damaging situation."

"She bit your earlobe," Freesia told him, squeezing my shoulder. "That was amazing, Violet. I'm not going to be able to sleep for days."

Doc reached up and tenderly touched his ear. "It stings like a son of a bitch. Were you trying to bite it clear off?"

"No. Sheesh, I didn't even draw blood this time."

He grunted his unhappiness at me and shifted under my weight, reminding me that I was still sitting on him.

I crawled off, kneeled next to him, taking his hand in mine. His skin was warmer again, the color coming back to his face ... and his ear, which was fire engine red.

I grimaced. "You shouldn't have gone in after me." I kissed the back of his hand and then pulled him upright. "It was too risky."

"I couldn't leave you alone with him." He rubbed the back of his neck with his free hand, holding tight to my palm with the other.

"Alone with who?" Cornelius asked, folding his tripod.

I hesitated, looking at Doc. Should I tell Cornelius about the albino? That might open up a slew of other questions I wasn't sure I was ready to answer yet.

"The dead guy," I said at the same time Doc spoke up with, "The ghost."

"Was that you trying to come through the mirror?" Freesia asked Doc.

His forehead wrinkled. "What do you mean?"

"After Violet woke up from her trance, or whatever it was," Freesia explained, "the mirror kept shuddering, like someone was pounding on it from the other side."

"That wasn't me." Doc's troubled gaze held mine.

Cornelius offered his hand to Doc. "I have a hypothesis about the mirror," he said as he pulled Doc to his feet. "I saw something similar in an old haunted hospital in Oklahoma."

I had my own hypothesis that included a white haired juggernaut with a big, sharp ax.

Freesia practically bounced with excitement. "What is it?"

"I need to analyze the video before I make any statements."

To whom? The press? I stood, brushing off my jeans, looking in the mirror. Could the albino see us from the other side right now?

Doc's reflection watched me, his forehead still covered in frown lines. "What's that on your hoody?"

I looked down over the material. "What?"

He touched a dark spot on the material above my left breast, then looked at his finger. "You're bleeding."

"I am?" I pulled aside my hoody, a sense of déjà vu rolling over me. My T-shirt had a red spot, too. Doc pulled my neckline askew. A cut in my skin was smeared with blood. My blood. "How did I ..."

The terror rushed back in, flash-flooding through me, overflowing my body with adrenaline.

"Doc," I gasped, clutching his shoulder when my knees threatened to give. "How did—"

Doc's finger on my lips shushed me. "You must have scratched yourself. We need to get you home. Tonight's been hard on you."

"But what if—"

"Freesia," Doc said, leading me toward the bedroom door. "Can you stay and help Cornelius clean up? I need to get Violet home. This much stimuli at once can be dangerous."

That was a bunch of horse hockey. I felt wound up enough to run a marathon right then.

"Of course." She shot Cornelius a secret smile that flew over his clueless head. "I'll make sure he's all taken care of."

And then some. I wondered how blatant she'd have to be for

him to realize she liked him. An ad on the Goodyear Blimp might do it. Or a billboard on Interstate 90.

"Cornelius," I said, "I'll call you."

"No, I'll call you. I have a lot of data to analyze from tonight. I'll probably be awake until seven-twelve in the morning, or maybe even seven-thirty-six."

"Make sure you're asleep by eight-o-two," I jested.

"Of course I will." He did not jest back. "It's irresponsible to stay up that late."

Doc shot me a raised brow. I shook my head and pointed toward the door.

"Don't bother getting a cab," I heard Freesia say to him as Doc led me out of the bedroom. "I'll take you back to your room ... I mean your hotel."

I admired Freesia's boldness. I might need to take a chapter from her book.

"Do you want me to go get the car and bring it around?" Doc asked as we stepped out onto the dark porch, quietly closing the door behind us.

"No, I'm good. What about you?"

"I'm worried about you."

"It's only a couple of blocks."

"You know what I mean. What happened in there was unprecedented." He wrapped his arm around me and pulled me against his side as we walked.

"I'm not even going to pretend that I understand anything that went on." I burrowed into him as I glanced around into the shadowed trees, afraid I'd see the albino stalking out of the darkness towards us.

"He's gone, Violet. You destroyed him somehow at Mudder Brothers, remember?"

"Then what was that swinging an ax at me in there? A nightmare? How were you able to get into my head? Or was I in yours? Why was the mirror showing me different realities? How did I end up with this cut?" Which was now throbbing since I'd given it a little attention.

He kissed my temple. "We'll work through this together. But

first let's go home."

I shivered in the brisk October air. "Mine or yours?"

"Mine."

After we climbed into the car, I dug out my cell phone. A text message from Aunt Zoe made my heart race for a more down-to-earth reason. "Oh, crap."

"What is it?" Doc started the engine.

"Addy has an earache." I should have known that cold wouldn't go away easily. Fall and spring's abrupt weather changes always found her body's weak spots. "I need to go home. She doesn't handle pain well."

"Okay, your house it is."

"To drop me off?" I didn't want him to leave me, afraid of the dark thoughts and fears that were sure to hit in the middle of the night. Or worse.

"Do you want me to drop you off?"

I was too emotionally spent to play games. "I want you to stay the night with me because I'm scared shitless of where I'll wake up if I fall asleep. But I can't ask that of you."

"Why not?"

"Because there's not going to be any hanky panky going on tonight, especially with Addy's earache. I just want you in the same house as me to make me feel safe."

"Then that's where I'll be." He turned up his street. "Let me grab a change of clothes and we'll be on our way."

"I don't want to make you do that."

"Christ, Violet, let me protect you for once."

Ten minutes later, we climbed Aunt Zoe's front porch steps. I paused at the top, frowning out at the darkness. "Was that a dream back there in that apartment?"

He took my face in his palms, his eyes glittering, reflecting the light leaking through Aunt Zoe's front windows. I breathed in the scent of his skin, letting it soothe my jangled nerves. "If I tell you my answer, are you going to believe me?"

"Yes."

Lowering his mouth, he kissed me slow and wonderfully, warming me from the inside out. I wanted to crawl inside his coat and curl up under his shirt until all of the bogeymen were shooed away.

He lifted his mouth, feathering kisses over my face, pulling me into his arms. "Violet," he said over my head.

"What."

"That was no dream."

The screen door creaked. "Mom?" Addy called, sniffling.

Doc released me. I kneeled in front of Addy. "My ear hurts," she cried, burying her head in my neck.

I hugged her tight. "It'll be okay, baby. I'll make it better."

"Can you make my ear better, too?" Doc said, his voice full of mirth.

"Mom," Addy looked up at me, her face pinched. "I had a nightmare. You were in the hospital and wouldn't wake up."

That was a weird coincidence. "I'm fine, baby. Let's go inside."

"Is Doc coming, too?"

"Yes, he's going to stay here tonight and watch over us."

She measured Doc for a moment. "Good," she said and took my hand, pulling me inside.

I glanced back at Doc. "Coming?"

"I'm right behind you."

Chapter Twenty-Two

Thursday, October 11th

Doc spent the night in my bed.

Unfortunately, I wasn't there with him.

Addy's earache had pained her until the wee hours of the morning. I woke to find myself leaning over onto her pillows, imitating the tower in Pisa. Addy's head was on my leg, which felt numb from the hip down.

As I sat upright, my gaze toured the room as I listened for sounds other than Addy's soft snores. Was that the murmur of voices coming from downstairs? I heard a chair scrape on the kitchen floor, then more murmuring.

I tucked a wisp of Addy's hair behind the ear that had given her so much trouble in the night. As much as I loathed earaches, I'd appreciated the normalcy of it throughout the dark hours as my thoughts circled over what had gone down at the Galena House. An earache I understood—an ax-wielding bogeyman from the past, not so much.

I slid out from under her, replacing my lap with her pillow. She moaned but didn't wake. I limped out of the room and closed the door behind me, leaning back against it while I stifled a yawn.

I hadn't dreamed all night. Not even a quick glimpse into some wispy world—shadow-filled or rainbow-edged. The dream machine in my brain seemed to be temporarily out of order. Or maybe I'd broken it completely yesterday.

After a quick check on Layne, who was sleeping with his butt in the air like he had done when he was a baby, I closed his door. I walked by the empty bathroom, hesitating outside of my bedroom door. I inched it open. My bed was made, my clothes that had littered the floor folded or draped over the mattress. Wow. I could get used to that. I was tempted to go sniff my pillows, see if I could smell Doc on them but decided to head downstairs and touch the real deal instead.

The third stair down creaked under my bare foot. The aroma of toast and eggs played carrot to my eager stomach. Harvey must be awake, working his magic with food.

To my surprise, I found Doc instead of Harvey standing at the kitchen stove cooking breakfast. I fell into the chair between Harvey and Aunt Zoe, blinking fully awake while exchanging good-mornings all around. It wasn't until Doc placed a mug of steaming coffee under my nose and tugged on a corkscrew of hair bobbing in front of my face that I remembered I hadn't stopped by the bathroom to spruce up before stumbling down here. I patted my curls, which were spiraling every which way.

Crud, I could probably pass for Buckwheat's blonde twin.

"You look fresh out of clown college with that hair." Harvey confirmed my suspicion. "I'm heading out to my ranch after I drop the kids off at school this morning. Want me to bring you back my rainbow suspenders?"

I nailed him with a glare in response.

He wheezed out his chuckles. "Be careful this mornin', Doc. She may take a bite out of more than just yer ear."

His ear? Oh, yeah. Last night's train wreck backed over me, leaving deep grooves. I groaned, covering my face with my hands, and leaned forward on my elbows. "What did you tell him, Doc?"

"He didn't say a thing," Aunt Zoe spoke up, clearing her throat. "Harvey noticed the teeth marks and Doc came clean about you two getting a little frisky."

My sex life and coffee for breakfast. Hmmm. I was going to need more coffee.

I peeked over at Harvey between my fingers. "You noticed the teeth marks on his ear? Jeez-louise, were you giving him a physical this morning or what?"

"I have keen powers of observation, girl." He knocked twice on the table. "You'd be smart to remember that."

"What else have you observed?" Doc asked, setting a plate with buttered toast and eggs cooked over-easy in front of Harvey, along with a bottle of hot sauce and ketchup. He pointed a spatula at me, "Hungry?"

I shook my head, but my stomach voiced its opposition. "Maybe a piece of buttered toast. But I can get it."

"Sit still and drink your coffee," he said, his smile making me forget how frightening I undoubtedly looked.

I ogled his backside as he stood at the stove, liking the cozy feel of him there with us. When I dragged my eyes off him, I found Aunt Zoe watching me watch Doc.

"I've observed a few things, too," she said, her gaze narrowing as she stirred her coffee.

Eek. I knew that look well. It meant she was going to be cornering me soon and asking some probing questions. I squirmed and hid behind my cup.

"Well, since you asked," Harvey said to Doc's back, "and since we're all sittin' here jawin' over good food," he piled his sunny-side up egg on top of his toast and sprinkled it with some hot sauce. "I have spied with my keen eye a few head scratchers." He took a bite of his egg sandwich, dabbing at the yolk that dripped into his beard.

"Willis, you don't need to shake your can of beans so much before you spill them," Aunt Zoe said with sarcasm. "You've got our attention, so let 'er rip."

Harvey shot her a gold-toothed grin. "All right, Miss Impatient, I'll start with you. I noticed your pickup was parked down near the fire station the last few days." When Aunt Zoe opened her mouth, he held up his hand. "Now I 'spose you're gonna tell me that you're parkin' down there rather than behind your store so that you can get yourself some exercise, that walkin's good for us and all that bullshit. But I suspect you're hopin' to catch a glimpse of a certain fire captain who's been moonin' over you lately like a lovesick teenager."

Harvey paused while Doc placed a plate of scrambled eggs and toast in front of Aunt Zoe.

"You can deny you still have a hankerin' for good ol' Reid

Martin until you're pushin' up daisies, but I think you're still moonin' a bit yourself what with the way you go for your shotgun whenever he comes around."

Aunt Zoe stabbed her eggs, shaking her head.

She was parking down by the fire station, huh? I wondered if Reid had noticed her pickup parked there, too. If not, I wondered if some little bearded, gold-toothed birdy might accidentally mention that fact to Reid while another little curly-haired birdy worked on softening her aunt up about going to dinner with the fire captain and trying to rekindle their friendship at least.

"I'm gonna give you a bit of advice from a lonely ol' man, Zoe," Harvey said, lining up his egg sandwich for another bite. "Life's short. Forget about stupid shit from the past and stay frisky as long as your equipment keeps workin' for ya."

"You should write greeting cards, Willis," Doc said from over by the toaster. "That one would be a top seller."

I snickered.

Harvey swallowed a bite of his breakfast. "My uncle tried that years ago. They didn't like his cussin' so much."

"Their loss." Doc replied while buttering my toast.

Maybe we could hook up for lunch somewhere private and he could butter my muffin, too.

Cripes, that sounded like something Harvey would say. The old buzzard was rubbing off on me. Next I'd be toting a shotgun around and saying stuff like *gol-darn* and *dad-gum*.

"But enough about my sentiments on life," Harvey said, "let's talk about your book collection, Doc."

Doc set my toast down under my nose. "What about it?"

"Why did you come to Deadwood?" Harvey asked.

"I answered this question before."

"Humor me. I'm an old man."

"Not that old," Doc said, leaning against the counter with his arms crossed.

"Old enough to know when I'm being honeyfuggled." He finished off his sandwich, wiped his beard, and turned in his chair to give Doc his full attention. "I suspect you came to this town for a reason."

"To start a business," Doc supplied.

"Partly maybe, but you could have started your business any place. After checkin' out the books you keep handy and payin' mind to places you don't frequent much, like Mudder Brothers during funerals, I suspect you chose this ol' ghost town for a reason havin' to do with your *rare* condition."

I frowned at Harvey. Had he figured out Doc's secret?

"My rare condition?" Doc kept a poker face.

I glanced at Aunt Zoe, she was eagle-eyeing Doc.

"You know," Harvey said, "that problem you have of gettin' the wind knocked plum out of ya when you share space with the dead."

Crap! He had figured it out. I shoved half a piece of toast into my mouth, chewing without tasting. What was Doc going to do? Would he lie outright to Harvey and Aunt Zoe? Should I lie outright for him? Or should I crack a joke, yell *FIRE*, or fall off my chair and pretend to have a seizure? I needed to do something distracting. Where were my kids when we needed an interruption, dang it?

"What are you saying?" Doc met Harvey's stare head on.

"I'm sayin' you see ghosts."

My pulse raced in a reckless three-beat gait. I had to do something. "Harvey, you're wrong. Doc can't—"

"Violet," Doc stopped me. "It's okay."

I groaned for him and picked at my toast.

"I can't usually see them," Doc told Harvey. "But I can sense they are there through other means, and I can switch places with them for short bouts."

"Hoo-haw!" Harvey clapped his hands. "I knew it! Damn I'm good."

Doc jammed his hands in his front pockets. "I'd appreciate it if you kept this knowledge to yourself for Violet and her kids' sakes."

"And to protect Doc's business," I added.

Harvey blew a raspberry, sounding remarkably like a horse. He needed to spend less time with four-footed mammals. "I ain't gonna say a word."

All eyes turned to Aunt Zoe.

"Your secret is safe with me, Doc. I appreciate your honesty." At his nod, she added, "And thank you for taking care of my niece."

Doc looked at me and shrugged. "She usually takes care of herself whether I try to help or not."

"She's stubborn as a mule," Harvey added. "And ornery to boot. She needs you around to keep her butt from ending up in jail again."

"Hey!" I slapped the buzzard's arm. "That was your fault."

"She definitely has a nose for trouble," Doc agreed, his grin crooked. "But she's easy on the eyes and has me wrapped around that little finger of hers. Besides, a bit of stubbornness is good. It keeps her feisty."

I huffed at Doc. I'd give him feisty all right.

"Better watch it, boy," Harvey said. "She'll bite your ear again and slap a saddle on you this time. That's how we used to tame stallions back in the day."

"Some men don't mind being saddled," Aunt Zoe said, sitting back in her chair. "I suspect you're one of those men, Willis. You're just too stubborn *and* ornery to admit it. Maybe we should talk to Miss Geary about saddles."

Harvey snorted. "I need to find me another filly. She put me out to pasture when that young stallion showed up."

I bit my lip to stop it from rattling out a string of insults about Miss Geary's so-called stallion, the no good, stinking rotten varmint.

"I haven't seen Mr. Black Sports Car around for a while," Aunt Zoe told him.

"Violet has," Harvey poked me in the shoulder. "Haven't ya, girlie?"

"Uhhhh…" I gave an Oscar performance of a deer caught in Harvey's headlights.

"Remember," Harvey pointed at the center of my face, "your nose twitches when you lie, so cough up the truth. Who's your friend?"

"He's no friend." I winced at Aunt Zoe, anticipating her reaction.

"Violet Lynn, what aren't you telling me?"

I felt Doc's hand squeeze my shoulder. I clamped onto it and told the truth. "The Jaguar belongs to Rex Conner."

Aunt Zoe's coffee cup slammed to the table, jarring my ears. "You've got to be kidding me."

"He was using Miss Geary to spy on us."

"Who's Rex Conner?" Harvey asked.

I glanced at the entryway to the kitchen, making sure neither of my kids was standing there. "My sperm donor," I whispered.

I had told the old man bits and pieces about my past with the kids' father after Harvey had met the bitch from hell, aka Susan.

Aunt Zoe leaned forward, her upper lip curled. "That son of a bitch was over there this whole time?"

I nodded.

"You mean he was just usin' Beatrice?" Harvey puffed his chest out. "Taking advantage of her generous nature?"

Generous nature? Is that what he called her burning up the sheets with a much younger man? I nodded again.

"What does he want?" Aunt Zoe glanced over her shoulder toward the dining room. "The kids?" she said quietly.

"He admitted to having a science experiment sort of curiosity about them but no interest in anything more."

"Then what?"

"Ummm …" I hesitated on my answer, not wanting to put a voice to the words, as if not saying it would keep it from being true.

Doc released my shoulder, heading back to the counter. "He wants your niece."

"Well," Aunt Zoe gripped her coffee cup with both hands, "he can't have you."

Harvey cracked his knuckles. "That two-timin' bull wandered into the wrong pasture this time."

"He wants what he can't have." I circled the rim on my mug with my finger. "Always has, always will."

"If I see that worthless bastard," Aunt Zoe said, "I'm going to string him up by his balls and use him for a piñata."

"You'll need to get in line behind Natalie," Doc told her.

"What about you?" Harvey asked him.

"I have other plans in mind."

Like what? I wanted to ask but wasn't comfortable with being the core of the problem at hand.

Doc folded the dishtowel and placed it on the counter. "I need to get going. Walk me out, Violet?"

I nodded and followed him into the dining room. His bag sat by the front door, waiting to go. The early morning air nipped at my bare ankles and feet where my thick robe didn't cover.

"Thanks for breakfast," I said, smiling up at him. "And for staying the night with me."

"Your pillows smell like you." He pulled me into his embrace. "Made me want to do wicked things to them."

I rubbed suggestively against him. "Like what?"

"Stop it right there, Boots."

"Spoilsport," I rested my head against his chest, feeling the steady beat of his heart on my forehead. "Have lunch with me today?"

"Sure. We need to talk about last night, share stories, match up details, and then talk to Cornelius."

I sighed. I'd been trying to avoid as much of that as I could since we'd left the Galena House. My guts churned whenever I started contemplating what it meant if it was not a dream. "Or we could have sex on your desk."

"You're evading, sweetheart." He tipped my chin up and kissed me, warming my lips and more. "I'll come to your office at …" he waited, his eyebrows raised.

"One o'clock." I was taking the late lunch today, watching the office until the others came back from theirs.

"One it is." He skimmed his knuckles down the side of my robe, brushing over my breast. "Wear your boots, vixen."

He left me standing there grinning like a big doofus in spite of the dark clouds overhead. I studied the gray sky as he drove off. They almost looked like snow clouds.

"Brrrr." I clutched my robe and hustled back inside.

Layne sat at the kitchen table when I returned. Addy was still sleeping. I kissed my son's head as he chowed down on the eggs Doc had left for him and then zipped upstairs to take a shower and get ready for work.

The sight of myself in the bathroom mirror made me hold the sides of my face and screech, imitating Edvard Munch's *The Scream* masterpiece. Old man Harvey was right; I looked like a freaky clown. I checked my teeth. At least I didn't have any food in them.

After a shower, a few spritzes of perfume, and a tooth brushing, I clomped downstairs in my purple boots. I passed Harvey and Layne on the way to the kitchen. They headed out the door after a kiss goodbye—for Layne, not the old buzzard who was still cursing under his breath about his ex-girlfriend being screwed over by my ex-boyfriend. I resisted commenting on the irony of it all, afraid he'd pinch me again.

In the kitchen, I poured some coffee in a travel mug, capped it, and turned to find Aunt Zoe standing behind me with her arms crossed and her chin set.

"We need to talk, Violet Lynn."

"Uh oh, that sounds like I'm in trouble."

"If you walk out that door without answering a few questions of mine, you will be."

"If this is about Rex," I started.

"It's not about that devil. It's about Doc." She walked to the table and pulled out a chair, pointing down at it. "Sit down for a minute."

"But I have to ..."

She pointed again.

I obeyed, tucking my dark orange peasant skirt under me. "... sit down and answer your questions."

She pulled out the chair next to mine and joined me. "Why did Doc spend the night here?"

Her question took me by surprise. She'd always been open-minded about my spending the night with Doc. It would knock me back a step if premarital sex under her roof was the reason for our *tête-à-tête* this morning. "Nothing happened. I spent the night in Addy's bed."

"I don't care if anything happened between you two or not. What I want to know is why he stayed?"

I still wasn't sure what she was getting at with her question. "Because I asked him to."

"What happened that prompted you to ask Doc to stay?"

I toyed with the button on my purple blazer, buying time.

She tapped her fingers on the table, waiting.

"I was afraid," I admitted.

"Of what?"

I hesitated again. "This is going to sound childish."

"Just say it."

"I was afraid of my nightmares." I picked at a loose thread on the button. "Afraid of someone showing up again when I fell asleep. So I asked Doc to stay because when he's around, I don't have bad dreams." I'd had a nasty one last night at the séance, though, and Doc was right there next to me. Then again, he'd told me that hadn't been a dream.

Aunt Zoe cocked her head to the side. I got the feeling she was weighing something carefully before saying it. "Violet, have you been trying to talk to ghosts?"

I hemmed and hawed, fiddle-de-diddled, and squirmed before whispering, "Sort of." I wasn't sure what I'd call last night's adventure. The word *séance* didn't really do it justice.

"Did Doc get you into this ghost business?"

"No, Cornelius did."

"Cornelius, your ghost whispering client?"

"Yes, that Cornelius."

"I thought you didn't believe he was legit."

"I didn't at first, but then I got roped into doing a séance with him and something happened."

"What?"

"I fell asleep and Wolfgang showed up in my nightmare. Only he kind of melted and turned into Kyrkozz."

"The demon from the skin-covered book I have hidden in the shop?"

"Yes, that Kyrkozz."

She crossed her arms. "So one séance adventure and you changed your mind about Cornelius?"

"Not quite just one."

"How many séances have you done with him?"

I chewed on my lower lip. "Four. Well, three and a half, since the deal up at Mount Moriah wasn't really supposed to be a séance. That was him teaching me how to reach out with my mind." I remembered the spittle in my palm afterward and shuddered all over again. "The other two were more like official séances."

"How long ago did the séances take place?"

"The first three were last month."

"And the fourth?"

"Last night."

"In Cornelius's hotel room?"

"No. We were in Ms. Wolff's apartment at the Galena House."

"Who's we?"

"Doc, me, Cornelius, and Freesia Tender. She owns the building so we had to include her in order to get past the police tape." I cringed. I probably shouldn't have told her about getting around Cooper's barrier.

Aunt Zoe rubbed her chin. "So Doc has been participating in these, too?"

"Not in the first one, that was Cornelius and me and some of his helpers. Then Doc came to the second one. The third one up at Mount Moriah was only Cornelius and me, and I already told you about last night's crew."

"What does Doc think about you being there?"

"He isn't thrilled, but I help him."

"Help him while he acts as a medium?"

"More like I help him after it's done. I have certain ways of bringing him back." When she leveled her blue eyes on me, I looked down at my hands. They were clenched. "I'm sure this sounds like I'm hovering just this side of deranged. Hell, a few months ago I would have rolled my eyes at the thought of doing a séance and laughed in your face if you'd told me I'd be believing ghosts really exist. But I've seen too much now." I puffed my cheeks and blew out a breath. "Way too much."

"If your main role is helping Doc, why have you had two séances without him? What were you doing during those? Learning?"

"Yes and no. Cornelius thinks I'm a conduit for channeling. He believes I have control of opening and closing channels." Jeez, this all sounded bonkers when said aloud in Aunt Zoe's happy lemon yellow kitchen.

"Are you a conduit?" she asked.

"No." I shrugged. "I don't think so, anyway." I twisted my hands together, thinking about my experiences during the séances. "Maybe I am." I frowned up at her. "This sounds insane, right? You must think I've lost my mind."

"No, sweetie, I don't think that." She took my hand and squeezed it.

"Thank you."

"But I don't think you understand what you are."

I sat there blinking at her for a moment. "You sound like Doc. He keeps insisting I'm something other than a single mom turned Realtor."

She smiled. "I'm liking that boy more and more, especially after the breakfast he cooked."

"He makes my stomach happy." Along with other key body parts.

"Do you believe in Doc's claim to have medium abilities?"

"I didn't at first." I scratched at some dried egg stuck to the table where Layne had sat. "But then I saw him go under a few times. He knew things that didn't make sense unless what he said about being a medium was true." I sucked a breath through my teeth and laid my cards on the table. "After what happened last night, I'm a one hundred percent true believer in him."

"What happened last night?"

"I somehow went through the rabbit hole with him and it got really weird. I ended up with a cut and some bruises when I woke up." I'd noticed the bruises on my butt and hips up in the bathroom mirror before I showered, figuring they were from when the albino had yanked me backwards.

"You were injured while talking to ghosts?"

"I wasn't only talking."

After a check over my shoulder for my daughter, I leaned in and told Aunt Zoe the whole séance she-bang. I started with Cornelius with his equipment outside the taxi and ended with Addy's earache, including everything about the ax-wielding juggernaut and my worries about his pale-skinned twin. I threw in the bits about Layne's picture in the mirror, the weird backwards writing, and Reid telling me Ms. Wolff wore wigs over her snow white hair. When I finished, Aunt Zoe was the one scratching at the table.

"Well?" I asked, leaning back in my chair. "Don't you wish you hadn't asked?"

She shook her head, her forehead still wrinkled.

"Are you going to lock me up and throw away the key? Because if you are, you're stuck raising my kids."

"I love Addy and Layne, but not enough to want to raise them on my own while their mother is alive and kicking."

I gripped the table edge, feeling decades older than my thirty-five years. "Tell me I'm not going nuts, Aunt Zoe."

She took my face between her palms and kissed my forehead. "You're not going nuts, kiddo."

"Then what in the hell is going on? How was I able to travel to the past and back through the mirror for crissake?"

"I need to think about this, Violet."

"Maybe you shouldn't. I'm afraid of what you'll come up with when you're done thinking."

She patted my leg. "In the meantime," she said, "I want you to do something for me."

"What?"

She held up her finger for me to wait and slipped out the back door. I heard Addy's footfalls overhead and then the toilet flushing. I was about to go up and check on her when Aunt Zoe returned and held a silver necklace out for me.

I took it, studying the odd looking charms linked onto it. "What are these?" I asked, trying to make sense of the symbols etched into the glass and metal.

"Protection."

Addy's footfalls reached the stairs.

I lowered my voice. "Protection from what?"

Aunt Zoe glanced toward the dining room, then leaned next to my ear and whispered, "From those who kill."

Chapter Twenty-Three

Protection from those who kill.

Hours later as I sat alone at my desk waiting for Mona and Ben to return from lunch, I was still pondering that answer. Addy's arrival in the kitchen had kept Aunt Zoe from explaining further, and I'd needed to head out for work, so we'd left our discussion with a "to be continued" status.

I fingered the necklace Aunt Zoe had given me as I had throughout the morning, lost in thought. She'd swallowed the news about Doc, me, the séances, and everything else without gagging on it even once. She'd always had an open mind about politics, spiritual beliefs, and my life choices in general, but all of this paranormal stuff was plain screwy.

Hell, I was still struggling to believe what all had transpired. I touched the cut above my breast, making sure it was still there. Yep, and sore to the touch, too. I'd scar, most likely. So bizarre.

My computer screen went dark again. That was the third time today that I'd drifted off in thought long enough that my computer got bored and went to sleep on me. Mona had asked me if I'd wanted her to skip lunch so I could go home early and get some rest. My absence wouldn't be noticed with Jerry and Ray out showing Honey and Dickie around—it was their last day of pre-show preparation before they headed back home to make plans to return with the whole crew. I'd waved Mona off, but her eagle eyes had been on me until she and Ben had left for lunch over a half hour ago.

I moved the mouse to wake up my screen and bumped my full cup, sloshing milky coffee onto my desk.

"Crud," I muttered and headed to the restroom to get a wet paper towel. I heard the front door open when I shut off the water. "Be right with you," I called out.

I dried off my hands and headed out front with the paper towel in hand. The sight of Rex sitting on the corner of my desk stopped me cold. He looked men's catalog slick in his black dress pants, open-necked pinstripe shirt, and fancy leather shoes. All he needed was a suit jacket slung over his shoulder and a pair of Ray-Bans and he'd be ready to shake his booty on the catwalk.

As I stood there glaring at him, he made a scene of inspecting my outfit from head to boot toe, whistling in response. "Nice boots, baby."

"Now what do you want?" I snapped. I was too strung out to deal with Rex and his bullshit this afternoon.

He clucked his tongue at me. "Really, Violet. You should work on being more professional with your clients."

Was that a dig about my tendency to get a little too personal with my clients? No, how would Rex know about that? Unless he'd been snooping around ... or hanging out with Ray.

"You're not my client."

"Oh, but I am. Your boss and I had a talk about me being your client just yesterday." His smarmy smile made me want to smash my keyboard over his head. "He assured me you'd be able to meet all of my needs and then some."

Correction, I was going to smash my keyboard over Jerry's head. I returned to my desk, wiping up my mess. "Rex, go away."

"Not until you give me what I want."

I threw the paper towel in my trash with gusto. "If you think you can come swinging back into my life and start making demands, you're more delusional than I remembered."

"I really like how feisty you've become. When you were young, you were so eager to please. It became boring pretty quickly."

"Oh, so that's your excuse for screwing around with my sister behind my back. You were bored with me. And all these years I'd assumed you'd been unable to resist Susan throwing herself at you."

"I don't need an excuse for my actions. You and I weren't married or committed in any other way at the time."

"No, I was just pregnant with your children. Silly me to expect you to remain monogamous."

"When I had sex with your sister, I was unaware you were pregnant."

"Would it have made a difference?" Not that it really mattered anymore. In the end, my heartless bitch of a sister had saved me from Rex. Irony was such a sadistic bastard sometimes.

He shrugged. "Who knows? That's the past. Why rehash it? What's done is done."

"Exactly. You and I are done, so why rehash our past by coming here?" When he tried to disarm me with a fake, charming smile, I sneered at him. "Don't try to insult my intelligence again by proclaiming an adoration for me that doesn't exist."

His smirk came easy. "Well, that youthful eagerness to please did show up during sex. Of all of the partners I've had over the years, you are one of my most memorable."

"Gee, thanks. I hope I have a Sexual Partner of the Month picture hanging somewhere to commemorate that."

He pointed at me. "See, this feistiness is new. I imagine your prowess during sex has increased accordingly."

Who talked like that? I shuddered, feeling like he had me under a microscope and was poking around my sexual reproductive organs with a long pair of tweezers.

"You can imagine whatever you'd like," I told him, "but that's all you'll do. The naivety and youthful ignorance that left me pregnant with twins is gone. When I look at you now, I see past the pseudo charm and the good looks to the rat hiding underneath it all, and I fantasize about taking a garden hoe and chopping you into tiny pieces."

Covering his mouth, he faked shock. "There's so much violence in you these days, Violet."

Rex must've been trading notes about me with Detective Hawke. "What can I say? You bring out the worst in me."

He leaned over my desk, leering down at me. "Does that violence cross over into the bedroom as well?"

I thought of sex with Doc—the way I'd bitten his shoulder, clawed his back, marked him as mine. My cheeks warmed. I pretended to focus on something on my computer screen. "My sex life is none of your business."

Rex's chuckle made the hairs on the back of my neck get all up in arms with pitchforks and torches. "It appears your sister and you have more in common than I thought. She was quite something in bed. Thinking back, I assumed she was trying to impress me at the time, to lure me away from you. It turns out the wildcat behavior during copulation is genetic."

Like I wanted to think about my sister copulating with my ex-boyfriend. I clenched my fists, telling myself that physical violence was frowned upon in a civilized society.

"Rex, is there something in particular as a Realtor that I can do for you today?"

"Yes, I need you to act as my wife."

I stuck my finger in my ear and wiggled it, then pulled it back out. "I'm sorry, I could swear I heard you say you wanted me to be your wife."

"To *act* as my wife."

"Oh, only act the part. I see."

"I'll need the children, too."

"The children? Do you mean the two small human beings you donated your sperm to create?"

"Yes, those two children. Quit being facetious, Violet."

I was being facetious? That was rich. I leaned back in my chair and crossed my arms over my chest. "You'll need MY children for what, Rex?"

"I need a family."

What? Had he turned over a new leaf? One with a conscience? Was he feeling remorseful for how he'd treated us over the years? "Why do you need a family? Are we going on tour? Is it for a production of *The Sound of Music*? Because if it is, I have to tell you that I'm really bad at staying on key, but I do twirl quite well in a dress. Would you like to see me twirl?"

Now I was being facetious.

"Are you done having your fun?" he asked.

"That depends on why you need a family?"

"Because my promotion depends on it."

I clamped my teeth together. It was that, or lean forward and bite his head right off in one chomp. Swallowing a lump of rage, I managed to speak without yelling. "Get out."

"I told you, I'm not leaving until I get what I want."

Did he have even an inkling how insulting this was after birthing and raising those two children without a single penny or word from him? There was a reason I'd insisted he sign off all rights of fatherhood after they were born and he'd shown absolutely no interest in them, and that was to protect them from being used rather than loved. Yet here Rex stood, thinking he could show up and borrow what could've been *his* family if he hadn't run away from responsibility a decade ago.

This was so not happening. Not now, not with my kids.

I pushed my chair back and walked over to the door. "Get out of my life, Rex." I meant that with every cell of my being.

He shook his head. "Not until you play your part and help me get what I want."

"Why do you need a family to get a promotion?"

"Because the board of directors in my company believes that employees with dependents are reliable and trustworthy. The only way I'll get the promotion I deserve is if my boss sees in person the family I told him I have." He pulled out his wallet and flipped it open, flashing a familiar photo of me and the kids.

He'd cut out the family picture I'd used on the marketing postcards I'd posted on bulletin boards this last spring, back when I was trying to drum up business as a new Realtor in town. Criminy, first Wolfgang had found that postcard, now Rex. Who was next?

"So you already lied about us?"

"Officially, you having birthed my children makes me a father, otherwise known as a family man." He slid his wallet back into his pants. "Now I need to borrow them, along with you, in order to get the promotion."

"No."

"I'd be willing to compensate you financially for your time." His gaze lowered to my chest. "Or reward you physically if your boyfriend isn't satisfying your needs. I was very good at bringing you to orgasm if you'll remember."

I hated him to death with my eyes. "You selfish bastard."

"Baring our teeth now, I see. Good." He sauntered toward me. "Are you getting excited?"

"What in the hell is wrong with you?" I gaped at him. "Did you hit your head somewhere in between the time you signed away your rights to those kids and today?"

"We were good together, Violet, and you know it."

"No, I was good, you were just average. But I was foolishly star struck, and you took advantage of my naivety and left me in one heck of a predicament." I glared at him. "I can assure you that I have absolutely no desire to take up where we left off physically, nor will I act the part of your wife or allow my children anywhere near you."

His face tightened, pinching into a cruel expression. "Do the children know my name?"

"No."

"Are you sure?"

His vile sneer made my heart pitter-patter in my throat. "Yes," I whispered.

"We made beautiful children, you and me." He reached out to touch my cheek, but I stepped back, bumping into the wall.

Goosebumps crawled up my arms at the creepiness in his gaze as he closed the distance between us.

"Our daughter has your eyes." His voice had lowered to a foreboding level. "Even the little flecks of gold amidst the hazel."

How did he know that? "Stay away from my children."

"Our son has my love of science. Based on some of his recent choices from the library, I bet he'd love to see what I do in the neutrino lab."

The son of a bitch had been playing ant farm again, this time with a magnifying glass. I jabbed him in the chest. "Do not come near my family again."

"Help me get that promotion and I'll be transferred out of your life for good."

"Go get Susan, she'd love to pretend to be your wife."

"I don't want Susan." He shoved me back into the wall, my

boot heel hitting the wood baseboard with a loud thud. "It took me too long to remove her from my life last time. I have children, so why not use them as they were intended."

A red fury hazed my vision. "Go fuck yourself, Rex." I shoved him back.

He stumbled over Ray's trashcan, using the desk chair to keep himself from falling. "You like it rough now, Violet?" He rushed me, grabbing me by my blazer lapels and yanking me against him. "I can play rough."

"Get your hands off of me, you arrogant asshole." I stomped down on his toe with my boot heel.

He yowled in pain, pushing me back into the wall again. This time both heels hit the baseboard with a loud clunk-clunk, along with my elbow.

"It's time for you to leave, Rex," I rubbed my throbbing elbow, stepping away from the wall. "Or I'll call the cops."

"If you don't help me get that promotion, I'll go public about being the father of your children."

I hesitated. I needed to shield Addy and Layne. If they found out about Rex, they'd want to know more, and then he'd really have me squeezed in a vise. "You signed a paper giving up the right to that title," I reminded him.

"Oops." He covered his lips like he'd done something wrong. "Oh no, I accidentally let the truth slip out. My mistake. I'm so sorry."

My fists itched to connect with his face.

"Violet, the solution is simple." He rolled up the sleeves of his shirt. "Dump your boyfriend, tell your kids I'm your latest lover, and act out a few scenes in front of the right people. Then I'm on my way and all of this frustration will disappear."

"First of all," I held up a finger, "if you come back in this office again, I'll slap a restraining order on your ass. Second," I held up another finger, "I don't know much about these family-loving higher ups, but I wonder how they'll feel when they learn that you left me pregnant and alone ten years ago. Or what they'll think when I mention that I spent the last ten years raising my children without a single penny of support from you." I walked over and stood by the front door. "Do you think they'll want to give you that promotion then, Rex? Or will it go to some other employee who's actually invested time, money, and love in a family?"

"You stupid bitch!" His calm demeanor crinkled, replaced by a snarl. His hand snaked out, latching onto my arm, squeezing my wrist hard enough to make me yell out. He tugged me, cussing and struggling, away from the door and dragged me toward the back hallway. "I'm going to teach you a lesson about obedience, Violet."

I tried to twist free, digging in my boot heels, but his grip clamped on tighter, shooting pain up my arm. "Let go of me!" I swiped the stapler off Ray's desk as we passed. "If you don't take your hands off—"

The front door slammed open, banging into the wall behind me. I registered footfalls on the wood floor right before Doc flew past me, smashing into Rex. Suddenly, my wrist was free. I stumbled backwards, bumping into Ray's desk.

On the other side of the desk, Doc had a handful of Rex's shirt, pinning the jerk against the wall.

"Don't touch her again," Doc said in a quiet but menacing voice.

Rex's face was blood red, his eyes wide with surprise or shock, I couldn't tell. He tried to peek around Doc. "Violet, call off your guard dog."

"He's not my guard dog." I crossed my arms.

Rex hit Doc with a sneer. "And if I touch her?"

I bristled at his veiled threat and beat Doc to the punch. "You'll wake up in a bathtub full of ice water with your kidneys gone."

Rex looked at me, his mouth catching flies.

Doc lowered his head. His shoulders shook in silent laughter.

"What?" I said to Doc's back. "That sounded badass, didn't it?"

Rex struggled in Doc's hold, but Doc had more upper body strength. Finally he stilled again. "Is that a threat, Violet?" Rex asked. "Because if it is, I bet the cops would like to hear about it."

Shit. I didn't want Cooper learning about this, or Detective Hawke. I jutted my chin. "If you want to take this to the police, Doc will be playing poker this week with Deadwood's only detective along with the Sheriff of Lawrence County." I wasn't sure if the sheriff part was true, but Doc had played with him in the past, so what the hell. "He'll be sure to let them know how you were assaulting and battering a single mother while she was alone at her job. I'm sure it'll help even more in that promotion pursuit."

I heard the back door creak open. My pulse fluttered in panic. "Doc," I whispered. "It's Mona."

He let Rex back down on his heels, stepping away from Rex as Mona sailed into the front office.

She stopped so fast when she saw Rex and Doc that Ben ran into her back. Her gaze shifted to me. "What's going on?"

I considered using the ol' Jedi mind trick on Mona, but instead fibbed with a big bright smile. "I was introducing Doc to Mr. Conner."

Rex straightened his wrinkled collar, his face blotchy with red spots. He avoided her scrutiny. "It was interesting conversing with you both." He headed for the door. "Violet, I'll be in touch."

"I wouldn't advise it," Doc told him.

"We'll see what she decides." With a sniff, Rex walked out under the gray sky and exited stage left.

"Doc? Vi?" Mona said, her forehead arched. "What just happened here?"

"Rex and I had a misunderstanding," I came clean, sort of. "Doc paid us a visit to help straighten everything out."

Ben chuckled. "I've seen misunderstandings like that before out behind the Blue Moon bar down in Rapid."

Mona placed her hands on her hips, drilling me. "You knew Mr. Conner before he became your client, didn't you?"

I nodded.

"One of these days, you and I are going to go to lunch and you're going to explain to me exactly how you know him."

"Okay." I owed her that as my friend. "But only if you promise me that you won't mention anything about this to Jerry." I turned to Ben. "Or to Ray."

"Mention what?" Ben asked, winking. He dropped into his chair and picked up the report he'd printed off earlier.

"My lips are sealed," Mona said.

"Thank you," I smiled at both of them.

Doc grabbed my purse from the back of my chair, handing it to me. "I'm taking Violet to lunch. We'll be back in an hour."

"Make it two." Mona waved us goodbye and sat down. "She looks like she could use a long lunch."

Doc led the way out the back door and across the parking lot to his car. He held open the door for me. While he walked around the back and slid behind the wheel, I sent Aunt Zoe a text message to make sure Addy was still doing okay.

"Where to?" he asked, his attention straight ahead.

"Your place." My phone dinged. I looked at it. Addy was fine and sleeping. Good.

The Camaro rumbled to life. He backed out and headed toward his house, his focus locked on the road.

I got the feeling he was silent for a reason, contemplating something, probably why he'd ever taken up with a woman who had so many problems. I swallowed a bubble of nervous jabbering and watched the houses go by out the window, trying not to think about what had just happened with Rex.

Doc pulled up in front of his detached garage and hit the automatic door opener. After we rolled into the bay, he closed the door behind us, killing the engine. It ticked as we sat there. I wasn't sure if I should reach for the door handle or apologize to Doc for messing up his world.

"Violet," he said, his hand still gripping the wheel. "I owe you an apology."

Huh? He did? I was the one with the apology, not him. I looked at his stony profile. This better not be the opening line for our breakup scene. "For what?"

"I lost control back there."

Ohhhh, this was about his control issues again. Whew! "Dear

me, Doc," I said, tongue in cheek. "Your control slipped. It appears you might actually be human after all."

He turned to me. "You jest."

"Of course I jest. I lose control every morning when I'm trying to get my kids ready for school. Do you have any idea how many times I have to tell them to get their dang shoes on before they do it?" I captured his hand, squeezing it. "I don't mean to poke fun, but if you're going to be involved with me and my kids, you're periodically going to experience a total loss of control. But try to take comfort in the fact that you'll always be more self-disciplined than me."

"Okay." A hint of a smile played on his lips. "He didn't hurt you, did he?"

"Not really." I pulled up my sleeve. There were no red marks or signs of bruising on my wrist. "He made me want to jump on his back and go ape-shit on his head, though."

"That would make a great circus act." He pushed open his door. "Come on, you probably need some food."

I always needed food. I stepped out of the car, coming around the front to where he was waiting for me at his workbench. "How did you know Rex was in there with me? Did you see him walk by your office window?"

"I heard noises through the wall." He hung a wrench on the pegboard over the bench. "Some yelling, a few thuds. It was enough commotion that I thought you and Ray were finally duking it out." He tucked a pair of pliers into a tall tool chest. "I came over to make sure you were okay. When I saw Rex manhandling you, I sort of snapped."

I leaned my hip against the workbench. "You moved so damned fast. I bet Rex didn't even know what hit him."

He rested his palms on the bench. "I remember looking in the door and seeing his hands on you. Next thing I knew I had him against the wall." He turned to me. "I can't remember anything in between except this roaring sound in my head."

I could tell by his taut expression that he wasn't thrilled about the whole thing. "I'm sorry, Doc."

"For what?"

"This mess with Rex is my fault."

"You aren't responsible for his actions, Violet." He reached over and cupped my jaw, rubbing his thumb down my cheek. "Or for my reaction when someone threatens you."

I sighed, feeling guilty for his conflict even though he'd let me off the hook. "I probably could've handled things better today, done less yelling maybe, but he pissed me off."

He lowered his hand, catching mine and lacing our fingers together. "What happened?"

"I wouldn't give him what he wanted so he played dirty, using the kids against me."

"What did he want this time?"

"A family."

"What?"

I explained what Rex was after and why, nodding in agreement when Doc let out a drum roll of expletives. "I couldn't have said it better myself."

"It's no wonder you want to remove his kidneys."

I chuckled. "It sure sounded good at the time."

"You certainly surprised me with that one, and your ex, too, going by his slack-jawed expression." Doc slipped his hand around the nape of my neck, pulling me toward him. "Have I told you lately how crazy you make me, woman?"

"You mean like Patsy Cline's version of crazy?"

His mouth tasted mine, tender with my lips. "I'm still working that out." He swooped in for seconds, this time seeking a response.

I closed my eyes, trying to block out the madness of the last twenty-four hours and just enjoy being kissed.

Doc's lips left mine too soon. "I need to make you lunch."

I'd rather have him for lunch. I glanced over his shoulder and noticed a familiar picture hanging on the wall next to the light switch. I leaned to the side. "What's that?"

Doc walked over and stroked his fingers down the poster of me in my Interstate 90 billboard stance with my blood red lips, teased hair, and kohl-circled eyes. "It's my babe calendar for the garage, minus the calendar."

"How did you get that?" I joined him in front of it.

"I pulled off the side of the road and took a picture, cropped it, and blew it up."

I pointed at my tousled hair. "I look ridiculous."

"Not ridiculous." He stared at the poster, his head cocked to the side. "A little wild maybe with the way they have your hair, but 'wild' on you is sexy. That silk dress really shows off my favorite curves, and those red lips remind me of how you taste when you're wearing that cherry flavored lip gloss." Doc stepped back, leaning against the front fender of his car. "I thought about hanging it over my bed, but then I'd never get any sleep."

I took off my blazer and hung it from a nail over the poster, covering half of it. "There, that's better."

Doc captured my hand and tugged me toward him. "Don't cover up my favorite poster."

"Can't we get you another one?" I placed my hands on his chest. "Maybe one of those motivational posters with a kitten or puppy on it?"

"I like my hot babe. She motivates me in all sorts of ways."

"Oh, yeah?" I pressed my hips into his. "Like how?"

"Let's go inside and I'll show you."

"No."

"No?"

I pressed again, feeling a response. "Show me here."

He palmed my hips, arranging me against him more to his liking. "In the garage?"

I nodded, reaching for the button on his khakis. I didn't want Harvey barging in on us. In Doc's garage, we were safe, hidden from the world for a moment. "Unless you're worried about getting your car a little messy."

He raised one eyebrow as I pulled down his zipper. "You know I have a perfectly soft bed?"

"Yes, I'm familiar with your bed." I slipped my hand inside the front of his pants. "And your shower. They're both nice," I squeezed him through his briefs, "and big."

He sucked a breath in between his teeth. "I'm glad you're happy with them."

"I'm over the moon with the whole package." My fingers found the waistband of his briefs. "Would you like me to show you how happy I am?"

He remained silent, his gaze locked onto mine as I slid my hand inside his waistband and felt my way south. His eyes darkened as I stroked. Watching the passion flare in his eyes and feeling the evidence of his lust for me had me licking my lips in anticipation.

"You do understand what's going to happen next, don't you?" His voice sounded taut.

"We're going to play doctor, Doc?" I ran the heel of my palm down him, chuckling under my breath. "Is this a thermometer in your pants or are you just happy to see me?"

"I'm always happy to see you, Boots." He pulled my hand out of his pants and spun me around so my butt was against the fender. Then he lifted me onto the hood, his lips taking mine in a hungry rush. I gave back as good as I got, wrapping my legs around him and locking my ankles behind his back. I hauled him closer, wanting him to make me forget about everything but his body possessing mine.

He caressed my breasts through my knit shirt, hefting the weight of them, teasing around the peaks until I couldn't stand it and stripped off my shirt for him.

"Nice necklace," he whispered as he lowered his mouth, arousing me through my pink satin bra. I gasped his name, holding him against me. He stepped back way too soon, his face flushed as he ogled me. His desire gave me a new confidence. I unclasped my bra, slipped it off, and tossed it on the hood behind me.

"Now what are you going to do?" I taunted, trailing my fingers over my skin, the flesh damp from his tantalizing tongue, cool to the touch.

"Damn," his breath came in short huffs. "You are …" he raked his fingers through his hair, his Adam's apple bobbing as he stared. "Damn."

"You already said that." I rubbed my boot up and down his thigh. "You want to see something, Doc?"

He glanced up at me. "I want to see everything."

I grabbed a handful of my skirt and teased it up over my knees. When his focus shifted downward, I slowly ran my other hand up, up, up. Tracing my inner thigh, I led his gaze, doing my best to tempt him into touching me and more.

His hands hovered over my thighs, fingers flexing. "Do you have any idea what you're doing to me?" he rasped.

"I know what I'm trying to do to you." I inched my skirt higher. "And I know what I want you to do to me."

His hands landed on my legs, his palms burning hot. "What do you want me to do?"

I placed my hands over his and guided him north, to my throbbing center. "Touch me."

His thumbs skimmed over the inner hemline of my underwear, tempting. "Like this?"

I writhed, my body ready for him last week. "More."

"Not until you lie back."

I hesitated. "I don't want to scratch your hood."

"Violet, it's just a car. Lie back and let me play, too."

I did as told, resting on my elbows so I could watch him. "What are you going to do?"

He pushed my skirt the rest of the way up, staring down at me. "Watch and see." He bent over and skimmed his lips along my stomach above the waistline of my panties. It tickled my nether regions and then some, making my breath hitch.

"Do that again," I ordered.

He obeyed, adding a brush of his fingertips to the mix.

I moaned, lying flat on the hood. The heat of the engine warmed my bare back while Doc worked his magic on me, his touch searing me from the waist down.

It didn't take long for him to have me thrashing, begging for more. He took me close to the edge and then pulled back, amplifying my need to feel him inside of me.

Threading my fingers through his hair, I lifted his head so he could meet my eyes. "I'm ready."

"I noticed."

"Let's make this a two player game."

"Are you going to start talking sports to me again?" He hooked his fingers in my underwear and tugged them down. "These need to go."

"Wait." I sat up. "Do you like them? I bought them for you."

"I'll write an ode to them later. Right now, they're in my way." He threw my panties over his shoulder and locked onto my hips, pulling me toward the edge.

"I've never had sex on a car before." I grabbed his shirt and lifted it. He knocked my hands away and took it off for me. It went the way of my underwear. "Have you?"

"Sure, I do it all of the time." He chuckled when I slapped his shoulder. He ran his hands up my legs, starting at the heels of my boots and ending at my waist. "No, Boots, I haven't. But I'm happy to give it a try. Wrap your legs around me."

I obeyed, leaning in to kiss his ear.

He pulled slightly away, eyeing me. "You're not going to bite that ear again, are you?"

"Trust me, you big baby." I pulled him back to me and brushed my lips over his ear, being extra tender with it. "See," I whispered, "was that so bad?"

He turned and kissed me hard, dominating me until I submitted with a sigh-filled moan. I rubbed against him, creating a delicious friction that made my body hum. "What are you waiting for?" I asked. "Written instructions?"

"Your skirt is in the way," he said, tugging on the cotton material that had somehow wrapped around me.

"Here," I said yanking it out of the way. "Is that good?"

"It'll be great in a moment," he said, fitting against me.

I bit my lower lip in anticipation, grinning at him. "Are you going to show me how hard you can hit the boards?"

"You're hopeless, Violet," he said and then drove into me, pulling me tight.

He was right. I was hopeless. I was positively gaga in love with him. I captured his mouth, wanting to taste him as he took me. His hands caressed and rubbed as he pushed me higher and higher with each stroke.

"Doc," I panted, gripping his shoulders, arching into him.

"Right. There. Don't. Stop."

"Like this?"

I didn't have a chance to answer. Pleasure steamrolled over me. I cried out his name several times, and then trembled for another round of ripples. When I came back down, I kissed him, lavishing his mouth the way I knew from experience would light his fire with a *ka-boom*. Then I dug my boot heels into him.

Groaning, he thrust into me a few more times before he seized up, his muscles straining. Then he buried his face in my neck, heating my skin with his exhale.

I stroked his bare shoulders, wishing we could hide out in here for a week. My butt bone ground into the hood, placing its vote for Doc's bed instead. I squirmed and he stepped back, adjusting himself while I pulled my skirt down, fastened my bra, looked around for my shirt, and pretended I wasn't a shameless, wanton woman when it came to his touch.

"Violet." He zipped his pants, looking toward the bench.

"Yes?" I followed his gaze. My underwear had landed on the counter.

"I really like those panties."

I laughed, wrapping my arms around his neck, pulling him in for a slow kiss, a finale of sorts. "Are you going to fix me something to eat or not?"

His lips curved, his gaze warm and heart-melting. "I'd peel grapes for you if you'd like on one condition."

"Name it." I touched the necklace from Aunt Zoe. "But if you're going to request that I join you in the shower, I get to choose the soap I use to wash your back." The cinnamon flavored was my favorite.

"I like it better when you hand wash my front. But first, what did …" He looked down at my necklace I was still fiddling with and stopped. "Where did you get that necklace?"

"Aunt Zoe gave it to me after I told her about last night's séance. Why?"

He frowned at me. "It has symbols from the book on it."

"What book?"

"That book about Kyrkozz that you gave to her."

Chapter Twenty-Four

"We need to tell Cooper how Ms. Wolff died," Doc said a half an hour later while I sat at his kitchen counter eating the chicken breast and salad he'd set down in front of me.

I'd told him my version of the séance while he stood at the stove, cooking our lunch. From waking up on the wrong side of the mirror in Ms. Wolff's bedroom to how I reached into the darkness with my mind and grabbed onto Freesia's hand to return to the present. The shrunken heads weren't news to him, since he'd been on the scene, too, viewing the events through the greaser's eyes. We'd both agreed that based on what Ms. Wolff's body looked like when Harvey and I found it, she had suffered the same fate as the other three in the past—a beheading via a freaky-ass, medieval looking ax. Or "scythe" as the albino had called it.

But just because we knew the where and when answers to the murder equation, and now we agreed on the *how* part, that didn't mean I concurred on the Cooper incorporation.

"No way," I told Doc, who joined me at the counter, his plate in hand. "He'll never believe us. And even if he did consider what we tell him, he'd wonder how we know this and the truth about you would come out."

Doc sliced off a piece of chicken. "I'm beginning to wonder if we should be more concerned if truths about *you* surfaced."

"Which truths?"

"All of them—Rex, Prudence, the demon book, the mirror trip, and who knows what else." Doc stabbed the chicken piece. "Next to you, big tuna, I might be a minnow."

We chewed on that in silence for a couple of chicken bites. Then I remembered a question that had come to me in the middle of the night during Addy's earache. "How did you get back inside the greaser's head? He was already dead when you wrote the word MIRROR on the wall, wasn't he?"

"I didn't go back in through the greaser."

"You didn't?" I ate the last of my chicken.

"When I was in that apartment in the greaser's point-of-view, right before you scared the hell out of me by rushing out of the bedroom to face off with the killer, I picked up a scent."

I swallowed a drink of water. "Of what?" Or who?

"Someone else was there watching, too. Another ghost."

Chills peppered my forearms. "Ohhh, creepy."

"After the greaser died, I woke up back in Ms. Wolff's apartment and noticed two things immediately—you had left the room and that same scent I'd picked up while inside the greaser was there with us, stronger than ever."

"Let me get this straight. You're saying the same ghost was in that apartment both in the past and present."

He nodded, slicing off another piece of chicken breast.

"But this new ghost hadn't been a live person during the ax-swinging party."

"Correct." He held out the chunk of chicken for me. "He was already dead."

I took him up on his offering, swallowing before I asked, "Then how did you get back to me and my juggernaut?" I thought Doc's ability only allowed him to see the events of a person's death, not anything posthumous.

"He took me there."

"The ghost took you back in time to me?"

"More like forward in time to you."

I stole another piece of his breast with my fork. "Clarification, please."

"We started with his death, and then … I don't know how but … it's like he wouldn't release me. He knew how to drag me to where we needed to go. He took control, like Prudence does each time, to the point where I can't easily get back out."

I frowned at Doc. "You went into the past to witness a man's death and then forward in time through his ghost to witness other deaths." I was struggling with this one. "That sounds beyond deranged."

He shrugged. "Maybe, but you traveled into the past through a mirror and showed up on scene in physical form to do battle with what I suspect is a paranormal being whose ax not only kills, but somehow withers or burns and shrinks." He shot me a sideways smirk. "How deranged is that?"

I stabbed a piece of his chicken with my fork and then pointed it at him. "Touché."

He leaned over and ate the bite-sized chunk.

"So who was this ghost? Was his death somehow related to the greaser's or what was going on in that apartment?"

He shook his head. "I think he built the Galena House."

"You mean Freesia's great great-uncle, Jake Tender? What makes you think that?"

After wiping his mouth on a napkin, he stood and collected our plates. "When I went back to the time of the ghost's death, his skin was dark, and he was still tall and muscled, even in old age. I'd seen pictures of Big Jake Tender in that history book you picked up from Ms. Wolff's apartment. She'd had the page with a shot of him standing in front of the Galena House bookmarked with an old photograph of what I now am pretty sure is the two of them much younger, standing next to one another at a parade. Jake was younger, anyway." He put our dishes in the dishwasher. "Here's the interesting thing I witnessed during his death, which was a heart attack by the way." Doc dried his hands and then leaned on the bar across from me. "I think Ms. Wolff was there with him when he died."

I frowned, doing the math in my head. "You mean as a little girl?"

"No. She had crow's feet around her eyes and her hair was bright white. She was leaning over me—I mean him, holding his hand. But she looked the same age as she did in the picture with Big Jake. Like she hadn't aged, except for her hair."

"You're sure?"

He rubbed his jaw, his expression contemplative. "Not a hundred percent, but pretty sure, yeah."

"Reid told me that Ms. Wolff kept wigs on those styrofoam heads in her closet. If she was alive when Freesia's great great-uncle was around, and she had white hair even then, you know what that means."

His eyes locked onto mine. "Ms. Wolff was one of them."

"She must have used the wigs to blend in over the passage of time." I chewed on my knuckles, the weight of all this heavy on my chest. "So what does that mean? Why did she call me that day? What is it she needed to tell me before she died that was so damned important?"

Doc came around the counter and took my hand. "Let's think about this somewhere more comfortable."

He led me over to the couch, pulling me down next to him. A stack of blankets were draped across the other end, evidence of Harvey's temporary residence. I leaned back against the sofa arm, stretching my legs perpendicular across Doc's, close and comfy with him like so many nights over at Aunt Zoe's in front of the boob tube.

"She knew she didn't have much time left." He slipped his hand under my skirt, stroking my bare calf. "Which is ironic considering all of those clocks on her ..." he trailed off, his hand going still.

"And she called me an executioner, which isn't the best way to make new friends."

"Violet," he looked at me, his brow pinched. "I can't believe I didn't put this together before now."

"Put what together?"

"The timekeeper. Ms. Wolff is the one Prudence keeps telling you to bring to her." He squeezed my shin. "It makes total sense now."

"Not really." He must be reading from a different script.

"We need to go see Prudence," he said.

"Or we could skip that and have another nooner."

His grin rounded the corners of his eyes. "You name the time and place, and I'll be there."

"I like the privacy in your garage."

"I like the softness of my bed." His hand crept up over my

knee, stroking my thigh. "Especially when you're naked on top of me." He leaned over and kissed me. "Now quit trying to distract me with your body."

"Is it working?" It was on me. My pilot had the engines all fired up again.

"No."

"Liar." I could feel otherwise and moved purposely against him.

He held me still. "When can you arrange a visit to the Carhart house?"

"I don't suppose taking off my shirt will dissuade you?"

"That will inspire me to do several things, but when I'm finished with you I'll still want to go see Prudence."

I sighed, fingering my necklace. "She wants those teeth, you know. If I show up without them, she'll be ticked."

"She's a ghost, Violet."

"Are you sure that's all she is?"

"Mostly." He pushed my fingers away and lifted the charms on my necklace, leaning closer to get a better look at them. "You need to ask your Aunt Zoe about this necklace, if there's a purpose for it."

There was. "She said I needed to wear it for protection from those who kill."

His gaze met mine, searching. "She said that?"

I nodded.

His focus returned to the charms. "It looks like colored glass over some kind of metal etched with symbols that I swear I remember seeing in that book."

"The metal is probably silver." I lowered my chin, trying to look at the pieces, too. "All of the other charm jewelry she's made for me over the years is silver and glass."

"I remember you mentioning the boot bracelet she made, as well as some pieces for your brother and your children."

"Yeah, she's made me stuff since I was a kid." I pointed at one of the charms. "See that symbol there? I think that's one of the runes stone symbols, isn't it? Several of the pieces she's given me have runes on them."

He let go of the necklace and sat back. "I have a feeling your Aunt Zoe knows a lot more about things going on with you than she's letting on. Take that mirror in her workshop that she said belongs to you. That's not a normal mirror, and after your trick with the mirror at Ms. Wolff's place, I'd like to pick your aunt's brain about you."

"That's not a good idea." Aunt Zoe knew I was pretty gonzo for him. After her past troubles with Reid, she might say something to see where Doc stands before I was too far gone. Unfortunately, I had a feeling she was already too late.

One eyebrow lifted. "You afraid she'll warn me off?"

"I'm afraid she'll scare you off."

He twirled one of my curls around his finger, his attention on my hair. "I'm not an easy man to scare."

Yet Tiffany's talk of marriage made him take flight. "Your ex did a good job of it."

"Tiffany?" He scoffed. "You're on a whole different level."

"Just out of curiosity, what are the various levels we're talking about here?"

He shifted me around so I straddled his lap. "How about I show you?"

Was he evading my question for a reason? Did he know I'd fallen for him and was trying to change the subject so I wouldn't voice it? Jeez, I hated this relationship shit. Maybe it was time we just laid this out on the table so I'd stop agonizing over it.

"Doc," I shifted, unwinding my skirt that had gotten all twisted tight around me. "Don't worry, I don't expect any kind of long term commitment from you."

He stilled, frowning at me. "You don't?"

"No. We're having fun here, enjoying each other's company for the time being."

His head cocked to the side. "Is this about what I told you in that hotel stairwell? About why I broke it off with Tiffany?"

I'd only obsessed about that for weeks now. "Not at all."

"Your nose just twitched."

I crossed my arms over my chest, wishing he didn't know my tell so well. "It did not."

"And there it twitched again." He unwound my arms and tugged me closer. "Violet."

"What?" His eyes were like rich, dark chocolate.

"If you're not in this for the long run, then I want out."

I blinked twice. "If *I'm* not in it? I'm the one with kids."

"Exactly. You should know better than to flirt and tease a poor, old bachelor like me, getting my hopes up."

"Flirt and tease? I made the first move with that kiss."

"No, I kissed you in a dark stairwell in this very house." He toyed with my skirt hem. "The first move was mine."

"If you'll remember, you told me you didn't want to get involved with your Realtor."

"You believe I asked you to represent me by chance?" He shook his head. "I couldn't stop thinking about you."

My heart was doing the Snoopy dance in my chest. "What are you saying, Doc?"

"I'm saying I don't want you to act the part of Rex's wife."

Whoa! I wasn't expecting that curve ball.

Before I could respond, he reeled me in for a long, slow, wet kiss that left me steaming. "I'm saying I don't share well with others," he said against my lips.

Neither did I.

His mouth trailed along my jawline, warming my earlobe. "I'm saying we need to tell Cooper how Ms. Wolff died."

I'd swear I heard the sound of a record being scratched. I pulled back. "That was a non sequitur, and I still disagree."

"Think about it." One of his hands slid yet higher up my leg. "We could ask if he'd return the teeth while we're at it."

I let out a harsh laugh. "He'll never go along with either."

"Never say never. I once said I'd never get involved with a blonde billboard model, yet here you sit on my lap, inspiring wicked thoughts about those sexy panties of yours."

"Now *you're* trying to distract me."

"Wasn't there talk earlier about you taking off your top?"

"It's not going to work. I'm not telling Cooper. He'll throw me in jail again for even mentioning the albino."

Doc reached waaayyyyy up under my skirt, his eyes widening

the further his fingers traveled. "Apparently, Boots, you've misplaced your underwear."

There wasn't much to be said for a long time after that.

* * *

Saturday, October 13th (Two days later)

"I still think this is a bad idea," I told Doc as he towed me through the tables and the scattering of people in the Purple Door Saloon to a back corner booth. The one next to it sat empty, giving us the privacy we would need. The smell of beer, burgers, and fried potatoes weighed heavy in the warm bar. The place wasn't as busy as it was on summer weekend nights. The tourist season had pretty much wound down, leaving Deadwood in the lull that hit every year until the snow started falling.

Sharp Dressed Man from ZZ Top with its eighties guitar riffs blasted from the jukebox back by the pool table. The song seemed fitting for Doc tonight in his black khakis and white shirt under his leather jacket. Had I known he was going to dress so slick, I'd have put more effort into my blue jeans and T-shirt getup.

"Who's going to bail me out of jail if you're in there with me?" I asked.

"Cooper is not going to throw us in jail for this." Doc helped me shuck my coat and waited while I slid into the booth. He shed his jacket, tossed it and mine onto the empty table next door so it looked occupied. "He may be a bit ticked that we went into the Galena House, but we did have Freesia there with us. It wasn't breaking and entering, at least not this last time."

He had a point. "Or trespassing."

"Exactly." He dropped down next to me.

The waitress bustled over, tossing thick paper coasters on the table. "What can I get you two to drink?" she had a smoker's voice, which seemed fitting for a saloon. Luckily the regular bartender wasn't working tonight. He wasn't fond of blondes for some reason and preferred to glare holes through me rather than serve drinks.

"Margarita on the rocks," I said. "Make it extra strong."

After hitting me with a raised eyebrow, Doc ordered whatever was on tap. When she left, he draped his arm around the back of the seat, his fingers stroking my shoulder. The heady scent of his cologne made me want to do naughty things to him under the table, but I kept my hands to myself.

"Did you talk to your Aunt Zoe about that necklace?"

"I haven't found the right time to bring it up." Between the kids and Harvey, we always seemed to have an audience. "I did talk to Freesia, though. She assured me that they put the apartment back together and erased all signs of our being there, including returning Layne's picture to the mirror."

"Good."

"Although that seems pointless with what we're about to do here tonight."

"For appearances sake, I think it's best to make it look like nobody has been in there but the police. What Cooper does with what we tell him tonight is up to him."

I rubbed my hands together to warm them. My nerves had me trembling for more reasons than the brisk October night. "Did I tell you that Detective Hawke thinks I'm a witch?"

Doc stared at me, his forehead knotted as if he were considering how I would look with a pointy hat and broomstick. Then he shook his head. "No, not a witch."

"Of course I'm not a witch," I said, poking him in the rib.

He grunted and started to grin, but then his gaze shot to the door. "He's here."

The urge to escape out the back door made my toes tingle.

Detective Cooper was dressed similar to Doc, only his leather coat was gray instead of black. Had someone neglected to tell me there was a monochrome dress code for the Purple Door on Saturday nights? He stopped by the bar and ordered a drink before heading our way.

The detective tossed his jacket onto the booth seat. "Are we expecting company?"

"You're it," Doc said, squeezing my shoulder in support. Or maybe he was holding me in place so I wouldn't fly out of there.

Now that I thought about it, his putting me on the inside was a calculated move, trapping me. Dang his foresight.

Cooper clasped his hands together. "So why am I joining you at the Purple Door tonight?" His gaze slid my way. "Based on Parker's spooked expression, I'm guessing this isn't a social event."

I turned to Doc. "I look spooked?"

He held up his index finger and thumb posed in a pinch.

I couldn't help it. Spilling my guts to Cooper about crimes I'd committed was up there with facing off with an ax-swinging juggernaut.

Before we could get rolling, the waitress brought our drinks, including Cooper's. When we passed on ordering food, she left with a sly smile at the detective. She and Mona should start a Detective Cooper Fan Club. They could wear matching handcuffs.

"What's this about?" Cooper asked, his gaze bouncing between Doc and me.

"Ms. Wolff," Doc spoke first. I was still searching for my tongue, which seemed to be cowering behind my uvula.

"What about her?"

"We know how she died," I spit out, and then drowned my tongue with margarita.

"We know the murder weapon," Doc corrected.

"You know what decapitated her?"

"We know what made her end up all shriveled and gnarled," I cut in again, and then swallowed another mouthful of liquid bravery. "And who's responsible."

Cooper's gaze gave away nothing as he examined our faces. "Why do I get the feeling something about this is going to make me unhappy?"

I tried to remember when I'd seen Cooper anything other than unhappy. "I told you this was a bad idea, Doc."

Doc sat forward, palms flat on the table. "Hear us out and then you can decide what to believe and go from there."

"I'm all ears."

"Ms. Wolff was murdered by either the white-haired killer

Violet and I battled at Mudder Brothers or his twin—the one she and Natalie saw in front of the funeral parlor in August."

"What do you mean *or*?" Cooper's focus slid to me. "You said he went up in smoke after you stabbed him."

I sat up straight, feeling defensive under the detective's scrutiny. "He did, but since there's no body as proof, I thought *we*," I emphasized the royal form, "weren't sure that smoke equals death."

Flashes of that night in the funeral parlor played through my mind ending with the albino's struggle to reach the scissor blades I'd jammed into his back. All of it still seemed so surreal, the way his face had morphed and his eyes had turned snake like. *You again*, he'd said in that ghoulish voice right before he'd ... hold up!

You again.

Holy shit! Did that mean he'd recognized me that night at the funeral parlor? He'd remembered chasing me around that apartment in the past with his ax? The time circle ramifications boggled my brain, making my hard drive chug.

"We aren't sure he's dead," Cooper interrupted my epiphany. "Nor are we sure you're sane, Parker."

Lately, I wasn't either. I wrinkled my upper lip at him.

"What was the murder weapon?" Cooper asked.

"A scythe-like ax," I answered.

"A wooden handled medieval looking weapon," Doc added, "with a blade on one side and a sharp point on the other. I could provide a rough sketch if you're interested."

"I'm still listening." Cooper tipped his beer and downed half of his glass.

I took the reins. "We think Ms. Wolff suffered the same fate as those three victims back in the fifties. You know, the shrunken heads murder case that was never solved." When he just stared at me, I felt compelled to throw out, "If you go back and research those three victims, you'll find the victims were of the same ilk as Ms. Wolff and the killer."

The detective's gaze narrowed. "Ilk?"

"White hair, pale skin, albino-looking."

"Are you insinuating that these particular so-called albinos are not human?"

"I'm not insinuating, I'm saying it straight up. Ms. Wolff and that ugly bastard I stabbed at Mudder Brothers and Caly from the Opera House are all the same species, which is not human."

Skepticism was as plain as the crooked nose on his face.

I looked to Doc for reassurance. He pointed at where I'd caught the edge of the ax blade.

"When the victims were cut by the killer's ax they shriveled up." I pulled the v-neck of my shirt aside, showing Cooper my new red scar. "Unlike me."

He glanced at the scar. "What do you mean unlike you?"

"He tried to slice me in half, but he missed." I pulled my neckline back in place. "Mostly."

"Who?"

"The albino."

"You just said he wasn't an albino."

"Fine, the big, white-haired juggernaut who probably cut Ms. Wolff's head off. The same asshole who decapitated those three back in the fifties."

"Explain to me again how you know he was the one who decapitated them?"

"Because I saw it."

"We saw it," Doc corrected, squeezing my leg.

"You both saw the 1950s murders?" He focused on Doc.

"Correct." I let Doc answer. Cooper didn't think he was nuts. Not yet, anyway.

"And you both saw him cut off Ms. Wolff's head?" Cooper's tone was full of disbelief.

I had the feeling he was just humoring us at this point, which made my jaw clench. I leaned over the table. "No, not Ms. Wolff. I saw him chop off the heads of those three in the fifties." My tone was clipped. "We had a séance in Ms. Wolff's apartment and I witnessed—"

Doc grabbed my shoulder and pulled me back to my corner of the ring. "Violet, let me explain."

I growled in my throat and snatched up my margarita.

Cooper shifted his steely gaze onto Doc. "Nyce, please tell me you didn't buy stock in Parker's story."

Doc stared into his beer. "There's something you need to understand." He swallowed a drink. "Remember how I knew the details of Wilda Hessler's death?"

Cooper nodded.

"How I knew that she didn't die from a broken neck after her brother pushed her down the stairs, but rather bled to death from landing on the dagger she'd been holding when she fell?"

What? That was news to me.

The detective nodded again.

"I didn't read about that detail in any obituary or any autopsy report. I'm not even sure if it's listed there."

"It's in the autopsy report." Cooper cocked his head. "If you didn't read that, how did you know?"

Doc tapped his beer glass. "Since I was a kid, I've been able to interact with dead people."

"Ghosts," I clarified, to make sure Cooper's thoughts didn't take the necrophilia route.

"I'm a medium," Doc held Cooper's stare. "I can't speak directly to them, but I can witness through their own eyes not only how they die, but any events that occurred in their lives right before death."

Not a peep came from the detective, his face granite.

"That's how I knew about Wilda Hessler. I fell down those stairs with her and landed on the dagger, I felt her pain and rage as she bled out."

"Are you saying you have a sixth sense?" Cooper asked.

"If you want to call it that, okay."

His eyes narrowed. "Are you fucking with me, Nyce?"

Doc shook his head. "While we're clearing the air, the Deadwood Police Station has two ghosts, as far as I can tell. Your house is ghost-free; however, your uncle's place isn't. He's got some traffic, but he already suspects that."

"Jesus," Cooper took another long drink, downing most of the glass. "Is this some early Halloween practical joke? You talk to ghosts and she's a witch?"

I rolled my eyes. "Doc can't talk to ghosts."

"Violet is no witch," Doc gave me a measured glance. "We're still not sure what she is, but hocus pocus is not in her repertoire."

Cooper's gaze darted between us. "You're both serious?"

"Yes," Doc spoke first. "We weren't thrilled about calling this meeting, but what's going on in Deadwood is bigger than any of us can handle alone. You need Violet and me to help with what you can't see, and we need you to keep the paths clear and the Detective Hawkes of your world off our backs."

"So you two can have more séances in restricted areas?"

"Something like that."

Cooper finished his beer. "I'm going to go to the bar and get another drink. When I come back, let's try this again, only without the supernatural shit." He left us alone.

I stirred my drink, noticing Cooper's stiff gait. "He doesn't believe us."

"Would you have a few months ago?"

"Not at all."

"Tonight is about planting seeds. Knowing Cooper, he'll wait to see what they turn into as they grow, and then come back with a lot more questions."

"I hope he doesn't wait too long." Or it might be too late.

Cooper returned. "So, let me get this straight." He slid onto the bench seat. "The albino-like guy, who may or may not be the same one who sliced George Mudder's head off the night Violet broke my nose, killed Ms. Wolff in her apartment with an ax. Do I have this game of Clue in the bag?"

"Or his twin did it." Doc replied.

"The nose was your fault," I stuck to my guns on that one.

After glaring back at me, he looked at Doc. "In your version of this game, why was Ms. Wolff murdered?"

"I'm not sure, but I think it has to do with Violet."

"Because of the phone call she made to Parker?"

"No. I suspect the phone call was a warning of something that's to come."

"Why Parker? Why not call the police?"

"Because Ms. Wolff knew about Violet and her history with others like her—other non-humans. Remember Violet's statement after the Opera House events? Dominic Masterson told her, 'It's in your hands now.' Maybe he knew Ms. Wolff, or maybe word spread somehow to her."

"There are a lot of maybes in your story."

Doc shrugged. "I have a feeling there are more to come."

Cooper took another drink, setting it down with a sigh. "You two must realize how ludicrous this sounds."

I scoffed. "You should try sitting on our side of the table."

"Who all knows about your theories?" he aimed the question at Doc.

"Only Violet and I have discussed it in this much detail, but Cornelius Curion, Freesia Tender, your uncle, and Violet's aunt all know I'm a medium. Only Zoe and I know the particulars about Violet's experiences."

Cooper scrubbed both hands down his face. "You two should have asked me before going into that apartment."

"Would you have consented?" I asked.

He fiddled with the coaster for a moment. "No."

"I didn't think so."

"Nobody at the station is going to believe any of this."

"That's why we're only telling you," Doc said.

"I'm not sure I believe any of it."

I looked at Doc. "Mark my words—this was a mistake."

"You once sat on the detective's side of the table."

True. I turned to Cooper. "Whether or not you believe us, I trust the badge you wear ensures your silence, right?"

"If I breathe a word of any of this, Parker, I'll be forced to have another psych eval."

Another?

I opened my mouth to ask what had prompted the first one, but Doc poked my leg, nudging his chin toward the door. Natalie stood near the bar, taking off her coat. She zeroed in on me and headed our way.

"Hey," she said as she drew near. "Your aunt said I'd find you here." She did a doubletake on Cooper and took a step back.

"Am I interrupting something?"

I hit the detective with a questioning look only to find his focus on Nat. When he just stared, I prompted, "Detective?"

The speed of sound seemed to have slowed to a snail's pace based on how long it took him to reply. "Ah, we're done here. I'll leave you to your evening." He reached for his coat.

"Bzzt, wrong answer, Cooper." Natalie dropped onto the bench seat next to him. "You can't leave yet."

"I can't?"

"Nope. Scooch over." She hip bumped him deeper into the booth and then leaned in close to him, sniffing. "Is that you?" She sniffed again. "Damn, you smell yummy. Oh wait, you're a cop. Let me rephrase that. Detective, you have a pleasant fragrance on this evening." She grinned. "Sir."

"Uh, thanks." Cooper's voice sounded thicker, garbled.

"Don't worry, I'll keep my hands to myself." Her chuckle had a self-deprecation ring to it. "I'm not interested in the handcuff/strip search routine these days."

"That's a shame," he shot back.

"Cheeky. Nice." She patted his forearm. "So, I need your professional opinion on something."

He toyed with his glass. "Are you and Parker planning on doing something illegal again? Or do you need a second opinion on where to put another tattoo?"

"You're in rare form tonight, Detective."

"It's Coop," he said, "and you don't know the half of it."

"You never let me call you Coop," I said.

"That's because you need to be reminded at all times that I'm a cop or you'll go out and break another law."

"He's got a point," Doc said, and then grunted when I elbowed him.

Cooper's gaze locked onto Nat's mouth. "What's your question?"

"First, Violet needs to answer something." She looked at me. "Are you going to let your ex blackmail you?"

I'd told her earlier about Rex's visit to my office and his family proposition, but a phone call from Jerry had interrupted us and put an end to the conversation.

"There's no way in hell that I'm giving in to that bastard."

Doc caught my hand, lifting it to his lips, his eyes molten.

The waitress stopped by to drop off Natalie's iced tea.

Cooper's brow knitted. "Is he bothering you again?"

"I told you he's an even bigger asshole than you," I said, smiling to take the sting out of my answer.

"The son of a bitch is about to lose his balls," Natalie said, reaching over Cooper to grab a couple of sugar packets. "And I have just the vice clamp and pruning shears for the job."

With her mind on sugar or Rex's cojones or both, Natalie didn't seem to notice Cooper's reaction as she stretched across him. Sitting directly across from him, I saw it all—the sharp intake of breath, the tightening of his shoulders, the slow blink of his eyes as she leaned into him, and the way he looked down at his forearm where her breast had touched after she sat back. Then he took a big gulp of beer. His eyes widened when he caught me watching, his neck and face darkening.

Busted!

There it was right in front of my face. *Cooper and Natalie sittin' in a tree, K-I-S-S-I-N-G.* Oh, my molies!

"Detective?" Natalie waved her hand between us, interrupting our stare off. "Yoo hoo."

He warned me with one last narrowed glare, and then turned to Nat. "What?"

"What happens if Vi files a restraining order and Rex ignores it?"

"Knowing Parker and you, I'd say such a foolish step by her ex would result in dismemberment."

Natalie grinned. "What's the jail sentence for penis removal by pruning shears?"

The bartender called for Natalie. "Be right back," she told us and slid out of the booth.

Cooper watched her go.

"She's innocent, I swear," I told him.

"I doubt that." He slid out of the booth and stood, grabbing his coat. "I need to go." He looked at Doc. "We're still on for poker Wednesday night, right?"

"Sure."

"That ability of yours—is that why you keep kicking my ass at cards?"

Doc chuckled. "No, you just suck at poker."

"Damn. I thought I had an excuse." He nodded at both of us. "I'll be in touch. Stay out of my crime scenes unless I'm there with you."

"Oh, wait," I said, holding up a finger. "One more thing."

"What?" His tone was full of suspicion.

"Could we have that box of teeth back from evidence?"

"Why?"

"That's another long story that will make you unhappy."

"No." He didn't even hesitate.

"Okay," I said, "feel free to think about it for a few days."

"Nyce, see you at the game. Parker, don't call me."

I watched him stride out the door and then looked at Doc. "I think he's warming up to me."

He kissed my forehead. "You played well with others tonight, Tiger."

"Thanks. Cooper likes Natalie."

"I noticed."

"Do you think she did?"

"You tell me." He finished his beer.

"I don't think so."

"Are you going to say something to her?"

I thought about that for a moment. She seemed so much more at ease with herself since she'd given up men, happier, less self-critical. Not to mention her admission that she was loving her independence from lust and regret. "Probably not."

"But you really want to, don't you?"

"Of course. It's Nat."

"And it's Cooper, who is already not happy with you for a multitude of reasons."

"That man needs a smiley face T-shirt to wear. Maybe he'd wear it if I pretended it was from Natalie."

"Violet."

"Okay, okay, my lips are sealed." For now. "What do you think Cooper will do about Ms. Wolff?"

"We'll see. Whether he believes us or not, he has some answers to ponder now about her death."

I finished off my margarita. "I still want to know why she called me. Why she had Layne's photo. What that writing in the drawer says." I fingered my necklace, wondering. "Do me a favor, Doc. Send me the picture you took of that drawer."

"Okay. Why?"

"I think I know who might be able to decipher it."

"Who? Cornelius?"

I stabbed the lime in the bottom of my glass. "Aunt Zoe."

Chapter Twenty-Five

Monday, October 15th (Two days later)

The lunch crowd at Bighorn Billy's had slowed to a trickle. Only a handful of patrons remained, including my once-a-week lunch buddy and me.

"What'd you do to Coop?" Harvey asked in between bites of his cheeseburger.

I squeezed a lemon wedge into my glass of iced tea. "What do you mean?"

"He's actin' like he's got his tail in a wringer lately."

That didn't tell me much. "He's been acting like that since I met him."

"This is different. The boy's all fidgety and frustrated. I can't tell which way that mule's gonna jump these days."

I shrugged. "Who knows what he's stewing on now? Maybe he's all buggered up about that foot ol' Red found."

Or maybe it was Doc's and my tale about Ms. Wolff's murder, or Detective Hawke's constant presence at his side, or a hankering for a certain brunette. The poor knucklehead probably had a shitload of problems keeping him up all night. It turned out Cooper wasn't made of steel joints and hydraulic fluid after all.

"I blame you." Harvey stuffed the last of his burger into his mouth.

"What did I do?"

He finished chewing and swallowing before answering. "Tossed a hornet's nest in his outhouse."

"You're the one who keeps finding creepy body parts out at your ranch, not me."

"No, you just find dead bodies mostly in one piece."

"Just finish up so we can get rolling. I have an appointment to get to and I don't want to be late."

"For what?"

"The hotel sale is a done deal. Cornelius takes over ownership of the Old Prospector Hotel this afternoon. He asked me to join him at the signing." Cornelius had told me on the phone earlier that he wanted my *juju* there to ensure success with his future plans for the place. I was happy to attend so I could make sure he didn't get distracted by a chatty ghost or certain busty redhead.

When I'd asked him if he'd finished analyzing his recordings from the séance, he said the video had shown me walking into the bedroom and staring in the mirror. That was it until the rest of them joined me. There was no paranormal instances caught on film. He'd sounded sad about it, too, like his balloon had slipped from his grip and floated away. When I'd inquired about the other recording equipment he'd brought, he told me the Galena House must have some magnetic energy field that interfered with his readings, because what data he had made no sense.

Focusing back on the things in my world that did make sense, I grinned at Harvey. "I should get a nice paycheck today or tomorrow and finally be able to buy a used car for the winter. You don't have to take the Picklemobile into the shop to get her heater working again after all."

"No wonder you've had that goofy grin on your face since we got here."

The goofy grin had a little to do with the sale finally being in my past and a lot to do with a certain brown-eyed man being in my future.

Ten minutes later, we crunched across the parking lot toward Harvey's pickup.

"So what is going on out at your ranch?" I asked, climbing into the cab.

"I already told you, I'm sellin' off my herd. I'm tired of dealin' with all of the kooky shit happening to my cows. Then I'm gonna get the old homestead cleaned up some more so maybe next spring we'll land us a big fish from the other side of the state. Turn my ranch into one of those fancy vacation properties that are so popular these days here in the hills. That's why I want you to find me an ol' Red a rental in town for the winter." He'd informed me of his plans last night while I'd been cleaning up the dinner dishes. "Doc's couch is mighty comfy, but I don't want him to start setting my boots outside the door each night."

"I meant what is going on with that foot? Has the sheriff's department been out to scour your property yet?"

"They had the dogs out there twice this week, sniffin' around everything, but I ain't heard nothin' else since." He started up the pickup and rolled out onto the road. "Where to? Back to Calamity Jane's?"

"I need to swing by the Galena House and drop off some paperwork for Freesia to sign."

"We sneakin' inside for another peep at the crime scene?"

"Not today. I don't want to miss the signing appointment because Cooper has me locked behind bars."

We rode in silence for a few blocks while I daydreamed about paying off some bills and buying the kids a couple of pairs of much needed shoes and new winter gear with the money I was going to make off the sale of the hotel property.

"I saw our lovesick fire captain last night at the bar up in Lead," Harvey interrupted my money-filled fantasy.

"He wasn't drowning his sorrows again, was he?"

"Nope. He was cueing up at the pool table, enjoying a game with one of his buddies. I asked him if anyone in particular had threatened to fill him with shotgun pellets lately and he got a big fat grin on his mug."

"What does that mean?"

"That's what I asked. He told me that he'd recently been called a low-down, rotten heartbreaker, but there'd been no talk about gettin' her gun. Said he considered that progress."

I'd keep my fingers crossed for him.

Harvey pulled up in front of the Galena House and cut the engine. "You want me to go on up there with ya?"

"No." I grabbed a pen from my purse and opened the passenger door. "I'll be right back."

"I'm gonna play me some cards then." He pulled out his phone.

I clomped up the sidewalk in my knee-high black boots, fantasizing about shopping for a used car. I didn't care much about the color. Something that didn't backfire every time I shut it off would be a real treat. Although the Picklemobile did a great job of announcing my arrival on scene when necessary.

I was at the base of the porch steps when the front door opened. I looked up with a smile for Freesia. The sight of the ax-carrying juggernaut pushing out through the screen door froze me like a rusted tin man. A squeak leaked from my lips. My bladder threatened to leak as well but held tight.

His bulbous dark eyes locked onto mine. I didn't remember them being that dark before, but then Caly had talked about wearing contacts, so maybe he was, too.

I held my breath, waiting for his reaction, all prepped for flight as fast as my boots would skidaddle.

His face remained flat and disinterested, no spark of recognition before he turned back to Freesia.

"I'm sorry for the inconvenience," Freesia said to him, all sugar and friendliness. "Until the police take down the crime scene tape, my hands are tied."

Why had he been trying to get into Ms. Wolff's apartment? Had he left a clue behind when he killed her? Something Cooper had missed?

"I understand," he spoke in that Slavic accent I knew so well from my nightmares. "I will come back at another time for my aunt's personal effects."

His aunt? What a load of manure.

"If you leave me a phone number," Freesia started.

"I am traveling for a few weeks." He bowed slightly to her. "Thank you for your assistance."

He moved with lithe grace down the stairs, joining me on the sidewalk where I was trying to play chameleon and blend into the background. As he neared, his eyes still showed no recognition, his face an unreadable mask. I could have been a kid's bike left on the grass for all he seemed to care.

His gaze left my face and locked onto my necklace. His steps staggered, his nostrils flaring wide. When he looked back up at me, I stared into narrowed vertical slits. Snake eyes!

Adrenaline spiked, but it was too late to run. I lifted my chin, holding his hard, chilling glare. My fingertips tingled as I gripped the pen, ready to stab him if he lashed out.

Then he blinked, and his dark eyes returned to normal. Without another glance, he stalked past me. I watched him go, not trusting my back to him. At the end of the sidewalk, he took a sharp left and made for the pine trees.

My breath shallow and fast, I watched him disappear into the thick shadows under the trees.

Holy funkendunkel! That was close. Was that the juggernaut's twin? Or had the killer just not recognized me? No, that had to be the twin, didn't it?

"He's Ms. Wolff's nephew," Freesia said from the porch.

No, that was the bogeyman in the flesh. I considered clarifying who he really was, but decided that ignorance may be best for her safety.

Shaking off the tension that had kept me locked solid for the last minute, I joined her on the porch. I scanned the tree line, afraid he might come sprinting back with that sinister ax in hand at any moment. "What did he want?"

"To collect some of his aunt's possessions."

I wondered if Cooper had contacted any relatives. I doubted it because I was pretty certain Ms. Wolff didn't have any. At least none still alive.

What did he really want? Something with the clocks? Something from her bedroom? Something Doc and I had overlooked?

I palmed my phone, pulling up Cooper's number.

Then I remembered the detective's parting words the other night: *Parker, don't call me.*

Maybe I should wait, talk to Doc first, let him call Cooper.

"He seems nice, but he scared the crap out me when I first saw him." Freesia said.

"Because of his looks?" That oversize, gangly armed Donald Duck thing he had going repulsed me every time. There was no getting used to that ghoulish mug.

"No, although that is a face only a mother could love."

Or a twin brother.

"I came downstairs," Freesia explained, "and he was leaning against the wall next to Ms. Wolff's door, all big and creepy looking."

She should see him come at her with an ax sometime. No wait, I didn't want her to witness that. "Just standing there?"

"Yeah, hanging out."

"That's weird."

"I explained to him about the police tape and Detective Cooper's rules. The guy was polite enough, but I think something was bothering him because he kept looking at the door." She touched her chest, all sympathy and caring for a monster who could have cut out my heart. "I can't imagine finding out my aunt was killed. He must be devastated."

Right, the poor, murdering bastard. Where was he hiding that ax? Was it stashed in the apartment somewhere? Was that why he'd come back?

"Did he mention what made him come by today? If the cops had contacted him?" As far as I knew, Cooper was still trying to keep this all hush-hush.

"No. He told me he was in town and wanted to pick up her things. That was it."

"You need to tell Cooper about this." If Freesia called, then I'd be even more removed from the gust of heat when his temper flared.

"About Ms. Wolff's nephew visiting?"

No, about the ax-swinging assassin standing outside of Ms. Wolff's apartment telling lies about his relationship to her. "Yes, you should let him know about it all, including a physical description of the nephew. He inferred the other day that he wanted to keep close tabs on the coming and goings here."

I didn't specify that he meant *my* coming and goings.

"Okay. I'll call the detective as soon as you and I finish with the paperwork you mentioned on the phone."

"Good."

Now to wait for the ax to fall—Cooper's or the albino's.

Both made me want to run home and hide under my bed.

* * *

Later that evening I walked Doc and Harvey out to Doc's car, kissing one goodnight and blowing a raspberry at the other.

"You sure you don't want me to spend the night?" Doc asked as I huddled inside his arms.

"We'll be okay." There was something about Aunt Zoe's house that made me feel safe and secure in spite of who I'd seen earlier. "He didn't recognize me at first."

"Maybe not, but something about that necklace sure snagged his attention." Doc stepped back. "I'm just a phone call away. I can be here in five minutes."

I huddled under my sweater in the brisk October evening as he backed out of the drive. The moon was out. Jack Frost was going to be busy sprinkling his diamond dust on thick throughout the early morning hours.

Back inside, I herded Addy and Layne to bed, spending a few minutes with each of them, talking about their plans and hopes for school the next day. After kissing their foreheads and tucking them in, I hesitated outside their bedrooms and listened to the sounds of them settling into their beds.

Their father's threat replayed in my head. No way in hell was I going to let Rex near them. If that bastard wanted to play dirty, I had no qualms about getting muddy.

I heard the phone ring downstairs. It was after nine. Who was calling? Had Harvey or Doc forgotten something? Was it Natalie catching up on today's events? Or was Reid trying to break through Aunt Zoe's wall?

Aunt Zoe waited for me with the phone at the bottom of the steps. "It's for you."

She mouthed the word *Cooper* as she handed it to me.

My gut jumped off a ten-story building.

"Hello, Coop."

"That's Detective Cooper to you, Parker."

"Whatever. Why are you calling? Do you need me to solve a new case for you?"

He sighed.

I imagined him squeezing the bridge of his previously broken nose.

"Parker, did I not explicitly tell you Saturday night not to go into Ms. Wolff's apartment without me?"

"I vaguely remember something about that."

"Then why did you?"

"I didn't." After several silent seconds, I added, "I'd swear to that on your *History of Hand Guns* bible that you keep on your coffee table."

"It's *The History of Recreational Firearms*, smartass," he corrected. "So, you're saying you didn't go into Ms. Wolff's apartment today and take Layne's picture off the mirror?"

"No, of course not. Why would I ..."

My lungs seized up, my vision tunneling.

The albino had been at Ms. Wolff's place today, standing

outside of the door. Now Layne's picture was missing.

"Oh, God," I whispered, looking back upstairs where I'd left my kids tucked into their beds.

"Parker?" Cooper's voice cut through my panic.

"Did Freesia call you about ... about ... " My brain was stuttering in terror.

"She did. You think the albino took the picture?"

"Who else would have?"

"Fuck." I heard the sound of a chair creaking. He must still be at work. "Before you freak out, let me ask around and make sure someone here didn't mess with it. I'll send someone over first thing in the morning to search for it. Maybe it just slid out of the mirror and Detective Hawke didn't look under the bed and dresser for it when he was there earlier."

"Cooper," I said, still panting. "Promise you'll call me as soon as you know."

"I will. Try not to panic, Violet."

That was easy for him to say. He hadn't seen what that damned ax could do firsthand. I had a feeling there'd be little sleeping done tonight and poor Doc would be stuck talking to a hysterical broad yet again.

I hung up and found Aunt Zoe standing behind me. She waved me into the kitchen. "We need to talk."

Like a zombie, I shuffled after her, my thoughts in Ms. Wolff's bedroom where my son's picture no longer was stuck in the mirror.

"Have a seat, Violet."

I fell into the chair she'd pulled out for me. She placed a steaming cup of something in front of me.

"What's this?"

"Hot lemon tea." She knew it was one of my favorites on a cold night. "Drink up." She lowered into the seat next to me.

I sipped the warm sweetened drink. "That was Cooper."

"I know." Oh, yeah, she'd answered the phone.

"Layne's picture is missing from Ms. Wolff's bedroom mirror." I took another drink and then spilled my guts about the albino I'd seen today and what he'd told Freesia. When I finished,

I looked up from my hands and frowned at her.

She reached out and squeezed my wrist. "You're strong, Violet. Stronger than you realize."

I cocked my head, trying to figure out why she was saying that at this particular moment. "Is that code for me to wear more antiperspirant?"

"No, it's me saying that you've grown your wings now and need to leave the cocoon."

Huh? I looked down into my drink. "Did you spike this with something?"

"Yes, sugar." She tapped her index finger on the table. "There is something you need to know—two things actually."

"Okay." I waited, uncertainty making those wings she'd mentioned flap inside of me. "What?"

"I figured out what that message says on the inside of Ms. Wolff's drawer."

I leaned forward. "Was it in Latin?"

"A derivative of Latin, actually."

"What did it say?"

"Only when the clock stops will your time be at an end."

I sat on that for a bit, replaying it over and over. "What does that mean?" Was it a general saying she liked to keep on the inside of her drawer or had she meant it for me in particular? If Doc's theory was correct and Ms. Wolff had been the timekeeper Prudence kept requesting, the saying may have a deeper meaning. But what?

"You tell me."

I sipped my tea, considering. "Well, Ms. Wolff did have two walls full of these spooky looking clocks."

"Spooky how?"

"They were black forest clocks, but not your usual happy German boys and girls and animals carved into them. Each is unique with these freaky, garish scenes."

Aunt Zoe tapped her finger again. "I want to see them."

"I'll need to clear it with Cooper." After she nodded, I asked, "What's the other thing?"

She stared at me so long I considered asking her the question again. Then she blew out a slow breath. "There's no easy way to tell you this."

"What?" My pulse throttled higher thanks to the apprehension lining her face. "You're killing me here."

"It's funny you should use that turn-o-phrase. When your great-grandmother died, I was placed in charge of keeping track of our family tree."

"I think you told me that before."

"This business with Ms. Wolff sparked a memory of something I'd seen in one of our family history volumes."

We had family history volumes? As in plural?

"But since so much of it is handwritten in German, I had to scour through several volumes to find it and then try to decipher what was being said. Some of our ancestors could've used some writing practice."

"Find what?"

She scooted her chair forward so that our knees were almost touching. Then she clasped both of my hands and stared hard into my eyes. "Long, long ago, back in Germany, they called some of the women in our family *Scharfrichter*."

"*Scharfrichter*? You mean ... " Ms. Wolff's voice echoed in my head.

She nodded once. "Executioners."

"You're kidding, right?" I laughed. It sounded shrill in the quiet kitchen.

She didn't.

"Are you ... what are you saying?" I must have misunderstood her.

"Violet Lynn," Aunt Zoe said, still holding onto my hands. "You come from a long line of killers."

The End ... for now

To share your thoughts and ideas on what is to come for Violet and her friends (and enemies) with others who have finished the fifth book in the Deadwood Mystery Series, check out Violet's Secret Book Club—a hidden page on my website.

(Note that you may be able to access this webpage only from a computer or certain kinds of devices.)

To enter the book club, type the password: Elvis
http://www.anncharles.com/?p=1474

Speed Dating with Ann Charles

I asked some of my wonderful friends in my Ann Charles' Purple Door Saloon group on Facebook to come up with questions for me to answer in one sentence for the end of this book—speed-dating style.

Why did you choose to move to Arizona?
Because of the outdoor activities available throughout the year along with the incredible views help my brain relax and the creativity flow.

When Violet is talking to Natalie down in Jackrabbit Junction, do you think about what's going on with Claire and her crazy family down there?
Definitely, because I would like to be hanging out at The Shaft with them, drinking, playing pool, and hiding from Deborah.

Why a chicken?
Because Elvis the chicken showed up to the casting call and her audition was phenomenal.

Have you ever entertained the thought of having a ghost dog helper in your books? Either a living dog who detects ghosts or one who has passed on and offers help to Violet or Doc? A cat would also do, if you know more about felines?
No, I'm afraid the dog or cat might eat Elvis.

What's the scariest paranormal event you've experienced?
There hasn't been one paranormal-wise because like Violet, I'm a dud when it comes to seeing ghosts.

How do you come up with the locations of the characters' houses?
I hang out in Deadwood and Lead and story ideas come to mind. (I'm afraid if I tried to analyze why my imagination chooses what

it does, it will get uppity and stop coming up with ideas altogether.)

When you are writing a book for one series are the characters from your other series living their lives in your head as well, just waiting their turn to be written down?
They are not waiting—they aren't that patient with me; they are stomping around, demanding my attention.

Will there be more crossover stuff in your series? I like the crossover from Deadwood to Jackrabbit with Natalie. Will you have other characters jump?
All of the characters in my series live in Ann's Universe, so there will be more crossover characters as I continue to share Quint and Claire and Montana's worlds with you.

In your FB post about Quint and Angélica from the upcoming book, LOOK WHAT THE WIND BLEW IN, you say you wrote the first draft years ago. Do you always do that? Do you have a shoe box full of drafts about your characters?
I don't always do that, but I do have several stories that I wrote before I was published, and some of them are tied to characters in my now-published books.

I have heard an author say that although she respects her readers, she doesn't write for them, she writes the story that she needs to tell. Do you feel the same?
I have a story in my head that needs to be told a certain way, and if I start letting others dictate what needs to happen in that story, my imagination will pick up its ball and leave, refusing to play with me anymore. (That's not good.)

Do you use events from your life in your books?
All of the time, but I've been advised by my characters not to tell you what's fact and what's fiction.

About the Author

Ann Charles is an award-winning author who writes romantic mysteries that are splashed with humor and whatever else she feels like throwing into the mix. When she is not dabbling in fiction, arm-wrestling with her children, attempting to seduce her husband, or arguing with her sassy cat, she is daydreaming of lounging poolside at a fancy resort with a blended margarita in one hand and a great book in the other.

Connect with Me Online

Facebook (Personal Page):
http://www.facebook.com/ann.charles.author

Facebook (Author Page):
http://www.facebook.com/pages/Ann-
Charles/37302789804?ref=share

Twitter (as Ann W. Charles): http://twitter.com/AnnWCharles

Ann Charles Website: http://www.anncharles.com

59327445R00240

Made in the USA
Lexington, KY
03 January 2017